"I Want to
Lied to
Announced.

Alana grew very still. Had he somehow learned the truth about Gilbert's death?

"You're taking too long to answer, Alana," he remarked, then moved toward her.

"Stay where you are!" she commanded, clasping the wet bath sheet closer. To her amazement, he didn't obey.

He halted less than an arm's length away and gently captured her chin. "Tell me what I want to know, and I won't have to hound you like this."

The timbre of his voice had deepened. Her breath caught when he released her chin, his knuckles brushing lightly upward across her cheek.

"I understand why Gilbert was enchanted with you. Your skin—it's as soft and smooth as a babe's." His hand moved to her hair. "Like silk," he whispered.

Alana could do naught but gaze at him. His eyes were fully dilated, glistening onyx ringed by a heavenly blue.

"You're temptingly beautiful," he murmured. Before Alana could react, his lips were on hers. His kiss was hot and searching, and to Alana's regret, far too brief. He pulled away and examined her face.

"How could a mouth that sweet be at the same time so very deceitful?" he questioned. "You have the ability to lure a man, even unto his death. Tell me: Is that what happened to Gilbert?"

Please turn the page for critical acclaim for
Charlene Cross. . . .

Booksellers Love
Charlene Cross's

SPLENDOR

"*Splendor* is all it implies and more. Absolutely wonderful! Charlene Cross is truly a superb author. Five stars!"
—Donita Lawrence, Bell Book & Candle

"Outstanding! I didn't want the book to end. I can always count on a good book from Charlene Cross."
—Mary Bracken, Book Depot

"This is a superb medieval romance that has you riveted right from the beginning."
—Joan Adis, Paperbacks & Things

"Another wonderful story from a fine author! I couldn't put it down."
—Donna Harsell, Windflower Books

"The best medieval I have read in a *long* time. Ms. Cross has a place of honor on my 'keepers' shelf."
—Jackie Skimson, Pages Etc.

"*Splendor* is an absolute treasure! Definitely a keeper. I will be selling a lot of this book."
—Bobbie McLane, Basically Books

"A fast-paced, surefire winner! An exceptional book, by an exceptional author. Destined to be one of the best Romance novels of 1995!"
—Kevin Beard, Journey's End Bookstore

"Wow! Charlene's done it again—a true attention-grabber, one that keeps the reader involved from beginning to end. . . . Her readers want her to 'write faster, faster!'"

—Merry Cutler, Annie's Book Shop

"This is Charlene's best to date. I loved this book, the characters jumped out at you and held you throughout."

—Adene Beal, House of Books

"The gradual awakening of love among the ravages of war and political manipulation is beautifully written by Ms. Cross. I thoroughly enjoyed this book."

—Tanzey Cutter, Old Book Barn

"What a wonderful story! I loved the characters! I couldn't turn the pages fast enough to see what would happen next! This book will fly off the shelves."

—Kay Bendall, The Book Rack

"*Splendor* is simply splendid! Charlene is a great story-teller!"

—Kathy Cross, Paperbacks Plus

"*Splendor* is filled with passion, intrigue, betrayal, and romance. A magnificent medieval to capture the heart. Bravo!"

—Yvonne Zalinski, Paperback Outlet

Books by Charlene Cross

Masque of Enchantment
A Heart So Innocent
Deeper Than Roses
Lord of Legend
Almost a Whisper
Splendor
Everlasting

Published by POCKET BOOKS

For orders other than by individual consumers, Pocket Books
grants a discount on the purchase of **10 or more** copies of
single titles for special markets or premium use. For further
details, please write to the Vice-President of Special Markets,
Pocket Books, 1230 Avenue of the Americas, New York, NY
10020.

For information on how individual consumers can place
orders, please write to Mail Order Department, Paramount
Publishing, 200 Old Tappan Road, Old Tappan, NJ 07675.

CHARLENE CROSS

EVERLASTING

POCKET BOOKS

New York   London   Toronto   Sydney   Tokyo   Singapore

For Andrea Kane—
whose friendship I treasure and
whose encouragement made this book possible.
Thanks, pal, for always being just a fax away.

The sale of this book without its cover is unauthorized. If you purchased
this book without a cover, you should be aware that it was reported to
the publisher as "unsold and destroyed." Neither the author nor the
publisher has received payment for the sale of this "stripped book."

This book is a work of fiction. Names, characters, places and
incidents are products of the author's imagination or are used
fictitiously. Any resemblance to actual events or locales or persons,
living or dead, is entirely coincidental.

An *Original* Publication of POCKET BOOKS

 POCKET BOOKS, a division of Simon & Schuster Inc.
1230 Avenue of the Americas, New York, NY 10020

Copyright © 1995 by Charlene Cross

All rights reserved, including the right to reproduce
this book or portions thereof in any form whatsoever.
For information address Pocket Books, 1230 Avenue
of the Americas, New York, NY 10020

ISBN: 0-671-79433-7

First Pocket Books printing July 1995

10 9 8 7 6 5 4 3 2 1

POCKET and colophon are registered trademarks of
Simon & Schuster Inc.

Cover art by Lisa Falkenstern

Printed in the U.S.A.

CHAPTER

1

~~~~

**Northern Wales
April 1157**

It was inevitable.

The realization came to Alana of Llangollen with absolute clarity.

To say that she had been unwise to hope the news of Gilbert's death would bring no more than an expression of sympathy from his king was a misstatement at best.

Downright foolish would qualify far better!

Still, her expectations had been high.

And Henry's response had been made altogether plain.

Some four dozen mounted men presently waited beyond the palisade, their leader demanding entry to the Norman castle that had been erected long ago on the land of her forefathers . . . land that was now part of her inheritance.

Alana turned from her chamber window to her

1

trusted servant Madoc. "Is Henry among them?" she asked.

Madoc shook his graying head. "I don't think so, milady. The one who is at the fore calls himself Paxton de Beaumont. He bears a pennon with a golden dragon on a crimson field. States he knew Sir Gilbert; says they were old friends. Even if he hadn't mentioned such, his knight's trappings and his arrogant demeanor indicate he is one of Henry's vassals. Looks to be Norman as well."

Madoc's contemptuous tone wasn't lost on Alana when he'd cited what he thought was Paxton de Beaumont's lineage. She understood her servant's hatred; shared in it herself.

Since the time of William the Conqueror, her countrymen had fought against the unprincipled invaders who sought to lay claim to her homeland. Almost a century later, the struggle continued, both sides perpetually gaining and losing ground.

Though Alana could in no way predict the future, she held an inherent fear that one day her small country would be swallowed by a marauding force too powerful to turn aside. As it was, her kinsmen may already have met their vanquishers, even looked into their eyes.

Isn't that why she'd sought to marry Gilbert? To ensure, whether the victors were Norman or Welsh, that her descendants wouldn't be driven from their home soil?

And a fine plan it was. Except Gilbert was now dead and she had no issue.

"You say there is a priest with them?" she asked.

"Aye."

"I wonder why."

Madoc shrugged. "Perhaps this Paxton de Beaumont considers himself a religious man."

"Or mayhap, like Gilbert, he thinks we are a passel of heathens whose souls are in great peril."

To Alana that was the more logical rationale as to why a priest would be in the company of such a small band of Normans. When would they understand that Christianity had come to her homeland long before their kind ever had?

"Where is Sir Goddard?" she asked, referring to the knight who was currently in charge of the isolated stronghold.

Madoc's dark eyes flashed with scorn. Contempt once more rang in his voice when he said, "As usual, he imbibed far too much wine last night. Midday has come and gone, yet he still sleeps, as do most of his companions."

Alana nodded, then again faced the window to stare at the woodland beyond the palisade.

Between the breaks in the trees, their new growth unfurling under the rays of the warming spring sun, she glimpsed the rippling river that snaked through the valley below. Today its waters were almost placid, far from the raging torrent of six months before.

Time swept backward to that fateful day.

From afar, she saw herself falling through space, experienced the breath-robbing plunge when she sank beneath the frigid waters, felt herself tumbling helplessly along the rain-swollen eddy, her body crashing against the rocks projecting from the river's bed.

Deprived of precious air, her lungs threatened to burst. Somehow she clawed her way to the surface, where she gasped and sputtered, only to be dragged to the bottom once more.

As Alana remembered, the cycle continued for no less than an eternity. That she hadn't drowned was a veritable miracle.

And Gilbert—the blackguard . . .

"Milady?"

Alana blinked, her trance broken. "What is it, Madoc?"

"Should I tell those at the gate to turn this Paxton de Beaumont away?"

She circled around. "Nay. We have no choice but to allow him entry."

"But—"

"We must. Otherwise he'll grow suspicious. We can ill afford his mistrust. Besides I'm certain he has come to secure what is rightfully Henry's."

Madoc's lip curled beneath his mustache. "Rightfully Henry's?" he repeated with a snarl. "These Norman dogs are far too brash. They invade our homeland, claiming it as their own. But just as with your dead husband, they also will know the wrath of our countrymen."

"That may be so, Madoc. But until we are able to drive these 'dogs' from our soil, we must temper our pride and act as though we accept them as our masters." Alana knew that was especially so if she hoped to keep the events surrounding Gilbert's death hidden from his king. "Since Sir Goddard is indisposed, order the gates opened and allow this Paxton de Beaumont and his men entry. Offer them food and drink. I will soon be down to bid them welcome."

Once Madoc exited the chamber, Alana moved to a small chest that sat against the opposite wall and took hold of her comb. At each stroke through her hair, the mass gathered forward across one breast, she wondered why their visitors had so boldly crossed the marches and Offa's Dyke into Cymru. *Wales,* she corrected, knowing the Normans also used the long-held Saxon term for her country.

She thought of the man who'd declared himself their leader.

4

Paxton de Beaumont.

His name sounded familiar, but she couldn't remember Gilbert's connection to the knight or even in what context her late husband may have mentioned the man. But then, Gilbert had told her little about his past or his prior friendships.

Alana wasn't surprised by the fact. Little more than six months into their marriage he had begun to converse with her less and less. The ensuing three years became a study in silence.

Yet, Gilbert did manage to communicate in other ways.

Though their relationship was strained, he craved his husbandly due. Save for the last four months of his life, he came to her bed each night, expecting her to submit, which she did.

Alana shuddered as she recalled how without preliminaries he would mount her. After several thrusts and a few grunts, followed by a lengthy groan, he rolled away and left her side. Freed of her obligation, she considered it a blessing sent from on high. Other women might believe differently, but to Alana, lovemaking was a loathsome act, something she hoped never again to endure from any man.

A knot had formed in the pit of Alana's stomach, marking her distaste. What was past was past, she told herself, vowing not to think about such things again. Right now, there were more pressing issues to consider.

With one last stroke of the comb, she plaited her hair, then wrapped the lone braid around her head and secured the coil, afterward donning a headrail. She smoothed her hand over her tunic, then drew her mantle around her shoulders. Taking a steadying breath, she left her chamber.

At the top of the stairs leading down to the great

hall, Alana affected an expression of bereavement. Over time, she'd learned to perfect her widow's mask and could execute it at will. She could even summon forth tears at the mention of her late husband's name. A ruse, yes. For when she'd first learned of Gilbert's death, she almost jumped for joy.

Presently Alana worried little whether her feigned grief was taken as genuine or not. It was Paxton de Beaumont who concerned her.

The knight's presence, she suspected, was at Henry's bidding. He'd traveled across the marches and into what most considered hostile territory in order to secure the castle for his king. But Alana doubted that was his sole reason for showing outside the gates.

She had a strong feeling Henry disputed her account about Gilbert's drowning. Suspicion of foul play was the underlying motive that brought his vassal to the secluded fortress overlooking the small tributary which flowed into what the English called the River Dee. She'd swear on her parents' graves this was so.

As Alana descended the stairs, she began to fret. Of all those who resided here, only two people knew what had actually transpired on the day Gilbert died: Madoc and herself.

Alone together in her bedchamber, they had prepared her husband's body for burial once it had been recovered from the river. By her own insistence, everyone else had been barred entry. Otherwise the telltale wounds marring his flesh would have alerted whoever saw them that the frigid waters hadn't been the cause of Gilbert FitzWilliam's demise. Nay. It was the plunge of an angry blade, many times over, that had ended his miserable life.

For her sake, and the sake of those whom she protected, Alana prayed Paxton de Beaumont never discovered the truth.

The bloodred pennon with its prancing dragon snapped in the wind above Paxton's head as he waited for the gates to be opened to him and to his men.

A strange land this Wales, he thought, glancing around him, his interest piqued.

With its rugged, slate-sided mountains, its forests of pine and oak, its open hillsides sheeted in purple blossoms of heather, the vapory mists rising from its frigid streams, the country displayed an eerie sort of beauty, one he'd never beheld in all his travels.

Wales, this land of strangers, puzzled him, especially its people.

An unruly lot, he decided, drawing on all he'd been told about the Welsh. If not bent on destroying their enemies, they were bent on destroying each other. For certain, no Welshman could be trusted. He wondered about the women.

Alana of Llangollen, Gilbert's widow—what was she like? As treacherous as her male counterparts? More to the point, was she the cause of Gilbert's death?

The last correspondence he'd received from Gilbert FitzWilliam was written on the eve of his friend's union to the *lovely Alana.* That was how Gilbert had described his bride in his letter, the missive arriving a good six months after the couple had wed. *Lovely* she might be, but Paxton would reserve opinion on Gilbert's widow until he met her himself.

For now, all he knew about Alana of Llangollen was she'd been offered in marriage by her kinsmen to the new lord who had been sent to fortify the motte-and-bailey castle that had long since been abandoned beyond the fringes of the Welsh marches. It appeared she was a token of peace. Or so Gilbert had implied.

Over the years, his travels having taken him far and wide, Paxton never learned if Gilbert was happy with his marriage. The next he'd heard of his friend was not from the man himself but from Henry, who, only two weeks ago on his return from Normandy, had reported to Paxton that Gilbert had drowned while attempting to save his wife from the raging torrents of a nearby river. Considering Gilbert's skill as a swimmer, the account had made both Paxton and Henry take pause.

In fact, Paxton's expedition across the marches was threefold.

First, he was to make certain the fortress remained in his king's possession, for unknown to the Welsh, Henry planned to invade their country, determined to rout Owain Gwynedd, a Welsh prince whose bold exploits nettled Henry to no end.

During the Anarchy, a time in which Stephen de Blois and Henry's mother, Matilda, vied for the throne of England, much of northern Wales was wrested back from Norman control. With Stephen dead, and Matilda's son now England's indisputable ruler, Henry purposed to reclaim the land that had been lost over the past twenty-two years, and he intended to do it soon.

The second reason for Paxton's journey was that he'd been asked to investigate the events surrounding Gilbert's untimely death. Henry didn't hold much fondness for the Welsh. He trusted them not. From all he'd heard about the breed, Paxton was of a like mind to his king.

The third, and most tempting—well, he hadn't decided yet if he'd accept Henry's offer or even if he'd follow his king's advice. But just in case he chose the course suggested by his king, he had a priest at hand, along with Henry's decree, signed and sealed. All Paxton need do was deliver it into the proper hands.

At last the gates creaked open, the group granted entry by one of the guards. Leading the way, Paxton guided his destrier through the wide portal, along the darkened passage beneath the gate tower, and into the courtyard, whereupon he examined the wooden structures that framed the area, including the small chapel. The buildings were surprisingly in good repair. Next he scanned the inhabitants who'd halted their tasks to view the newcomers with wariness.

"There are an inordinate amount of Welsh manning the place," Graham de Montclair commented as he rode up beside Paxton.

Paxton looked at his companion and fellow knight. "Aye." He again scanned the yard. "And one of them comes our way."

"Good day to you, sirs," the man hailed, halting before the pair. "My name is Madoc. My mistress has sent me to bid you welcome. Once you've seen to your horses, she asks that you come into the hall, where refreshment await you and your men."

"Thank you for your courtesy, Madoc," Paxton said while dismounting. He stepped in front of his steed. "Where is your mistress? I'd like to greet her personally, if I may."

"She's inside." The man jerked his head in the direction of the large building standing opposite them. "She waits for you there." He hesitated, then cleared his throat. "I presume Henry has sent you?"

The Welshman's expression indicated he was most eager for a response, but Paxton countered with a query of his own. "Do you pose the question for yourself or for your mistress, Madoc?"

9

"Since we don't often have visitors, my mistress assumed you were sent by Henry. I hoped to confirm such, so I could inform her in what capacity you have come."

"I will address her myself on that matter," Paxton replied. "For now, tell me: Who is in charge here?"

"That would be Sir Goddard. He's not risen as yet, nor have his men."

Paxton peeked at the sun's angle. Marking it was well past noon, he wondered at the laxness of those who were to defend the castle. He glanced around him to note it was the Welsh who protected the gates. "Then wake him," he stated, "and tell him I am here. I'll meet him in the hall."

Handing the reins to his squire, Paxton motioned to Sir Graham. Together they crossed the yard toward the building where Alana of Llangollen said she would meet them.

Tall, self-assured, he came through the door, his companion behind him. Removing his helm, he raked his long fingers through his thick raven hair, its lustrous length settling against his broad shoulders.

From where she stood at the foot of the stairs, Alana had no trouble distinguishing which of the two men was Paxton de Beaumont.

Prideful, he was. Commanding as well.

His head held in what Alana deemed an arrogant fashion, he surveyed the vast room, from ceiling to floor, and wall to wall. He appeared unimpressed, the accoutrements within the hall apparently not conforming to his tastes. But then, if he understood anything about the Welsh, he'd know they gave themselves not to excess but to modesty.

It was then he spied her.

His gaze fast upon her, he strode toward her, his movements fluid and masculine.

Praying he wasn't as discerning as he appeared, Alana steeled herself for their first encounter. Shoulders squared, her mask in place, she waited.

"Alana of Llangollen?" he inquired when he stood before her.

"Aye."

He bowed his head, then regarded her closely. Alana was at once fascinated by his deep blue eyes and the long black lashes framing them. Her heart skipped a little as she met him stare for stare. Her reaction both confused and surprised her.

"I am Paxton de Beaumont, knight and vassal to Henry, king of England, duke of Normandy and Aquitaine. I am also an acquaintance and friend of your late husband. Please accept my condolences. I was grieved to hear of his death."

Deceptive tears were beckoned forth, and Alana gazed up at him through their shimmering screen. "Thank you for your kind words of sympathy. It has been six months, but I feel Gilbert's loss as though it were yesterday. That I was spared and he . . ."

She allowed the rest to fade, her voice becoming choked. She drew a jagged breath, another ruse she'd perfected.

"Regrettably," she continued after a suitable pause, "naught can change what has happened."

"Regrettable indeed."

There was a harshness to his tone, and Alana wondered if he mistrusted her manifestations of grief in both word and aspect. She measured him, but his face was an unreadable mask. Alana remained wary.

"I hear you've brought a priest with you," she said, again curious as to why he'd done so. "Is that true?"

"It is. Does his presence trouble you?"

"Of course not," Alana announced, thinking he'd sounded rather defensive. "It's just that we are not often visited by a priest. I thought if he is willing, he could say a mass for Gilbert, something that was not afforded him when he died."

"I'm positive Father Jevon will agree. I'll speak to him about your request, but it will have to be done later. Presently, I believe he is inspecting the condition of the chapel. At least, that was where he was headed when I last saw him."

Alana clenched her teeth. She might be mistaken, but by what she'd gathered from Paxton's statement, even the priest believed they were a crass lot, disrespectful of the Lord's house, hence his frantic dash to the chapel.

If Father Jevon expected the place to be little more than a hovel swathed in cobwebs and caked with dust, he'd be very disappointed. The building and its furnishings, though sparse, were in superior order. Thus, the pompous priest could say his prayers without fear of begriming his robes.

Alana constrained her rising anger at these Normans, understanding she *must* be gracious. "Thank you," she said in response to Paxton's offering to arrange a mass. She glanced at the table. "Come. After your long journey, I'm certain you are in need of refreshment. Food and drink have been prepared for you. I ask that you partake of our meager fare and accept it in way of welcome. But first, I offer you water so you may wash your feet."

He frowned down on her. "Wash my feet?"

"That is our custom. It is how we show favor to all our guests." She tilted her head to study him. "You seem uncertain. Does the concept of such a practice displease you?"

12

Far from it, Paxton thought. Though he'd prefer to sink to his neck in a hot bath, he wasn't in the least put off by the notion of merely washing his feet.

"I consider your custom to be most acceptable, but I wouldn't call myself a guest. The term is reserved for those who intend to stay only a short—"

Paxton swallowed his words as a commotion sounded at the entry. Turning toward the disturbance, he assessed the man who had found his way into the hall. Unkempt, his reddish hair knotted and dirty, several days' worth of stubble shading his haggard face, he stood just inside the door, wearing naught but his braies and a mail shirt.

"Where is this Paxton de Beaumont?" he inquired loudly, swaying on his feet.

Paxton's jaw hardened. Surely this wasn't Sir Goddard. If so, the knight was a sad testament to his profession. "Here," Paxton called across the way.

Staggering toward Sir Graham, who stood a few yards inside the doorway, the man spun none too steadily in Paxton's direction. He set his course, his bare feet crushing the fragrant grasses covering the floor. Halfway to his destination, he weaved around the central hearth where he batted at the smoke curling outward and upward toward the beamed ceiling. "Are you Paxton de Beaumont?" he asked on reaching his target.

The man's stale, wine-laden breath struck Paxton square in the face. He stepped back from the repulsive sot. "I am," Paxton replied, noting the man's faded blue eyes were bloodshot and watery. "And I suppose you are Sir Goddard?"

"Aye. Did Henry send you?"

"He did."

The man jerked a nod. "More stomachs to feed," he

13

grumbled. "Come with me, and I'll show you where the garrison is lodged."

Paxton was astounded by the statement. "You have separate quarters?"

Sir Goddard snorted. "Aye." His eyes narrowed on Alana. "'Tis the only way to ensure we'll not be murdered in our sleep."

The man's belligerence wasn't missed by Paxton. He examined the woman who stood at his elbow. Her long-lashed, dark eyes, which had captivated him from the first, remained fixed straight ahead. "Do you have reason to fear for your lives?" he asked the knight.

"'Tis well known not a Welshman can be trusted."

"Still the entire yard is filled with their ilk," Paxton countered. He didn't disagree with the knight's statement, just questioned the man's reasoning. "Why is that, especially if you feel they are untrustworthy?"

"'Twas Sir Gilbert's doing. And hers. They're her kin. Had the fool sent them all back into the woods, where they belong, he might be alive today."

Paxton noticed Alana hadn't moved nor had her expression changed. She was indeed lovely. An incomparable beauty, in fact. Paxton would be the first to admit that, based on her comeliness alone, most any man would be pleased to have her as his wife, including himself. But that was not to say she was incapable of treachery, something he was determined to discover. "Are you saying her kin were responsible for Gilbert's death?"

"Not them. 'Twas her," Sir Goddard proclaimed, swaying on his feet. "Had he not gone into the river after her, we wouldn't have pulled his body from the waters a day later. 'Tis her fault that he's dead."

The allegation, its insinuation sharpening Paxton's attention, brought a quick reaction from Gilbert's widow. She stiffened, spearing Sir Goddard with a condemning look.

"As always, you are feeling the effects of your night of drink," she accused. "Likewise, your hatred of my people has once again made itself obvious. Tell Sir Paxton why you have not sent us into the woods. Go on. Tell him."

Sir Goddard curled his lip at Alana. Deep-seated malice sparked in his eyes. Paxton felt certain there was more to the man's malevolence toward Alana than her heritage. When no response came forth from the knight, he instructed, "Do as the lady has bidden you and tell me why the Welsh are here."

The man shifted his gaze. As he did so, he lurched sideways. "I don't have to explain myself to you."

"Oh, but you're mistaken, sir. I want an answer and I want it now."

"By whose authority do you order my reply?"

"By Henry's authority. And by my own."

Amazement showed on Sir Goddard's face. "Your own? Don't tell me you're the new overlord of this forsaken piece of land?"

"This piece of land and everything on it," Paxton announced, "including you. Answer my question before I have you bound and hung headfirst over the palisade."

A discontented snarl erupted from the man before he said, "There's no mystery to it. They remain as laborers to keep the place in order. 'Tis not befitting for a knight to toil at such menial tasks."

"I presume they are paid for their work."

"They are fed and have a place to sleep."

"And are they allowed to come and go at will?" Paxton inquired.

"If you're asking if they are held prisoner behind these walls, the answer is no."

"I beg to differ with you," Alana interrupted. "Nary a man has left this place without some mishap befalling him once he's passed through the gates."

"If you're speaking about young Aldwyn," Sir Goddard bit back, "he was punished for his thievery."

"He took no more than two days' supply of food to hold him until he reached his dying mother's side," she returned. "You sought not justice in your punishment. Instead, because of your twisted logic, you enacted naught but a grievous cruelty."

"'Twas justice," Sir Goddard insisted.

"By whipping him, then severing his right hand? In my judgment, such a penalty goes beyond what is morally befitting, especially when in fact there was no crime."

"He deserved what he got," the knight snapped.

"Why? Because he is Welsh?"

Paxton was aware that by Henry's own edict thievery was to be severely dealt with. Sir Goddard had acted in accordance with the rule, yet under the circumstances, some compassion seemed in order.

The lad was not a soldier, therefore duty wouldn't have prevented him from attending his mother as she passed from this life to the next. Likewise Paxton doubted the castle stores were in such a critical state that two loaves of bread and a brick of cheese would have been missed.

The only conclusion he could draw was that the knight had been deliberately cruel. The suggestion that the maiming occurred because Aldwyn was Welsh appeared to ring true.

Because of the knight's actions, animosity and dissent were roiling inside the castle walls, creating a constant threat of revolt. Knowing he couldn't chance such an occurrence, Paxton came to a decision.

"Sir Goddard, as of this moment, you are relieved of your duty at this fortress. Find your way back to your quarters and begin packing your belongings. I'll expect you gone from here in an hour."

"With pleasure," the man stated. "You're welcome to this wretched place and its ill-borne inhabitants. 'Tis a cursed land. Why Henry seeks to retain it under his authority is beyond me. I offer you a word of caution, Paxton de Beaumont. Keep the slut far from you, lest you also end up dead."

Paxton watched as Sir Goddard rolled on his heel and staggered toward the door. Feeling a light pressure against his arm, he focused on the small hand that had settled there. An instant later, he found himself staring into a pair of entrancing eyes . . . eyes that held for a man an exciting promise, the reward of which was ecstasy, delirious and wild.

His reaction was spontaneous. Lust seared his veins, sparking fire in his loins.

Surprised by his response, Paxton understood Gilbert's attraction to the Welsh beauty. With her woman's form covered from head to toe in a headrail of homespun linen and a tunic of caddis wool, her allure was in no way overt. Nevertheless, beneath her modest, grief-stricken facade, she was a temptress, a seductress. Was she a murderess as well?

Her soft voice broke through the haze of desire clouding Paxton's thoughts as she whispered his name. He forced himself to heed her words.

"Thank you for sending Sir Goddard away. Ever since Gilbert's death, he's been exceedingly barbarous and spiteful. Truly, I'm grateful Henry has appointed you as our new overlord."

Keep the slut far from you, lest you also end up dead.

Sir Goddard's warning attacked him anew, and

Paxton was eager to be away from this bewitching siren before he found himself forever caught under her spell.

Or, like his friend, he lost his life.

The open doorway beckoned to him. It was time he inspected the rest of the garrison and judged which men should depart with Sir Goddard and which of them should stay.

While he eased Alana's hand from his arm, intending to take his leave, his mind conjured forth a gruesome picture of what could have been Gilbert's pallid, lifeless form when pulled from the river.

The truth.

One way or another Paxton aimed to have it.

"Today, Alana of Llangollen, you may be grateful Henry has made me your new overlord," he responded, his tone grating. "But know I have not been sent here to ease your burdens. Far from it."

He admired how she withstood his abrasiveness. She hadn't so much as flinched. But he wasn't through.

"My authority is all encompassing," he continued, his inflection equally as emphatic. "Everyone here will observe my commands. As to Sir Goddard, in the long run, you may find I am not barbaric like he is, but let it be known: Should the situation warrant, my form of justice is every bit as forceful and as swift as his." He captured her chin between his thumb and forefinger; her full attention as well. "Grateful?" he queried. "Come to me a few weeks hence and tell me your feelings then. I'll wager anything you'll not be as welcoming of my presence as you now are."

With that, he strode from the hall.

CHAPTER

2

The hour allotted to Sir Goddard to gather his belongings and make his departure was almost spent.

Stationed to one side of the courtyard, Alana watched the knight. His actions were brusque, his mood glum. Close by, a dozen men, whom Sir Paxton had also deemed unfit to serve at the fortress, behaved in a similar manner.

"'Tis good the bastard is leaving," Madoc bit out near her ear.

"Aye," she said. But she wondered if she should have agreed so readily.

She wanted the knight gone, yet her emotions were mixed. If the truth were known, she felt at an impasse.

On one hand, she was ecstatic that the loathsome man would soon be on his way. Conversely, though, she feared his replacement would be far more worrisome than Sir Goddard ever was.

Come to me a few weeks hence . . . I'll wager anything you'll not be as welcoming of my presence as you now are.

Paxton de Beaumont's words were branded in her mind. She doubted he would be half as malicious in his dealings with her people as Sir Goddard had been, but she still fretted over how he intended to treat them.

Forceful and swift. Those were the terms he'd used to describe his form of justice.

He'd promised no barbaric acts, which Alana believed meant no beatings and no severing of hands. But he'd made it very clear: His adjudication would be effective and executed with haste. Did that mean, instead of torturing the alleged offender, he'd simply kill him?

Alana turned her gaze to the man in question and was entranced by what she saw.

Sunlight bathed his burnished hair, haloing his head in a blue-black light. The shimmering rays glistened off his mail hauberk, creating a silver aura from his shoulders to his knees.

A celestial host, she mused at first. Then remembering he was *Norman,* she dismissed the notion, equating him to one of Hell's own demons instead.

Her senses restored, she studied him. Positioned a half-dozen yards from her, he appeared at ease, as though he hadn't a care in the world.

Only a fool would regard him as being heedless. Beneath his indolent facade, he remained alert, ready to react at the slightest provocation. He was powerful, his skills unmatched, a warrior of the highest caliber. Oh, how she prayed that he possessed compassion and understanding as well.

He must have been aware that she watched him, for he turned his head. Their eyes met, and the air between them quickened . . . sizzled with the same vitalizing energy of an approaching storm.

From observing nature's fury, the rains coming often to her homeland, she knew the feeling to be exhilarating but dangerous.

The same as he.

The concept alarmed Alana, and she looked away, but didn't act soon enough. To her total dismay, he came toward her, halting no more than a hand's breadth from her.

"I take it you are eager to see Sir Goddard on his way," he commented.

Alana dared not face him. The strange stirrings inside her, which she was at a loss to explain, had not subsided. She felt at her most vulnerable. One glance, and what confidence she held would be utterly destroyed.

And along with that frailty of emotion came the possibility that he might unearth her secret. He was far too discerning, and Alana knew she couldn't chance his discovering her deception. Too risky, she thought, positive all would come to ruin.

"A twinkling of time would not be soon enough to have him gone," she said, staring straight ahead.

"I cannot promise a 'twinkling,' but I can assure you he'll be away from here shortly."

As his response met her ears, several of Sir Goddard's companions mounted their horses. The others were following suit. "He won't be missed," Alana returned, noting how the knight made a last minute check of his steed's saddle. "The man is a beast."

"Perhaps that is so. But after Sir Goddard is gone, you may find that you've spoken too soon."

"Never will I believe that."

"Never?" he asked. "You might think that now, but

once you've dealt with me, you may in fact be wishing him back."

Forgetting her resolve not to look at him, Alana turned around. Had she been right in her assumption? Would he be far more worrisome than Sir Goddard ever was? Though the warning was distinct, no such threat marked his features.

His mood was lighter than when he'd left the hall, for an easy smile touched his lips, dimpling each sun-bronzed cheek. "I thought that would get your attention."

She blinked. "My attention?"

"Aye. You refuse to face me while we speak. Why?"

The answer was simple: He both fascinated and frightened her. Not that she would tell him such. Nevertheless it was true.

Once again she found herself captivated, his lazy-lidded eyes reminding her of a clear morning sky. It was then she heard what she thought was the roll of thunder.

The sound swelled in her ears, and the ground vibrated beneath her feet.

"Milady!" Madoc shouted.

Alana glimpsed the charging horse, its large hooves biting into the earth, clods of mud slinging into the air.

Just as she thought she'd be run down, Paxton thrust himself between her and Sir Goddard's steed. As the beast was reined in, its shoulder struck Paxton full in the chest. He grabbed hold of the bridle and steadied himself, checking the horse's tossing head at the same time.

Offering no apology for the scare he'd given either of them, Sir Goddard stated, "We are ready to take our leave."

"Then be gone with you," Paxton grated, releasing

the harness. "You should be at your destination by tomorrow night."

"We'll be at Chester Castle sooner than tomorrow night. *That* I can promise you." Sir Goddard looked to Alana, then back at Paxton. "I suggest you sleep with your sword nigh, else you might find yourself slumbering for all eternity." He turned his horse and set it into a canter toward the gate tower.

When Sir Goddard and his companions had passed through the opening, the gates closing behind them, Alana breathed a relieved sigh. She would thank Paxton for coming between her and what would have been certain death had the horse trampled her, but she decided not to.

On extending her appreciation once before, his retort had been clipped and unfriendly. By the looks of him now—his jaw set, his eyes cold, his body rigid, Sir Goddard's cautioning words no doubt the reason —she believed if she voiced her gratitude his rejoinder would be delivered in much the same manner as it had been when they were inside the hall.

"The fare that was laid for you on your arrival grows stale. Do you wish to partake of some refreshment?" she inquired, thinking she was on safe ground.

"Have those who traveled with me been fed?" he countered, his tone formal.

"Except for the priest, aye. I've yet to see him, but I imagine he's still in the chapel. As for the others, their bellies are full, their plates and cups empty."

"Then clear the tables. The priest can eat later."

"But you must be hungry. Or, at the very least, thirsty."

"I'll take my sustenance at supper. Right now, I have more important matters to attend to."

He spun on his heel and crossed the yard, Alana staring after him.

"What do you think he's about?" Madoc asked once Paxton had entered the door of the building that housed the garrison.

"I'm not certain." An uneasy feeling was growing inside Alana. "But pray, Madoc, his haste has only to do with his wanting to acquaint himself with those who have remained and the workings within the fortress itself and not about Gilbert. Especially not about his death."

"And you saw or heard nothing unusual before or after Sir Gilbert was pulled from the river?" Paxton asked.

The man shook his head. "Nay, sir. The Lady Alana was distraught . . . so pitifully woeful, the same as anyone would be when stricken with such a sudden shock."

"Her tears—were they genuine?"

"As far as I could tell—aye, I'd say they were." The man paused briefly. "I need to add that, despite her apparent grief, she insisted on preparing the body for burial herself. Considering the agony she was suffering over her loss, I thought it to be a loving gesture."

Feeling frustrated, Paxton rubbed the back of his neck. "Aye. One would think so." He straightened from the small table where he leaned a hip against its scarred wooden top. "Thank you for your help. You are dismissed."

Watching the young soldier as he made his way from the room, Paxton decided he'd learned nothing of consequence. From the time he'd entered the garrison, he'd set to questioning each man about the day Gilbert died. One by one, they gave the same accounting. It was no different with this man.

The door closed behind the last of the twenty who Paxton had found fit to continue serving at the fortress. Unfortunately, he still lacked proof that the circumstances of Gilbert's death were anything more than what his widow had related to Henry: an accidental drowning.

Yet Paxton remained wary.

Though Sir Goddard was an unkempt drunk, the man wasn't a complete fool. Something had to have given him the impression that his life and the lives of each of Henry's men were in jeopardy . . . that Gilbert's death was not as it appeared.

Too late Paxton wished he'd questioned the knight more fully before sending him on his way to Chester and to young Earl Hugh, under whose command Sir Goddard served. He'd now have to ferret out the answers he sought on his own. And he would start his search with Alana of Llangollen.

A hollow gurgling noise disrupted the room's silence. Paxton's hunger was unmistakable. "What hour is it?" he asked, his gaze pinpointing Sir Graham.

The knight stepped from the corner where he'd been standing quietly. "It's nearly dark. I imagine our supper awaits us. I say we make our way to the hall before there is naught left us but crumbs."

"Your suggestion is sound," Paxton returned, his stomach declaring its emptiness again. "Lead the way, sir."

Hunger driving them, the pair exited the room, then the building. As they made their way across the courtyard, Paxton heard the hum of voices coming from the hall. On entering, the aroma of roasted meat filled his nostrils; his stomach rolled with the ferocity of a lion's roar. He and Sir Graham found a seat.

While Paxton set to nourishing his body, the issue of Alana's innocence or guilt kept plaguing him. Not just because he hoped to avenge his friend, but because of the opportunity that could be lost.

The third reason why he had crossed the marches—and to Paxton, the most enticing reason of all—was the promise from his king that he and his issue would be made permanent overlords of this fortress, of this portion of land on which it sat, and of all the inhabitants for miles around. But the pledge came with one stipulation: Paxton must gain for Henry the sworn allegiances of all those Welsh whom he would oversee.

His status was that of a knight-errant, his services bought by Henry. With there being no hope of his ever receiving an inheritance of his own, the notion that he could be the master of a vast region, along with part and kind, appealed greatly. Yet the area of his promised domain was here in Wales. And the Welsh had no inclination toward being tamed. Least of all by a Norman.

Paxton recalled those moments with Henry, just a fortnight ago, when the offer had been extended. Then, as now, he'd been troubled by whether the Welsh would accept him as their overlord, and Henry as their king.

Worried that he might not be able to fulfill the requirements set forth, he must have allowed his uncertainties to show. Henry didn't miss his dubious look. His eyes narrowing, Henry had scoffed at Paxton, asking if he had not the wit nor the fortitude to subdue such a cloddish lot as the Welsh.

"You know I have both the intelligence and the nerve," he had countered, taking umbrage at Henry's barb.

"Then hear me, Sir Paxton," Henry had said. "You have served me well, and I wish to reward you. We both know the Welsh are unpredictable, and that what I have asked will not come without effort. Therefore, as your king, I shall attempt to make it easier for you to receive that which you most desire."

With a quick wave of his hand, Henry had signaled to a robed cleric, who in turn dipped his quill into the inkwell, then waited to put words to the parchment.

Clearing his throat, Henry had then announced, "By royal decree, you will become the new husband of Alana of Llangollen. All properties, whether belonging to her late husband, Gilbert FitzWilliam, or given to her by inheritance from her deceased sire, Rhodri ap Daffyd—which, according to the moldering bastard's claim, is the land where the old Norman fortress presently sits—will pass into your possession on the day of your nuptials. Once she is your wife, it shouldn't be too hard to gain the allegiance of her people."

Paxton had objected to Henry's prescribing that he should wed the woman who may have slain Gilbert. Besides, he'd doubted Alana of Llangollen would accept any such edict as binding. She was, after all, Welsh.

Henry had bristled at Paxton's stated opposition. "The day she married Gilbert she made herself my subject," he'd snapped. "She will obey me, or she will pay the penalty.

"As for Gilbert's death, we don't know if it was as she said: a drowning. Or if it is as we suspect: a vicious murder. If she suits you, I suggest you marry the woman. If she doesn't suit, marry her anyway. The only time you need lie with her is when you wish for her to conceive a legitimate heir. Should it be pleasure you seek, and she doesn't satisfy, find yourself a comely wench and take her as your mistress. If, in the future, you do discover that Alana of Llangollen was indeed instrumental in her late husband's death, bind her over to me, and I shall deal with her treachery myself.

"All but the latter is a suggestion. If you don't elect to marry her, that is your choice. I thought it would be helpful if I were to intercede, thus my decree. However, as I've just stated: If she is behind Gilbert's death, she is to be brought before me so I may sit in judgment over her. The offense will not go unpunished. On this point, I will have it no other way. Is that clear?"

Paxton had answered in the affirmative, then Henry had made him swear an oath that, if the proof of her guilt were found, Alana would be given over, even if she became Paxton's wife.

His king's offer was tempting, and Paxton wanted nothing more than to be lord and master of his own estate. But the condition remained: The Welsh must swear allegiance to Henry. Without Alana of Llangollen at his side, Paxton saw the quest as being almost impossible.

Yes, he could bring them to their knees by force, continuing to rule over them by the threat of the sword, but the prize he so coveted would soon become tarnished under a constant battle of weapons and of wills.

Which brought him to the piece of parchment that was twice folded and hidden in a leather pouch tied to his belt.

Though Alana was quite beautiful and most appealing, the prospect of them ever marrying seemed far-fetched. They had differences aplenty, a huge discrepancy being their heritages.

But the main obstacle was trust.

Unless he was fully assured of her innocence, Henry's decree—stated more formally on paper than from the king's own mouth—would remain tucked away. Likewise, the priest could keep to his prayers, while delivering, daily, a morning mass.

Lifting his gaze from his plate, which was close to being depleted of its fare, he scanned the hall, searching for the woman in his thoughts. To his surprise, he found her among the servers.

For the longest time he watched her, impressed by the fact that she didn't place herself above her countrymen. She filled the cups, replenished the trenchers, working as industriously as those he considered to be beneath her. He noted too that she kept to the opposite side of the room, far from him.

Reflecting on how she first refused to look at him during their conversation in the yard, Paxton wondered why she shied away from him. Did he unnerve her that much?

He couldn't imagine he'd done anything to elicit such a response. Unless . . .

"Do you still believe Gilbert's death to be an act of murder?" Sir Graham asked after tossing off the last of his wine. "From what we were told, nothing indicates such."

The statement drew Paxton's attention. Just as with him, Sir Graham had also eaten in silence, his blond head bent studiously over his plate. Obviously, his companion's thoughts had been centered on the last several hours and the twenty men who had paraded in and out of the garrison.

Paxton waited until the knight's cup was refilled. When the flagon was moved toward his own cup, he placed his hand over its rim, shaking his head. "No, it doesn't," he said after the server had moved on. "But if someone wanted to hide the truth badly enough, that someone could quite possibly succeed."

Graham's green eyes widened. "How?"

"Tears of bereavement have been known to soften many a man's heart, even if they are false."

"Then you think his widow was faking her grief . . . that she is the culprit?"

"My suspicions lean that way."

"Suspicions are not proof."

"Perhaps not," Paxton said, his gaze again finding Alana. "Call it gut instinct, if you like, but I say she's hiding something. If she didn't murder Gilbert, she knows who did. One way or another, she's involved, and I intend to prove that she is."

"I must warn my uncle," Alana whispered to Madoc hours later.

The pair stood just inside the doorway to the hall. Circled around the hearth, the castle's inhabitants slumbered on the floor behind them.

"Let one of us go in your stead," her servant insisted, his voice kept low. "'Tis far too risky. Unlike his foregoer, he hardly touched his wine. He may still be awake. If you're caught trying to slip through the side gate, he'll become suspicious."

She glanced through the opening at the building where Paxton de Beaumont and his men were chambered, all of them having retired there for the night. No light shone from its windows. "I'll not get caught. Besides acquainting Rhys about the present situation, I must speak to him about other matters as well."

"Then let me come with you," Madoc countered. "The night wood is no place for a young woman alone."

"Have you forgotten my heritage?" she asked, now inspecting the yard. "I can run these hills and forests as good as any man." She shook her head. "Nay, Madoc. I must go by myself."

"Once you reach your uncle's, stay there and do not

return. This one is far more astute than was Sir Goddard. If he learns the truth—"

Alana's fingers fell over Madoc's lips. "I have to return. Whether Henry says otherwise or not, this land is my inheritance. It belongs to me and to you and to all the Welsh who dwell here. I'll not desert what is mine. Nor will I leave my friends to fend for themselves against these dogs." She again glanced at the yard to see no one was about. "I'll be back before dawn."

Before Madoc could issue another protest, Alana was out the door, heading for the side gate. The sky was cloudy, masking the moon's glow. The better for her, she thought, knowing her trained eye could see twice as far in the dark as any Norman's. The air smelled of rain. She prayed the skies didn't open until she'd crossed the river and was back.

Rhys—she had to get to him so she could warn him and her cousins that Sir Goddard was no longer at the fortress. The knight had been lax, mainly because he continually kept his face in his cup. But his replacement was every bit the warrior that Sir Goddard had failed to be. Paxton de Beaumont, along with his men, as well as the twenty others he'd chosen to stay, could fend off her countrymen with ease, no matter how large their numbers.

Not that Rhys planned to attack, but she must apprise him to stay on the opposite side of the river, far from the stronghold which overlooked the valley and the heavy wood. They could no longer meet as they once had, as they planned to do tonight. The risk was far too great.

On silent feet, Alana traveled from the sheltering shadows of one building to the next. Halfway along the side of the last structure, she spied the gate. Seeing no one guarded the outlet, she broke into a run. Just as she cleared the building, a hand snagged her arm, pulling her up short. Though she nearly screamed at full voice from the sudden scare, a soft cry was all that escaped her lips. She stared at the man who had grabbed her. . . .

Paxton de Beaumont.

"What are you doing?" she asked, attempting to shake from his hold.

"It would seem that is my question to you." He looked at the gate, then back at her. "Where were you planning to be off to at such a late hour? Does your lover wait for you in the wood?"

Glaring up at the tall knight, Alana clenched her jaw. *Hardly.* She'd die before she lay with a man again. Yet, considering the strange feelings that Paxton had evoked in her earlier, she wondered if that were true.

"I was going to Gilbert's grave," she said, dismissing the last of her mind's meanderings as pure nonsense.

"His what?"

"His grave," she lashed back. "It lies just beyond this gate, in a clearing, in the wood. Sir Goddard would not allow me to leave the fortress. So, at night, when he'd fallen drunk on his pallet, I would make my way to Gilbert's resting place to offer a prayer for his soul."

Paxton remained silent for such a long time Alana feared he didn't believe her. The tension drained from her when he said, "I'm not Sir Goddard. It is best you remember that. When the sun has risen, we shall both go to Gilbert's grave, so I may offer a prayer for him as well. For now, you will return to the hall. To make certain you do, I will accompany you."

As she was escorted back the same way she'd come, Alana thought of her uncle. Somehow she had to get word to him.

Madoc, she decided, certain, from now on, she'd be constantly watched.

Not Madoc, she concluded, knowing Paxton de Beaumont was too clever by far. Someone else would have to take the message. Someone he'd not suspect.

Maybe Aldwyn.

No. He'd lost far too much as it was. She couldn't chance that he'd next lose his life. Even so, Rhys had to be warned.

They halted outside the doors to the hall. Alana waited for Paxton to release her arm. But he held her fast. "Is there something else you wanted?" she inquired at long last.

"A truthful answer from you."

Alana lifted her chin. "What is the question?"

"Did Gilbert drown? Or did you murder him?"

CHAPTER

3

~~~

Angry silence was Paxton's reward.

Torches blazed in their holders, illuminating the courtyard at strategic points throughout. But no light shone at the spot where they stood, and Alana's eyes lay in shadow. Nevertheless, he felt her irate stare . . . a stare that threatened to cleave him in two.

Seconds passed, the question of whether or not she had murdered Gilbert hanging between them like a razor-sharp sword. At last he heard her indrawn breath.

"If you wish to name me as the cause of Gilbert's death, you are welcome to do so. Had I not taken that fateful plunge, the river sweeping me along in its eddy, he might be alive today. Instead he lies in his grave . . . pulled from the same waters that nearly ended my own life. I did not force him to do what he did. He made the choice himself. So blame me if you will. Sir

Goddard certainly does. Why should I hope it would be any different with you?"

Paxton's fingers tightened around her arm when she strove to break free from his hold. "Because I am not Sir Goddard," he replied sharply.

"Given the nature of your question, you couldn't prove it by me," she snapped, still resisting his grip. "If you do not believe my accounting of the events, ask your counterparts what transpired that day. Ask them what they saw when they found my husband's body and brought it back to the fortress."

"I have."

Her fruitless struggles ceased. "And?"

"They saw nothing that would indicate Gilbert's death was anything other than a drowning," he admitted, relaxing his hold somewhat.

"Yet you choose not to believe them. Why?"

Paxton was unable to answer her query. What was he to say? Though he lacked the needed proof, instinct told him she murdered Gilbert? Or, at the very least, had some sort of involvement in the deed?

Such an argument would be given little credence when set before his king. But Henry apparently shared the same intrinsic feelings as did Paxton. Gilbert had died. The question was how.

"You, sir, have prejudged me," she announced when he stayed quiet for too long. "And you've done so for no other reason than because I am Welsh."

"You're wrong."

"Am I? Had Gilbert been married to a woman of Norman blood would you be asking the same question of her?"

Paxton again held his reply, her query stirring around inside his mind. Was she right? If Alana had been Norman and not Welsh would the question ever have been asked?

"You claim not to be anything like Sir Goddard," she said. "But I say you are. The two of you are a perfect match, especially in way of your prejudices."

Her words hit him like a wave of cold water. He wanted to deny her accusation, to deny he held any bias against her ilk, but he couldn't. In truth, he'd deemed her guilty, had done so before he'd ever set eyes on her. The motive, he now realized, was indeed her heritage.

He breathed deeply. "I withdraw the question. Likewise, I apologize for having asked it. But, as you are currently aware, I'm having great difficulty believing Gilbert drowned. He was an expert swimmer . . . in fact, he was the one who taught the skill to me."

"That day his ability was not enough," she said. "We had experienced a heavy rainfall the night before, far heavier than usual. The current was exceptionally swift, the river churning like a boiling caldron. I didn't see Gilbert come in after me. Once I hit the water, I was far too busy struggling to keep my own head above the surface as I was being swept downriver. I was terrified, certain I would die. My lungs felt as though they might burst. Had it not been for a tree limb stretching across my path, which I somehow caught hold of, I wouldn't have survived. Luck was with me. Gilbert, however, did not share in the same good fortune as I."

Paxton noted how she trembled under his grasp, how her voice quavered when she related the incident. She'd been reliving the horror of that day, the horror of losing her husband, the horror of almost forfeiting her own life. His heart lurched, compassion filling him.

Releasing her arm, he raised his hand and touched her face to find it was wet with her tears. "Put your misery to rest, milady, and think of that day no more. The hour grows quite late. It is time you retire. Tomorrow, as promised, we will visit Gilbert's grave. Till then I bid you good night."

"Tomorrow," she whispered. Turning, she hurried into the hall.

Once the door had closed behind her, Paxton expelled his breath.

The moisture from her cheek yet clung to his fingertips. Tears of grief. Or were they feigned?

Though he tried, he couldn't seem to rid himself of his suspicion. Part of the reason, he acknowledged, had to do with her being Welsh.

The wind ruffled his hair, and the first driblets of rain struck his shoulders and splattered the ground. His gaze remaining fixed to the door, Paxton ignored nature's own tears. Rather he sought to calm his thoughts and clear his mind.

Until tonight, he hadn't known the extent of his prejudices, perhaps because he was unaware that he harbored any. He was not alone though. Intolerance was a shortcoming of all humanity. Unfortunate but true.

Lost in a self-examination over his feelings about Alana and her race the rain pelted him with force, but he felt not a drop. He was soaked to the skin when he was able to at last concede that, in itself, her heritage was inconsequential. She deserved to be judged solely on her character. This he understood.

Yet . . .

Paxton whirled around and stalked through the growing puddles toward the garrison.

His mental study had been for naught. Whether it had to do with her being Welsh or, more likely, because of some innate sensation that kept twisting at his gut, his skepticism about Gilbert's widow refused to subside.

A tragedy or vile treachery—which was it?

Paxton knew he'd not rest until the answer was made clear.

New growth sprouted from the forest floor, peeking up and around the decaying leaves littering the damp ground. Tree limbs waved at a canopy of puffy white clouds and patches of blue sky, a cool breeze stirring through their tops. Undulating mists rose from the turbulent river below, the ethereal vapors disintegrating into nothingness once they met the sun's rays. The air smelled fresh, invigorating, cleansed from the night's heavy rain.

In the center of the small clearing, Alana gazed down on Paxton's bowed head. He knelt on one knee beside Gilbert's grave, his eyes closed in reverent prayer.

While Alana stood behind him, she was busy offering up silent prayers of her own. Whereas Paxton's were for Gilbert's soul, hers were for herself in way of thanksgiving.

Between lauding every saint that came to mind, she wondered what she would have done if Paxton had not stopped her near the gate, but had instead followed her into the wood and across the river, to see her meeting with Rhys. She imagined him lurking behind a tree, listening to every word, discovering the truth about her deception. Would he have slain them then and there?

Alana silently extended special praise to St. David, the patron saint of all Wales, leader against the Saxons, and she hoped, her own personal protector against Paxton de Beaumont and all his kind.

Staring down at the elongated patch of earth that Father Jevon, at Paxton's request, had sanctified earlier—a mass being said also—she was more than certain that if St. David hadn't been watching over her last night she'd now be lying in a newly prepared grave, Gilbert's death avenged.

Rhys—she had to get word to him.

Listening to the rush of water as it swelled over the rocks and crashed against the boulders lining the river below, she knew it would be several days before anyone could safely cross to the other side.

Unknowingly she chewed her lower lip as she fretted.

With her not having showed at their appointed meeting place, Alana was aware her uncle would be worried. Though thwarted in her endeavor, she was glad she hadn't been able to traverse the river. She'd not have gotten back if she had. She just prayed Rhys wasn't foolish enough to come looking for her, nor that he would attempt to cross the cataclysm himself.

A twig snapped underfoot. Alana gasped when she felt a hand on her arm. Blinking, she saw Paxton standing before her. She was so lost in her thoughts that she hadn't seen him rise. He stared down at her, his face somber.

"I spoke to you, several times," he said, "but you were far away. I presume you were again thinking about that day."

She looked to the grave and its carved stone marker. Praying God would not smite her for her deceit, she beckoned forth false tears. "Whenever I come here I always think about that day." She raised her chin, allowing Paxton to see the shimmer in her eyes. "How could I not?"

"Your grief is understandable. But you must not

allow yourself to dwell on the incident. To do so will only make you ill."

Alana was amazed when his thumb brushed against her cheek. His touch was tender yet brief, much as it had been the night before. And like last night, she found she was again affected by his sympathetic ministrations, more than she wished to admit.

Her heart fluttered erratically; her face suddenly felt flushed; oddly, she was left breathless. Never had a man made her feel this way.

Taking command of her emotions, she decried the strange responses he always managed to evoke. She hadn't wanted to think about their effects last night, and she certainly didn't want to think about them now.

He pulled his hand from her face to gaze at the tear on the tip of his thumb. Then his hand fell to his side. "I thank you for bringing me here and allowing me the opportunity to say farewell to Gilbert."

"It was kind of you to offer a prayer for him," she countered, hoping he hadn't detected the differences in her physical demeanor. "I know he would be gladdened that you thought so highly of him." She paused, then approached the one subject that had been needling her since his arrival. "Gilbert had mentioned your name several times with affection, but I don't know much about your friendship or how it is the two of you had met. I'd very much like to learn these things, if it isn't too much trouble."

He chuckled. "I doubt he mentioned me with 'affection,' considering how competitive we were. Despite our rivalry, we did become good friends.

"As for how we met, Gilbert and I were first pages, then squires at the house of Varaville in Normandy. We learned our skills there, while serving both a father and a son. Eventually we squired for different knights before we finally earned a pair of golden spurs of our own.

"The last time I saw Gilbert was five years ago, prior to my being called to service at Cartbridge Castle, north of Derby in England. I visited him at Chester, where he was under the command of Earl Ranulf. I was gladdened to see him well and happy." He inclined his head. "Now that I've told you what you wanted to know, I'd like to hear the same from you. How was it that you met Gilbert?"

"I was here when he and his men arrived."

He arched his brow; disbelief showed on his face. "What ho! Are you saying you'd usurped Henry's own castle?"

"Henry was not king then. 'Twas Stephen who ruled England. But nay. This land was my father's. Because of the conflict, first between Stephen and Matilda, then between Stephen and Henry, the fortress had long since been abandoned. Instead of destroying it, we utilized it for ourselves. When my father died, all this became mine."

"As I say, you appropriated the castle from Henry."

Alana bristled. "How can someone appropriate something when it already belongs to him? You Normans are all alike: arrogant and greedy. You're never satisfied with what you have, perpetually wanting and taking more. Did it ever occur to you that you're not welcome here?"

"Aye, it has occurred. Nevertheless we are here, and here we shall stay."

Alana noticed they were practically nose-to-nose. Not exactly a favorable position to be in, she concluded, then pulled back a step. Her anger, however, did not subside. "Henry's interference here may one day meet with defeat, then you'll all be sent packing. But this talk about your king is inconsequential. It was Earl Ranulf who sent Gilbert here, for he was the one who had claimed this land. And like Gilbert, he is now dead."

"Which brings us back to Henry," Paxton stated. "Since Ranulf's heir, Hugh, the current earl of Chester, is but ten years old and cannot possibly defend any of his holdings with either his wit or his sword, Henry has taken it upon himself to act in the boy's stead. Hence my own presence here."

Alana couldn't refute his argument. Earl Hugh was only six when his father died—poisoned, it was said, by William Peveril, who was angered because his lands had been given to Ranulf by charter from Henry.

When the news of Ranulf's death eventually reached the remote castle, Gilbert had worried over whether any rebellious Welsh from outlying areas would spawn an attack against them. Earl Hugh, because of his age, was unable to command, and Henry had not yet ascended to England's throne, while King Stephen's rule was as lax as ever when it came to his holdings in Wales.

In the end, Gilbert's unease had been for naught, for no such aggression ever came. But much of northern Wales did see an upsurge of violence as Owain Gwynedd was spurred to action, his quest to reclaim his homeland from the Normans continuing unto this day.

"Have you no response?" Paxton inquired, for she'd been quiet way too long.

Alana met his gaze. "Nay. 'Tis as you say. The castle is Henry's."

She didn't believe that one whit, but had conceded such simply to appease him. She'd allowed her anger to be fueled, which helped her cause not at all. The more vocal she became about who owned this land, the more his suspicions would rise. It would be better for her to remain docile, for everyone's sake.

At her prolonged silence, their tempers had cooled. An easy smile graced Paxton's once stern visage. He was obviously pleased that he'd won the point.

Turning, Alana moved away from Gilbert's grave; Paxton followed. Near a large oak, she stopped and pivoted around to again face him.

He gazed at her a long while, then as though they'd never locked horns, he said, "Llangollen—doesn't it lie south of here on the River Dee?"

"It does."

"How far?"

She leaned against the thick trunk, its rough bark pricking at her back. "Ten miles. And Chester is a little over ten miles to the east."

"If Llangollen is where you were born, how is it your father claimed the land here?"

Another sensitive subject, Alana thought. Not to him but to her. It was one she'd sooner forget, especially the strife that followed Daffyd ap Cynan's death. "My family has lived here for centuries," she replied. "When my grandfather died, my father accepted his inheritance."

She refused to tell him that on Daffyd's death, his two sons had warred mercilessly over their inheritance. Rhodri, the elder son, and Alana's father, finally won out, but it was at the cost of his own brother Hywel's life. To her, some things were best left in the past, and this was one of them. At least her cousin, Gwenifer, held no grudge, and for that Alana was thankful.

"What prompted you to ask such a question?" Alana inquired.

He shrugged. "Your name and our locale—they don't match. Let's say I was just curious." He paused. "Your mother—I presume she is also deceased?"

"Aye. She died when I was eight; my father when I was fourteen. She from a fever; he from an accident."

"An accident?"

"He was thrown from his horse."

"You have no other kin?"

"Certainly. You've spoken to some of them. Most live here with me."

She hadn't lied exactly. Just had neglected to mention her relatives beyond the river. Again she thought of Rhys, praying he stayed away.

Paxton stepped closer. "You must have been a very young bride. Were Gilbert here, I'd accuse him of having robbed the cradle."

Alana couldn't help but smile. "I shall take that as a compliment. However, when Gilbert and I had wed, I was older than most brides. Presently I'm in my twenty-first year."

"You look to be six-and-ten."

"Had he lived, Gilbert would now be seven-and-twenty. I presume, since you squired together, you are the same age."

"I'll be six-and-twenty on the day of the Feast of All Holy Martyrs. Gilbert wasn't as quick to learn as I. Though we were knighted at nearly the same time, overall it took him a bit longer to receive his spurs. I said we were competitive, didn't I?"

Wasn't as quick to learn as I. The phrase stuck, and Alana vowed to remember it well. "You indicated you were rivals. But in defense of Gilbert, he was quite capable in his own right."

Capable of his own duplicity, Alana thought. And because of his deceit, he rested beneath the earth, cold, stiff, and rotting, the worms eating at his flesh.

"Tell me," she said. "Has your curiosity about me been quieted? If so, I have a few questions of my own to ask."

"Such as?"

"You were interested in my parents. What about your own? Are they living?"

"My mother is. My father died eight years ago. He was returning to our estate from the last Crusade, when he was apparently beset by a band of thieves. A passerby found him two miles from our home alongside the road. He was stripped of his possessions, lying nude in a ditch. His wounds were grievous but not so grievous that he could not have mended. But a cold rain had fallen on the region the night he was attacked. He took a congestion in his lungs. That was what did him in." Paxton shook his head. "It always amazed me that he could travel half the world away to battle against hordes of heathens—even risked the plague!—and return to Normandy with nary a scratch, only to die from the croup."

"How very sad," Alana said, thinking that life was forever filled with twists and turns, no one ever really knowing what might happen next. "Your mother—is she in Normandy?"

"Actually she is now in Aquitaine. She has remarried and is very happy. My older brother is in Normandy, content with his wife and four children. The last I heard, they were all well."

As he'd spoken, his hand met the tree near her head. With each word, he leaned closer and closer. Alana was now staring straight into his eyes. They were so hauntingly blue, clear and unshadowed. She'd never forget their color nor the way their owner gazed at her.

Those strange feelings erupted in her once more, and Alana's breath grew short. "I should get back to the fortress," she said, slipping away from the tree.

Paxton caught her arm. "Before you go, I have one more request of you. I'd like to see where it happened."

By *it* Alana knew he referred to the supposed mishap that had befallen Gilbert and herself.

"If taking me there is too difficult for you," he continued, "I'll understand. I ask only that you turn me in the right direction."

Her heart fluttered wildly, but this time in fear. Was he still questing for answers? Did he believe, even after six months, he might find some clue, some offering, that would inevitably point to the truth: Gilbert was in fact murdered? If he found something, would it in turn implicate her?

Alana examined his face, seeking her own answers. Her trepidation subsided when she realized he would discover nothing at the site where she'd tumbled into the water. No blood, no signs of a struggle, naught that would suggest anything malicious had occurred. At least not to Gilbert.

Paxton's deep voice broke through her thoughts. "I can see the concept of accompanying me unnerves you. Just show me the way, and I'll find the place on my own."

Unsettling memories of that fateful day had thus far prevented her from returning to the particular area alongside the river. She'd not guide him to the location now, save for one thing: Rhys could be, at this very moment, wandering the opposite bank, hunting for a feasible spot where he could cross over. If she spied him first, she could warn him off. Likewise, if he came upon them while they stood beside the river, she'd be able to wave him back in the wood. Either way, she couldn't allow Paxton to go alone.

"I'll take you there," she said.

"Are you certain you want to do this?"

"Yes. Seeing the place once more might at last help me put the incident to rest." She raised her skirts and turned toward the river. "Come. It's down the hill, and a short way up the bank."

Alana's feet descended the steep slope with inherent familiarity. Halfway to the river, she looked back to see Paxton was well above her. He swayed from tree to tree, clutching at its bark, attempting to keep his footing as he gingerly tracked along the soft ground.

One misstep, and he could end up on his backside. Worse yet, he might slide a short distance, only to find himself straddling a tree. Worst of all, he could take a straight shot down the incline and into the river, never again to be seen.

To Alana, the prospects were humorous . . . save for the last one, of course. She didn't want him dead, just away from her homeland. However, the other two possibilities she would readily allow.

As she continued to watch his inept moves, she somehow kept her laughter from bubbling forth.

What great warrior he? she wondered, a smile playing on her lips.

Conversely, though, she took pity on him and amended the notion, knowing that he usually did battle in an open field and not the thickness of a wood. At another time, she would wait for him, permitting him to catch up. But not today. She had to get down to the river and see if Rhys was about.

The sound of the raging torrent was deafening.

Standing several feet back from the river's edge, Alana tried to ignore the turbulent force as it rolled, dipped, and swelled, to flow violently past her. She scanned the opposite bank, relief filling her when Rhys was nowhere to be seen. Then it happened. The surging spray leapt forth, striking her in the face.

Stunned, Alana stared at the roiling water. Like a

living, angry being, it appeared to reach out to her, beckoning her forward.

Closer.

The voice was masked in the river's roar, but Alana heard its call nonetheless.

Closer, I say.

Mesmerized by the gyrating motion, Alana heeded the summons. She stepped to the water's edge and gazed at the eddy rushing by at her feet.

Closer still, the voice coaxed.

It was as though her foot belonged to someone else. From afar, she saw it extend out over the water, the swells stretching up to meet it.

Come join me.

Alana felt herself going forward when abruptly she was jerked back.

"Christ, woman!" Paxton thundered, spinning her around. His fingers bit into her shoulders as he shook her. "What do you think you're doing?"

Snapping from her trance, Alana stared up at him. His face was ashen, while the tempest of some unknown emotion raged in his eyes. Was it anger?

"I—I don't know," she whispered, then looked at the water. Her headrail, which had been shaken from her, snaked along the surface, then disappeared as it was sucked under. Realizing what she'd nearly done, she felt the blood drain from her own face. She attended him again. "I heard a voice."

Confusion knit his brow when Paxton asked, "What voice?"

"It came from the river."

"The what?"

"The river. I heard it calling. 'Closer,' it said. Then, 'Come join me.' " His eyes flickered with incredulity just before his harsh expression softened. "You don't believe me, do you?"

"I believe your coming down here was a mistake. You weren't prepared. The rushing water, your grief —they almost sent you over the edge—literally. Killing yourself won't bring Gilbert back. Come." He urged her away from the river. "Let's make our way up to the fortress."

"Don't you want to see where it happened?"

"No. Not now."

"But you had such difficulty getting down here," she protested.

A sigh escaped his lips. "Can we see the place from here? If so, point it out."

"That jutting rock," Alana said, her forefinger aimed at the outcrop, the water gushing around it. "They found Gilbert's body a mile or so downriver, caught in some brush against the opposite bank."

He glanced at the torrent streaming by them. "Was the water as turbulent as this?"

"Worse," Alana said, knowing she'd never beheld such fury in the river as she had that day.

"Come." He took hold of her hand. "I've seen enough."

As Alana allowed him to lead her back up the incline, his footing far more secure than it had been on his descent, she wondered about the voice she'd heard. Had it been Gilbert beseeching her to join him, so he could take his revenge?

Though Alana didn't believe in ghosts, she nevertheless puzzled over the notion that her dead husband's spirit had indeed been calling out to her. Deciding the plausibility of such was utter nonsense, she dismissed the concept altogether.

In all likelihood, it was her own qualms crying out to her. Why she should feel any guilt over Gilbert's death, especially when she'd never done so prior to this day, Alana couldn't say. She was glad Gilbert had died. Why then had she been caught in the depths of a trance?

The water—she'd not faced it in such turmoil since the day she'd experienced her harrowing fall, only coming and going when it was tolerably still.

Maybe being confronted by its raging force had provoked recollections from the depths of her mind . . . recollections she wasn't even fully aware of now. Perhaps that was what had induced the temporary madness she'd just suffered.

Lifting her gaze from the trail, Alana looked at Paxton.

There was an unnatural stiffness about him, his hard strides taking them, without effort, straight up the hill. He was clearly angry. But she couldn't tell if the emotion was aimed at himself or at her.

He'd saved her from certain death by catching her before she'd stepped off into the river. For that she was grateful. But his belief that she'd intended to commit suicide, her grief the reason, was ludicrous.

Still, the misconception might work to her advantage. If she were able to convince him she truly mourned Gilbert's loss, even to the point of wanting to take her own life, he may cease with his tormenting questions, his doubts about her at long last laid to rest. But in order to make this happen, she needed to gain his sympathy, his concern, his compassion.

To that end, Alana knew her tears would serve as her greatest weapon. She was already adept at bringing them forth at the blink of an eye. The most hardened of men were known to have been brought to their knees on seeing a woman cry. Why should it be any different with him?

Beware, a small voice cautioned. *Your intention is that he console you, thereby ending his perpetual*

*inquiries about Gilbert's death. But what will you do if
that solace is offered only in his arms?*

Alana felt his hand tighten around hers as he pulled
her up the last few yards to the top of the hill. Onward
they went, passing Gilbert's grave, and up the short
incline, to the side gate. All the while, his grip
remained sure and firm, yet never hurtful, just as she
imagined would be his embrace.

The small voice, Alana knew, was her own, and the
thought of a man holding her in his arms caused her to
inwardly cringe. But what choice did she have when
there was so much else to consider?

Again inside the courtyard, Paxton's shouted command to grant them entry having been obeyed, he
stopped their progression midway between the gate
and the hall.

"Henceforth, you'll not be allowed by the river
unless someone goes with you . . . that someone pref-
erably being me," he stated. "I'll not risk another
episode like the one we just experienced. Is that
understood?"

When he referred to her near accident, something
flashed in his eyes, the same something that had
sparked in them while they were beside the river.
Unable to discern exactly what the glimmer was, she
decided to test him. "Had I gone in, there would have
been one less of my ilk for you to worry over. In fact,
I'm surprised you intervened, considering you believe
I killed Gilbert."

"I told you my reason as to why I doubted the
account of his death, but after seeing the force of the
water, I can now say his skills were ineffectual at best.
It's a miracle you survived. The saints protected you
that day, milady. Today as well. Next time, they may
turn a blind eye.

"In response to your amazement that I saw fit to intervene, I did so because I do not wish to see you placed next to Gilbert this soon. You are far too young and have years of life ahead of you. Therefore you are forbidden to go to the river without me. In fact, given your precarious state of mind, I just might allay my worries by placing a guard on you at all times."

So, he was concerned, Alana thought . . . afraid she would doubtlessly take her own life. That's what had flashed in his eyes both times: alarm. Her near tumble into the river had given him a scare, one like no other he'd ever experienced. Would her plan work?

"I'm not addled," she shot back, mock tears springing forth. "I told you I heard a voice. The river—maybe it's angry because I didn't die alongside Gilbert."

"Or maybe you feel guilty because you survived and he didn't." He touched her cheek, then captured her chin, forcing her to look at him. "Alana, don't torture yourself this way. Gilbert is gone. You can't change what has occurred. Let it go and allow yourself to heal."

Reprehensible was the word Alana chose to describe how she felt about deceiving him this way. His gaze recounted that he was genuinely affected by her tears, that he abhorred the idea she might seek self-destruction over life without Gilbert. What a truly horrible person she was. However, if she were forthright with him, the consequences promised to be heavy, for she doubted he'd believe her. Therefore, she had no alternative but to play him false.

"'Tis hard," she whispered, a tear rolling down her cheek.

He watched it fall, then whisked it away. "I know, but you must try. Promise me you'll do that much."

Again praying God didn't smite her, Alana sniffed, then nodded.

"Good. Now seek your chambers and wash your face, then allow yourself a rest," he said in a fatherly fashion. "I'll see how you're doing shortly."

Alana offered no protest when he turned her toward the hall. Her head bowed, she made her way across the remainder of the yard, certain her plan had taken hold.

Sympathy, concern, compassion—he had shown her all of these. Another stint or two of tears and she'd win him over completely.

With a much-desired victory this close at hand, Alana wondered why she felt so very untriumphant.

A woman's tears were his downfall, especially when they flowed from eyes as lovely as Alana's.

Stalking along the riverbank, Paxton remembered how his heart had wrenched when that lone crystal droplet had welled over to slip down her soft cheek. At the time, he'd felt for her and was sorely tempted to take her into his arms. There, in his protective embrace, she could wail away her sorrow, his words of reassurance soothing her, until her grief was spent.

If that had been his intention, why, then, did his suspicions still linger? Probably because he knew some women's tears to be false.

"How many more times do you insist we do this?" Sir Graham asked above the water's roar, as he trekked along behind Paxton.

"For as many times as it takes."

"We've done this thrice, and the results remain the same. Besides, that scrap of cloth in no way resembles a man's body. Not in weight and not in size. I say we're wasting our time."

Paxton stared at the sodden piece of linen that he'd plucked from a snarl of brush by the water's edge. On Alana's entering the hall, he'd called upon Sir Graham to accompany him back down to the river. Once there, they went in search of her headrail, Paxton having shaken it from her head after he'd prevented her from stepping off into raging torrent.

Close to a mile downstream, they found it, snared by a tangle of limbs. What troubled Paxton was that it had ended up on this side of the river, not at all like Gilbert's body had, against the opposite bank.

Determined not to make too much of it at first, he'd carried the headrail to the jutting outcrop Alana had indicated as the place where she and Gilbert were situated that fateful day, wanting to see if the current bore it differently from there.

Three times he'd dropped the cloth into the water; three times he'd retrieved it from the exact spot where he'd originally found it.

By every indication, the river's run kept all debris to this side of the bank. So, why had Gilbert been found across the way?

Perhaps Graham was right. The headrail in no way compared in size or in weight to a man's body. Besides, Gilbert may have been able to swim for some distance before he was sucked under, his futile attempt carrying him into another sluicing current, which would explain why he was given up on the other side.

But as Paxton studied the violent swirl and tumble of the water, he believed the premise unlikely. The river's force was greatest alongside the bank where he stood. Therefore one would conclude that whatever the element—whether it be a flimsy piece of cloth or a man's body weighing twelve stones—it would surface in approximately the same spot where he found Alana's headrail.

Paxton had no way of proving that. Not unless he wanted to take his chances and plunge into the river from the outcrop to see where the current carried him.

Far too drastic, he thought, knowing it was doubtful he'd survive.

"Do you wish to attempt it again?" Graham asked.

"Nay," Paxton responded, wringing the excess water from the cloth. "Just as you've said: The results will be the same. There's no sense in expending our energies when it will obviously be for naught."

"Good," Graham chimed. "All this walking has given me an appetite. Let's take ourselves back to the top, so I may raid the kitchens for something to eat."

At Paxton's nod, the two men began ascending the hill toward the side gate. On the trek upward, Paxton's thoughts remained on Alana.

The voice—had she actually heard it? Or was that also a ruse?

What wasn't a trick was that she had well-nigh stepped off into the river. Had he been an instant later in descending to the grassy bank, one wink shy in grabbing her, she'd have gone in, to be swept away in the current. This time he doubted she'd have survived. Praise God that he'd caught her in time.

On entering the fortress, Paxton found he was more confused than ever. Her tears, the voice, her near mishap, the current, the headrail—damnation! What was he to believe?

He and Graham were almost to the doors of the hall when a shout sounded from the gate house; Paxton looked to its source.

"A rider comes," the guard called from the tower.

Paxton glanced at Graham, then the two loped

across the yard toward the main gates. Climbing the ladder to the walkway, each peered over the palisade. Paxton emitted a curse when he saw how the man swayed precariously while slumping forward in the saddle.

"Open the gates," he commanded, then retraced his steps down to the yard, Sir Graham following close behind him.

Breaking from the fortress, the two men rushed toward the rider. While Graham grabbed hold of the stallion's reins, Paxton caught the man as he toppled from the saddle.

An angry tic pulsed along Paxton's jaw when his eyes confirmed his thoughts. Bloodied and worn, the man in his arms appeared near death. Then Paxton watched as the man's eyelids cracked open.

"Attacked. All dead."

Sir Goddard rasped the words for Paxton alone to hear. Then the injured knight fell unconscious.

CHAPTER

4

"Trouble is afoot," Madoc announced.

Alana sat up with a jerk and stared at her servant.

Abiding by Paxton's orders, given when they were in the courtyard on their return from the river, she'd gone to her chamber, washed her face, then taken to her bed.

Until a moment ago, she'd been lying there pondering what it would take to convince Paxton that Gilbert's death was accidental, albeit a lie.

Though he was affected by her tears, their use might not be enough to fully allay his suspicions. And therein lay the snag. Just how much would she be willing to sacrifice in order to protect those who were involved?

For a long while, the question weighed heavily in her mind. The answer never came to her, her deliberation ending when Madoc burst into the room.

"What sort of trouble?" she asked, swinging her legs off the bed.

"Come," Madoc said, striding from the door toward the window. "'Tis best you see for yourself."

Meeting Madoc at the opening, Alana looked down on the yard to observe a man being carted toward the garrison by Paxton and Sir Graham. Her brow furrowed as she viewed the unconscious man more closely. Her heart froze when recognition took hold. "Sir Goddard?"

"Aye. He's back. If we're lucky, he'll die from his wounds. 'Twill save us the misery of having to suffer through his surly moods and his endless accusations."

Alana was filled with foreboding. "Where are the others?" she inquired of the dozen knights who had accompanied Sir Goddard from the castle.

"Dead."

"Did Sir Goddard say who attacked them?" she asked, praying it wasn't Rhys or her cousins. And if it had been, at the very least, she hoped the knight hadn't identified them as being her kin.

"That I cannot tell you. I was in the yard when a shout sounded from one of the guards in the gate house. Sir Paxton and Sir Graham rushed up to the wall walk. Just as fast, Sir Paxton ordered the gates opened, he and Sir Graham coming back down.

"Inquisitive as to what was going on, I followed to the entrance. I heard Sir Paxton repeat to Sir Graham what Sir Goddard had said before he'd passed out. 'Attacked. All dead.' Those were the words Sir Paxton used."

"I must get to the garrison," she said, turning from the window.

Madoc caught her arm. "Milady, it would be wise if you were to stay here. I'll go in your stead."

"Nay. I must go myself. Should he awaken I want to

be there to hear all he has to say. I must learn whom he accuses. Pray, Madoc, it is not the person or persons I think."

"Your uncle?"

"Either he or one of my cousins . . . all of them, for that matter."

"I'll come with you," Madoc stated.

"First go to the kitchens and collect the chest of medicinals. Our offering to tend to his wounds will give us a plausible excuse as to why we are there. I'll meet you inside the garrison."

Madoc nodded, then Alana and he quickly left her chamber.

Paxton was straightening from the pallet on which the unconscious Sir Goddard lay when he saw movement at the door.

Alana . . . what was she doing here? She answered his silent query before he could ask it.

"I saw you from my window," she said, stepping farther into the room. "I thought you might need assistance in caring for him. Madoc has gone to fetch the chest of medicinals. He should be here shortly. In the meantime, if there is anything I can do, please let me know."

Her words surprised Paxton. The depth of her loathing for Sir Goddard was more than just appreciable . . . it was a living, breathing entity. Therefore, in offering such aid, she was either being exceptionally charitable or exceedingly false.

"I've yet to check his wounds," Paxton replied, curious as to the true motive behind her sudden show of benevolence. "But I would welcome an extra hand, especially if its owner is proficient in the art of healing."

"I'm not as skilled as Madoc," she said, staying

where she was. "He is the one you want. Until he arrives, I'd be willing to see what I can do."

Paxton tossed aside the chain mail hauberk that he and Graham had removed from Sir Goddard prior to Alana's entry and motioned her forward.

Once at his side, she stared down on the injured knight. Her small jaw was clenched, marking her enmity. Hesitant at first, she slowly lowered herself to her knees. Paxton did likewise. At her instruction, he and Graham removed the knight's bloody tunic.

"He doesn't appear to be in any serious danger," she said after examining the wounds along Sir Goddard's torso. Her slender fingers probed close to the deep gash at the man's shoulder. "I'd say this one is the most serious of all, but not so serious as to cause worry. I don't see any indication of poisoning. Madoc will be better able to tell if there is. If his wounds don't fester, he'll survive."

Paxton nodded, then watched as she again explored the area on Sir Goddard's shoulder. If she were averse to touching the man, she certainly didn't show any signs to imply such. Still, Paxton imagined it was difficult for her to do so, considering her dislike and distrust.

He was admiring her forbearance when Sir Goddard awakened from the realm of the sleeping dead. The knight grabbed Alana's wrist, crushing it in his hand; she gasped.

"Get this Welsh bitch away from me," Sir Goddard commanded, "lest I also end up in my grave." Alana fell back on her bottom when he thrust her from him. He moaned from the exertion. "'Twas her kin who killed my companions. Keep her from me, I say." With another groan, the man again lost consciousness.

Though Sir Goddard's words had been somewhat

garbled, Paxton hadn't missed a one. Turning his gaze on Alana, he asked, "Is he right? Were your kinfolk the culprits?"

"Nay," she answered, rubbing her wrist. "His loss of blood has made him delirious."

"That could be so. But he could also be very much aware of his attackers' identities. If you know something, it would behoove you to tell me now. Because later, should I discover that you have been hiding the truth, you'll wish you had never held your tongue."

"You saw Sir Goddard and the others leave. Did anyone depart the castle after them?"

Paxton knew that they hadn't. "No one followed," he conceded.

"You have your answer then," she said. "I imagine when he says they were my kin, he is referring to the fact that they were Welsh. That in itself is not surprising. With your presumptuous encroachment on our soil, it stands to reason that my countrymen would want to expunge you from it. You are the ones who are infringing here, not us."

She came to her feet.

"Now if you will excuse me," she stated, "I shall return to my quarters. Madoc will care for him. Or, better yet, you may care for him yourself. Sir Goddard doesn't trust us. Nor do you. Should something happen to him, we'll be the ones who are held at fault. I hereby withdraw my offer of assistance. A pleasant good day to you."

Paxton had risen from his knees at the same time Alana did. The bitterness of her words still rang in his ears as she marched toward the door. She nearly collided with Madoc when she reached the opening. Taking the casket of medicinals from his hands, she set it on a nearby table.

She looked back at him, pointing to the small chest.

"Whatever you need to tend to his wounds is in there," she announced before she turned away. Waving her servant ahead of her, she disappeared from sight, Madoc with her.

"Do you think Sir Goddard is, as she suggested, delirious?" Graham asked. He had also come to his feet and now stood shoulder to shoulder with Paxton. "Or do you believe he is correct when he said her kin were involved?"

Staring at the empty doorway, Paxton shrugged. "It is difficult to say. But just as it is always wont to do, the truth eventually manages to surface, whether we like it or not. I suppose, my friend, time will one day give us the answer."

Worry was Alana's constant companion. She slept with this feeling of distress; moved through the daylight hours with it sitting on her shoulder. The fear that something terrible might happen never left her.

Since the hour Sir Goddard had been brought through the gates, close to a fortnight ago, the tension inside the fortress had expanded to the point of near explosiveness. The knight, not having taken the poisoning into his blood, would survive, and the threat of retribution was now spent. Even so there was cause for concern.

Sir Goddard's claim that the troop of knights had been attacked by Alana's kin as they made their way toward the plains of Chester quickly passed from mouth to ear throughout the castle. As expected all trust between Henry's men and her people had soon abated.

Alana had no way of knowing if the assertion were true, for she'd yet to hear from Rhys. But whether it had been her kinfolk who had fallen upon the group or another rebellious band, who were altogether unknown to her, didn't really matter. Paxton's stand was that the perpetrators were *Welsh*. That was all he needed to know.

From her vantage point at her chamber window, she examined the man in her thoughts. He stood on a raised platform overlooking the palisade and the new construction beyond.

The day after Sir Goddard had found his way back to the castle, Paxton ordered that a ditch be dug around the perimeter. Once completed it would gird the entire stronghold.

Currently crushed rock was being hauled up from the riverbed, the water having subsided to an easy flow, whereupon it was dumped into the small section that was finished, to serve as a base for the massive wall that was to be erected.

This new barrier promised to climb significantly higher and be far thicker than its present counterpart. Piece by piece, the old wooden structure would be dismantled, impenetrable stone rising in its place.

Alana sighed. Though the changes were being implemented in order to fortify against the Welsh, it was her own people who labored at the task.

So far they worked arduously and without complaint. But one word, one misstep from either side and things could easily erupt in disaster. She just prayed that tempers held—hers and Paxton's included—so the tenuous truce between all those concerned wouldn't be broken.

Paxton let loose a shrill whistle, then waved his arm. Alana knew it to be his way of signaling that this day's work was done.

As usual, though several hours of daylight remained, he didn't press her people beyond their limits, insisting they toil until they fell in their tracks. He was wise in this respect, knowing that a weary man produced less in way of his labors. Alana was thankful he was so perceptive.

The first of the laborers began entering through the gates, carrying their tools with them. Unlike the Normans, the Welsh, who as a whole refused to give themselves over to gluttony, partook of only one meal a day, usually in the evening. Therefore Alana knew there would be hungry stomachs to feed.

With one last cursory glance at Paxton, who was climbing down from his high perch, she headed for the door and the hall.

A short time later, Alana was busy refilling the cups as she made her way along one of the tables, where a simple meal of lagana—a broad, flat cake of bread— broth, and chopped meat was being consumed.

Milk brimming inside the goblet, she set the filled cup beside the empty trencher and close to the man's hand, its owner slumping over his plate. She started to withdraw, but gasped when he caught her wrist.

Frowning down on him, she gazed at his covered head. He slowly turned, peering at her from beneath his hood. Alana's heart nearly stopped.

"Dylan . . . what are you doing here?"

"I'd think that was obvious, Cousin." His handsome features were further enhanced when a lazy smile broke beneath his mustache. "I'm here to see you, of course."

"But how did you get in here? The guards—how did you ever manage it?"

"With so many laborers moving about outside, it wasn't hard to join in with them. I fear, though, I'm not as industrious as they . . . or should I say: not as seasoned?" He released her wrist and turned his palm upward. "I've got blisters, and they hurt like the devil."

Staring at the broken, bloodied skin, Alana felt for him. "Oh, Dylan, how could you do this to yourself?"

"Easy. I don't work with my hands . . . not if I can help it. Being older and wiser than my brothers, I leave the hard chores for them."

"One day they shall catch on, and when they do you'll suffer for it . . . worse than you are now." She glanced to the table where Paxton sat. He and Sir Graham were deep in conversation. Probably discussing the new construction, she decided, relieved his concentration was elsewhere and not on her. "Your hands need attending to," she said, again looking at her cousin.

"Even more importantly, we need to talk."

"Meet me in the kitchens, and we shall do both."

While Alana continued down the line, refilling the cups, Dylan rose from his seat and made his way from the hall. After the pitcher was empty, she followed the same path her cousin had taken, with the excuse she needed to get more milk, the Welsh seldom partaking of wine.

Dylan was lounging against a table, a hip perched on its top, when Alana entered the kitchens. "Don't dawdle," she commanded, switching the pitcher for the chest of medicinals that was kept on a shelf. "Come. Let's find a place where we'll less likely be heard."

Sequestering themselves in a storeroom, Alana took hold of Dylan's hand and turned it toward the candle that burned close by. "Give me your other hand," she ordered. When he complied, she inspected the broken blisters on it. "I suppose you joined with the other workers because your father wanted you to check on me?"

"Do you assume I'd simply throw myself into their

65

labors because I thought they needed a helping hand?" he asked incredulously. "Indeed, my father sent me. It's been two weeks since he's last seen you. He's been worried about you, the same as I . . . the same as Meredydd and Caradog."

"How are they?" she inquired of her uncle and her other two cousins as she opened the chest. "Are they well?"

"Aye, they are well, considering their worry."

She sprinkled some herbs onto a dab of grease, stirring the whole into an ointment. "You know then that Sir Goddard is no longer in charge here," she said, smoothing the concoction across the palm of Dylan's right hand.

"Aye," he responded, his dark eyes meeting hers. "One of the watchers reported seeing the loathsome bastard leave alongside his companions. The next day, Father saw you by the river with the tall Norman . . . this Paxton de Beaumont."

So, Rhys *was* in the woods after all, Alana thought. She was glad her uncle hadn't emerged from the cover of the forest that day. By keeping himself secreted, he had at least some inkling as to why she hadn't been able to meet him.

"You already know his name?" she inquired, surprised by Dylan's use of it.

"Not until today, when young Aldwyn offered me a dipper of water. He was able to tell me some things, but not all that I want to know."

She had finished with his right hand, having wrapped it in a linen bandage, and was now attending to his left. "Which is?" she asked while applying the ointment.

"Is he treating you well?"

"Who . . . Paxton?" She saw Dylan's nod. "He's not mistreating me. He is, however, suspicious of my account of how Gilbert died. I fear he intends to keep digging until he unearths the truth. You must tell Rhys to stay far from the fortress. Paxton is not like Sir Goddard. He rarely takes more than one cup of wine. He is skilled and astute. There is no laxness about him, nor about the men who serve him. They are all warriors, Dylan. Once you cross back over the river, do not come here again. Tomorrow I want you gone."

The other bandage tied off around his hand, he flexed his fingers. "Not unless you come with me," he stated. "That's why Rhys has sent me . . . to take you where he's assured you'll be safe."

"I cannot leave."

"Why?"

"Because I will not desert my father's people."

"What about your mother's people. Don't we count for anything?"

"You know you do. And that too is why I cannot leave here. He already mistrusts me. Should I suddenly disappear, he'll know I was playing him false . . . lying, not just to him but also to Henry when I told them that Gilbert drowned. I'll not risk his coming after me in his need to see justice is done. If he found me in your company . . . well, I'd hate to think what would happen then."

"If he does come upon us," Dylan returned, "you can be certain he'll meet the same fate as your husband did."

"He won't be alone, Dylan. Even if he were, don't you think there will be retribution? If not from his men, then certainly from Henry. I cannot and will not see my family slaughtered, no matter which side it is." She paused and regarded him closely. "On the day Sir Goddard and the others left here, did any of you follow them?"

Dylan's eyes were at once shuttered. "'Tis best that

you don't question me on that. The less you know the better off you will be."

A sinking feeling encompassed her. "You've answered my fears. Why, Dylan? Is it too much to ask that you try to keep peace with our enemies?"

"That is the point, Alana. If we sit back and do nothing, they will continue to encroach. This land is not theirs. Therefore they must be driven from it. If it means killing them to ensure their expulsion, then it will be done."

She shook her head in defeat. "One day Henry's anger will erupt, and he'll ride against us. I don't mind telling you I'm afraid of the cost."

Dylan's fingers caressed her cheek. "You worry too much. If Henry rides against us, we'll be ready."

"But the slaughter—I couldn't abide it if you, or Rhys, or your brothers were to die."

"Hush," he whispered, his finger falling over her lips. "Death does not frighten us. Becoming slaves to a conqueror does. This land is ours, Alana, and we will fight to the very last man to keep it that way."

She caught his hand and pressed her cheek to his palm. "I know. But I'd much prefer a peaceful settlement."

"Unfortunately, that will not come . . . not without bloodshed." He placed a gentle kiss on her forehead. "Come. We should get back to the hall before this Paxton de Beaumont becomes suspicious and starts searching for you. I noticed he watches you inordinately."

"Only because he hopes I'll err in some manner, thereby giving him the clue he's looking for."

Dylan shrugged. "Perhaps. But you are quite lovely of face, Cousin. And he is a man. His intense interest might have something to do with your being a woman."

"Pah!" she exclaimed, slamming the lid on the chest. "His only interest is to discover how Gilbert died, naught else."

"We'll see. But I warn you, if he lays a hand on you, he'll wish he hadn't. Rhys was against your marrying Gilbert, but in your perpetual desire to keep the peace, you insisted the union go forth. You know how that ended."

"Do not fret, Dylan. One Norman was more than enough for me. I promise you: There'll not be a second."

He arched an eyebrow. "Husband or Norman?" he inquired.

Because there were few secrets kept between them, Dylan was aware of her distaste for the marriage bed, hence his query. "Both," she said. "Now get back to the hall before we are found."

He pulled her into his arm, giving her a hug. "I'll tell Rhys you refused to leave here. He'll not be pleased, but I'll make certain he abides by your wishes. For now, at least."

"Thank you, Dylan," she whispered, returning his embrace. Of all her relatives, he was her favorite. Perhaps it was because they were so close in age, Dylan being only two years her senior. "I knew you'd understand." She pulled back. "Tell your father that I'll try to get word to him as to what is happening with me. When we part in a moment, for safety's sake, I believe it's best we stay at opposite sides of the hall. And whatever you do, once you depart altogether, don't come back. Not one of you, do you hear? As long as Paxton de Beaumont remains here, stay far from the castle. For all our sakes."

"We'll keep to our side of the river. But be assured, you'll be watched." He kissed her cheek. "Farewell, Alana. Stay well."

"A safe journey to you, Dylan," she called as he made his way to the door. Genuine tears stung her eyes when he closed the panel, for she was sad to see him go.

Where was she?

Paxton scanned the room from corner to corner. He hadn't noticed exactly when Alana had slipped away, but in his estimation, she'd been gone far too long. He was about to rise, intending to search her out, when he saw her coming from the direction of the kitchens, a pitcher in each hand.

He continued to watch her. Soon he found himself fascinated by her graceful moves as she glided alongside one of the tables, refilling the empty cups with milk.

She was incredibly beautiful, but it was her unaffected manner that actually held him spellbound.

The method in which she held her head when she pondered something, the way her lips fanned out into an impish smile when she was amused, the spark of joy that lit her face when she was happy, the dark fire that flashed in her eyes when she was angry . . . and of course, her tears—he could never forget her tears!— all these things caused his heart to pound and his loins to stir.

Damn! He wanted her. Would even consider taking her as his wife. If he could only rid himself of his doubts.

"I thought you said you were going to see how Sir Goddard was faring," Graham stated. "Have you since changed your mind?"

"Nay. I haven't changed my mind. In fact, I'm going to his quarters now." Paxton came up off the bench. "Keep a close eye on the Lady Alana for me, will you? I trust her not."

"That's obvious enough," Graham remarked. "As for myself, it is with great pleasure I accept my duty. After all, she is quite pleasing to the eye."

Paxton leaned close to Graham's ear. "Sir Gilbert thought that as well. He now lies in his grave. I suggest you temper your interest, or you might soon be lying beside him."

Not waiting for a reply, Paxton crossed the hall to the door, heading for the garrison and Sir Goddard's quarters.

On entering the storeroom, which had been cleared to accommodate the knight, his cursing and moaning disrupting everyone's sleep within the barracks. Paxton clenched his jaw when he saw the man was guzzling deeply from his cup.

"Is it so difficult for you to remain sober at least one night?" he asked as he crossed to the table where the knight sat.

Wiping his mouth with his arm, Sir Goddard turned red-rimmed eyes Paxton's way. "'Tis the only way I can forget." He waved at his bandages which were scattered across his chest and torso. "Besides, it eases my pain."

Paxton caught Sir Goddard's wrist as he reached for the flagon to refill his cup. "And what was your excuse prior to the unfortunate occurrence that recently befell you? Or were you trying to forget something then as well?"

"What do you think?" the knight snarled, shaking Paxton's hand from his wrist. "This forsaken outpost and the people in it are enough to cause any man to seek his cups, so he can relieve his misery."

Paxton seized the flagon just as Sir Goddard's hand met its handle. "First, we talk," he said, holding the container fast. "Afterward, you may drink yourself into oblivion, if that is your preference."

Casting Paxton a dissenting glare, Sir Goddard soon uncurled his fingers from the handle. "What do you want to talk about?" he asked, slumping over his empty cup.

"The Lady Alana," Paxton stated, seating himself on the extra stool.

"Ah, the bitch herself," Sir Goddard announced, his gaze meeting Paxton's across the table. "What do you want to know about the slut?"

Paxton bristled at the terms used to describe Alana. "I know your opinion of her, so you may save the aspersions on her character. Just answer my questions. And try to do so in a more chivalrous manner."

Sir Goddard snorted. "Whatever you desire. Now get to the interrogation, so I can get back to my wine."

Paxton's eyes narrowed. The man was totally lost to the drink. He could not and would not be helped. "Who, if anyone, assisted the Lady Alana from the river the day Gilbert died? Where was she found? Who sounded the alarm? Tell me all that occurred."

Sir Goddard frowned. "No one assisted her. She came stumbling into the fortress sometime after dark, looking a fright. She was asking for her husband. 'Where's Gilbert? Find him. I need him,'" the knight whined, mimicking a woman's voice. "It was then we knew something was amiss, for none of us had seen either of them since early that morning, when they left through the side gate.

"We told her such, and that's when she began babbling about falling into the river, insisting we go searching for Gilbert, because she feared he may have jumped in after her.

"With torches in hand, a band of us accompanied her to the point where she said it happened. We found no trace of Sir Gilbert . . . even crossed to the other side of the river to walk the bank. The rain started again, so we gave up our search. We found him the next morning, a mile downstream."

It was Paxton's turn to frown. "If the water was raging, how did you get across the river?"

"Easy. By way of the footbridge."

"Footbridge? Where?"

"It no longer exists. Before I cut it down, it spanned the river about a half mile up from where Gilbert's body was found. The ropes still hang from the trees where the bridge was anchored."

"Why did you destroy it?"

"To keep her kin from coming and going whenever they fancied. I figured the harder it was for them to cross over, the better off we'd all be."

Paxton drummed his fingers on the table's surface. "The day I arrived here you claimed you never prevented her folk from leaving the castle whenever they wished. Now your words indicate otherwise. Did you or didn't you hold them captive?"

Sir Goddard looked puzzled. "Hold them captive?"

"Aye. The bridge—you said you had cut it down to keep them from coming and going whenever they fancied."

"I wasn't talking about her kin here at the castle. I was referring to those across the river."

Paxton jerked to attention. "She has kin across the river?"

"Aye. They are a raucous bunch, far more worrisome than any of the group who live here. None of them are to be trusted," Sir Goddard stated, "but the ones across the river can be trusted least of all. That's why I destroyed the bridge. Though it didn't keep them from crossing over, the downing of the structure made it less convenient for them to do so."

"Then when you said her kin attacked you, it was those across the river that you were referring to?"

"Aye. Who else did you think I meant?"

"Since I was unaware she had other relatives until now, I thought you just meant your attackers were Welsh." Paxton believed that because he'd allowed Alana to convince him that it was fact. "Did you recognize any of them?"

"Nay. Their faces were painted, as is their custom when they fight. But they were her kin all right. No doubt they saw us leave . . . followed us until they found the opportune time to attack.

"We were in a valley when the clamor started—drums pounding, trumpets blowing, shouts sounding. In a twinkling, they came streaming down around us, tossing their darts. Arrows and lances were flying. We had no time to react."

The knight shuddered from the memory and reached for the flagon. Paxton made no attempt to stop him. "Where do these relatives of hers live?" he inquired, watching as the wine sloshed into Sir Goddard's cup.

"In a crude ringwork, about four or five miles west of the river."

"Have you been there?"

"Nay," the knight said, after swilling his drink. "But I've heard that is where they live." He drained the cup, again reaching for the flagon. "Sir Gilbert—rest his soul—was there and told me about the place."

Paxton had come here seeking answers. They were given to him. But during his grilling of Sir Goddard, more questions had arisen. And there was only one person who could respond to the new queries that abounded inside his head.

"I shall leave you to your wine," he said, rising from the stool.

Sir Goddard grunted his agreement, and Paxton headed for the door.

The instant he entered the hall his eyes began searching for Alana. Not seeing her, he marched toward Sir Graham. "Where is she?" he asked on reaching Graham's side.

A deep line creased the area between Graham's eyebrows as he stared up at Paxton from where he sat on the bench. "And a pleasant good evening to you," he remarked, chiding Paxton for his abruptness.

"Amenities are not high on my list of priorities at the moment. Tell me: Where has she gone?"

"She took herself up the steps to her chamber. I believe she has retired for the night."

Paxton didn't hear the last of Graham's words, for he was striding toward the stairs and the gallery above.

Once he reached her chamber, he didn't bother announcing himself by knocking. He released the latch and proceeded inside.

The sight presented to him caused his blood to rush and his loins to stir.

For Alana had just stepped from her bath.

CHAPTER

5

~~~~

Maledictions galore came to mind, each and every one to do with Paxton and his parentage, but stunned silence was all that Alana could manage at his unconscionable invasion into her chamber.

Did the man possess no sense of decency whatsoever?

Obviously not. Otherwise he would have at least knocked.

Gauging him, she retained a death grip on the linen bath sheet, hugging it to her breasts and hips. It was then she shivered.

The insuppressible reaction was caused not by the room's chill, the cool evening air flowing through the open window and skimming her wet skin, but by the effect of Paxton's intense gaze.

Her heart tripped faster as his hooded eyes caressed her from head to foot. Never had a man looked at her with such ardent interest, not even Gilbert.

Words of protest had formed in her throat, but refused to pass over her tongue. Her cheeks flamed with equal amounts of indignation and embarrassment, her face growing hotter and hotter.

The spasms choking her voice subsided, and Alana at last admonished, "How dare you infringe on my privacy. Take yourself from my chamber this instant and close the door behind you."

To her utter dismay, he stood firm. Then a knowing smile spread across his face, a dimple showing on each sun-bronzed cheek.

"And if I decide not to leave, what will you do then?" he asked. "Eject me?"

He laughed wickedly, tauntingly; Alana hugged the bath sheet even tighter.

"I fear milady is at a disadvantage," he continued. "You're protected by only a flimsy piece of cloth. Should you attempt to toss me out into the hall, the ensuing struggle will, in all likelihood, dislodge the thing altogether.

"As a result, my curiosity will be rewarded, my eyes no longer robbed of what they desire to see. On the other hand, your embarrassment will increase, all your secrets having been revealed . . . almost all, that is.

"Therefore, considering what *could* happen, I suggest we stay as we are. Believe me. It will be far safer, especially for you."

By the way he surveyed her, his irises having deepened to a midnight blue, Alana had little choice but to acknowledge that he was right. She was tempted to tug at the tail of the bath sheet, wrapping the whole around her, but she feared any movement might unveil far more than what she meant to hide. With her blush now fanning down to her shoulders, she elected to stay as she was.

"I hope you have an adequate explanation as to why you barged in on me like this," she stated, fighting against her nervousness. "Justify your rudeness."

"I want to know why you lied to me."

Alana grew very still. Had he somehow learned the truth about Gilbert's death?

The prospect frightened her. *Remain calm,* her inner voice commanded. Battling her panic, she asked, "L-lied to you? W-what are you talking about?"

"I'm talking about your kinfolk and about your negating Sir Goddard's claim that they had attacked and killed his fellow knights."

Alana unknowingly clutched the wet bath sheet closer. A puny shield, she thought, once she absorbed what she had done.

She scrutinized Paxton's face. Sir Goddard—he'd told Paxton about Rhys and her cousins, something she had purposely neglected to do.

"You allowed that no one followed them," she said, pretending to be ignorant of his meaning. "Have you since changed your mind?"

"Nay. As I previously agreed: No one followed from the castle. But when I let you convince me that Sir Goddard's ramblings were about the *Welsh* in general, I was unaware that you had family living across the river. You failed to tell me about them, didn't you, Alana? Why? Is it because you're trying to protect them? Were they the ones who attacked Henry's men, slaying all but Sir Goddard?"

Alana nibbled at her lower lip. What was she to say? Dylan had confirmed, in a roundabout way, that her kin had assailed Sir Goddard and the others. The lies. Each was mounting one on top of the other. Would she be able to keep them all straight?

"You're taking far too long to answer, Alana," Paxton remarked. As he did so, he took a step toward her.

"Stay where you are," she commanded, clasping at the bath sheet. To her amazement, he didn't obey.

"For each second you delay in replying," he announced, "I shall come a step closer. One . . . Two . . . Three . . . Four . . . Five . . ."

Mutely, Alana stared at him. It was as though she had lost her voice. Before she found it, he'd crossed half the distance to her. "Stop!" she shouted.

He paused and cocked his head. "I don't hear your response." He picked up his pace. "Six . . . Seven . . . Eight . . ."

Alana stumbled back a step. "How can I respond when I don't know the answer?" she cried, praying he'd not come any nearer. "I've not spoken to nor have I seen Rhys in weeks."

"And who is Rhys?" Paxton asked, still striding forward.

Tall and powerful, he intimidated her. Her heart was pounding erratically while strange feelings whirled inside her stomach. Dear God! Why didn't he leave her alone?

"My mother's brother," she blurted, feeling suddenly faint. "Please don't come any closer."

He halted less than an arm's length away. Reaching out, he gently captured her chin. "Tell me what I want to know, and I won't have need to hound you like this."

His light touch nearly undid her. Her knees wobbled. Positive her legs would give way, she was both surprised and grateful that they held her firm.

"I-I don't know who attacked Sir Goddard," she insisted, hoping he'd accept her at her word, wishing he'd now depart. "As for relatives, I have many. Some are as far south as Swansea. Others as far west as Harlech. Even more to the north at Conwy. Do you expect me to know their movements at any given hour of the day?"

"I'm not interested in the others . . . just in those across the river. And, of course, in you."

Alana noted how the timbre of his voice had deepened. Her breath caught when he released her chin, his knuckles brushing upward across her cheek.

"I understand why Gilbert was so enchanted with you. Your skin—it's as soft and as smooth as a babe's." His hand moved to her hair. "Like fine silk," he whispered, allowing the tresses to cascade from his fingers.

Mesmerized by his words, his gentle touch, Alana could do naught but gaze at him. His eyes were fully dilated, glistening onyx ringed by a heavenly blue.

He cupped her right shoulder. His fingers played there for a second or two, then trailed slowly down her back. "You're temptingly beautiful," he said, the thumb of his other hand caressing the curve of her mouth.

Before Alana could react, his lips were on hers.

His kiss was hot and searching, and to Alana's regret, far too brief. He pulled away and examined her face.

"How could a mouth that sweet be at the same time so very deceitful? You have the ability to lure a man, even unto his death. Is that what happened to Gilbert?"

Alana stiffened as anger surged inside her. Wiled by his honey-coated words and his masculine charm, she'd nearly fallen for his ploy, almost responded to his kiss. She was glad she'd kept some of her wits about her, not giving into the magic of the moment.

Her eyes narrowed on him. "It is as I've told you, and as I've told Henry: Gilbert died trying to save me.

"You speak of deceit, so let us discuss your assertion. You maintain that you are Gilbert's friend, yet you enter what was once his chamber, and without preamble; approach his grieving wife, who is not properly dressed; refuse to leave when she commands it; then you attempt to seduce her while in the same breath you call her a liar. Who is the one filled with deceit? You show no respect for Gilbert's memory nor for me as his widow.

"I have answered your question. If you do not believe what I say, then cross the river and ride upon my kin and discover for yourself if they attacked Sir Goddard. I warn you, though: They are over three hundred strong, where you and your men number less than seventy. Attack them, and you'll not survive. Leave them alone, and you'll have no trouble. The choice is yours.

"Now take yourself from my room and give me the privacy that is due me . . . the privacy Gilbert would expect from a man who was indeed his *friend*."

She spat the last word from her lips. His eyes shuttered, Paxton viewed her at length. Then to Alana's relief, he spun on his heel and strode from the room.

Still clutching at the bath sheet, she pressed her fingers to her lips and stared at the closed door. Heat yet prickled low in her stomach while her heart continued to flutter. Even now she could feel his mouth on hers.

The inflated numbers she'd given when speaking of her kin promised to ensure Rhys's safety, along with the hundred or so people residing in the ringwork, nearly half of them being children.

Her lies had worked, just as she'd hoped.

But at what cost?

Again remembering the effects of his kiss, as well as her desire to respond, Alana felt certain she'd somehow betrayed herself.

Paxton leaned against the wall in the narrow corridor just behind the gallery and only a few feet from Alana's door.

He was amazed by his temerity, astounded by his lack of gallantry. Never had he behaved so brazenly toward a woman, especially not toward a friend's wife.

Reason followed that he'd acted as he had because he'd never faced a situation such as this. The fairer sex usually approached him, not the other way around. But then he'd never walked in on a woman who was fresh from her bath.

Groaning, Paxton remembered how tiny beads of water had trickled down her satiny limbs. He'd been tempted to catch each droplet with his tongue, at the same time tasting the sweetness of her skin.

And the bath sheet.

He recalled how the damp linen clung to her alluring breasts to outline their fullness as jutting nipples thrusted impudently against the cloth.

And her enticing hips.

Though she made every attempt to hide them, he was granted short glimpses of their seductive roundness. Likewise he was allowed to view the sleek length of her thighs, the turn of her calves, the slimness of her ankles, and the smallness of her feet.

He thought of their close quarters. How easy it would have been to strip the cloth from her, unveiling her completely.

The notion had tempted. That he hadn't acted on the urge was a veritable miracle. Paxton knew that if he had, his loins would not still be throbbing, hot lust yet blazing inside him.

Even so, he'd been enchanted enough by her beauty that he braved to touch her, to kiss her, and yes, afterward, to taunt her.

He'd gone searching for the truth. Now that he found it, it wasn't at all what he'd expected.

He desired Alana, wanted with every inch of his masculinity to lie between her outstretched thighs and bury himself inside her, physical gratification his reward. He could have her too. All he need do is summon the priest and present her with Henry's decree.

I suggest you temper your interest, or you might be lying beside him.

The words that he'd uttered not so long ago to Sir Graham about Gilbert twirled through Paxton's mind, peaking into a dizzying crescendo.

His lust soon quieted, and he pushed away from the wall to stride the corridor toward the stairs and the hall.

Alana was beautiful, but she was equally as treacherous. Understanding such, Paxton decided he'd be wise to heed his own warning.

Alana clutched at the kegs stacked beside her as a wave of heat coursed through her when she remembered Paxton's kiss. The fiery flames licked outward, then shot low in her belly; the effect left her breathless, shaken.

From last night until this very afternoon, she couldn't stop thinking about that moment . . . couldn't stop thinking about *him*.

Damn him for playing havoc with her emotions— the insufferable blackguard!

Angered with herself that she allowed him to have

such control over her, Alana pushed away from the kegs and began counting the sacks of meal piled in the corner of the storeroom.

She'd come here to get away from him, to get away from her memories by occupying her mind with something else. After tallying their food supplies over and over, coming up with a different number each time, she knew it was no use. Her shoulders slumping, she sank down onto the bags of meal.

What was wrong with her?

It wasn't as though she'd never been kissed before. Gilbert had done so often enough . . . at least at the beginning of their marriage.

But like everything else between them, things eventually changed. His kisses came less and less frequently. Carnal satisfaction was all that he was interested in.

Alana shuddered.

Thinking about Gilbert had left a sour taste in her mouth. In the end, she'd grown to despise him. Even more so, she'd despised the thought of his touching her.

Lovemaking—how disgusting!

She frowned.

If she actually believed that were true, why then had she dreamed about Paxton, the two of them locked in a heated embrace, his hard body thrusting, hers eagerly receiving each deep stroke of his rigid manhood?

Flames again leapt to life inside her as she was seized once more by the images that were played out in her nighttime fantasies. Her face burned, for the passionate enactments were far too real; Alana gasped for breath.

This would not do.

Allowing herself to imagine them as lovers was a

waste of time. He was Norman, an enemy to her people. Dylan, who Madoc reported had safely crossed back to his side of the river that morning, had warned her that if Paxton ever touched her he would pay . . . dearly, at that. Did she want another man to die, simply because of her?

Besides, the oaf had called her a liar, hinting that she was a murderess as well. In the first instance, he was right; the second, he was wrong. Just knowing he distrusted her should make her want to shy away from him.

Unfortunately, and to Alana's chagrin, that was not the case.

Misery of miseries! she thought, coming up off the sacks to her feet. This foolishness had to stop.

Determined to complete her inventory, she faced the bags of meal and began counting.

The door opened behind her.

Believing it was Madoc, she turned with the intention of asking for his help. Her smile faded when she saw who had actually entered the room.

"Well, well. If it ain't the murdering little bitch herself," Sir Goddard snarled, a look of vengeance in his eyes.

CHAPTER
6

Fear prickled along Alana's spine as she realized the extent of the danger she faced.

She appreciated fully how much Sir Goddard hated her, how much he hated all her kind. The greater portion of his loathing, she knew, could be attributed to Gilbert's demise. With the additional deaths, his abhorrence had been compounded another twelvefold. He wanted revenge, and the feral gleam in his eyes said that she was about to receive her due.

Alana's first reaction was to scream. On any other day, the act would bring quick results, with half the castle rushing to her aid.

Today, however, everyone was either out in the yard or beyond the castle wall, working diligently under Paxton's command on the new construction.

Knowing she was on her own, she backed against the sacks of meal, her eyes frantically scouring the area for a viable weapon.

The small knife in her belt would be no match for the man's cunning and strength . . . no match for the enmity driving him.

True, she might be able to deliver a few jabs or a stinging cut—perhaps even two—before he disarmed her, but nothing so drastic as to immobilize him.

Her search for something to use in her defense went unrewarded, and Alana decided the application of her own wits might be the best protection of all.

"I presume you've come to restock your daily supply of wine," she said, squaring her shoulders. "The vats are against the wall, the flagons on the shelf beside them."

"I know where the vats are," he snapped.

Staggering more fully into the room, he slammed the door; Alana jumped.

"Aye, I came for more wine," he continued. "I'll get it too . . . once I'm finished with you."

For a drunk, he was exceedingly agile. Before Alana had time to draw her knife, he was upon her. Grabbing her wrists, he forced her back onto the sacks, his ponderous girth pressing down on her.

"Get off me, you oaf!" she demanded. She struggled against him without success. He was far too powerful. "Off me, I say!"

"Nay. 'Tis time you got what's coming to you."

Her heart pounded in her ears, exertion and trepidation taking its toll. So much for her own wits, she thought, hysteria bubbling up inside her.

His massive weight crushed her chest. As she sucked air between her teeth and through her nose, she felt her stomach roll. His stench was sickening, days' old sweat and stale wine wafting from his body and breath. "You're filthy and you smell. Likewise you're disgusting."

He laughed sharply. "Had you been a Norman

wench, I might have taken the time to bathe for the occasion. But you're naught but a Welsh bitch. Low-born scurf, that's what you are." He smiled coldly, exposing his decaying teeth. "I always wondered what Gilbert saw in you . . . why he wanted a slut like you in his bed." Drawing her arms upward along the coarse sackcloth, he caught her wrists in one hand. He lifted himself, his free hand settling between them. Simultaneously, his knee burrowed between her thighs. "'Tis time I discovered what the mystery is all about."

She knew it was coming, knew it as surely as she knew her name. Even so, she still wasn't prepared.

When Sir Goddard's meaty hand grabbed her hard between her legs, massaging her with brutish force, Alana flinched and stiffened. Tears stung her eyes, then welled and streamed across her temples and into her hair as she tried without success to squirm away from his lewd manipulation.

She whimpered openly, a silent cry screaming through her mind: *Merciful God! Anything but this!*

Paxton climbed down from the platform where he'd been overseeing the day's construction to spy Sir Graham standing in the middle of the courtyard shaking his head.

"You appear perturbed," he said on reaching Graham's side. "What troubles you?"

Graham met Paxton's gaze. "The damn fool nearly ran me down on his way to the hall. No apology, mind you. Just a surly 'get out of my way.' Something has to be done about his drinking. He smells from lack of bathing, his bandages are filthy . . . he's of little use to anyone, least of all to himself."

Paxton didn't have to be told the *fool's* name. He'd dismissed the man once from his duties because of his inability to perform. It was now time he and Sir Goddard had a heart-to-heart talk. Whatever it took, Paxton was determined to see that the man became and stayed sober, even unto the point of having the sot shackled permanently to his cot.

"Where is he?" Paxton asked.

"I imagine he's by now in the storeroom swilling from a wine vat. Why waste energy staggering back and forth for a new flagon each time he comes up dry when it's far easier to remain next to the source itself?"

"See to the construction, will you? I'll be back shortly."

Paxton's words flew over his shoulder at Sir Graham, for he was already striding toward the hall.

Alana's struggles continued to be futile. Her headrail had been torn from her hair, her lone braid whipping against the sacks as she fought to keep Sir Goddard's mouth from hers. Her skirts were bunched up high on her thighs, his fingers pulling them higher and higher. Then she felt his hand working between them as he attempted to free himself from his braies.

"Nooo!" she cried, nausea and bile churning up to her throat.

She wanted to swoon, felt she might, but if she did, there would be no way to fight him off. But if she didn't faint, she'd always have to endure the disgusting memories of his defilement.

Her skirts were now around her hips. His other knee joined with the first as it rammed between her thighs, both spreading her wide.

Saint David . . . someone . . . anyone help me!

The answer to her silent plea came from Sir Goddard. "Now, bitch, I'll see what you're worth."

Gritting her teeth, Alana closed her eyes and prayed: *Let this horror be over.*

And it was.

One second Sir Goddard was atop her; the next, he was gone.

Her eyes sprang wide at the release of his constraining weight. She saw him flying through the air. He landed in a heap on the floor, halfway across the room. He didn't move.

Relief flowed through her as her gaze sought the man who had saved her.

Paxton.

He stood mere inches from her, flexing his hand. He looked at her, and she shivered, for the fury in his eyes was a fearsome thing to see.

Pray that his rage was never turned on her, she thought, afraid of the aftereffects. Just as Sir Goddard had crumpled under the blow of Paxton's fist, she also would not fare well."

"Cover yourself," he said.

The coldness in his voice stunned her. She watched him with care as she pulled her skirts down past her knees. Afterward she slid from the sacks and stood on wobbly legs, facing him.

"Do you blame me for this?" she asked, noting how he avoided meeting her gaze.

"Nay. I blame myself." As though it pained him, he turned his eyes to hers. "I should have known he'd try something like this. If I'd been a second later in coming—God's wounds!" he exploded. "I can't bear to think what would have happened to you. He didn't—"

Alana's fingers covered his lips. "No. Nearly, but you came in time."

She stepped closer and slipped her arms around his

90

waist. The action obviously surprised Paxton, for he seemed not to know what to do with his own arms. In truth, Alana had surprised herself as well.

She pressed her cheek to his broad chest. The steady beat of his heart was in itself comforting to her. "Thank you for saving me."

With a soft groan, Paxton returned her embrace. "You're welcome," he whispered huskily. "More welcome than you'll ever know."

It was then that the trembling set in. Alana began to shake uncontrollably while her teeth started chattering. This had happened to her once before, just after she'd dragged herself from the swollen river.

She didn't want to think about that day nor to think about what had almost happened now. All her physical and emotional reserves were suddenly drained, and she desired only to find her bed, so she could rest and regain her stamina.

Apparently Paxton understood her need, for he said, "Let's get you to your chamber and into a warm bed. You're clearly reacting to the terror of the moment, along with the panic you sustained when you thought no one would rescue you."

Gently he set her from him, then supporting her, nodded in the direction of the door.

Clinging to him, Alana allowed him to guide her across the room. When they came nigh to Sir Goddard, her tremors became more pronounced. Paxton pulled her to him, assuring his protection.

"What is to happen to him?" she asked, surveying Sir Goddard with care.

"If by some chance he manages to survive the night, he'll be gone from here just after dawn, tomorrow."

Her eyes grew wide. "You're not planning to kill him, are you?"

"The thought has crossed my mind."

"Set the notion aside. He's not worth your anger nor the loss of your honor."

"What then would you have me do?"

"Send him into the wood, alone," she said, forgetting her sworn obligation to protect her kin. "He'll soon meet his own doom."

If Paxton had caught her slip of the tongue, he didn't show that he had. Perhaps he'd overlooked the implication. Better still, maybe he'd missed it altogether.

Deliberating on which of the three it might be, Alana was relieved when he declared, "Your suggestion sounds tempting. I'll consider it closely."

He kicked Sir Goddard's limp leg from their path as they passed by him. Whether from the wine, from Paxton's debilitating fist, or from a combination of the two, the man was oblivious to the blow.

The knight had better hope he remained such, Alana thought. For by the hard tic in Paxton's jaw, she was certain Sir Goddard hadn't suffered the last such punishment from her rescuer.

And sunrise was yet a long way off.

Shortly after dawn the next morning, Paxton watched as the huge gates were swung wide on their hinges. Beside him, Sir Goddard was trussed to his saddle, ready to make his departure.

Just as he'd promised, Paxton had considered Alana's suggestion about turning the knight loose into the wood alone. In the end, though, he decided to send the man to the Chester Castle with instructions that Sir Goddard be held there. When Henry arrived to begin his campaign against Owain Gwynedd, he could deal with the bastard. With luck, Sir Goddard would feel the full wrath of their king, his crime against Alana avenged.

Looking up at the knight, Paxton noted the man's posture was slumped, his demeanor subdued. Several bruises showed on Sir Goddard's face, the marks an exact match to Paxton's fists. His jaw hardened and his eyes narrowed as images of Alana struggling ineffectually against the sot flashed through his mind.

Never had he felt such rage toward any human prior to yesterday's events. Even now, he could feel his fury rising. The desire to kill the odious brute mounted inside him. One furtive glance, one simple word, and his control, held only by a fine thread, would snap.

"Hear me, and hear me well," Paxton said through clenched teeth. "You leave here alive only because I have allowed it. You go to Chester, where you will await your fate. Hope, sir, that your judge is merciful. If he is not, you have no one to blame but yourself." Paxton hadn't mentioned Sir Goddard's arbiter by name, for Henry's movements were to be kept secreted. "Hear this also," he continued. "If by some off chance you go unpunished for your crime and are set free, never come this way again. Understand?"

Sir Goddard grunted an incoherent reply.

Paxton couldn't tell if the garbled sound was emitted as a sign of agreement or if the croak was from the man clearing his throat.

It mattered not.

Should the bastard reappear, it would be his last such act of defiance.

With one final glare at Sir Goddard, Paxton turned toward Sir Graham, who was seated atop his horse, waiting.

"Once you reach Offa's Dyke, leave the others behind." His voice was kept low so only Graham could hear him. "From there, you and the two who will accompany you are to escort Sir Goddard to Chester. See that he is incarcerated, with orders that he be held for Henry. If he gives you any trouble on the way, slay him and leave his body to the scavengers. I'll expect you back here in three days . . . definitely no more than four."

"Do you think your plan will work?" Sir Graham asked. "I'd hate to be left out there in some wood like the others who were slain."

Paxton shifted his gaze to the two dozen Welshmen who were to accompany the four knights on their journey. He'd chosen the lot, hoping to avert another tragedy. "It should work. They know the consequences if they fail to bring you back alive."

"Which in itself is naught but a hoax, right?"

Paxton shrugged. "I haven't decided yet. The threat hangs above their heads. They have no way of knowing if I'll follow through or not."

"Well, just in case they didn't fully grasp what you said the first time around, I'd appreciate it if you would repeat it to them again, so there is no misunderstanding."

"If you have qualms about going, I'll take your place."

Graham shook his head. "Nay, you're needed here. Besides, like my two fellow knights, I volunteered. No one is forcing me to go. Though why we don't let her kinfolk dispatch the bastard, here and now, is something I've yet to determine." He waved Paxton from his side. "Go on. Give your speech. I'll feel far better once you have."

Paxton reached up and clasped Graham's forearm. "God's speed to you. Make certain you watch your back."

"That I will," Graham responded, releasing Paxton's arm. "Your speech, sir."

Paxton moved to the center of the yard. "Heed me . . . all of you!" he called, his gaze sweeping the Welsh, Madoc included.

The man's presence among the group was in way of additional assurance toward Graham's and the two other knights' safe return. Given Madoc's loyalty to Alana, Paxton doubted the man would allow any underhandedness to occur.

When Paxton had everyone's attention, he said, "I will repeat my orders to you so that everything is made quite plain. You are to escort these men to Offa's Dyke. Once there, you will keep to your positions while Sir Graham, who is in charge of this expedition, and his companions take Sir Goddard on to Chester. On their return, you will escort the three of them back to the castle. Whether it is going to or returning from the marches, you will protect these knights with your very lives. If Sir Graham and his men do not return here as hale and stout as the day they departed, the Lady Alana will suffer—greatly, at that—for your carelessness." He locked eyes with Madoc. "If you do not wish to see her harmed, I suggest you take your duty to heart. You are to be back here in three days. Is that clear?"

A collective rumbling of ayes, along with an equal number of nods, ran through the group.

"Good," he announced. "Now be off with you."

The troop of men began filing through the yawning gates, the four knights at the center. As Paxton watched them go, he prayed Graham and his men would come to no harm. Sir Goddard he couldn't care less about. Still the edict had been given for all four of them.

And if Graham and the two men who had volunteered to accompany him did suffer from some mischief, whether it was theirs or another tribe of Welsh running these hills, would he then follow through on his threat against Alana?

There were others besides those riding with the four knights who had heard his discourse. A good commander always kept his word, never broke a vow. Therefore, he realized the only acceptable course would be to exact punishment on her.

The gates were now closing.

Paxton drew in a deep breath.

Pray God they returned in the allotted time, he thought. And pray that his comrades remained safe.

He sighed heavily. The last thing he wanted to do was scar Alana's soft back with the biting sting of a whip.

But a flogging was far better than the alternative . . .

Which was death.

He was very clever, Alana decided, as she turned from her chamber window, the last of the men having passed through the gates.

She'd heard everything, his words rising distinctly in the crisp morning air.

As she began to listen, she was at first startled by his directive, frightened by what it could mean. Then she understood the significance of it all.

Her own people acting as escorts for the four knights ensured there wouldn't be a repeat of the slaughter that befell the first group after they'd left the castle, especially when the Welsh were ordered to guard the Normans with their lives.

Paxton's added threat against her safety was also an ingenious maneuver. The intent was that they would not fail her. Yet Alana wondered if any of these measures would work.

Rhys was unaware of Paxton's promise to take retribution against her should Sir Graham and the others be injured or killed. Though Alana doubted her uncle would harm any of his own race, in his eagerness to liberate his beloved Cymru of all Normans, he might feel it necessary to attack the group.

His wild cries and his menacing actions would no doubt scatter the less stouthearted among those who protected the four knights, their flight leaving the Norman warriors at Rhys's mercy. She could only imagine what would happen to her then.

Yesterday, Paxton had shown her compassion by giving her comfort after he'd freed her from Sir Goddard's clutches. In three days, however, he might be forced to inflict on her his own form of reprisal.

Having witnessed Paxton's rage while it was imposed on Sir Goddard, Alana wondered if her punishment would be as swift and unerring. Would it also be as brutal?

Turning, she looked through her window at the trees beyond the river. She hoped for once Rhys tempered his lust for Norman blood, otherwise she'd be made to suffer for what Paxton would doubtlessly term as *Welsh atrocities.*

Alana wasn't just worried about herself. She was concerned about Sir Graham and his two companions. Sir Goddard she cared not a whit about. Then there were those who were sworn to protect the knights—her own kin.

Remembering their solemn expressions as Paxton delivered his decree as to their conduct, she knew they'd taken him at his word, had accepted that she would be severely disciplined if anything happened to the Normans in their care. With that treatise hanging over their heads, they would indeed stand against Rhys, fighting unto their deaths.

The thought of having one side of her family battling against the other nearly undid Alana.

She had to get word to Rhys ... to Dylan ... to someone across the river.

But how?

A familiar name came to mind. She disliked the thought of using him, yet she had little choice.

Spinning on her heel, Alana headed for her door, going in search of Aldwyn.

"What are you doing?" Paxton asked.

"Skipping stones," came the reply.

Frowning, Paxton watched as the lad picked up another smooth rock. He then cast it with his left hand across the surface of the river. Paxton counted six skips. Not bad, he thought.

"Mind if I try?"

"'Tis your choice."

Paxton found a similar stone as to the one just thrown. Positioning himself, he hurled the thing, sidearm, at the water.

Three skips and it sank.

"You could use some practice."

Paxton heard the smugness in the lad's voice. "Agreed," he said, "but it has been years since I tried this." He picked up another stone. "When I was your age"—Paxton estimated the lad to be about fourteen—"I averaged ten skips. My record was seven-and-ten."

"Pah! No one is that good."

"I was."

Paxton tossed the stone. It skimmed the water's

98

surface twice, then faltered and disappeared. With that the competition was on.

After six rounds of the pair casting their stones, Paxton losing every time, he asked, "What's your name, lad?"

He need not have done so. By the boy's missing right hand, he knew the answer. In fact, their meeting beside the river didn't happen by chance.

From the wall walk where he stood, Paxton had seen Alana speaking with Aldwyn. Their conversation was brief, their countenances serious. A short time later, Aldwyn had slipped through the side gate. Paxton had followed. Thus their present interaction.

Aldwyn stated his name, then cocked his head. "I'd think you'd have more important things to do than skipping stones."

"Not today. The construction is on hold at present." Paxton shrugged. "It being such a fine day, I thought I'd just dally about." He cast another stone, watched it skip, then looked at Aldwyn. "Why are you at the river?"

"Building my strength and dexterity," he answered, skipping another rock. "With the loss of my right hand, I had to learn to do everything with my left."

Paxton nodded. "I imagine it has been difficult."

"At first, it was. I was fumbling with things all the time. I'd get angry and wanted to give up. But Alana made me practice. She was always after me to try different things. When I got good at one, she had me move on to something else."

"Such as skipping stones?"

"Aye. She's challenged me to a contest. Told me just a little while ago that I'd better practice. Said she'd hate to embarrass me by beating me, she being a female."

Paxton smiled to himself.

So, his suspicions were for naught. The two having their heads together was nothing more than Alana's wanting to goad the lad into improving himself so that in the future his disability would in no way deter him.

In that instant, Paxton's respect for Alana grew. Where many would look upon the lad as a beggarly cripple, shoving him aside as they went, she had taken a different tack. In Aldwyn she saw potential. She believed in him, and she wanted him to believe in himself.

By the way Aldwyn cast the stones, the last one skipping across the water ten times, Paxton knew the lad would fare quite well. He possessed determination, and was quickly becoming skilled with his left hand. And Alana was the driving force behind both accomplishments. Aldwyn could not have asked for a better friend.

After tossing a few more stones, Paxton said his good-byes, then started back up the hill. Halfway to the top, he turned to look down on the dark-haired, dark-eyed lad whose courage he admired.

Paxton stared at the spot where he'd stood only a few minutes before. A puzzled frown creased his brow, for he saw naught but the rippling waters and the grassy bank.

Aldwyn was gone.

Nightfall had come, and just like the curtain of darkness that had descended on the fortress, the moods within had grown equally as black.

With supper over and her chores finished for the day, Alana strolled the dimly lit courtyard, wanting to be away from the oppressiveness inside the hall.

She was concerned, and with good cause.

Paxton's promised reprisal against her should Sir

Graham and his men come to harm had precipitated a change between Welsh and Norman alike. Though neither side trusted the other, caution always being the preferred course of action for both parties, never were they this wary, this suspicious, nor this restive, not even on Sir Goddard's return with the news of the slaughter.

As she made her way toward the side gate, the leaning of her direction having become a matter of habit from months of sneaking out into the night wood, Alana questioned whether she should attempt to lift her kinfolks' spirits by telling them that they could put their fears aside.

Around midmorning, Aldwyn had returned from his appointed task, apprising her that he'd gotten word to one of the watchers who was positioned in the woods not far across the river from the fortress. With Alana's communication delivered, the man had set off toward the old ringwork, promising that Rhys would be informed of the situation immediately.

Yet Aldwyn's recount of the man's hasty departure, along with his added aside about how the man had gone waxen in appearance on Aldwyn's repeating her message, had given Alana reason to wonder if her uncle was preparing to ride against her kin and the four knights. At the time, she could only pray that the watcher had arrived prior to Rhys's striking out in pursuit of the group. Or, ultimately, and more importantly, that word was gotten to her uncle before he attacked.

Uncertain if her prayers had been answered, she hesitated in raising her kinsmen's hopes, only for them to be dashed a few days' hence.

Besides, there were other raiding bands of Welsh who preyed on anyone who dared to cross Offa's Dyke, whether coming or going, supporters of Owain

Gwynedd in particular. Even if Rhys had received her message in time, Sir Graham and his comrades could yet fall under a different hand. The risk remained high, and Alana was well aware that the days ahead promised to be long ones. If the knights returned safely, the tension inside the fortress would subside. And if they didn't . . . what then?

Alana found she was beside some barrels and crates stored near the side gate. Hoisting herself, she sat atop one of the barrels. With feet dangling, she began to ponder the extent of her punishment, wondering what form it might take.

Her imagination took flight, and she saw herself suffering from a myriad of penalties that ranged from the mortifying embarrassment of being made to stand naked in a cold, pelting rain, to—horror of horrors!—being drawn and quartered.

So absorbed was she in the scenarios that popped in and out of her mind—especially the one where Paxton forced her to become his paramour—that she didn't hear the footsteps drawing nigh. She nearly leapt from her skin when she felt a hand settle on her shoulder.

"Lost in your thoughts?"

Paxton's familiar voice triggered a quick response. As flames of embarrassment licked up her neck to her face, she couldn't help wonder if that one vignette, which repeatedly played in her mind, had somehow beckoned him to her side.

The mental pictures of them being locked in an ardent embrace refused to subside. Alana instantly went on the defensive. Her breath rushed from her lungs as she snapped, "Don't ever scare me that way again!"

"I called out to you, twice," he stated, edging a hip onto the barrel next to the one where she perched. "I was certain you heard me . . . until you jumped, that is." He tilted his head. "You sound agitated. Why?"

Thankful the lighting was such that he couldn't conceivably see the flush on her face, Alana kept her gaze pointed forward. After what had been spinning around in her head, how could she ever look at him?

She responded to his query with a question of her own. "If someone just took ten years off your life, wouldn't you sound agitated?"

"Not as agitated as you are. What's wrong . . . besides my scaring you?"

Still plagued by her wild imaginings, which she now deemed as distasteful, she felt his scrutiny. Oh, why didn't he just go away?

"Nothing's wrong," she muttered.

There was a prolonged silence, then he said, "Alana, I may not know you as well as I'd like, but—"

"What do you mean by that?"

She shot the words at him, her gaze affixing itself to his face. That he seemed taken aback wasn't surprising.

"Mean by what?"

The thought occurred that she might be over-reacting, her own guilt the cause. Even so, Alana forged ahead. "Not *knowing* me as well you'd like."

Again there was silence. Then the light of dawning streamed across Paxton's face. "I wasn't referring to *knowing you* in the biblical sense, if that's what you've assumed . . . at least not this time. But then, you didn't allow me to finish my sentence, did you?"

Alana couldn't say why her power to reason had gone awry. Perhaps it was due to the strain of her worrying over her kinsmen and Paxton's men. Maybe she could owe it to her fear of what would happen to her if the knights didn't return safe and sound. Or most probably, she could blame it on Paxton and the strange emotions he always managed to evoke whenever he was near. Whatever the cause, somewhere in the back of her mind, she understood she wasn't thinking straight. Still, she hopped on his words like a cat on a mouse.

"So!" she exclaimed, bounding down from the barrel to face him. She burrowed her fists into her waist. "You *have* thought of me in that vein, have you?"

Just as fast Paxton slid to his feet. "Several times," he growled, standing toe-to-toe with her. "In fact, milady, if you must know, I've thought of you in that *vein* more often than not!"

Righteous anger filled her, and Alana's eyes narrowed. "You men disgust me. First, it was Gilbert demanding his husbandly due, always wanting to ease his needs. Never mind my needs. No! He cared little about the loving sort of tenderness that should be shown to the woman who was his wife.

"Then, of course, it was Sir Goddard. Because of his hatred of me and my heritage, he tried to punish me by defiling me. Thank God the bastard is gone!

"Now it's you and your offensive fantasies about us. What makes you think I would welcome your advances, inside your head or out! Men!" she blasted his gender again. "You're all naught but a bunch of rutting beasts! I scorn the lot of you."

Though she didn't realize it, her words were more telling than she knew. She expected a cutting reply in defense of his own sex . . . waited for it, in fact. To her astonishment, he merely released a long breath.

"What? Have you nothing to say?" she goaded, eager for a fight. Her fist itched, almost painfully so, for Alana wanted to poke him straight in the nose.

"Aye, I have something to say. Considering what

you've suffered from two of the men you mentioned, I can understand your feelings of disgust."

Before she could utter a protest, he caught her face in his hands, assuring he had her full attention.

"But I tell you this, Alana of Llangollen: If we were to make love, those feelings of abhorrence would quickly ebb. I'm not selfish like Gilbert was. Nor am I brutal like Sir Goddard whose lone intent was not an act of lust but one of violence. In my arms, you'd find ecstasy, an emotion you've obviously never enjoyed.

"You're not a complete innocent, who has no understanding of what a man and a woman do when secreted behind the curtains of their bed. Imagine how it could be between us. Long, slow passionate kisses, our tongues mating, sending a burst of heat deep into our bellies; urgent but gentle caresses, our skin tingling, eager to experience each new magical touch. Envision us together, along with the pleasure our closeness could bring. Once our desire for each other can no longer be contained, I'll join with you. And you *will* welcome me, Alana. This I promise you." His fingers threaded into her hair, urging her to him. "When you're inclined to share this sort of intimacy with a man who knows how to make a woman's body tremble with longing, when you're ready to savor the rapture only I can give you, come to me. Until then, remember this."

His mouth captured hers in a kiss that was at first soft and teasing. Then his lips became demanding, devouring, and his tongue plunged to search and to probe.

He was a master at this, Alana thought as sparks showered inside her igniting a fire in her loins. She moaned as she remembered what he'd said about the burst of heat. She thought to respond, but was denied the chance.

"Remember," he whispered on drawing back. With that he abandoned her.

Frozen in place, Alana stared after Paxton as he disappeared into the shadows. Her mind raced as her fingers rose to her lips. They were wet, bruised. And, yes, still hungry for his.

Undeniably his suggestive words and tantalizing kiss had stirred her blood. Both had left her breathless and wanting.

She was tempted to go after him, shout that she was willing to accept his invitation. Yet she held back.

He'd promised her joy, pleasure, ecstasy, rapture— all delights of the flesh.

But Alana sought far more than those things that were carnal in nature.

Before she gave herself to any man again, she required something that came from his very soul, something she doubted Paxton could ever offer, something she was unsure she'd accept.

That something was a pledge of love.

CHAPTER

7

Paxton was not in the best of moods.

The past two nights had taken their toll. With his worry over Graham's safety, and the safety of the two men who had accompanied his friend, along with his fretting about whether or not he'd have to punish Alana, which in itself might provoke an uprising among the Welsh inside the fortress, he'd had little sleep.

Then there were the recurring visions that came to him during those short periods of intermittent slumber.

God's wounds! He never knew his dreams to be so real, so vivid. He could have sworn he was actually living them.

They were always of Alana.

She lay naked on a soft bed of wildflowers in a glade within the deep wood, slender arms beckoning for him to come to her. Stripping from his clothing, he'd lie beside her. Soon they were fully joined, limbs entwined, she welcoming each of his unerring strokes. But before he could reach his climax, she attaining her own, he'd come fully awake.

His heart would be pounding, his breath coming in hard pants. Likewise his sweat soaked his pallet while his manhood ached with a merciless throb.

After five such episodes of this for two nights on end, he was worn and tired. If the occurrences continued to haunt him as they had, he was certain he'd soon go mad.

A long sigh rushed through his lips as he pushed the half-empty trencher of bread, cheese, and chopped meat across the table. He and his men were gathered in the hall to break the fast, while the Welsh were already hard at their chores. He had no appetite. At least not for food. His eyes sought and found Alana. She was what he wanted.

Her ethereal likeness flashed through his mind, and Paxton felt his loins stir.

Damnation!

He shoved himself up off the bench and stalked toward the entry in want of some fresh air . . . and, he hoped, some peace of mind.

Remember.

The command rolled through Alana's thoughts while she watched Paxton stride from the hall.

How could she forget?

Every time she so much as glimpsed him she recalled his kiss. Without a doubt, she'd always believed he was exceptionally handsome, his face and form a work of perfection. Until the other night, his startling blue eyes were what had held her captivated. Now her fascination lay with his lips. The memory of their mastery hadn't left her. Even now she could feel their tantalizing play.

The ghostly sensation caused Alana to groan. This had to stop!

There was only one way to end the wild fantasies that were constantly flitting about in her head. She had to openly tell him she'd never seek his attentions, never propose that he make love to her.

Certain this was the answer, she set the empty trencher she held on the table and skipped along toward the door, determined to put this whole outlandish incident to rest.

By the time Alana reached the courtyard, Paxton had vanished from sight. She glanced at the garrison, then scanned the wall walk to see if he were there. Her shoulders slumped when she didn't see him, for her courage was fast waning.

Then she heard his called command to open the side gate. Gathering up her skirt, she was at once after him.

Paxton leaned a shoulder against the thick trunk of an oak. Plucking several acorns from the dozen or so he'd scooped into his hand, he idly tossed them in the vicinity of a ground squirrel. The small creature scurried from one golden brown nugget to another, feasting on one, storing the other in its cheek.

A twig snapped behind them. The squirrel hastened into the cover of the leaves, and Paxton turned to see who'd come upon him.

Alana.

Paxton cast the remainder of the acorns into the wind, then straightened from the tree. "Milady," he greeted, wishing it had been anyone but her. "What are you doing out here?"

"I want to speak to you . . . if I may?"

"You don't have to ask my permission to talk to me, Alana." He noted how her small teeth worried her lower lip. "I presume you wish to discuss what happened the night before last, correct?"

"Yes."

She stayed at a safe distance. Considering what had thus far occurred between them, Paxton guessed she was unwilling to venture any closer. "Do you expect me to apologize?"

"An apology is not necessary."

Paxton was surprised. "No?"

"No."

Her response was curt, and Paxton braced himself, waiting for the tirade he felt certain was to follow. Not a word came forth. He might have left it at that, except he wasn't in any humor to play games. "Lost your nerve, have you?"

"My nerve?"

"Aye. You tracked after me in order to air your feelings. Now you are suddenly hesitant to approach the topic. Either have at it or take yourself back up the hill. Which do you say?"

Her eyes flashed as she squared her shoulders. "I say you are insufferably rude. You're *Norman,* therefore such coarseness is to be expected. But that is neither here nor there. The other night was partially my fault, and I shall accept my portion of the blame. However, if you are under the assumption that I shall one day come to you, begging for your favors, you are mistaken, for it will not happen. So, if you're harboring any such fantasies about us, I suggest you forever put them to rest." Her chin rose, and she stared down her nose at him. "There. 'Tis said."

Her posture was moralistic, her tone petulant, and at her final word, Paxton expected she might stamp her foot for emphasis. His eyes narrowed as he emitted a loud snort. Who exactly was she attempting to gull?

He offered her a deliberate grin. "And a fine speech it is, milady," he stated. "'Twould be believable, save for one thing."

Her bravado faded, and she grew very still. "What thing?"

"My kiss. Remember?"

Alana sputtered in protest, but he waved her off.

"Don't try to deny it. The very fact that you followed me into the wood tells me you haven't forgotten it." As galling as it was, neither had Paxton. He became more surly. "What occurred between us was a mistake. That much I'll admit. But let it be known that the incident would never have happened had you not cut me off in midsentence. Instead of allowing me to finish, you twisted my words and concluded something that was totally unjustified, all in the space of one breath."

"Twisted your words?" she asked incredulously. "What illogical sort of logic are you trying to foist on me now?"

It was obvious she had not a clue as to what he meant. *"Knowing you*—does that sound familiar?" He didn't give her an opportunity to answer. "You call me rude, a fault that comes with my being *Norman.* In reply, I say you are equally as rude, if not more so. And the failure, milady, has nothing to do with the fact that you are Welsh. In the courtyard, had you the courtesy to hear me out, you would have discovered that I was concerned about you, for your worry was evident. But no! You came up with this ridiculous idea that my only interest in you stemmed from some sordid desire to bed you."

"You admitted as much," Alana interjected in haste.

"I don't deny that. But my craving for you is no greater in measure than what I've felt for a hundred other women who are all now part of my past."

A lie, Paxton thought, but the flames of Hell would be doused and cooled by the waters of the entire North Sea before he'd admit differently.

"'Twas your own purple little mind which came up with this nonsense that I wanted to *know* you intimately," he snarled. "To play along, I allowed you to believe it was true."

Another falsehood, he conceded in silence. He couldn't explain why, but the longing he felt for Alana was far superior to any yearning he'd ever experienced. And that vexed him. Especially when she may have murdered his friend.

"So, milady, you may blame yourself for all that transpired the other night. You may also be assured it will never happen again—not unless by word or by deed you should invite it. Therefore, I suggest you proceed back up the hill, for if you tarry, you can wager I'll take that as an open invitation to alleviate my carnal urges."

With a gasp, she lifted her skirts and turned away, when in afterthought, he called out to her. She circled around.

"In response to your concerns, I don't want to punish you, nor do I want to make you an example of what will happen to anyone who disobeys my commands. Hope, Alana, that Aldwyn got to your kin across the river in time to prevent another slaughter, for if Graham and his comrades don't return safely, I will have no choice but to fulfill my promise. Now go."

Paxton watched as Alana whirled around, whereupon she scrambled up the hill and through the gate. Once the portal closed, he leaned against the same tree where he'd been resting his shoulder before she'd come upon him. He looked off into the distance, beyond the river, thoughts of her punishment uppermost in his mind.

He noted how her dark eyes had widened in surprise when he'd mentioned Aldwyn and her kin. No doubt she took him for a fool, believing he'd not catch on to the little hoax that she and Aldwyn had perpetrated.

Skipping stones, indeed.

He'd almost fallen for the ruse, but Aldwyn's sudden disappearance had given him away. He didn't go after the lad for one simple reason: The message from Alana to her uncle was meant to help protect Graham and the two knights on their journey to and from Offa's Dyke. Likewise, it was meant to help protect her.

Which of the two was more important to her, her own safety or the knights', he didn't know. But for her sake, and certainly for the sake of his men, he prayed this Rhys fellow restrained his lust for Norman blood and opted instead to safeguard his niece.

Paxton sighed heavily, his thoughts growing more ponderous by the moment.

This being the third day—the day that Paxton had ordered Graham and the others back to the castle— the group should be showing outside the gates sometime before nightfall.

As a precaution, though, for Paxton understood there could be mishaps—a horse going lame, a rider injured in a fall, the band of men and mounts drawing off course and getting lost—he decided he would wait until the evening of the fourth day before he took any action against Alana. If by then Graham and the others had not returned, there would be nothing left for him to do.

Regrettably, she would be flogged. And though the thought pained him, *he* would be the one who plied the whip.

A candle burned late into the night.

Twisting and turning, the tiny fire ebbed and spat on its wick, as though it were gasping for its last breath, but Alana paid the dying flame no heed.

Secured in her chamber, she stared through her open window at the countless twinkling gems scattered across a midnight blue sky, wishing she were high among them.

If not up there with the stars, then someplace else . . . someplace far away, someplace where she was safe and free from worry. Anyplace but here, she thought.

Briefly she prayed that this night would linger forever, for she lived in dread of what was to come on the morrow. But she knew that was impossible. As it had done in ages past, the sun would top the horizon once again. But this time, the dawn would mark the fulfillment of Paxton's promise and the commencement of her own misery.

Not that long ago, sunset had signaled the end of the fourth day. Though her hopes were now dashed, Alana had always trusted that the group would return. But with the coming of twilight, the reality that something terrible must have happened to Sir Graham, to his two companions, to Madoc, and to the two dozen Welsh who'd accompanied them to Offa's Dyke became ever so clear, not only to her but to Paxton as well.

Shortly after dusk, he'd approached her in the hall. The tension inside him was evident. His frown had deepened as had the lines near his mouth. His whole body was unnaturally taut. But where she thought she'd see anger in his eyes, she instead saw remorse. With him, he carried a hastily sewn gown made of sackcloth.

"Tomorrow, when you rise, you'll don this and naught else," he'd said, shoving the makeshift piece of clothing into her hands. "Not long after sunrise, you'll be taken to the yard for your punishment."

"And what is my punishment?" she'd asked.

"Flogging . . . ten lashes and no less."

Alana remembered how her heart had lurched at hearing those words. Apparently she'd paled also. Likewise she'd been unable to mask her fear.

None of this was lost on Paxton, for he'd taken a step closer to her. "I shall try to go easy on you. Even so, I know you will suffer. The edict was given, and I have no choice but to follow through on my promise. You know this, don't you?"

"Aye," she'd responded, then squared her shoulders. "I assume, then, it is you who will be administering my punishment."

"It will."

"Then so be it."

At that, Alana had moved away from him, carrying the sackcloth with her.

The shabby creation presently lay next to the waning candle on the table that stood behind her. With one last bright flicker, the flame died, leaving her in darkness.

Staring at the stars, their brilliance appearing to have increased tenfold, Alana admitted she was afraid. But above her fear for herself was her concern for the men who were her kin, for Sir Graham and his comrades, and certainly for Madoc, her trusted friend.

Had Rhys intentionally ignored her message to him? Or had her directive gotten to him too late? If he had slain the knights, her people too, why hadn't he tried to get word to her? Surely Dylan would have come. But then she'd ordered him to stay across the river. And if Rhys hadn't attacked the small company, was it possible they had still fallen, perhaps by the hand of the Welsh prince, Owain Gwynedd?

Myriad questions abounded in her mind, but one stood at the fore: Where were they?

In the courtyard below, Paxton was wondering almost the same thing as Alana.

What was the delay? Where were they? Damnation! Were they all dead?

From the shadows, he'd been watching Alana at her window, saw the candle flame flicker and die.

With darkness masking her, he sank to the bench that he'd moved outside the garrison's door and took up the whip with its dozen yard-long braided leather strands, their ends knotted. Next he grasped the container that sat beside him. Aided by the residual light from the torches scattered throughout the yard, he stared at the memento, a last remembrance from his father.

His fingers ran the surface of the solid gold flask which was encrusted with jewels. Inside was a precious perfumed oil. Both were said to have come from Persia. Mayhew de Beaumont had procured the treasure on his way to Jerusalem. When a close friend and fellow knight was to return to Normandy because of a recurring fever, Paxton's father had sent the gift, along with several other valuable articles, ahead with the man.

From the time he'd received the keepsake from his mother, shortly after his father's death, Paxton had kept it close to him. Tonight, he'd use the flask's contents for the first time.

Pouring some oil into his hand, he worked the lubricant into the ends of each strand of the whip in an attempt to soften the leather. For Alana's sake, he hoped his efforts took the bite away and left her skin unbroken. But he feared his pains would only slightly lessen the severity of her wounds. No doubt, there would still be scars.

The concept angered Paxton, for he was thinking of Alana's uncle. If the man was the cause of the group's not showing up, if Rhys was knowingly allowing Alana to be punished because of his own bloodlust, Paxton swore he'd take revenge on the bastard. Whether they were three hundred, five hundred, or a thousand strong, he'd have his due. This he swore.

As he kept to his task, he glanced at the darkened window, wondering if Alana was yet at its opening.

In battle, he'd felled some of the fiercest opponents, but in all his life he'd never so much as raised a hand to a woman.

Could he?

The question plagued him, had done so from the moment he'd given his edict. But tonight it did so with a vengeance.

His extra efforts aside, one thing was certain. After tomorrow, should Gilbert's death be proved an accident, and if Paxton were to ask for Alana's hand in marriage, she'd refuse him. Not even Henry could force the issue. Her hatred would be too strong. And so would her kin's.

The offer his king had made him was doubtlessly lost to him. Just the same, he had to stand by his word. Alana's punishment would go forth.

He had no choice.

But did he have the nerve?

The answer, Paxton knew, would come shortly past sunrise on the morrow.

His robes slapping against his legs, Father Jevon skipped alongside Alana as she was escorted from the hall by two of Paxton's men.

"Are you certain, my child, that you don't wish to make a confession before you are taken to the post and bound? Even God's blessing may ease your pain in this time of trial and tribulation."

The priest had been haranguing at her about her immortal soul from the time she'd been taken from her chamber to the present, and Alana was fast becoming annoyed. It was as though he expected her to die from the beating. If her wounds festered, she knew it was possible.

Once again, as it seemed wont to do from the instant she'd awakened just before dawn, her fear rose inside her. Quickly, she tamped it down, allowing her anger to take precedence. Her indignation and rage would serve as her mainstay. It was the only way she'd get through this.

Her gaze pinpointed the thin man whose complexion was so pallid that he appeared next to death himself. "I have nothing to confess," she lied. "As for a blessing, bestow it on your Norman brethren. They are the ones who will need it once this is all said and done."

Father Jevon ignored her words. A litany of Latin flowed from his lips as his hand waved in the air, in the sign of a cross.

Alana barely heard his utterances, for her attention was on the crowd that had gathered.

Her people stood around the yard's perimeter. Eyes glistened with tears in faces of stone. Anger churned beneath the surface of the Welsh who looked on. Aldwyn was also there, his face nearly as pale as the priest's. With their swords drawn, Paxton's men acted as a barrier between her kinsmen and herself, ready to fell any man, woman, or child who broke past their ranks.

Alana's gaze jumped to Paxton, who was positioned near the whipping post that had been erected in the center of the yard a short while ago, the implement of punishment clutched in his hand. His expression was unreadable.

Didn't he realize the depth of her kinfolks' animosity nor the path their enmity would take once the whip struck?

Alana understood fully the outcome, and her fear leapt to the fore once more.

A bloodbath, she thought. And the carnage would befall Welsh and Norman alike.

Paxton would, in all likelihood, be the first one slain, her people's fury driving them in aggregate straight at him. If any of her kinsmen were lucky enough to survive, they would then suffer the full potency of Henry's wrath, which would be an awesome thing indeed.

Whether now or later, Alana couldn't allow her kinfolk to be slaughtered. Nor could she abide the thought of seeing Paxton torn limb from limb.

To prevent these things from happening, she had to impress on all those concerned that she wasn't afraid, then she had to brave her punishment without flinching, without crying out. A monumental task, she knew. Yet, should she show the least little sign of distress, the result would be chaos.

Knowing she lacked the superior strength that was needed to accomplish her aims, Alana accepted Father Jevon's blessing, then uttered a prayer of her own. Soon she found herself beside the whipping post, staring Paxton in the face.

"Are you ready?" he inquired flatly.

"As ready as I will ever be," Alana said. "Are you ready?"

He didn't respond but nodded at the two men who had accompanied her from the hall. Taking her arms, they turned her toward the post and bound each wrist with strips of leather to the cross beam. The two men then stepped away.

Looking over her shoulder, Alana saw Paxton had moved close behind her. His hands were then high on her back. She swallowed hard as he rent the sackcloth down past her waist. The cool morning air coursed across her bare flesh when he spread the torn cloth wide; she shivered.

Alana's heart thundered wildly, and she said another prayer, waiting for Paxton to step away. Save for his taking the whip from beneath his arm, where he'd tucked it, he kept to his place.

Strained silence was all that either of them could manage. Alana shivered again, for he was so close that she felt his breath fan across the top of her uncovered head, its warmth trailing down her exposed back.

Oh, misery of miseries, why was he prolonging the act?

As Father Jevon droned on and on with his litany, she drew a steadying breath and gathered her courage. "Be on with the deed," she commanded. "Or has our new overlord lost his mettle?"

The question dangled between them.

Her tone was purposely berating, and Paxton understood her intent was to prod him into fulfilling his promise to punish her. He was the first to admit his spirit wasn't in this. How could whipping her change the fate of Graham and the others?

It wouldn't.

Yet something had occurred to him while he'd watched her walk from the hall to the post, something that hadn't come to mind previously. What if the message she'd sent via Aldwyn to Rhys was not designed to warn her uncle against attacking the group but was meant to spur him on instead?

If that were so, he'd be justified in chastening her.

But he didn't know if what he'd conjectured held any credence whatsoever.

"I thought Normans prided themselves on not being cowardly. Or are you the exception?"

Alana's words made Paxton wonder if she were impatient to be abused. "Nay. I simply have no taste for beating a woman."

"You gave the edict, then announced I'd be punished if the group didn't return. Will you now forswear your vow?"

"I cannot."

"Then be done with it," she said and turned her face to the post.

Paxton stared down on her sable brown hair and the lone braid that trailed along the center of her back. He could delay no more. Taking hold of the braid, which was like silk to the touch, he tucked it over her shoulder, then stood aside.

Untamed emotion rioted through him as he shook loose the whip's softened tentacles. His gaze swept the area. Spying the look of hatred in the myriad of Welsh eyes that were firmly fixed upon him, he clenched his jaw. He understood their hostility, for he felt it himself. He detested what he was about to do to her, loathed himself for doing it. But it had to be done.

Slowly, he looked to Alana's smooth back. His hand gripped the whip's leather swathed handle until his knuckles whitened under the force.

Ten lashes and her flawless skin would be forever scarred.

He drew back his arm, and there it stalled.

A curse exploded through his lips.

The whip was falling from his hand when the shout sounded from the gate tower.

To Paxton's utter relief, the cry announced the group's return.

CHAPTER

8

"**W**hat the hell delayed you?"

Graham had ridden through the gates before the others and had just dismounted from his steed when Paxton's words attacked him. He was clearly stunned by the hostile greeting.

"'Twas the Lady Alana's cousin," he replied, his eyes gauging Paxton with care. "We came upon her attendants and her yesterday, well past noontide. The cart carrying her coffers and other belongings had lost a wheel and couldn't be repaired. By the time we made litters to transport the lot, dark was nearly on us. In lieu of risking another mishap, we camped for the night." He looked around Paxton's shoulder. "What goes on here?"

Behind Paxton, and at his instructions, Alana was being loosened from the post by the two soldiers who had escorted her from the hall. "If you'll recall, I gave you three days in which to return from your expedition, else the Lady Alana would be punished for what would be conceived as your demise. I even allowed you an extra day to make certain I didn't act without cause. This marks the morning of the fifth day, Graham. I nearly striped her back because I thought you were dead."

"I can see that," the knight stated, his tone contrite.

"Then explain your need for the additional day," Paxton demanded, his anger simmering just beneath the surface.

"I had trouble convincing those at Chester that they should incarcerate Sir Goddard and hold him until further notice. When sober, he is quite eloquent. In fact, he gave a rather credible impression of his being a worthy knight who'd been accused wrongly. It became a matter of my word against his. Hence it took me an added day to make everyone see that not all is as it appears."

"How did you accomplish the deed?"

"I didn't do a thing. Sir Goddard once again fell into his cups. He sealed his own fate. He now sits in the castle dungeon with naught but water to slake his thirst."

Paxton glanced over his shoulder at Alana to see she was rubbing her wrists. "Graham, I could throttle you," he said, turning back to the knight. "Believe me, had Alana felt the force of the whip, you'd now be gasping for air. You knew you were a day late. Why then did you stop to help this cousin of hers? At the very least, you could have left some of the men behind, while you and the rest came on ahead."

Graham looked at his feet. "Regrettably, I didn't think."

"You're damned right you didn't think!" Paxton blasted. "As long as I've known you, you have never been remiss in your duty. I cannot imagine what would cause you to behave . . ."

Paxton's words faded as he caught sight of the young woman who was now riding out from under the shadows of the gate tower.

"Arresting, isn't she?" Graham asked.

Indeed she was, Paxton conceded in silence. In fact, he was awestruck by her beauty, which even he had to admit surpassed Alana's notable fairness. Considering this, he nearly forgave Graham for his negligence.

Nearly was the most that Paxton could offer his friend.

As knights, both he and Graham had sworn an oath, pledging always that their duty would come first. Thus, no woman, no matter how lovely she was, should be afforded the power to distract either of them from fulfilling their obligations.

If anyone understood this it was Paxton. Yet he'd been indecisive about punishing Alana, so much so that the whip had slipped from his fingers prior to the call proclaiming the group's return. How then could he fault Graham when in his own way he also had failed?

"Unhand me!"

The sound of Alana's voice induced Paxton to turn around, whereupon he saw her struggling against the holds of the two men who had freed her from the post.

"Release her," he commanded.

He was rewarded with a scathing glare, then lifting her chin, she snatched up a handful of her sackcloth gown. "Gwenifer!" she cried as she dashed toward her cousin's mount.

"Cousin? Is that you? Merciful Lord you look a sight. What is happening here?"

The words flowed from Gwenifer's lips as she alit

from the gelding with help from one of her attendants. She immediately clutched Alana to her.

"Where is this rogue Norman who has replaced Gilbert as your new overlord?" Gwenifer asked on drawing back. She looked around, her gaze stopping not far from Paxton's foot. "What is that . . . a whip? Alana, tell me: What is going on here?"

Paxton saw Alana's mouth open, but before she could respond, her cousin pressed her aside.

"You there!" Gwenifer called, wagging a finger at Paxton. "Are you the one who's in command here?"

"Watch how she walks," Graham whispered near Paxton's ear as Gwenifer moved their way. "An angel cannot be as graceful."

Paxton marked the fluid movement of her body, especially the sway of her hips. Though they were covered with a fine linen chainse, a tansy-yellow silk bliaud, a bloodred camlet mantle, then atop that a hooded woolen cloak of sapphire blue, she wielded them in a way that was certain to attract a man's notice.

"Aye, she proceeds with a certain elegance," Paxton admitted, "but she chatters too much."

"Mayhap, but her voice is more musical than a harp," Graham countered on a sigh.

One with its chords having gone awry, Paxton thought, knowing he'd go altogether mad if had to listen to her for very long. She sounded like a fishwife!

Apart from that, there was something about her that inspired a wariness within him. Paxton didn't understand the sensation nor could he explain why it had come upon him. Nonetheless the feeling was there.

"You," Gwenifer stated, halting before him. "Are you this Paxton de Beaumont that Sir Graham mentioned to me?"

"I am," Paxton replied, thinking, her temperament aside, she was even more lovely up close.

Her hair was the same color as Alana's, a deep sable brown; her skin was smooth and creamy and without flaw; but where Alana's eyes were the color of the rich dark earth, Gwenifer's were a light hazel and speckled with golden dots of sunshine. Right now, they sparked with fire.

"I presume you have something you wish to say," he finished.

It was Gwenifer's turn to assess Paxton. He withstood her scrutiny as her gaze ran over him from head to toe. Then her eyes met his. What he read in their depths said she was pleased with what she saw.

"I do," she stated, her abrasive tone having softened. "But it comes more in the way of questions, milord. Why is my cousin dressed in sackcloth? And why is there a whip lying close to your feet? Has she offended you in some way . . . so horribly, that you must punish her this brutally? I know Gilbert would at times become very angry with her, but never to the extent that he thought to beat her. What has she done?"

"She has done nothing," Paxton returned. "The matter is now ended. Fortunately for Sir Graham, your cousin was not harmed."

"Sir Graham?" she asked, her eyes darting between the two men. "What has he to do with this?"

"Come, Gwenifer," Alana declared, coming upon the threesome. "Let's go into the hall. I'll explain everything while I dress."

Paxton was aware of her approach, noted how Madoc trailed behind her. The man now peered over Alana's shoulder at him, eyes flashing with malice. The look Madoc sent him indicated that Paxton might be soon wiping the man's spit from his face.

Unable to hold Madoc's gaze, Paxton scanned the yard. The Welsh had not yet dispersed. They watched and waited. It was as though they weren't quite certain their kinswoman was safe. His attention then fell on Alana.

"No one is more relieved than I that this is over and that you are unscathed," he said.

As was her habit, she elevated her chin in the same condescending fashion that he'd seen more often than not; then just as he anticipated, she bestowed on him a withering stare. Without reply, she turned away and urged her cousin across the yard.

As he watched them go, Paxton sighed inwardly, mindful that it would be a long while before she forgave him, if ever.

What had he expected? That she would fall at his feet in gratitude that he hadn't beaten her?

With her face to the post, she had no way of knowing the whip had left his hand, no way of appreciating that he wouldn't have followed through in chastising her, even if the group hadn't returned.

In time he'd tell her these things. For now, though, he'd keep his distance. A wise choice, considering her mood. Not to mention her anger.

Paxton frowned.

Thoughts of Alana's ire prompted him to remember something Gwenifer had said: *I know Gilbert would at times become very angry with her.*

He hadn't realized the significance of her words when she'd first uttered them, but he did now.

What exactly was it that prompted Gilbert's anger? Moreover, did his displeasure with his wife somehow lead to his death?

His friend's demise was one of the main reasons he'd been sent to the castle. Because of his worry over

Alana, and whether or not he'd have to punish her, he'd nearly forgotten that.

With his concerns at last put to rest, how Gilbert died was again at the fore of his mind, and Paxton was suddenly determined to discover if there in fact might be something to this small bit of news that Gwenifer had handed him.

That, coupled with Alana's slip of the tongue about Gilbert's selfish use of her in their marriage bed, was beginning to paint a picture about the couple's relationship. The portraiture was still hazy, but it appeared that all was not wedded bliss.

He needed answers, and of those here, Gwenifer might be the most willing to divulge the information he sought.

Unless he was mistaken, which he doubted, her eyes did say that she held a certain feminine interest in him. If he were to apply his masculine charms to advantage, he could very well succeed in getting at the truth.

Mulling the concept over, Paxton decided it was worth a try.

"How long has he been here?"

Alana poked her head through the neck of her chemise to see Gwenifer trailing her finger over the top of the table. "He who?" Alana asked, kicking the crumpled sackcloth away from her feet.

Gwenifer looked at her fingertip. Finding no dust, she allowed her hand to fall to her side. "You know who. Paxton de Beaumont, of course."

Alana would rather forget she knew him at all. "Three weeks, I suppose."

"You suppose? Don't you know?"

"I'm not in the habit of marking off the days as each

one goes by. Much has happened since his arrival. Truly, I cannot remember when he came. I do, however, wish he'd go away."

"I take it you don't like him, then," Gwenifer said.

An understatement, Alana thought. "Let's just say he annoys me."

"Why?"

Alana studied Gwenifer closely. Was her cousin interested in Paxton? She pictured the pair together, both perfect human beings in the physical sense. They would make a striking couple. For some reason, the thought nettled. "Because he's Norman," she snapped. "Why else?"

"Gilbert was Norman. You married him, didn't you?"

"Aye, but I am now widowed, and thus I shall stay." Alana inclined her head. "Why the questions, Gwenifer? Are you taken with him?"

"Nay. It's just that he seemed very contrite about his almost having whipped you . . . well, I was wondering why you were so angry with him when he expressed his relief that he hadn't caused you injury. You would have been scarred, you know. You may have died had your wounds taken the poisoning. At the very least, you should be thankful he held off as long as he did."

On their way up to her chamber, Alana had told Gwenifer about Sir Goddard's attacking her, informed her of Paxton's edict and his use of the Welsh as a means of protecting Sir Graham and his two companions as they made their way to and from Offa's Dyke. She'd also apprised her cousin of the time limitation imposed on the group for their safe return to the castle.

Some of this Gwenifer had apparently gleaned from Sir Graham as the group traveled toward the castle. At first, her cousin had been very sympathetic, but now Alana thought she was acting rather odd.

"Are you saying that you think I should fall at his feet and thank him for not beating me?" she asked incredulously. "If so, Gwenifer, it shall never happen."

"I didn't say anything of the sort. What I'm suggesting is this: If you hope to keep our kinsmen and his knights from each others' throats, I think it would be wise to make peace with your new overlord. Did you not see the hatred in our kinfolks' eyes. I did, and you had been released from the post, unscathed, by the time I rode into the courtyard.

"Think about it, Alana. The less strife there is among those here the easier it will be for us all. Only you have the power to see that everyone stays calm. Therefore, swallow your pride and offer him your friendship."

Alana wondered what Rhys would think of Gwenifer's proposal. Not much, she decided. But then anything that passed from her cousin's lips would meet with his disapproval.

Rhys disliked Gwenifer with a passion. He'd never told Alana just why he harbored such an aversion toward her cousin, but he'd warned Alana against Gwenifer, saying she was not to be trusted.

Alana had disagreed with Rhys, for Gwenifer had never shown any malice toward her, not even after the terrible family tragedy when Hywel ap Daffyd, Gwenifer's father, was slain by his own brother Rhodri, who was Alana's father. There had never been anything between the two cousins but affection.

Reviewing Gwenifer's words, Alana had to admit her cousin was right. "And how do you suggest I make friends with a man whom I can barely abide without it appearing as though I'm betraying my own kin?"

"Betraying your kin?" Gwenifer chimed. "Really, Alana, you sound as though you think that by showing the man some common courtesy or that by working with him in mutual accord to ensure peace between both sides it would be received in the same manner as if you were to become his whore. Everyone here knows where your loyalties lie. You don't have to fawn over the man. Just proceed in an amicable fashion, and I'm sure the tension within the castle will soon abate."

Most times, Gwenifer was wise to a fault, but she was yet unaware that Paxton doubted Alana's account about Gilbert's death, which in itself was bound to keep the uneasiness between them churning.

Gwenifer, like everyone else who had been at the castle the day Gilbert was pulled from the river, believed Gilbert had drowned, and Alana never told her otherwise.

From childhood, they had shared many of their most private thoughts with each other. Gwenifer even knew that Alana's marriage was not the most stable. She also knew that the union was loveless.

But in order to protect her cousin, Alana had purposely kept the truth about Gilbert's death from Gwenifer. It was one secret that her cousin would never learn.

"What are you thinking?" Gwenifer asked.

Alana shrugged. "Nothing of consequence."

Gwenifer laughed. The light musical sound filled the room. "Come now. Do you really believe Paxton de Beaumont is of little consequence?"

"I wasn't thinking about him. But, aye. He *is* of little consequence."

That was the second time she'd lied to her cousin. The first was when she'd said that she could barely abide him. In one way that was true. But in another . . .

God's blood! Why did the blackguard intrigue her so?

"He is quite handsome," Gwenifer said, a bemused light shining in her eyes.

Becoming annoyed with all this talk about Paxton, Alana snapped, "You believe that of every man."

"Not every man. Just of those where it's true. Paxton de Beaumont is one of those men."

Alana inclined her head and studied her cousin. Gwenifer was angling for something. Had she somehow ascertained the truth . . . that in actuality Alana was fascinated with Paxton? If her cousin was hoping to extract a confession to that end, she'd not get it.

Then another thought struck.

Though Gwenifer had denied any interest in Paxton, she may have done so because she feared she'd be intruding on her cousin's domain. Alana held no claim to Paxton, and as far as she was concerned, Gwenifer was welcome to him.

"Gwenifer," she said. "A second ago you told me that you weren't interested in the Norman. But by the way you keep talking about him, I detect you weren't exactly telling me the truth. If in fact you are attracted to him, and if you wish to pursue a relationship with him—though, for the life of me I cannot conceive why!—I tell you that you are free to do so. But I caution you this: From my own experience, I think you would be happier with a man of your own ilk. The differences between Gilbert and me were insurmountable. For your own sake, make certain that you choose wisely when you choose your husband."

Gwenifer again laughed. "My husband? Alana, please. I have no intention of marrying Paxton de

Beaumont. I simply find him attractive. Besides, after the way I behaved on my arrival, I have a feeling he'll now keep his distance."

"You were a bit shrewish," Alana offered.

"Only because I was appalled at what I saw. It unsettled me more than you can imagine when I became aware that you might have been put under the whip. Were we but a moment or two later in arriving, you would have suffered unmercifully. And I would have blamed myself that you had."

"Why would you blame yourself?"

"If Sir Graham and the others hadn't come upon us in the wood, offering assistance because of that broken cart wheel, they would easily have been here yesterday." Tears sprang to her eyes. "It pains me so to think of what might have happened to you. I just cannot bear it."

Alana moved to Gwenifer's side. "Do not fret, Cousin," she said, placing her arm around Gwenifer's shoulders. "Saint David was watching over me."

Gwenifer sniffed. "How do you know that?"

"'Tis as you've said. Paxton held off far longer than most men in his position would have. He gave an edict, promised to punish me if it wasn't obeyed, then was forced to follow through on that pledge. For some unexplained reason, he waited. And because he did, the group came just in time, you with them, everyone being safe. I cannot look upon all this as a mere coincidence. Saint David was watching over us all. I'm certain of it."

"If you believe that to be true, I suppose I should also."

"You should," Alana said. "As for the illustrious knight himself, unlike myself, Cousin, you are able to build a rapport with every male you come upon. I see no reason why you cannot do the same with him."

Gwenifer pulled from Alana's hold and slowly walked to the window, where she stared down on the courtyard. "You refer to Gilbert, don't you?" She paused. "Are you angry with me because he and I were friends?"

Viewing her cousin's back, Alana had to concede that she had been somewhat jealous of Gwenifer's skill to engage Gilbert in conversation. But then Gwenifer's temperament was far different from her own. This morning was possibly the first time she'd ever heard her cousin's voice raise in ire. It may very well have been the last.

She and Gwenifer were quite the opposites in that vein. Where one was calm the other was most volatile. Unfortunately Alana knew herself to be the latter.

There was no denying that her biggest fault lay with her own inability to curb her emotions. When she was angry, she let the world know. If she was truly sad, she allowed her tears to flow.

Conversely, Gwenifer always appeared to be in control. Perhaps it was because Gwenifer held such confidence in herself. And why not? She was close to being perfect.

More often than not, Alana had envied her cousin's composure. Yet the question always arose: If Gwenifer carried the same burden as Alana did, would she still be as poised?

Unlike Alana, she wasn't responsible for the welfare of her kinsmen nor had she married Gilbert for all the wrong reasons, making her own life miserable as a result.

Which brought Alana back to Gwenifer's inquiry.

"Angry with you because you and Gilbert were friends?" she asked. "Nay." It was the truth. "At least you were able to make him laugh, something I could never do."

Gwenifer turned around with a smile on her face. "You know, after my journey, I find I'm exceptionally thirsty," she said while loosening the strings to her cloak. "Once you've finished dressing, what would you say to our going down to the hall and having ourselves a cup of milk together?"

"I say that would be quite nice."

Alana donned her white linen chainse and a bliaud of deep blue flannel. She was not as brightly nor as finely dressed as Gwenifer, but then simplicity and modesty were more suited to Alana's tastes.

"How is your mother?" Alana asked, hoping to put all talk of Paxton de Beaumont aside.

"She's in good health." Gwenifer patted the brooch that she'd attached to Alana's mantle. "There. I believe we are ready."

"And your stepfather—is he also in good health?" Alana asked as she drew on her headrail, her braid bound around her head.

"He's as hale as ever," came Gwenifer's reply. "They are both very happy living beside the River Clwyd. I believe they will be satisfied to live out the rest of their years there."

Alana remembered how after Hywel's death Rhodri ap Daffyd had looked after Gwenifer and her mother, Rhodri's sense of duty and remorse over slaying his only brother the reason. Besides, mother and daughter had no place to go. But Marared was forever resentful, and no one ever faulted her for her feelings of bitterness, but life with Marared around was not easy.

After a year of the woman's constant haranguing and badgering, everyone's nerves were on edge. Fortunately, through contacts of Rhodri's, a marriage was arranged for his widowed sister-in-law, one that was considered a good match.

Marared accepted the proposal, and she and Gwenifer left Rhodri's protection and began a new life by the River Clwyd, which was well north of the fortress. Gwenifer, showing no revulsion for her father's kin the way her mother had, visited often over the years. Though she came unannounced, she arrived at the most momentous of times.

Gwenifer had been here when Alana's father had tumbled from his horse, the fall killing him. She'd come shortly before Gilbert's demise and sought to console Alana, believing her cousin was truly grieved.

Why Gwenifer would think that her cousin actually lamented Gilbert's loss, Alana couldn't say. Gwenifer knew their was no love between the couple. In fact, as Alana recalled, it was Gwenifer who shed the most tears. But then she and Gilbert were friends, therefore Gwenifer's tears were genuine, where Alana's were not.

And Gwenifer was here now, at another time of tribulation for Alana. A godsend, Alana thought. For if Gwenifer, with her exceptional beauty and poise, could capture the interests of Paxton de Beaumont, maybe he'd forget all about delving into Gilbert's death, which would alleviate Alana's fears and worries.

"I'm glad to know your mother is again content," she said, wondering just how she could foist Gwenifer off on Paxton.

Considering Gwenifer's beauty, Alana doubted she'd have to play matchmaker for the pair. Awed, Paxton would no doubt approach the irresistible Gwenifer without any prompting. For her own sake, Alana prayed that he did.

"Are we ready for that milk?" she asked, then headed for the door.

"Indeed," Gwenifer said, drawing up alongside Alana. "I hope you will ponder what I said about approaching your new overlord and befriending him."

They were now out on the gallery. Minding the differences between Paxton and herself, Alana questioned whether they could ever be friends.

"I'll think about it," she said, knowing that was all she'd probably do.

"Are you certain that I have your permission to befriend him myself?" Gwenifer asked near her ear.

Over the railing that edged the gallery, Alana could see Paxton standing not far from the hall's entry. He was talking to Sir Graham. As though he were somehow aware that the cousins would soon be descending the stairs, he looked up. But his eyes were on Gwenifer not on her.

A hollow feeling suddenly settling inside her, Alana dragged her gaze from the hall below. "I have no interest in him, Gwenifer. You are more than welcome to the rogue."

"You're certain?" Gwenifer asked again.

Was she? Alana wondered. Paxton was the only man to light a fire in her blood. But he was Norman and she was Welsh. Then there were the lies about Gilbert's death. Too much stood between them.

Alana glimpsed the floor below and the man standing there. His gaze was still on Gwenifer. And apparently so was his masculine interest.

"Aye," Alana said. "I'm certain."

CHAPTER

9

Alana stood at the castle mews. Scraps of raw meat lay inside a bowl that she held in her hand.

She chose one of the morsels, then taking care to keep her fingers well back, she shoved it through a vertical break in the cage.

The trained falcon snatched the meat in his sharp beak. With its talons pinning the meal to its perch, the bird tore at the flesh, swallowing it greedily.

Alana turned to Madoc. "They should be allowed to fly," she said of the five hawks and four falcons. "They haven't hunted for weeks."

Not receiving a response, she studied the man. His brow furrowed into deep lines; he looked to be a far way off.

"Madoc . . . did you not hear me?"

He blinked. "Milady?"

She viewed him a bit longer. "You seem pensive. Is something troubling you?"

"Aye. But you don't like anyone to be critical of your cousin, so I'll hold my tongue about her."

"You refer to her attentiveness toward our new overlord, correct?"

Madoc's lips drew into a tight line as his eyes narrowed. "Aye. In the two days that she's been here, she has chased the Norman from one end of the yard to the other."

"And he has done the same with her," Alana interjected. With her words, an odd sort of pain settled in the middle of her chest. "They apparently hold an attraction for each other."

"That may be, but if she had any loyalty toward her own kind, she'd not be running after him in such a bold manner. 'Twas the same with your husband, always talking and laughing with him. Such actions do not sit well with her kinsmen, especially when they look upon this particular Norman as their enemy."

"Why this particular Norman?" she asked as she shoved another piece of meat between the bars of the next cage. The hawk seized its meal and tore into it the same as the falcon. "Did they feel any differently toward Gilbert?"

"We accepted him because you chose to marry him. You did so, hoping to protect us. But you and I both know that was a mistake. That he paid for his treachery with his life is only justice. As for this Paxton de Beaumont, we hold no liking for him whatsoever. He meant to injure you with the whip and would have done so had we not returned when we did. Your kinsmen cannot forget that, milady. Nor can they abide their kinswoman behaving like the Norman's whore. Something has to be done, and done soon, else tempers will erupt. I fear the consequences if they do."

And so did Alana. "I was unaware that they felt so strongly about this. Madoc, you must speak to them and tell them for me that I do not hold any malice against Paxton for what almost happened. I was not harmed, and he did say he was relieved that he didn't have to use the whip. As for Gwenifer, I was the one who encouraged her to make friends with Paxton."

"You?" Madoc cried, eliciting a screech from one of the hawks. "Why would you do that?"

Alana looked around to see if anyone had heard him. "Because I thought that if his interests were elsewhere, such as on Gwenifer, he'd stop delving into Gilbert's death. If he ever learns the truth, we're all doomed."

"Did you tell her what actually happened that day?"

"Nay." Alana hated that she was using Gwenifer in this way. Especially since it was besmirching her cousin's character. "'Tis as before. Of all here, only you and I know."

"Then she is in fact attracted to the Norman," Madoc muttered.

"She is attracted to men in general," Alana defended. "Because she had the misfortune of being born a female, Hywel paid her little heed when he was alive. Her stepfather shows her no interest now. That she seeks a man's attention speaks for itself. Besides, she is beautiful. Men are naturally drawn to her. It has been that way all her life. Because she feels at ease with a man and is able to speak to him freely does not mean she is his whore. Nor should anyone here think that. Whether it is true or not. I want you to pass the word that Gwenifer is assisting me by having befriended the Norman. Let them know that, whatever it is he tells her, she brings the information to me."

"And does she?"

"She is unaware that she does, but yes, she tells me much about him."

The truth was that Alana was becoming annoyed with Gwenifer's constant chatter about Paxton. Each night when she and Gwenifer retired to Alana's chamber, for Alana would not allow her to sleep in the hall with the others, her cousin went on and on about the knight.

So far the one-sided conversation lent itself to how wonderfully charming, how exceptionally handsome, how very virile Paxton was. It got to the point that Alana felt she might retch if Gwenifer were to say his name one more time. Believing the ache that grew inside her was naught but indigestion, Alana ignored the unsettling feeling altogether. And though it vexed her, she allowed Gwenifer to babble on, hoping at some juncture she would learn something of consequence.

"Will you do this for me?" Alana asked.

Madoc drew a long breath. "Aye. As long as what she does is intended to benefit her kinfolk, I see no reason why she cannot continue behaving in the same manner that she has. I'll tell them that it is all a ruse. But if I were you, milady, I would try to temper her a bit. If her itch for the Norman should get out of hand and it is discovered that he's bedded her, there's no telling what will happen."

The concept that Paxton and Gwenifer at some point might find themselves in the throes of passion, whereupon they made love, disturbed Alana far more than she wanted to admit. Save for Gwenifer's reputation, the prospect shouldn't really bother her. Should it?

"I'll keep watch over her, Madoc. You can be assured of that."

"And I will help you."

"Good," she said, then finished feeding the remaining hawks and falcons. She set the empty bowl aside, retrieved a scrap of cloth, and wiped her hands. "While you go about spreading the word, I also have something I must do. I'll meet you later in the hall."

Tossing the cloth into the bowl, she set off to find Paxton. If peace were ever to prevail inside the fortress, Alana knew it had to begin with her.

"You are forever asking about Alana and Gilbert," Gwenifer stated as she inclined her head. "Why are you so interested in the pair?"

Paxton looked down on Gwenifer as they idly strolled the courtyard.

The construction had been put on hold for the time being, for not much would be accomplished until the strained relations within the castle had eased.

The Welsh were still angry with him over Alana's near whipping, and Paxton understood that, with their attentions held other than on their work, accidents might occur while arguments could arise.

He'd not risk any harm coming to even one of them, for it was certain to invite further dissension.

With his days free, he had plenty of time to entertain Alana's cousin, probing for answers as he did so.

Apparently he was being far too obvious with his questions. Believing that subtlety would have served him far better, he decided it was a bit late for that now. Then maybe not.

"Why am I so interested in the pair?" he repeated, then saw her nod. "Because Gilbert and I were friends. We knew each other from the time we were pages. He died far too young, and I was just wondering, in the years since I last saw him, if he was happy.

I'd like to believe he was. It would ease my mind if you were to confirm such."

"I'd think Alana could answer your question better than I. The last I saw of her, she was by the mews. Why don't you go ask her?"

Paxton knew where Alana was. He'd glimpsed Madoc and her through the opening between the buildings as he and Gwenifer had ambled close by the area. But the responses he wanted had to come from Gwenifer.

"Most times," he said, "those closest to a situation cannot answer objectively, while those who stand at a distance can." He shrugged. "'Tis not important. I simply thought you might be able to confirm that what I had hoped for Gilbert was in fact true."

"I believe Gilbert was happy. As for Alana . . . well, I have my doubts."

"And why is that?"

"The difference in their heritage . . . her loyalty to her kin. It was not easy for either of them. Then there's Alana's temperament. She can be quite emotional at times. She is quick to anger, which can be most worrisome to a man. Gilbert felt the force of her ire, more than once. She never was able to contain herself, which may have added to her unhappiness. But then that is Alana. What more can I say?"

Yes, that *was* Alana, Paxton reasoned in silence, remembering how she'd turned on him. Her fury was like a raging tempest, wild and untamable. But the challenge was there. Which in itself made her all the more enticing.

As he viewed Gwenifer, whose hair in the sunlight shimmered like the finest silk ever woven in the farthest reaches of the Orient and whose skin was so smooth and creamy one would think it could belong only to an angel, he conceded she was beautiful, both in appearance and in manner. Her poise alone would impel many a man to seek her as a wife.

For Paxton, though, Gwenifer lacked the one element that to him was the most vitally essential. She was lost to the sort of fiery inner passion that could make his blood burn and cause his whole body to ignite in an inferno of desire. She was lost to the one thing that Alana possessed.

He wanted Alana more than any woman he'd ever known. But the same question kept gnawing at him: Could he trust her?

"Did my response ease your mind any?" Gwenifer asked as she spun around in front of him.

Hell no!

Paxton felt like shouting the words, but he managed to keep them inside—just barely. Gwenifer's statement about Gilbert being happy while Alana was not had given rise to more queries that needed answering.

And this matter about the dissimilarity in their heritage, along with Alana's loyalty to her kin—if these were two of the main obstacles that stood between Gilbert and Alana, what made him think it would be any different between Alana and him?

Like Gilbert, he also was Norman. And Alana's loyalty to her people was as strong as ever. Possibly stronger. A fine mess, Paxton thought.

"I'm glad Gilbert was happy," he said, though doubting it was true. A man who took delight with his young wife would not treat her so coldly when bedding her. As for Alana, he was aware of her sentiments, for she'd been the one who'd let that piece of information slip. "But I'm also grieved that your cousin was deprived of joy. Was it always so between them?"

Gwenifer pursed her lips. "You know, it is a lovely day . . . the sort of day that we Welsh aren't always blessed by, since it most often rains. Why can we not enjoy the sunshine without all this wearisome talk about Alana and Gilbert?"

Paxton was becoming chafed by the issue anyway. There would be time to question Gwenifer further. A slow smile spread across his face. "So what do you propose?"

"A walk in the wood, perhaps?"

He took her arm in his. "Whatever the fair Gwenifer desires."

Alana had taken two turns around the courtyard and still couldn't find Paxton. She'd even peeked into the hall, thinking he might be there. He wasn't. As she presently made her way toward the garrison, she saw Aldwyn crossing the yard. Calling out to him, she motioned him to her.

"Milady?" he inquired when he came upon her.

"Have you seen Sir Paxton?"

Aldwyn's jaw tightened. "Aye."

Alana waited but that one word was all that broke from his lips. "Well?"

Jerking his head in the direction of the side gate, he said, "He and Gwenifer went out into the wood together."

Alana noted a tinge of discord in his voice. She placed her hand on his arm. "Aldwyn, please don't be upset by what you see. Gwenifer is, in actuality, assisting me. Her association with the knight is meant to help us all in the long run."

"Are you certain of that?"

Alana nibbled at her lower lip. Was she certain? Or was her use of Gwenifer to keep Paxton occupied merely done in order to save her own skin?

In one sense, she'd misled Madoc, and now, more explicitly, Aldwyn. Gwenifer's purpose in pursuing

Paxton was in no way meant to help her kinfolk, but was done for personal motives alone. Alana knew this and had encouraged such.

Her biggest worry had always been Paxton's unearthing the fact that Gilbert was murdered, for she feared that whatever retribution was meant to fall would descend not just on her but on all her kin. But now there was something of a larger concern.

Except for Madoc, her kinfolk were unaware of Alana's deception regarding Gilbert. And despite Madoc's assurances to the whole that Gwenifer's affiliation with Paxton was no more than a ruse meant to extract information from the knight, they might be unwilling to see anything save that a woman of Welsh blood was consorting with a Norman.

The consequences of such could be grave if tempers were to erupt. A riot could ensue. What chance would her people have against Norman swords when they were armed with naught but rakes, hoes, and shovels?

Alana was aware that this grand plan of hers had become unworkable. She needed to put a stop to Gwenifer's association with Paxton. Or, at the very least, curb these intimate walks in the woods.

Without further acknowledgment to Aldwyn, she headed toward the side gate.

The woods had come fully to life.

Hidden among the high branches of the oaks, birds twittered merrily. Below them, sunlight dappled the forest floor, its beams shining through the breaches among the unfurled leaves.

Scattered alongside the path that Alana took to the river, wildflowers spread their petals, basking in the warm glow. Small creatures scurried into hiding at her approach, as quiet as it was.

Midway to the stream, she heard laughter. Paxton's

and Gwenifer's to be exact. The sound was heard to her left, and Alana veered from her original course to head in the direction of their voices.

On nearly silent feet, she trekked through the trees, Paxton's deep tones and Gwenifer's musical responses drawing her onward.

The voices became ever louder.

Making her way around a large pine, Alana glimpsed the pair. Though she didn't know why, she ducked back behind the tree. Pulling several boughs down, so that she could see the couple, she peered at them through the jutting needles.

It never occurred to Alana that she was spying. Something inside her simply said she needed to watch. It wasn't long before she wished she hadn't pried at all.

Across the way, Gwenifer, in all her grace and beauty, reclined against the trunk of a tall oak, smiling up at Paxton. His hand braced against the bark near Gwenifer's head, Paxton returned her smile as he leaned toward her.

Alana couldn't hear their words nor did she want to. It was unsettling enough to see Paxton lift Gwenifer's hand, his lips brushing the tops of her knuckles.

With her heart sinking like a heavy stone in water, Alana spun on her heel and made her way from the wood.

Halfway up the path, she remembered why she'd followed them in the first place. She'd have been far wiser if she'd waited until their return. But in her constant desire to ensure peace between Welsh and Norman alike, she just *had* to rectify the situation then and there.

Oh, why did she care what Gwenifer did?

Her cousin was two months shy of her own age.

Therefore she was old enough to make her own decisions.

And all this worry over loyalty and prejudices and how the slightest little thing might be perceived between either faction within the castle was beginning to grate on her nerves. Why couldn't they for once resolve their problems without involving her?

Then there was Paxton—the insufferable rogue.

First he was kissing her, then he was kissing Gwenifer. Didn't he have any mores whatsoever? Or was this some kind of a lark for him, playing one cousin against the other?

As far as Alana was concerned, he'd meet his end before she'd ever allow him to touch her again. Before she was *supposed* to hate him simply because he was Norman. Now she *did* hate him simply because he was Paxton de Beaumont, an unscrupulous lout!

In truth she'd grown weary. She wanted—needed! —to get away from here, away from all this strife and turmoil. If it were *only* possible.

Looking up, she saw she was two strides from the gate. In short order, the panel opened after she demanded entry. She crossed the threshold with such determination and with such speed that she almost upended Father Jevon, who was standing in her path.

Steadying himself on his feet, he said, "My child, I've been looking for you."

"Why?"

As Alana continued her march across the courtyard, the priest skipped alongside her. "I've been praying," he stated.

"For what poor soul this time?"

"For yours."

She made no effort to slow her pace. "You're wasting your breath, Father," she said. "'Twould serve you better if you prayed for Sir Paxton's. He's the one who needs your prayers, not I."

"I've been praying for his soul as well."

"Do you think it helped?"

"I hope so . . . in fact, I'm certain of it. That is why I came to search you out. I would like for you and Sir Paxton to meet with me. There is much to discuss. Your hearts and souls must be made right with God before either of you can go forward with the ceremony."

Alana skidded to a halt. "Ceremony? What ceremony?"

Father Jevon blinked. "Surely you are by now aware of Henry's edict?"

Edict! If there was such a thing, this was news to her. "Concerning what?" she asked, her eyes narrowing.

"Why, your marriage to Paxton de Beaumont, of course."

CHAPTER

10

Alana stared at the priest as though he'd just sprouted a set of donkey ears.

"My marriage to Paxton de Beaumont?" she asked, thinking he was very much an ass if he really believed she'd wed the rogue.

"Yes, my child. It has been decreed by Henry that the two of you shall unite in wedlock."

She should have known. From the instant she'd learned there was a priest amidst the small group, she'd wondered about his presence. Stupidly she'd allowed herself to believe he'd come to save their heathen souls. If that was one of his reasons for being here, it was a lesser one, for now she knew his main purpose was to perform the nuptials between Paxton and herself, and it was at Henry's bidding.

This couldn't be happening! "I have the right to refuse, don't I?" she asked, her emotions spinning around and around like a top gone askew.

"By ordinance of the Church, you do have the right to reject any man," Father Jevon responded. "But since your king has ordered the marriage, I'd suggest that you think twice before spurning his decree."

Alana was awash with relief. "Henry was Gilbert's king, Father Jevon. Not mine. Therefore he has no say over anything I do."

"Oh, but you're wrong," Paxton announced.

Alana's gaze shot over Father Jevon's shoulder to see Paxton was standing only a few feet behind the priest, Gwenifer beside him. So involved in her conversation was she with Father Jevon she hadn't noticed their approach.

Her ire rose, and her chin lifted. "I think not," Alana said, squaring her shoulders.

Paxton came forward to stop mere inches from her. "The day you married Gilbert you made yourself Henry's subject, Alana. Those are our king's words, almost verbatim. He also said that if you were to disobey him, you would not like the consequences of such an action. Henry's temper is notorious. If I were you, I'd think again before I challenged him in any way."

"I won't marry you," she bit out.

"We'll see."

He turned back to Gwenifer, whose face had gone pale. Alana's heart went out to her cousin, for they'd both been duped by Paxton.

"You are due an explanation, but that will have to come later," he told Gwenifer. "For now, I'd like to speak to Alana alone. Therefore I ask that you go into the hall and wait for me."

Gwenifer nodded, then with her poise appearing to be fully intact, she did as Paxton had bade.

How could her cousin be so calm? Alana wondered, knowing her own composure was precisely nil. She had to get away from Paxton before the anger inside her erupted with such fury that both men would cower at its force. She made a move to depart, but Paxton caught her arm. Once the door had closed behind Gwenifer, he turned on the priest.

"I thought, Father Jevon, that we agreed you would keep silent until *I* gave notice that Alana and I were to be married."

"But I was certain you had come to that decision." Paxton's jaw hardened noticeably, and the priest dropped his gaze to his feet. "'Tis now obvious that you hadn't. Mayhap it is time I retired to the chapel to say my prayers."

"An excellent idea, Father," Paxton declared, his tone biting. "Say several for yourself while you're at it."

"I will, my son. Believe me I will."

In growing irritation, Alana had listened to the exchange. After the priest had shuffled off toward the chapel, her gaze leveled in on Paxton, and she demanded, "Take your hand off me, Norman."

"Nay," he answered, then began guiding her toward the side gate.

"What are you doing? Where are we going?"

"To the wood so we can have a private talk."

"You scurrilous son of the devil—there is nothing to talk about," she announced, her heels now digging into the ground.

The effort was a waste, for he pulled her along with ease.

"I won't marry you, and you cannot make me," she insisted.

The words were uttered as he practically dragged her out into the wood. Alana looked around in surprise, for she hadn't even heard him order the gate opened.

He hauled her down the path, then turned into the trees. Glimpsing him, she saw the tic in his jaw. That in itself should have warned her. But when she marked that he was taking her to the same area where he'd taken Gwenifer, she let her anger fly.

"I hate you, Paxton de Beaumont . . . hate you with every inch of my—"

The air whooshed from her lungs as her back suddenly met the trunk of a tree. Blinking, she stared into Paxton's face as he pressed her against the rough bark.

"Do you, Alana? Are you certain you hate me? Or do you feel something else entirely but are afraid to admit it."

"You're insane."

"Am I? I heard you come through the wood a while ago, knew you were watching Gwenifer and me. If you hated me that much, why didn't you show yourself and demand that I keep away from your cousin. You had the power to order her back to the castle, Alana. All the Welsh listen to you. They'd never disobey you, Gwenifer included. But you did none of these things. Instead you scrambled back up the hill as though you were being chased by a pack of ravenous wolves. Why?"

Alana's heart was hammering in her ears. Oh God, he knew she was there, knew she was spying! She felt her embarrassment rise and sought to deny his claim as she snarled, "You're imagining things, Norman. I was never in the wood while you and Gwenifer were here."

"You weren't? Then come. Let's go ask the guard. I'll wager he'll say otherwise." He pulled back slightly. "Come along."

"No." The word was but a miserable groan that trembled in her throat. "Why are you doing this?"

"To prove that you don't hate me. But you *do* desire me, Alana. The same as I desire you. That's why you ran from the wood. You couldn't abide seeing me with Gwenifer. That's the truth of it, isn't it?"

She'd die before she'd admit that he was right. He could beat her within an inch of her life. He could kill her altogether! She'd never, ever tell him that what he'd guessed was fact.

She felt her tears rising ever closer to the surface. She had to be free of him before she started blubbering like a fool. "Get away from me, Norman," she said, surprised that she had managed that much. "If you want the truth, here it is: You repulse me."

He pressed into her more fully. "And I shall prove otherwise," he whispered close to her mouth.

Then his lips were on hers.

As his mouth ravaged hers in a hard, tantalizing kiss, Alana didn't know what she had expected. She'd challenged him, and he had to prove her a liar. Which, misery of miseries, she was.

The heat inside her was building. Her skin burned, and her arms ached unbearably to hold him. Yet she resisted.

Remember.

The word he'd uttered after kissing her once before came to mind just as his tongue plunged between her lips to forage at will, and she could no longer hold back. She moaned and gave herself over to his mastery.

His kiss deepened as he moved his hips against her. She felt the evidence of his desire and knew hers to be equal by the sudden moistness between her legs.

Then his open lips slid across her cheek. "You want me," he said, his hot breath fanning against her ear. "And God knows I want you. But we will not come together, Alana . . . not until we've said our vows."

"I won't marry you," she whimpered.

He nibbled at her ear. "You will."

"Nay."

He pulled back and looked into her eyes. "You will, Alana. You lied to me when you said I repulsed you. I learned today that you've lied to me before."

Her stupor of desire disintegrated, and she grew very still. "W-what do you mean?"

"Rhys."

She felt her stomach turn upside-down. Had he discovered the truth about Gilbert? "What about Rhys?"

"He is not three hundred strong but only a third of that, half of which are children. I'd say the odds are now suddenly on my side."

Gwenifer—she'd told him, Alana thought.

"If you continue to refuse me, I might have no choice but to ride against him. But if you cooperate with me, your kin across the river will remain safe." He caught hold of her chin. "You will marry me, Alana. 'Tis only a matter of time. When I say the moment is right, you *will* become my wife."

With that he dropped his hand and backed away from her. Too stunned to move, Alana watched as he began striding from the wood.

"Are you coming?" he inquired on turning back to her.

She shoved away from the tree and trailed him toward the path.

Marriage, she thought. And to another Norman. Yet, considering his threat, what choice did she have?

The question was posed, and the answer came with clarity . . .

Absolutely none.

* * *

"I don't understand," Gwenifer said. "If you were intending to marry Alana, why then were you prone to seek my attentions? In the wood, you were . . . well, I'm inclined to believe you were merely trifling with me."

Paxton studied Gwenifer. He'd thought it was the other way around. From the second she came down the stairs on the day of her arrival, Alana beside her, she'd been more than a bit congenial toward him. But then he'd accepted her overtures—had encouraged them in fact! He'd even presented her with a few overtures of his own. His motives, though, were not to promote an intimate relationship. Far from it.

What was he to tell her: His advances were fostered only as a means to glean information about Alana?

And this matter about their being in the wood. In truth he was trifling with her. Even so, he couldn't very well tell her that he'd orchestrated the intimate scene between them simply because he knew Alana was watching.

Paxton sighed inwardly. He'd built a certain rapport with Gwenifer, and for reasons that were purely selfish, he didn't want the harmony between them to fall into ruin. There were yet questions that needed to be answered. He despised using her this way, but there was little else that could be done.

Likewise, it was obvious that he'd managed to injure her feelings, and he didn't want to hurt Gwenifer further. But he knew, at some point, her pride would suffer again. Yet there was no way around it.

Releasing his breath, he came up off the edge of the table where he'd perched himself in a secluded corner of the hall. In a few steps, he was beside her.

"Henry gave the edict that Alana and I were to be married. But he also said the decision of whether or not the marriage would go forth was in fact mine. Of all here, only Sir Graham, the priest, and I knew of the decree. And that is the way it would have stayed if Father Jevon, in his eagerness to perform his duties for both God and king, hadn't made Alana aware of Henry's directive."

"Considering her reaction, do you still plan to wed her?"

"I haven't decided."

Gwenifer inclined her head. "Do you love her?"

Did he? He wanted Alana, desired her like no other. But love? "Nay," he said, believing the statement to be true.

Gwenifer's face brightened, then once again grew serious. "Before you decide," she said, "I caution you to remember the differences between Gilbert and Alana, which are identical to your own. Not much happiness came from their union. In light of that, are you willing to opt for the same?" Those words said, she left Paxton's side.

As he watched her go, Paxton frowned. To spend his life in misery—is that what he wanted?

Not really.

Yet, if there were strife between Gilbert and Alana, it was probably Gilbert's own fault.

Paxton knew his friend well. Unfortunately, selfishness had been one of Gilbert's deficiencies. That he hadn't managed to overcome the failure was made clear when Alana had let slip the tidings about the lack of warmth in their marriage bed.

As for himself, he might not love Alana, but he knew how to make love to her. She'd not be left wanting. Never by him. And to that end, they did have one thing in common: mutual desire.

Likewise, the pleasure that they would derive from

each other was certain to form a bond between them. In time, they might come to love each other. But even if it were only in bed, some joy was bound to come from their union.

The one thing that made him hesitate was the question of trust. But once that was resolved to his satisfaction, nothing would stand in their way. Their marriage would go forth.

The knowledge pleased Paxton, for on that day, just as Henry had promised, the castle, its inhabitants, and all the land, as far as the eye could see and beyond, would at last be his.

And so would Alana.

Upstairs, Alana wrung her hands as she paced the floor of her chamber.

Blessed Saint David! she thought. Surely there had to be a way to stop this farce of a marriage.

Over and over again, she bewailed the notion of them becoming husband and wife. But other than running a sword through the rogue, she could think of no way out.

Damn Henry's edict! And damn Paxton as well!

The condemnations shot through her head just as the door to her chamber opened.

Gwenifer! Of all people, she was the last person Alana wanted to see—except for Paxton.

"I just finished talking with Paxton and came to see if you were all right," Gwenifer said. "Oh, Alana, I cannot believe this is happening."

Neither could Alana. It probably wouldn't have come this far if it weren't for Gwenifer and her loose tongue. It was time her cousin learned a few hard truths, mainly about Paxton.

"Close the door," Alana ordered, "then come over here and sit down."

At first, Gwenifer faltered, then she secured the room. "Are you in some way angry with me?" she asked as she made her way to the chair. "Believe me I had no knowledge of Henry's edict. If I had, I certainly wouldn't have made a fool of myself over your affianced the way I did. Besides, you were the one who encouraged me to seek him out."

Alana bristled at the term *affianced,* especially when she thought *bastard* would suit him better. Biting her tongue, she attempted to calm herself, then waited until Gwenifer sank into the chair.

"That's one of the things I want to talk to you about," she said. "It appears, Gwenifer, that Paxton de Beaumont has played us both for fools. I'm in no way angry with you, and I take full responsibility for having encouraged you to build a relationship with him, if that's what you wanted. Of course, at the time, neither of us knew about Henry's edict."

"No, we didn't." Gwenifer nibbled at her lip. "Do you intend to marry him?"

"It seems I have no choice."

"But the priest said you could refuse. Surely that is your way out if you wish to take it."

"Not anymore," Alana said.

"Why?"

"Because in your intimate talks with Paxton, you let something slip, and he is now using it against me."

"That's impossible!" Gwenifer cried. "I never told him anything of consequence. Certainly nothing he could use in way of coercion."

"Did he perchance ask about my kin across the river and how many they numbered?"

"I suppose he did."

"And did you tell him they were just a hundred strong?"

"I guess I did," Gwenifer answered. "But how could he use that against you?"

"He has threatened to ride against Rhys and destroy them all."

Gwenifer blanched. "But why?"

Drawing a breath, Alana explained about the slaughter of the first group to leave the castle. "Sir Goddard somehow made it back here. He told Paxton that it was my kin who attacked them. When Paxton first questioned me, I evaded answering him as best I could. I didn't know if Rhys had assailed the knights or not."

"You lied to him?"

"Not exactly. I just didn't inform him about Rhys and the others. He knew that none here had followed the group on its departure, so he let the accusation pass, believing it was naught more than a wounded man's delirious ramblings."

"But he soon learned otherwise," Gwenifer commented.

"Aye. When he was recovered from his injuries, Sir Goddard told Paxton about Rhys. Paxton in turn confronted me."

"And that's when you lied to him."

"I had no choice," Alana said. "I feared he would retaliate against Rhys for the Normans who were slain. In order to protect my mother's kin, I told him that they numbered over three times the sum of his own men. It worked. With the odds being against him as they were, he decided not to seek his revenge."

"But today I unwittingly told him the truth, and now he is holding it over your head. Oh, Alana, whatever can we do?"

"For one, you are to stay away from him. Otherwise, just as you did today about Rhys, you might give something else away that he'll use against me in some other manner."

"Such as?"

"I don't know." Alana did know, but she wasn't about to voice such to Gwenifer. "What else has he been questioning you about?"

"He's been asking about you and Gilbert . . . about your relationship."

Alana's heart skipped a beat. It was just as she'd feared. He still discredited her accounting of how Gilbert died and was tapping Gwenifer for information. "And what did you tell him?"

Her cousin shrugged. "That you had your differences, but that Gilbert seemed happy. Was that acceptable?"

Alana supposed so—if, in fact, that was *all* her cousin had told him. "Aye," she said, not wanting to make an issue of it. "Please, Gwenifer, do as I've requested and keep away from him. And whatever you do, don't tell anyone about Henry's edict. I don't want the others to know that I've been ordered to marry another Norman."

"I promise I won't say a word." Gwenifer rose from the chair. Fine lines creased her brow as she began to tap her upper lip with her forefinger. "This matter about Paxton culling information from me," she said. "What if we were to turn the tables on him? What if I were able to extract some information from him? Whatever I learn, I'll bring it straight to you. What do you think?"

Alana sighed. "Thanks to Father Jevon, I believe we have discovered all there is to know."

"I'm not so sure about that."

"Don't tell me there is something else . . . never mind. Tell me!"

"Well, you say Paxton is forcing you to marry him by threatening retribution against Rhys, correct?"

"Aye."

"Yet, when I spoke to him just a short while ago, he told me that Henry issued the edict, but it was Paxton's choice whether or not he married. His king allowed him the option."

"And?"

"When I asked if he was going to marry you, he said he hadn't decided."

"What else did he say?"

"He said he didn't love you. But then you don't love him. So that's really of no consequence. I think that was all—for now."

Didn't love you.

As the words repeated themselves in Alana's mind, she wondered if Gwenifer had asked him about his feelings point-blank. Or had he tossed that little tidbit out on his own?

Ignoring the small twinge of pain near her heart, Alana decided she cared little who brought the subject up. Nor were Paxton's feelings toward her of any importance. The only thing that concerned her was stopping this marriage.

"If you were to remain on amicable terms with him, what good do you think it will do?" Alana asked.

"I'm not fully certain. But I do know, if I'm made to keep away from him, we won't have any inkling as to what he is up to. I doubt we gain anything that can be used as a threat against him. But I'm sure we can learn what his plans are and when he means to execute them."

Alana was hesitant. For all Gwenifer's good intentions, her scheme might in the end have an adverse effect. What if Gwenifer again let something slip?

Yet knowing Paxton's own designs and schemes in advance might somehow give Alana the upper hand.

She already knew that he hadn't decided if he was going to wed her or not, which meant some hope still existed. She'd not be aware of his lack of resolve if it were not for Gwenifer.

"Stay close to him," Alana said, "but make certain you keep your own tongue silent."

CHAPTER
11

⁓

"There are rumblings within the castle, milady, that will not be quieted," Madoc said. "Your cousin's blatant actions toward the Norman are stirring a lot of unrest. If something isn't done, I fear there will soon be anarchy."

Alana looked away from the cage, for she and Madoc were again at the mews feeding the hawks and falcons. Studying Madoc closely, she noted his face was drawn, and the lines near his mouth and eyes had deepened over the past four days.

Knowing Madoc as well as she did, Alana could not deny he was worried that chaos would be upon them in quick order. But what was she to do?

"Did you explain anew to them that Gwenifer is assisting me by gleaning information from him?" As she wiped her hands on a damp rag, the last bird of prey having been fed, she saw Madoc's nod. "Why then are they so unwilling to accept that?"

"Her getting information from him is not what rankles them," Madoc said. "What they cannot accept is the way she's going about it. All this laughing and smiling and looking into each other's eyes— seems to me she could show some restraint and comport herself in a manner that states she possesses some modesty. Instead she practically tosses herself into his lap the instant his backside hits a bench inside the hall."

Madoc's words were, to a certain extent, an exaggeration.

Yes, there were moments when their laughter filled the hall, the sound capturing everyone's attention. And there were times when they bestowed on one another an engaging smile, which elicited some pointed looks from Gwenifer's peers.

Likewise there were instances where their eyes would meet and they would gaze at each other as though they were entranced. On these occasions, a low grumbling of disgust traveled through the hall.

Alana had noticed these things, the same as her kinsmen had. But Gwenifer had done nothing so bold as to cast herself at Paxton. Not yet.

As Alana reviewed Gwenifer's behavior, it was now apparent that her cousin was being a bit *too* friendly toward Paxton.

However, Gwenifer wasn't totally to blame for her actions. Alana had allowed her cousin to conduct herself in whatever manner she wished, confident that sooner or later something of significance would come to light.

Yet in the time since they'd agreed to the arrangement, Gwenifer had brought not one word of import to Alana. That Paxton preferred venison over rabbit wasn't exactly newsworthy!

Despite Alana's disappointment, Gwenifer re-

mained her one link to Paxton, her one hope that
something of consequence could be learned. Even
though she was faced with an insurrection among her
kinsmen, she was unwilling to sever that connection.

But she could quell Gwenifer's exuberance toward
the Norman with a quick word of warning. That in
itself should be enough to ease the tension among her
people. At least she trusted that it would.

"I will speak to her," Alana said. "But I want you to
remind the others that she does what she does to help
us all."

"I'll talk to them again," Madoc stated. "But, I
caution you: They had better see some change in her,
and see it soon, else she'll be the one to suffer if they
don't."

Alana hadn't realized her kin might actually turn on
Gwenifer. "Go, Madoc, and pass the word. Let them
know if they think to harm my cousin—their own
kinswoman—I will not be the least bit pleased. Tell
them that they must have faith in me on this. Hurry."

He kept to his place, eyes narrowing on Alana.
"What do you hope to learn from the Norman that is
so important to us all?"

Alana was wondering the same herself. She hadn't
told Madoc about Henry's edict. And apparently
Father Jevon was now keeping his tongue between his
teeth, for no one else appeared to be aware of it either.

The truth was that if Paxton decided to force the
issue, demanding that they marry, she could do little
except comply. Running away might be her only
reprieve. Though the notion of taking flight was
tempting, she knew she couldn't desert her kin.

"I don't know, Madoc," she at last said. "All along
my one worry has been that he will somehow learn the
truth about Gilbert."

"Save for you and I, no one knows what really happened. Not here."

"As to just how he died, yes. But of the men who retrieved his body—what if one of them recalls noting something unusual?"

"Like what?" Madoc asked.

"The stains and cuts on the front of his tunic."

"Those were hidden by mud and grass when they pulled him, facedown, from the river. Besides, I burned his clothing, then buried the remnants when the rains started again. The evidence is gone. There's no proof that he didn't drown. You worry for naught."

"You may be right. But if Paxton should come upon something, the only way we might be made aware of it is through Gwenifer. It's not just my safety or yours that is at risk. Everyone here might be in jeopardy. His retribution could encompass us all."

"Including those across the river," Madoc said, nodding.

"Aye. That is why Gwenifer is keeping so close to him. Whatever she learns, she brings the information straight to me. Now go speak to the others, please."

"I will, milady. And this time, I will make them understand."

Alana watched as he scurried off to do her biding. Once he disappeared from sight, she wandered farther back into the yard, away from any activity, for she needed to be alone.

The mental burden she carried was beginning to weigh far too heavily. If there were ever a time she wanted to flee from her responsibilities, run from the uncertainties she faced, it was now.

Why couldn't the world, as she knew it, be free from all this strife and friction, its inhabitants living in peace and harmony? Moreover, what was it that resided in the human soul which prompted this constant quest for power, this untamable desire to dominate?

Alana wasn't thinking solely of the Normans. The Welsh were equally as covetous.

Without question, her countrymen were quick to band together against an outside invader, but when the threat was ended, they were fast at each other's throats, always grappling for control.

Fools all, Alana decided. For no matter who the perpetrator might be—Saxon, Norman, Welsh—the conflict in her homeland was neverending.

Weary of deliberating about mankind's weaknesses, she put such thoughts from her mind and strolled aimlessly toward the herb garden.

Before she reached the spot, she heard someone shout Paxton's name. The call sounded angry and had come from the vicinity of the hall. Alana didn't hesitate. Lifting her skirt, she set off in the direction where the cry had broken the air.

When she rounded the building's corner, a loud din of voices drawing her, she came to an abrupt halt, for she was startled by what she saw.

At the entrance of the hall stood Paxton. Behind him was Gwenifer and Sir Graham. Before the trio was a line of Normans, their weapons ready. They served as a shield between the castle's overlord and the mob of Welsh that confronted him.

Alana's eyes searched the belligerent crowd. She saw Madoc among them. Aldwyn, too. Their actions told her that they attempted to calm her kinsmen as they urged them to disperse.

Her heart sank. What she'd hoped to avoid had actually come to pass. Not wanting to see either side suffer any harm, she dashed forward, intending to put a stop to the brewing madness.

Unfortunately Alana insinuated herself between the

crowd and the men-at-arms at the worst possible time. She didn't see the rock that was hurled, but felt its force as it struck the side of her head.

"Milady!"

Madoc's cry echoed in her ears as sparks showered inside her head. Somewhere beyond the haze encompassing her, she knew she was falling, even thought she heard Paxton swear with explosive intent. But she couldn't be sure. For at the very instant she landed, face first, in the dirt, everything went black.

Paxton strode through the center of the hall, around the hearth, then on toward the stairs, an unconscious Alana held fast in his arms.

A vigorous expletive erupted inside his head as he gazed down on her wan face.

Her left cheek was caked with dirt and bruised from the tumble she'd taken. Her headrail had fallen away when he'd lifted her limp form from the ground, and he could now see her dark hair was wet and matted with blood at the site of her injury, just above her right ear.

She'd been hit hard and had gone down like a sturdy tree ripped from its roots by a fierce wind. The thud, when her body had hit the ground, had reverberated through the yard, the crowd having gone silent when they realized she'd been struck.

Paxton remembered the collective look of horror on their faces, saw how they had paled in response. They regretted their actions now. Would probably give anything to erase that one moment in time. But they couldn't. And Paxton vowed that if he ever learned the identity of the individual who cast the stone, which he understood was meant for him, he'd kill the bastard.

The stairs and gallery were behind him, and Alana's

chamber door loomed just ahead. "Open it," he said to Madoc. The man had been scampering along behind him, followed by Sir Graham and Gwenifer.

Madoc did as bade, and Paxton walked across the threshold, carrying Alana to the bed, where he settled her in the center of the mattress. He edged a hip onto the bed beside her.

"Alana?" He lightly smoothed his hand across her brow. His knuckles trailed down her uninjured cheek. "Wake up."

There was no response, not even a flicker of her eyelids.

He looked at Madoc, who was poised close to his shoulder. "Get the chest of medicinals."

"Is it bad?" Madoc asked.

"She has a cut and a nice-size knot. When she awakens, she'll no doubt have a severe headache. Other than that, 'tis hard to say. Now do as I ordered." Paxton's gaze skipped to Gwenifer, who hugged the door frame. "Go with Madoc," he commanded. "Get some clean cloths and bring some hot water from the kettle by the hearth."

Gwenifer didn't move. "What brought this on? What made them behave in such a manner?"

Everyone knew she referred to the crowd. "'Twas your behavior—yours and his," Madoc snarled as he marched to the door. He stopped only inches from Gwenifer. "Cavorting with each other the way you are—they don't like it. 'Tis worse with him than it was with Sir Gilbert. Should have been you who got stoned." Madoc shoved past her and was gone.

Paxton heard the man's accusing words, noted Gwenifer's stricken expression as she digested them.

"They hate me," she whispered.

"Nay," he said, not moving from Alana's side. "They hate the fact that you're associating with a Norman." He looked to Graham. "Go with Gwenifer and assist her in bringing the cloths and water." His gaze moved back to Gwenifer. "Sir Graham will offer his protection while you get the things I require."

Graham turned and withdrew from his position midway between the door and the bed. Once he was beside Gwenifer, he took hold of her arm. "No harm will come to you," he said, then urged her from the room.

The instant they were gone Paxton again beheld Alana. If anyone should be made to bear the blame for what had happened to her, it was he.

In his quest for answers about Gilbert, he had encouraged Gwenifer's advances. Had deliberately done so while being fully aware that at some point the Welsh would revolt.

It had rankled them that one of their kinswomen should dare to consort with their enemy before their very noses. He knew the risk. Despite that knowledge, he'd forged ahead, eager to seek Gwenifer's attention, welcoming any information she could offer, inviting trouble as he went.

Alana must have recognized the effects of his and Gwenifer's companionship. Why then didn't she attempt to cease their, as Madoc so aptly put it, *cavorting?*

It mattered not. The damage was done. Rightly Paxton condemned himself, for it was Alana who was made to suffer.

Sighing, he reached for her braid, then unplaited the strands. Afterward he combed his fingers through the dark tresses, spreading them over the pillow that was hidden below the wadmal bedcover.

Again gazing at her face, Paxton saw beneath the

dirt streaking her cheek the telltale marks of a bruise. His gut twisted as he damned himself and his own foolishness.

This incessant search for answers where none existed had to end. Gilbert's death was as Alana had stated: an accidental drowning. No more would he try to prove otherwise.

The decision came to him as he felt her scalp and measured the size of the bump that was rising there. Alana moaned at the action; Paxton watched as her head rolled away from his hand.

Her lashes fluttered, and he soon found himself looking into her captivating eyes. "How do you feel?" he asked, lightly stroking the uninjured side of her head.

She glanced around her, then stared at him in confusion. "What am I doing here?"

At the same time she posed the question, she caught the fact that his hand was in her hair. As though repulsed by his touch, she pulled away and tried to sit up. She groaned as she clasped her head and fell back onto the pillow.

Paxton fought the urge to shake his head in self-disgust. Did she truly despise him that much? "I suggest you stay lying down," he said. "If you keep yourself still, your head won't pound to the extreme that it just did. Do you remember being hit by the rock?"

"I remember," she grumbled while gingerly feeling the lump. She pulled her hand away to look at her fingers. "God's wounds! I'm bleeding."

"Aye. But the wound is not serious."

"Easy for you to say when it's not your head that's split open and aching like the devil."

"The stone was meant for me," he stated, ruing that she was the one injured instead of him.

"Aye. 'Tis not *that* hard to figure who was the actual recipient of their hatred."

"Woman, you amaze me," he said, a frown marking his brow. "If you recognized the extent of their anger, why the hell did you throw yourself in the middle?"

"Had I known the rock was coming, I wouldn't have," she snapped. She shot him a glare. "Why are you hovering over me like some witless nursemaid? Go see to Gwenifer." She shoved at his chest, attempting to dislodge him from the bed. "By all that has happened, she may be in need of your protection."

He caught her hands, securing them against him. "Sir Graham is with her. Besides, it is not her health that concerns me but yours."

"My health is fine. I'm stout and hale!" she proclaimed, jerking her hands from beneath his. "Now take yourself from my chamber so I may lie here in peace."

"I'll depart from your side only when Madoc returns with the chest of medicinals. Not before." He paused. "You know, Alana, mayhap you should accustom yourself to being near me. One day soon, you and I will be sharing this chamber. In fact, we'll be consummating our marriage in this very bed."

Her eyes widened. She sputtered several times before she managed to blurt out, "You must be mad! After what just occurred, do you really believe my people will allow the two of us to wed? Think twice, Norman. The dissension today was but a mere sampling of what is in store for you and your men if you decide to force the issue. There will never again be any harmony and accord among us."

"That's only if you continue to act as though you hate me. If you were to pretend to love me, even just a little, and if you were to convince them that I'd always be fair and honest with everyone here, I'm certain they'll eventually come around."

"I doubt it."

He shrugged. "Then I will chase them all away into the wood."

"And I'll go with them."

"Nay. You will stay here." His gaze settled on the mattress, and he ran his hand over the cover near her hip. "Imagine, Alana. In the not so distant future, our children will be conceived here in this very spot." He looked up to see she'd turned her head aside. "What's wrong?"

"If you are desiring heirs, then you've chosen the wrong woman. I'm barren."

The last word seemed to be said with a mixture of relief and heartbreak. The relief was obvious, for she'd hoped he'd now reject her. The heartbreak was also obvious, for she did want children, just not his.

"Why do you think you're barren?" he asked.

Her head swung back on the pillow so fast that she squinted her eyes against the pain. "Why do I think . . . ? Because Gilbert and I . . . well, after all the times we . . . Do you see me attending any children who affectionately call me Mother? Nay. I'm barren," she repeated.

Paxton smiled. "If you are without issue, Alana, it is because of Gilbert and not because of you."

"How do you know that to be true?"

"Because I have personal knowledge that it is true . . . or at least, that it is possible."

"Explain."

He inclined his head and surveyed her. "'Tis obvious Gilbert never told you this, but years ago, as squires, he and I were practicing at jousting. As we lumbered along toward each other on the old geldings we rode, the tip of my lance was aimed too low. It glanced off his shield, striking him in the groin. He was in agony for nearly a fortnight afterward. 'Twas almost a fortnight more before he could walk with any indication that his legs were not actually bowed nor that his back wasn't permanently hunched over. For a man, the injury he suffered was devastating. I think Gilbert wished he had died. He recovered, but the incident may have rendered him incapable of producing an heir."

"He never told me." She nibbled at her lip. "Even so, you could be wrong. I might be the one who is unable to bear a child."

"I'll take my chances."

Her brow furrowed. "I don't understand why you would want to marry me. I'm aware that you don't love me. We come from two different worlds, therefore we have nothing in common. This whole affair will bring nothing but unhappiness to us both. Why do you persist in seeing that the wedding goes forth?"

Paxton held his tongue as he studied Alana. So, Gwenifer had carried his words to her cousin's ears. Was that why Alana hadn't ended this supposed friendship between Gwenifer and him? Because she was searching for answers the same as he?

He wanted to laugh with uproarious glee. Poor Gwenifer had been caught in the middle of them both. Wisely Paxton remained sober.

"Marriages have been built on even less than what we have, Alana. At least we share something that many couples lack altogether."

"And what is that?"

"Mutual desire. It will be the magic elixir for us both." He rose, for he heard someone moving along the gallery. "Rest now. I'll check in on you later."

"I won't marry you," she said when he was halfway to the door. "I swear I won't."

At the threshold, Paxton turned back to her. "You will, Alana. The instant you are able to be up and around, I suggest you start making the necessary preparations for our wedding feast."

She opened her mouth to initiate her words of protest, but he curtly ordered her to be silent.

"Know this, milady," he continued as her jaw snapped to. "Whether the plans for such are complete or not, whether you're still lying in that bed pretending your injury has kept you there, our nuptials will take place in one week. Stand in opposition to me on anything I've just said and your kin across the river will suffer. This *I* swear."

CHAPTER

12

It was noon the next day when Alana marched into the chapel in search of Father Jevon. It was no surprise that she found him on his knees before the altar, his hands clasped and head bowed in prayer.

Alana was not one to be purposely rude, but her patience had worn thin. There were questions she wanted answered, and his petitions could very well take all day.

"I want a word with you," she announced, her tone brusque.

The priest did not move. Nor did he acknowledge her.

The moments stretched in endless succession; the continued silence became unnerving to her. Alana was tempted to poke his shoulder, thinking maybe he hadn't heard her, when he crossed himself and came to his feet.

"I presume it is about your wedding," he said.

"Then he informed you about it?" she returned.

Father Jevon nodded. "Sir Paxton came to me early this morning and told me to prepare for the nuptials. I must confess that I was gladdened by his news. Despite my prayers, my past endeavors have all ended in failure. With Sir Paxton's and your union, I now feel as though there is once again hope."

His *past endeavors,* Alana understood, were his frustrated attempts at saving what he thought were her kinsmen's beleaguered heathen souls.

Only a handful of her people had ever attended the daily masses that were held in the chapel. In fact, since their inception, the sums had dwindled until now there were none.

It never occurred to the priest that, if he'd also been of Welsh blood, the chapel walls might have threatened to burst. Instead he laid their disinterest on their inherent link to Satan, which was accredited to Adam's sin and Eve's deceit.

Conversely though, since many of the Normans attended mass with regularity, Paxton going on occasion, Father Jevon felt that their souls were in no peril.

The man was a fool if he believed that were true, for in reality, the transgressions of his ilk were as numerous and as grave as those that he ascribed to the Welsh. But she doubted Father Jevon would ever comprehend that. He was too pompous by far.

"I want to know what is expected of me in this marriage," she said, getting back to why she'd approached him. "I'd also like to know what sort of protection the Church might offer me if I find myself to be exceptionally unhappy."

The priest inclined his head. "Do you foresee that you will be unhappy?" he asked.

"It has nothing to do with my foreseeing such." A lie, Alana thought, but it could not be helped. "Paxton and I come from different backgrounds, which will, in all likelihood, cause us problems. I was unable to give Gilbert children. It may be the same with Paxton. If I continually disappoint him, he could become angry with me . . . so angry that he might strike me."

Father Jevon frowned. "I have seen nothing in his temperament that says he's predisposed to beating a woman."

Alana stared at the man. "You were there when I was tied to the post. He would have whipped me— and without a shred of mercy, I'll wager!—if the call hadn't come announcing Sir Graham's return."

Father Jevon smiled. "You are wrong, my child."

Was the man daft? Alana wondered. "I am not wrong. He would have beaten me if the group hadn't showed when they did."

"Since you were facing the post, you may have every reason to believe such. But I was in a position to see something that you were not. Sir Paxton had released the whip, my child. It was on its way to the ground when the call came about Sir Graham and the others. And yesterday, he was most angered and distressed by what had happened to you."

"Why do you say that?"

"Because his blasphemy was heard throughout the yard. I saw him charge from his position at the hall's entry the instant the stone struck you. He was almost at your side when you hit the earth. He knelt beside you and turned you over with care. Afterward he smoothed the side of your face, then lifted you into his arms. From where I watched, there at the chapel door," he said, nodding at the place, "he appeared quite concerned and very protective of you. Considering these things, I doubt, my child, he would ever strike you for any reason."

The priest was of no help to her. She was searching

for confirmation about something she thought was true. Rather than giving her the answer she sought, he was extolling Paxton's qualities and lauding his character. Perhaps she needed to try a different tact.

"I wasn't aware he had dropped the whip," she said.

In fact, the news had surprised and dismayed her. She'd been quick to accuse and to berate him for nearly beating her. Why hadn't he defended himself and set her straight? By what the priest had said, it was clear that she could no longer hold the incident against him.

"And I had not an inkling that he was so troubled by what occurred yesterday," she announced. "I suppose I have misjudged him."

"I'm glad I was able to ease your worries about his nature. As I've said: I doubt he'd ever be abusive to you."

"Theoretically speaking, Father," Alana said after she'd assessed him at length. "Let's say a man and a woman marry. Even though there is no love between the couple, the wife intends to be obedient to her husband, assisting him in whatever way he asks.

"At first, things go well, but after a while the husband becomes disinterested in his wife. As time passes, the husband finds he is most unhappy, thus he seeks to put his wife aside.

"Let's say there are no grounds for the dissolution of their marriage, but he wishes to be rid of her anyway, mayhap even to the point that he entertains thoughts of murdering her. What protection does the Church offer for the wife who has always served her husband well but discovers she is no longer wanted by her mate?"

"There have been instances where a woman has sought the security of a convent," Father Jevon replied.

"Even if she is married?"

"Yes, but—"

"Might she do this even if her husband has proved himself to be loving and kind?"

"If her heart is such that she feels that serving God is more important than serving her husband, she may indeed sequester herself. In doing so she must remain chaste and pure, for she is no longer her husband's possession but has placed herself under the dominion of the Church. In effect, she has made herself the bride of Christ.

"In any event, my child, if you're asking this for yourself, I would hope you'd at least see what your marriage is like before you place yourself in a convent."

The last of the priest's words were called out to Alana since she was now heading toward the chapel door. She had found the answer she'd wanted, therefore, in her opinion, nothing more needed to be said.

"'Twould benefit you if you were to quit your pacing," Graham commented.

Paxton halted in midstride and spun toward his friend. "'Tis the day of my wedding," he said. "Why shouldn't I pace?"

"Because the Welsh will think that their valorous Norman overlord is suffering from an attack of the jitters. Is that the impression you want to give?"

Paxton looked around the hall to see most eyes were upon him. "Nay, that is not what I want."

"Then find a spot and stand there. At least give the appearance that you have your wits about you, even if you don't."

Releasing a long breath, Paxton did as Graham bade, but his nerves were no less jumpy, his thoughts no less muddled.

He prayed he'd made the right decision in forcing Alana to marry him. He'd barely seen her over the past week since he'd given his proclamation. When he did come upon her, she'd been pleasant and, amazingly, docile.

Paxton wondered at her change in mood. He'd expected her to fight him at every turn on this. But since the hour he'd told her they would be married, using the threat of retribution against Rhys and the others as leverage, she had offered no opposition. He knew she'd seen the priest. Perhaps Father Jevon had convinced her that her fate was sealed. Maybe she had at last accepted that it was.

Scanning the faces of her kinsmen, who were gathered in anticipation of seeing the bride, Paxton remembered how he'd called them together, just four days ago, and announced the impending nuptials.

The Welsh were not approving at first, not until Alana had spoken to them. In a calm voice, she told them that she was going into this marriage willingly, said she did so with their interests at heart, asked that they would offer their blessings and put their past hatreds aside so that they could all live in peace.

If her words had had any effect on them, Paxton was unable to tell. Their grumblings had stopped . . . for the time being at least. The question was whether or not her kin would one day give their allegiance to Henry. That done, all this would be his. Alana as well. Though he desired to have his own fiefdom, in the end, Paxton believed she might be the greatest prize of all.

An elbow met his ribs, and Paxton looked to its owner.

"I suggest you cast your attention on the stairs," Graham said, nodding in that direction.

Paxton swung his gaze to the steps. What he saw

made his heart trip in the oddest fashion; his breath was suspended in his chest.

Beautiful was the only way he could describe her. The word was paltry at best.

Since this would be her second marriage, she presented herself unveiled. It was as though he saw her for the very first time.

In the light that streamed through the high window above the stairs, her sable brown hair, which was swept away from her face and secured by jeweled combs, the long tresses flowing down her back to her waist, shimmered like rich samite silk.

Dressed in a snow-white chainse and a soft yellow bliaud, its hem and sleeves embroidered with threads of gold, she carried herself proudly down to the hall, looking like a luminous ray of sunshine.

If just a particle of the radiance that presently enveloped her were to insert itself into their lives, their future together promised to be forever bright. Paxton basked in the thought, hoping it would soon come true.

The instant her feet hit the floor of the hall, he stepped forward and extended his hand. She had no father, brother, or close relative to offer her to him as was the custom, so it was agreed they would walk to the chapel door together.

"Are you ready to begin the procession?" he asked, seeing there was only a hint of a bruise still on her cheek.

She said not a word but gave her assent with a nod. Paxton then guided her through the hall, out across the yard, to the chapel door, where the priest awaited them.

Sir Graham and Gwenifer followed directly behind them, the others trailing them. Glancing over his shoulder, Paxton noticed the Welsh stood to one side, the Normans to the other. It was evident their long held prejudices remained.

When Father Jevon began the ceremony, he excluded the part about the bride being given away and went straight to the ritual where the ring, which had been blessed earlier, was presented.

Paxton lifted Alana's uncovered right hand, its bareness denoting she was a widow. As he slipped the ring, a family heirloom given to him by his grandmother, on and off the first three fingers of her hand, he said, "In the name of the Father, the Son, and the Holy Ghost."

Afterward he placed the ring on her left hand and made the pledge, "With this ring I thee wed, with this gold I thee honor, and with this dowry I thee endow." Once the words were said, Alana prostrated herself at his feet, showing her submission.

Seeing her thus, Paxton wanted to pull her to her feet. But the Church, and most men, expected a woman to honor her new husband in this manner, the act stating he was her superior. Though he allowed the display now, he vowed she would never again bow to him. He desired that she be his equal, not his subordinate in life.

When she rose, he directed her through the doors into the chapel, where Father Jevon gave the blessing. Mass followed, and when it was over, Paxton came from his knees to his feet, bringing Alana with him.

As he looked into her upturned face, his heart swelled. She was his wife. And tonight, he would at last bed her.

Remembering how she'd sworn she would not marry him, he grinned, gladdened that he'd won. "The deed is done, Alana. Your kin are safe and you are forever mine," he whispered before he kissed her soundly.

Alana's face beamed with satisfaction when he pulled back. But it was not his show of affection that had brought the smug expression to life. Of this Paxton was aware.

Cocking his head, he studied her, then asked, "Why do you appear so triumphant, my wife?"

She smiled. "You are my husband, 'tis true. But the designation you bear is forever in name only."

"What are you saying?"

"As of this moment, I have decided to take the veil."

CHAPTER

13

"Like hell you will!"

Paxton's voice thundered through the chapel to shake the very rafters.

The onlookers grew still, stunned by his profanity. He was furious, and Alana thought to cower, but she stood her ground.

"What madness is this?" he asked, gripping her shoulders. Then his blazing eyes turned on Father Jevon. "You! What sort of nonsense did you put into her head?"

Having been wide-eyed and speechless, the priest quickly found his tongue. "W-why none," he insisted, his pale face showing even more ashen.

"She came to you the day after she was injured," Paxton snarled. "Why?"

"She talked about a couple who were unhappy in their marriage . . . asked what sort of protection the

Church could offer if a husband wanted to put his wife aside."

"And you told her she could sequester herself in a nunnery," Paxton finished for the man, his gaze now on Alana.

Her chin lifted as she said, "Which, my husband, I have done . . . or I will do, just as soon as I make the journey to the nearest convent. Until then, I will keep myself in this chapel, under the Church's protection."

Paxton's eyes narrowed. "I think not," he growled.

Alana gasped when he swept her up into his arms. "Put me down!" she demanded.

"Nay," he said, then turned to Father Jevon. "Priest, get to yon hall and bless our marriage bed—now!"

"But—"

"Do it!"

As Father Jevon scurried toward the chapel door, Paxton following him, Alana saw her schemes unraveling like the frayed threads of a rotted tapestry. She'd hoped to get back at him for forcing her into a marriage she didn't want. Becoming a nun was her one recourse, her one way of thumbing her nose at the Norman.

Yet, while he carried her from her professed sanctuary, his intent being to bed her, everyone aware that it was, she saw hatred fomenting in her kinsmen's eyes.

This had to end before tempers flared. "Paxton," she said, her hand rising to his cheek. "Put me down, please. They watch us. To them, what you are doing is tantamount to rape. Don't let your anger with me become the cause of a clash between everyone here. 'Tis our wedding day. Let's not ruin it."

One stride away from the door he stopped. His gaze locked with hers. "Do you still want to become a nun?"

"Nay," she said while shaking her head.

"And this night you will lie beside me willingly, so we may consummate our marriage?" he asked.

Alana noticed how his voice grew husky, his eyes darkening to a midnight blue. She felt her stomach flutter in the strangest way. "Aye, I shall come to you willingly," she said, both dreading and desiring that she would. The latter surprised her, considering her abhorrence to the act.

"Then we shall wait," he announced and set her to her feet. "Come," he called to everyone inside the chapel and out. "Let us go enjoy the bride's ale."

The hall hummed with the sounds of merriment, laughter rising toward the ceiling just like the smoke curling from the central hearth. But it was the Normans who celebrated.

Alana watched the throng from her position at the table of honor. The Welsh sat to one side; the Normans to the other. One set of faces were grim; the others joyous.

That her people objected to her marrying another man of Gilbert's ilk was more than apparent. But like with Gilbert, they had held their tongues, allowing her to make the determination of whether or not she would wed herself. The problem was, in this instance, she'd had no choice. But her kin didn't know that. Even so, to them her decision was the wrong one. Gauging them now, she knew they'd be eternally unforgiving that she had married Paxton.

She looked across the way to where her new husband stood. Gwenifer had procured a harp and was playing the instrument for Paxton, Sir Graham, and several others who had gathered around.

As with everything Gwenifer did, the chords she plucked rose in perfect unison, filling the air with a haunting sound. All who listened were entranced. But then it was hard to tell if it was the woman or her talent who drew them.

Glancing at one of the windows, Alana saw the sun was sinking ever faster toward the western horizon. At sunset, or shortly thereafter, the marriage bed would be sanctified, she and Paxton receiving another blessing from the priest, so they may be fruitful. Then she would be expected to prepare herself for her wedding night.

Lying naked in the same bed she'd shared with Gilbert, she was to welcome Paxton when he came to her not that long after. She was to pay honor to him as her husband by being submissive, eagerly accepting his advances as he set himself to consummating their vows.

Her insides quivered at the thought. She was so very fearful of the moment he would come to her. Unlike her first time, she knew what to expect, but dreaded it just the same. Paxton had once promised that when they came together their joining would not be at all like what she suffered with Gilbert. But how could she be assured that he spoke the truth?

Just thinking about her past experiences made her stomach turn. Lord, there had to be some way out of this!

The more Alana conceptualized what was to come, the more agitated she became. Her mind tumbled and tossed with a flurry of uncertainty. Her people despised her; her new husband paid more heed to her cousin than he did to her—not that she cared. Then there was that horrid point when he would climb atop her.

The turmoil stirring within her drove Alana from her seat. She had to get away, even if it was no farther than to the yard. On swift feet she headed to the hall's entry. Once outside she drew a deep, cleansing breath and tried to calm her thoughts.

Rain. She could smell it. Though she saw only high wispy clouds, she knew a storm approached. A near tempest, she thought. Just like the one that whorled around inside her now.

For no apparent reason, Alana found herself heading toward the side gate. As she went her thoughts rolled and churned.

Oh, why hadn't she fled long ago when Gilbert had died? What exactly was it that had driven her back here, the dark secret she'd vowed to keep buried deep inside her?

Rhys had told her it was risky for her to return home. But she'd insisted, believing it was the only way to protect them all.

This land that she so loved—what had it brought her but misery. And her kin—this time their displeasure with her seemed insurmountable. And Paxton—if he ever learned the truth about Gilbert, he'd kill her.

It might be cowardly, but never did Alana want to run from her troubles as much as she did at this very second.

If she could only—

Alana halted in her tracks, staring at the side gate. Was she seeing things or was it actually standing open?

Blinking, she eyed the gate again. It *was* open.

She glanced around the area, looking for a sentry. She saw none and took the few steps needed to reach the portal, whereupon she peeked outside.

There, a half-dozen yards into the wood, was the guard. His back was turned to her as he relieved himself against a tree.

Anticipation rose within her. Beyond this gate was her pathway to freedom. Knowing she could bear no more of the chaotic turmoil that dominated her mind and soul, Alana took to the wood.

Halfway down the trail to the river, she heard limbs snapping and leaves stirring underfoot behind her. Then her name resounded through the trees in a thunderous roar. The voice was distinctive, angry. And it belonged to . . .

Paxton!

Alana sent herself running along the path with a flurry of stretching legs and pounding feet. Her heart was in her throat, fear of his catching her driving her onward.

"Alana, stop!"

His shout filtered through the hammering in her ears. He was gaining on her. Still Alana pressed on. She had to be away from him, away from what he represented.

The disconnected mass of thoughts once spinning inside her head drew together into complete clarity. The reason she'd been so restive, so desirous of escaping the castle was because she couldn't abide the concept of being trapped in another marriage that promised to be much the same as her first.

As it was with Gilbert, Paxton didn't love her. There would be no joy or laughter, no communion of hopes and wishes between them. Silence and moodiness was all that would be allotted to her, the express need to ease his physical wants the only time he'd seek her out.

She couldn't bear living in the same hell again. She wouldn't!

Alana was now at the river, but she didn't look back. Sliding down the bank, she hopped from boulder to boulder that rose from the riverbed, then when the giant stepping-stones were no longer afforded to her, she splashed through the shallows and up the opposite bank. It was then she turned to see Paxton bounding across the stream in the same fashion that she had.

God's wounds! She hadn't expected him to be this close.

Hiking her skirts, she dashed off into the wood, hoping to find one of the watchers. He would take her to Rhys, the swiftest way possible.

But Alana suddenly shifted course, away from the direction of the ringwork. Paxton may give up his chase. Gathering his men, he could then ride on her kin, burning and pillaging, destroying every man, woman, and child who dared to stand against him.

Her heart threatened to burst as Alana darted through the thicket. She heard Paxton crashing through the brush behind her. Closer and closer he came.

Up ahead was a small clearing. A little way beyond that was a steep hillside. Hidden in its rocky face was the entrance to a cave, naught but a slice in the slate. There she could take refuge, but that was only if she could outdistance Paxton.

Alana broke into the glade and ran for her life. Midway across she heard Paxton's boots digging into the soft earth; his pants sounded not that far behind her.

"Damn it, Alana," he growled. "Give it up!"

She never thought he could be this swift. Not from the uncertain steps he'd taken the first time he'd been in the wood. She was wrong about his agility. She was losing ground fast. Then she felt his fingers raking at her back.

"Nooo!"

The cry passed through her lips as she tried to break away from him. But, as his hand snatched at her again, she stumbled. She attempted to right herself, but couldn't. Alana went sprawling into the patch of grass and wildflowers dotting the floor of the glade; Paxton came down nearly atop her.

"Damn it, woman," he grated, flipping her over onto her back. He clamped his leg over her thighs. "Why didn't you stop when I told you to?"

His eyes were charged with fury, and Alana's fear bounded to the fore. "I won't," she said, her head rolling on the ground. "I won't."

Paxton's brow furrowed in obvious confusion. "You won't what?"

She squeezed her eyes shut, tears stinging them. Her sobs rose to her throat. She tried to choke them back, but to no avail. "I-I won't live like I did before. I won't be made to feel that way again. I won't, I tell you!"

He caught her face between his hands, stemming the toss of her head. Then he ordered, "Alana, look at me."

She refused his command.

"Look at me!" he demanded. "Please."

That one word, along with the soft tone in which it was uttered, caused Alana to open her eyes. His face, only inches from hers, no longer appeared harsh and angry. Concern marked his features instead. She said nothing, just gazed at him.

"You won't be made to feel like what again?" he asked.

"Like a whore . . . like the only thing of value I have to offer a man is my body."

"That's the way Gilbert made you feel," he stated.

"Yes. And I won't be made to feel that way again."

His jaw hardened. "Gilbert was a fool, Alana. An arrogant and vainglorious fool. I told you before I am not like him. Why won't you believe me?"

His eyes said he was sincere, but Alana was yet unsure. "You say you are not like him, but how am I to know?"

The question she posed had only one answer. Paxton understood this when he said, "I will prove what I say is true. Then you will have no more doubts."

"So you say."

Paxton was gazing at her lips, soft and inviting. The urge to taste them came just a hair short of overpowering him. "Aye," he whispered. "So I say." The words were delivered so close to her mouth that he felt his own breath fanning back at him. The need to feel her lips under his could no longer be suppressed. "Kiss me, Alana, then you will know."

He didn't wait for her assent, but opened his lips and covered her alluring mouth. She whimpered as she first resisted his urgings, but Paxton was determined to make her respond.

His teeth nibbled lightly at her lower lip, then his tongue played along the same path, to tease and to tantalize. He'd make her forget Gilbert's selfishness, wipe those unhappy memories away. He'd give her joy and fulfillment. This he promised himself.

With his hands still framing her face, he pressed down on her chin with his thumb. The action parted her lips, and his tongue plunged between.

At his invasion, she attempted to pull away, but he held her head still.

Delving deeper, he tasted the sweetness within. As his tongue plunged and withdrew, imitating the ritual that was to come between them, he gained his first response from her. Alana moaned. Her warm breath traveled into his mouth. Smiling to himself, he deepened the kiss. Soon she would be his.

Tentatively Alana's lips began to match the slant of his. As they grew more pliant, meeting each of his promptings, her tongue mating with his, Paxton rejoiced. She set a fire in his loins the way no other woman ever had. He wanted to be inside her, thrusting and withdrawing, watching her face as he brought her to the pinnacle of her own desire, watching as she sailed over.

His lips broke from hers, to slide across her cheek. As his eyes cracked open, he saw the blur of color surrounding her head. The fragrance of wildflowers filled his nostrils. It was his dream come true.

In his mind's eye, Paxton once again beheld her slender arms beckoning him to her, again saw her satiny thighs open, inviting him to lie between them. There he would find his pleasure; there he would spill his seed. With the knowledge, the fire inside him became a blazing inferno.

"I want you, my wife," he said near her ear. "I want you now." He drew his hand from her face to her breast where he captured its fullness. Through her bliaud, her chainse, and her chemise, which he was tempted to tear away, he caressed her. "Give yourself to me, Alana. Let me show you what ecstasy is."

"Nay."

Her response surprised him, as did the plaintive quality of her voice. He searched her face. Against the contrast of color that surrounded her, she looked starkly pale. "Are you afraid of my being inside you?"

Yes!

The affirmation screamed through Alana's head, but the word stayed just behind her lips.

Paxton read the answer on her face. "Why?" he asked, clearly bewildered.

Memories of Gilbert and how he'd driven into her, without care, leapt to mind. Swallowing, Alana attempted to look away from Paxton, but he caught her chin, forcing her to attend him.

"Answer me. Why are you afraid?"

"'Twill hurt, just like it always did."

An oath hissed through his lips as he stared off at some distant point. "The bastard," he grated, his eyes growing cold. When he next gazed at her, he levered himself up and away from her, then ordered, "Take off your clothes."

Alana gaped at him, fear rising inside her. If she thought he would be considerate of her needs, allowing her to escape his lustful demands, she'd been mistaken.

While she lay there staring at him, trepidation filling her whole being, he'd pulled his bloodred tunic, a golden dragon emblazoning its front, over his head. He spread it on the ground beside her, then he tore away his undertunic, placing it next to the first.

Poised on his knees, he planted his hands at his waist. "Did you hear me?"

Alana's voice was trapped in her throat. When she didn't respond, he gripped her shoulders and dragged her up from her back to face him. Then his fingers were low on her hips, lifting her bliaud. "Don't!" she cried, swatting at his hands.

He caught her arms. "You are my wife, Alana. You are to obey me in all I say. Now, remove your clothing."

His eyes said he'd brook no disobedience. Unable to hold his gaze, she scanned his broad shoulders, her attention settling on his chest.

Dark hair lightly furred its muscled expanse, darting down his rippling abdomen into his braies. His body—what she saw of it—was a work of perfection.

"Well?" he questioned.

Swallowing hard, Alana gripped the hem of her bliaud and, with shaking fingers, pulled it over her head. Next came her chainse. As soon as both garments had fallen from her hands, he spread them on the grass beside his.

"Your chemise, woman," he said.

Alana shook as she stripped the last scrap of protection away. Naked from her head to her knees, she crossed her arms over her breasts. Then she was being lifted, placed onto the discarded clothing.

"Lie back," Paxton ordered.

My God! He was going to ravish her. And there was nothing she could do to stop him.

Aware it was so, she nonetheless obeyed him. As though in a daze, she stared at the sky, her arms still clamped across her chest. The clouds were thickening. Rain, she thought nonsensically. It was coming.

She felt him at her feet. He stripped first one wet slipper from her, then the other. Next he removed her hose. Now she was fully nude. She trembled as the breeze blew across her skin, shuddered from the understanding of what he was about to do.

One of his boots thudded against the ground, then the other. His stockings and braies followed. Alana refused to look at him when he reclined beside her.

He stared down on her for the longest while, as though memorizing each inch of her, then in a husky voice, he ordered, "Close your eyes, Alana. Close your eyes and let yourself feel."

Her quivering worsened as she squeezed her eyes shut. He took hold of one wrist, then its mate, pulling her arms away from her breasts.

"You're beautiful," he said, and she jerked when his tongue touched her nipple.

Alana thought to cover herself, but his hands pinned hers to the ground.

"Be still," he commanded, his warm breath skimming against the moist bud.

Sensation rioted through her as he again began to lave the peak with his tongue. The feeling both frightened and excited her. Then he was suckling at her like a babe. Fire shot through her, a blaze burning low in her belly. Alana groaned, and Paxton moved closer, pressing his engorged member against her hip.

Her eyes came wide as she felt how hard he was, how large. She attempted to sidle away, but his leg trapped her thighs, holding her in place.

"Don't move away from me," he said as he shifted against her, edging closer. "Let me make love to you, Alana, in a way Gilbert never did, in a way I always will."

His eyes were darker than midnight, lids heavy with desire. Alana knew he wouldn't hurt her, knew he intended only to give her pleasure. Ecstasy—how would that feel?

"Close your eyes," he told her again.

This time Alana obeyed him willingly. She felt him lean nearer. His lips traced her jaw, then nibbled their way to her mouth. He kissed her fully, deeply, but when she was ready to respond, he withdrew, his lips and tongue sliding to her neck, then downward still. Again he laved her nipple. Alana felt it rise, harden painfully. She gasped as his teeth nipped lightly.

He kissed the peak, then his fingertips replaced his mouth. His caress was gentle, teasing, eliciting the most delicious sensations inside her.

From her breast, his fingers trailed feather-light to her abdomen. Where each one touched, Alana felt her belly constrict then ease. Lower and lower, he played, until his fingers were in her curls.

Alana stiffened instinctively. She tightened her legs, and caught his hand.

"Open to me, sweet." He twisted his wrist, shaking her hand away. "I promise I won't hurt you."

His pledge, and the way in which it was said, made Alana relax. Gently he spread her legs, fingers grazing back into her curls.

When he touched her there, Alana was tempted to catch his hand again, but she fought against her fears. His fingers delved with care, then slid into her folds. His actions were tantalizing. She grew moist and arched toward him.

"That's it, love," he whispered as he probed her secret place. "Allow yourself to know what pleasure really is."

Alana moaned as he slipped his finger inside her. He withdrew then plunged. His thumb trifled with the bud, making it erect.

Her skin was afire, her loins throbbing. Then Paxton was kissing her again.

This time Alana responded with a passion she'd never known or imagined was possible. Her fingers threaded through his thick locks, forcing his head closer. Eagerly her tongue entwined with his, and when he began to imitate the motion of his hand, she groaned with delight.

"Touch me," he said on drawing back.

His hand coming from between her legs, he pulled her own hand from his head, down his chest.

Alana marveled at the crispness of each hair covering the broad expanse, was amazed by the smoothness of his skin, the tautness of the muscle beneath. He pushed her hand lower to his belly. Her knuckles brushed his erection.

"Touch me," he repeated.

As Alana took him in her hand, he shuddered. Air hissed through his teeth, then a groan vibrated in his throat. He urged her to stroke him, his own hand atop hers. When she attained the rhythm he desired, he again attended her, fingers probing and teasing.

She wanted his lips on hers. "Kiss me," she breathed.

His eyes darkened even more. "With pleasure."

His mouth was on hers, devouring and hungry.

Alana never knew lovemaking could be like this. Her heart hammered wildly as her hips began to writhe against the wizardry of his hand. She was shaking inside, wanting something, unaware of what it was.

Paxton suddenly ended his kiss and rose above her. His knee edged between her thighs, followed by the other. He knelt before her, his manhood hard, erect, its crown glistening and wet.

"'Tis time we join," he stated. His fingers still priming her, twirling inside her and out, he leveled himself above her and braced his weight on one hand. "Guide me there. Show me the way to paradise, love."

Wanting also to know what heaven would be like, Alana couldn't resist his request. She took hold of him and directed him to her. He was opening her folds in anticipation of their meeting, and when they touched, sparks showered through her belly; Alana released him, allowing him to take command.

His knuckles grazed up over her stomach as he eased forward, gliding into her. There was no barrier to stop him, and he soon filled her completely.

Both hands now beside her shoulders, he gazed down on her, eyes glazed with passion. "Now for the ecstasy—yours and mine."

He sank to his forearms, covering her, and when he began to move, Alana was amazed that there was no pain. His short strokes were delivered with ease, almost lazily. He seemed unhurried, wanting to enjoy each sensation as it came to him. This was nothing like what she experienced with Gilbert.

"Move with me," Paxton said, his voice husky with desire.

Was that how it was done?

The question floated through her mind as his hand burrowed beneath her hips, raising her to him, urging her to learn the rhythm that he orchestrated.

With each of his deepening thrusts, the feeling within Alana increased. Sensation abounded. She clutched his shoulders and gazed at where they were joined, watching as he drove in and out of her. Soon she was matching the pulse of his hips with an eagerness that surprised her.

Then he seized her bottom, stopping her movements. He buried himself and swayed against her. Alana's eyes widened. The new attack on her senses threatened to send her sailing into oblivion. She started to pant. Something was blossoming in her loins, something she never knew existed.

She looked at Paxton to see the mark of pride and satisfaction on his face. He knew what was happening to her, had given it dawning.

"Go with the feeling, Alana. Let it take you where it may."

He continued the magical sway of his hips, lifting himself, then brushing against her in the most enticing way, teasing her to fulfillment.

The rush of excitement became unbearable as her craving mounted. She arched her hips and back, allowing him do what he wanted. Then it happened. It was as though the sun had burst inside her. Heat flooded through her to stream from her pores, moisture flowed from her as she was racked by spasms of rapture, frenzied and wild.

Somewhere beyond this she heard Paxton's voice. "Ah, love, your caresses are bewitching." Then his lips were on hers, hot and wet.

His kiss intensified as he thrust into her, faster,

deeper. In a few more strokes, he jerked his head back. His cry of ecstasy echoed through the glade as he shuddered and spilled his seed at the crest of her womb. Then he collapsed against her.

Alana bore his weight. He lay so still, she at first feared he'd died. Then his laughter rumbled in his chest. Pulling back, he smiled down on her.

"Sweet Jesus, I've never come that hard before," he declared.

His words stabbed at her heart. She knew there had been others before her. Else he'd not be this adept. But his mentioning such, especially on this occasion, had hurt her. But then he didn't love her. And she didn't love him. If that were the case, why did she feel so forlorn?

Yet joined with her, he was rolling to his side, carrying her with him. He grabbed one of their garments, draping it over her shoulders. Then he pressed her head against his shoulder. He held her close in his arms.

"And I don't think I've ever been this sleepy, either," he mumbled.

As Alana gazed up at him through her lashes, she saw his eyelids were growing heavy. Soon they closed completely. After a bit, his soft breaths of slumber stirred her hair.

Lying quietly, Alana once more felt herself becoming restive. He'd shown her what lovemaking could be like, left her desirous of experiencing the same again. The joy they had shared was unimaginable, indescribable. Though he didn't love her, he desired her. But Alana wondered, after time, when their passions cooled: What would become of her then?

The old fears rose in her anew. Silence and coldness —she couldn't bear that sort of existence, not with

Paxton. And what if he someday learned the truth about Gilbert. She couldn't withstand his hatred, his censure.

But why?

Then Alana knew.

Despite her claims to the contrary, she was falling in love with Paxton de Beaumont.

The realization stunned her. She lay so very quiet that she forgot to breathe. When she next did, it was on a disjointed sob.

Nay, she thought. She couldn't possibly hold feeling for this man, this Norman. He was her enemy. And her executioner, if he ever learned the truth.

Anxiety pummeled through Alana. To love Paxton would be an act of betrayal—to her kinsmen, to her heritage, and to herself.

As Alana searched the angles and planes of his handsome face, she knew the passion they had shared was now a memory she would always treasure. He'd promised her ecstasy and the vow had been fulfilled. But those joyous feelings would never come again, for it would end here.

She knew what she must do.

To save herself and her sanity, to protect her heart and her life, Alana understood that she had no choice but to . . .

Run.

Paxton came awake with a start.

Thunder rumbled through the glade again. He examined the sky to see the black clouds rolling ever closer. His gaze dropped to the area beside him, seeking Alana. The air was instantly suspended in his lungs and his brow furrowed. He jerked his head to the opposite side of where he lay.

She was gone!

On an oath, Paxton bounded to his feet. Standing there, nude, he searched the perimeter of the glade and the trees beyond. A flash of yellow caught his eye as it disappeared deeper into the wood.

Lightning jumped through the clouds, thunder crashing down around him. Paxton was too busy fumbling with his clothing to pay it any heed.

Donning his stockings, braies, boots, under and over tunics, he spun around, searching for his sword. Then he remembered: This being his wedding day, he hadn't worn it.

With another oath, which was more vivid than the first, he dashed off in the direction where he was certain he saw Alana vanish from sight.

What the hell was she up to? he wondered as he now darted through the trees. God's wounds! She was the most annoying creature he'd ever come upon. And the most exciting, he conceded. "Alana!" he shouted with sudden rage, his eyes scanning the wood.

Then he spied the telltale yellow ahead. She was at the top of the next hill. Clenching his jaw, Paxton took off at a full run.

When he reached the rise where he'd seen her, he stood there searching the hillside beyond. Nothing.

Where was she headed?

Rhys, he thought.

The sky lit above him, thunder cracked, while the treetops began to sway, the wind whipping through them with fury. He was nearly at the crest of the next hill when the heavens opened, drenching him to the skin.

Slipping and sliding on the sodden leaves that cluttered the forest floor, he didn't know how far he'd come or how far he had to go, but he instinctively headed due west, the direction where Sir Goddard said the ringwork lay.

Why had she run from him? What made her think she could escape him? Why the hell did she want to?

The questions shot through his mind as his anger drove him onward. When he got hold of her he would . . .

Paxton was loping through a small glade when he skidded to a halt. From out of the trees beyond the clearing stepped four men, their spears aimed straight at him.

Backing away, he spontaneously reached for his sword and hissed a curse when his hand came up empty.

Then Paxton stiffened as the point of a spear met the center of his back.

"Move ahead, Norman," a voice commanded. "Else I'll skewer you like I would a pig."

Paxton had no choice but to obey.

CHAPTER

14

It was well after dark when Alana stumbled through the ringwork's iron-banded log gates, several of her distant kinsmen granting her entry.

She was cold and wet and nearly in tears. Most of all, she was fearful of the questions Rhys would pose when he saw her.

The rain beat down on her in force as she took the familiar path that wound past several circular buildings, their conical-shaped thatched roofs pitching sharply downward, ending just a few feet above the ground. The cooking fires that usually flamed just outside each hut had been drowned out. Not even a curl of smoke or wisp of steam rose from their ashes.

Alana's feet slid on the muddy trail as she wended her way ever closer to the safety of her uncle's home. Just as when she left him, her thoughts were on Paxton.

He had followed her, shouting her name. Ignoring

his call, she'd plunged onward through the trees. Was he yet roaming the wood searching for her? Or had he turned back when the sky had opened, knowing the river would soon be impassable?

For his sake, Alana prayed it was the latter. She would hate that he was lost in the dark in the forest in a torrential rain.

And for her own sake, if he did make it back to the fortress, she hoped the deluge that was upon them prevented him from crossing over for days to come.

By then, Alana thought to be far away from here. Away to the northernmost climes. Possibly to Anglesey, well beyond Paxton's reach.

Her uncle's hut was just ahead, and Alana tripped along more quickly, wanting to seek its safety. Ducking beneath the thatch that was cut away above the door, she rapped on the wooden panel. As she reached for the latch, the door was jerked open.

"Alana?"

Dylan stared at her as though he were seeing an apparition.

"'Tis me," she said, wanting to throw herself into his arms and sob out her misery, but she resisted the urge. "Might I come in?"

"Forgive me." He stood back and waved her inside. The instant she ducked through the door, he took her into his embrace. Almost as fast he pulled away. "My God, you're sodden. Come, let's get you out of those clothes."

Alana followed Dylan deeper into the circular hut, which was naught but a large room. Glowing coals lay in the clay hearth that was situated in the room's center. Fragrant rushes were scattered across the dirt floor.

The place was crudely furnished—a few benches and stools, a table for food preparation, several storage chests, and four rush-filled pallets covered in rough cloth.

Swords, spears, darts, and longbows with arrows and their quivers were neatly stacked to one side. The dwelling stated that it was inhabited solely by men. Even so, the place was warm and, in some ways, quite comforting.

"Where are your father and brothers?" she asked, noting she and Dylan were alone.

Dylan had crossed to the far side of the room to fetch a piece of toweling from a chest. "Rhys is visiting at another hut," he called over his shoulder. "Caradog is with him. Meredydd is off in the wood somewhere, getting soaked the same as you."

Having retrieved a length of flannel, he was soon at Alana's side whereupon he began drying her hair.

"What are you doing here?" he asked. "Did your Norman overlord chase you off? Or did you have the good sense to escape him?"

Alana froze beneath the cloth that was ruffling along her scalp. Though Dylan had been jesting with her, he'd come so close to the truth that it frightened her.

She was loath to reveal that she and Paxton had wed. Rhys would be livid! But what excuse could she possibly provide as to why she'd come here, as to why she wanted to exile herself to Anglesey, without telling all?

None, she decided.

The towel came away from her head, and Dylan peered around her shoulder at her. "Well? Are you going to answer?"

"'Tis a little of both, Dylan," she said at last.

His dark mustache lifted at the ends as he smiled. "I had figured he'd soon pique your anger to the point of absolute madness. What did he do to drive you out into a rain such as this?"

"It wasn't raining when I left." She looked about the room. "Do you mind if I get out of these wet garments and into something dry?"

"Forgive me again." He handed her the toweling and strode off to another chest. "Caradog is closer to your size, but I'd not be offering you any of his clothing. He hasn't washed it in weeks."

Nibbling at her lower lip, Alana watched as Dylan rifled through the chest. Again she wondered what she would tell him. The lid slammed shut and he came to his feet.

"Here we are," he announced, shaking the folds from a short tunic and a pair of braies. Beside her once more, he gauged the length of the tunic to her own height. "I doubt you'll be needing these." He tossed the braies over his shoulder at the chest and handed her the tunic.

"For modesty's sake, I think I *will* need those," she returned as she marched away from him to snatch up the discarded braies.

Dylan crossed his arms over his chest and turned his back to her. "It's not as though I haven't seen your legs before, Cousin. In fact, I've seen a lot more than that. If you'll recall, I was the one who taught you to swim. And I did so while we were in the altogether."

"If you'll recall, Cousin," Alana replied, as she quickly stripped from her clothes, "I was eight and you were ten. A lot has changed since then."

"Aye, it has. And definitely for the better."

Her wet garments lying on a bench, along with her slippers and stockings, Alana dried herself off, then donned the braies, folding the hems of each leg.

"So," she heard Dylan say as she tightened the drawstring about her waist and tied it off. "What exactly did he do to cause you to run from him?"

Alana drew on the tunic. "I could be running to something and not from. Had you thought of that?" she asked as her head came through the neck opening.

"Unlikely, Cousin. You're here because something has frightened you. Tell me what it is."

Alana came away from the area where she'd dressed, her wet clothing and slippers in hand. She still didn't know what to tell Dylan or just how she should broach the subject when she did. "I came for a visit, that's all."

His arms yet crossed over his wide chest, Dylan was now facing her. He scrutinized her face. "A visit, hmm?" He shook his head. "Alana, thus far I've been more than patient with you. Without pressing, I've waited for you to apprise me as to exactly why you've come here. But I'm not a fool. You wouldn't be running through the wood in the dark in a drenching rain such as this unless something has happened. What has the Norman done to make you flee?"

Dylan knew her too well, and Alana now conceded there was no way around it. "I shall explain everything, but first you must swear that you won't tell your father, your brothers, or anyone here what I am about to divulge to you."

His brow furrowing, Dylan inclined his head. His frown deepened, and he captured her chin, inspecting her more thoroughly in the candlelight. His face suddenly became a harsh mask.

"Christ's blood, Alana! You're bruised. He struck you. Why? Damnation! He didn't—"

"Nay," she cut in, knowing what he was thinking. "Not exactly."

"What do you mean 'not exactly'? Either he ravished you or he didn't. Which is it?"

"Swear to me you won't tell."

"I'll swear nothing. If the bastard used you in an unseemly manner, your kin have the right to avenge your honor. I'll kill the cur myself."

Alana caught his arm as he made for his weapons. "Dylan, he didn't strike me. The bruise came by an accident of my own making. And he certainly didn't rape me." She swallowed, then drew a lengthy breath. "Dylan, he is my husband."

Dylan stared at her dumbfounded. "You *married* him?"

"Aye. Now swear you won't tell."

"If I want to hear the whole of this, I suppose I have no choice. I swear," he said. "Now explain why the hell you married him."

"I had to, Dylan. He threatened to ride against you if I didn't. Besides, Henry ordered that we marry. 'Tis done and nothing can change it."

"Why did you run away?"

"That I cannot tell you. 'Tis private. But with my having fled, I fear he may yet ride here and destroy all of you. He is aware of your numbers. With his knights and men-at-arms, he has you outmatched."

Dylan snorted. "If necessary, we can gather five times our present strength and have them here by tomorrow morning, ready to fight him."

"How?"

"Our neighbors to the north and west will gladly join against any Norman who dares to attack us. All we have to do is send runners to alert them. So, if you married him simply to protect us, you shouldn't have."

"Could you find enough men to defend against Henry and all his knights?" she asked.

"We could try, and might very well succeed. Owain Gwynedd would be more than happy to unite with us against England's king."

"I fear, Dylan, all this fighting and death may be for naught. One day, whether we like it or not, we will be made to accept another's rule."

"If that ever comes to pass, Alana, it will be a long while off. You know your countrymen would much rather die fighting than meet their ends lying in their beds. We will not give in to a conqueror. We will *not* accept another's rule." He paused and viewed her closely. "What happened to your staunch loyalties to your own kind? You never used to be this much of a naysayer. Not even Gilbert was able to defeat your assuredness that we would one day prevail. But this new Norman—well, the fight has suddenly gone out of you. Has he somehow managed to cloud your thoughts and win your sympathies?"

"Nay," Alana asserted. "My sympathies lie with my own kind. 'Tis the worry that has taken the fight from me."

"What worry?" he asked.

"The worry that you, your father, your brothers— all my kin!—will one day die."

Dylan chuckled. "'Tis the way of it, Alana. Death will come to us all eventually."

"That's not what I'm talking about and you know it," she snapped. "At the rate you're going, with all this vengeance and warring, you'll die far sooner than need be."

"And what would you have us do? Simply give in and allow them to swarm over us?"

"Nay," she said shaking her head. "That's not what I want. As for my assuredness that we would prevail, if I had believed that, I wouldn't have married Gilbert in the first place, being termed a traitor because I did."

"Rhys has since forgiven you for defying him. He thought you married Gilbert FitzWilliam merely to secure your birthright—the land. But I know you did it in hopes of ensuring peace between us all. The deed was rectified though. At least it had been until—when did you marry the bastard?" he asked.

"This morning."

Dylan looked at the dripping clothes in her hand. All at once he threw back his head and laughed. "So, the bridegroom lies abed alone, does he? Is that what made you run . . . your abhorrence to the marriage act?"

As Alana recalled Paxton's wondrous lovemaking, the tiny flame that lingered in her loins blazed anew. Her skin was at once flushed; she ached for the man she'd deserted. Abhorrence? Nay. Not after Paxton.

"I must warn you about something," Dylan said.

Alana blinked, surprised to see him standing across the way. While she stood there, speechless, thinking about Paxton, he'd taken the sodden garments from her hand. He was now spreading them over the table. Her slippers lay in the rushes by his feet.

"Warn me about what?" she asked, the fire inside her now banked.

"Rhys has been harping about your marrying one of us again. When he sees you, I'm certain he'll try to press the issue, which is now decidedly dead. Since you refused his own proposal of marriage twice, I thought you should know he now has plans for us, Cousin. Be prepared."

Alana was in no way startled by the statement. The Welsh intermarried frequently in order to keep their bloodlines pure. Uncle and niece, cousin and cousin, brother and sister—it was quite common they should join. And though the Church insisted it was incest, a mortal sin, the Welsh cared little. The practice had gone on for centuries, and Alana imagined it would continue until they were forced to stop.

Dylan was now striding toward her. "I would wed you—if you weren't taken, that is—except the love we have for each other isn't that sort of love."

It was true. She held deep affection for Dylan, but she could never envision them as lovers. Nor he her. "So what do I tell Rhys once he begins hounding me again?"

"Nothing. But be forewarned: With your staying here on a permanent basis, he'll be after you constantly. Mayhap we could pretend to cohabitate. That should appease him. In a year's time, I could set you aside, paying you a stipend for your trouble."

What Dylan had proposed was the natural way for a couple to come together in Wales. The young woman's family was paid in advance for her services, then the couple lived together, usually for a year, to see if they could abide each other before taking their vows. If it didn't work out, the prospective groom simply returned the young woman to her family, another payment given for their trouble. It was similar to handfasting as it was called by others.

"And how do you propose we pretend anything of the sort, especially with the five of us living together in one hut?" she asked. "Your father will know we aren't cohabiting."

"You mean because we aren't making love in the middle of the night?"

Alana tossed him a quick glare. "You know what I meant, so you need not have mentioned it."

Dylan chuckled. "Because of your abhorrence. You know, Alana, had you married a man of your own ilk at the start, you wouldn't be suffering from such disgust now. Unlike the Normans, we Welsh know how to treat our women."

Alana doubted it would be any better than the way Paxton had treated her. But then she would never know. "'Tis beside the point. Your plan won't work. Rhys will know."

"He won't know if I build us a hut of our own. Unless my father intends to stand outside with his ear to the door, he'll be totally ignorant of what's happening on the inside." Dylan shrugged. "'Tis only a suggestion. Take or leave it as you will."

"Thank you for your concern, but I doubt Rhys will be harping at me for long. I won't be staying here, Dylan."

Surprise showed on his face. "Where do you propose to go? Not back to him?"

"Nay. I cannot."

"Then where, Alana?"

"To Anglesey. Will you take me? If not, I shall journey there on my own."

Dylan viewed her at length. "You're that desperate to escape him, are you? So much so that you'd risk life and limb by traveling there by yourself. Why?"

Alana couldn't hold Dylan's gaze. "'Tis private, I said."

"Private?" Dylan returned. "Nay, Alana. The answer is written on your face. You're running away from your home, from your kinsmen, from all you hold dear because you've fallen in love with the Norman. 'Tis true, isn't it?"

Alana didn't have time to either confirm or deny Dylan's words. In that instant, the door burst open. Along with the wind and rain blowing inside came Rhys, Caradog behind him.

Her uncle stopped in his tracks. His head tilted while his dark eyes examined her. "Niece?" he inquired as though he didn't believe what he saw. Then his laughter rumbled forth as he threw his arms wide. "By Saint David's own shroud! You're really here!"

Rhys enveloped Alana in his embrace, almost

smothering her. Apparently aware that he was getting her wet, he pulled back and grasped her shoulders.

"Damn my eyes, I never thought I'd see you again."

Though she was smiling at her uncle, who was an older version of Dylan—still muscular, still handsome—Alana knew his jubilation would soon fade, understood the questions would come. She wasn't disappointed on either count.

"What are you doing here? The Norman—did he do something to chase you off?" He caught her chin, the same as Dylan had. "You're bruised. He didn't punish you after all, did he? By God, if he—"

Alana hushed Rhys when she placed her fingers over his lips. "I came for a visit, but if you keep badgering me, I'll take myself back the way I came. I will answer you this: The bruise was by my own making. He didn't punish me, and he didn't chase me off. Let that be the end of it."

"For now, Niece, I will accede to your wishes. But we will talk, and soon." He looked down at himself. "I suppose I should change my clothing."

Before Rhys could move, the door opened again. This time Meredydd entered.

"Alana," he greeted brusquely. His gaze shifted to Rhys. "Father, I need to speak with you."

Her cousin and uncle moved aside. Alana watched as Meredydd whispered in Rhys's ear. Her uncle frowned, then nodded. The two broke apart.

"There is something that needs our attention, Alana. We shouldn't be gone long. Caradog can entertain you until our return." He turned to his eldest son. "Dylan, come with us."

Wondering what could be so pressing as to take the three men out into a driving rain, Alana stared at the door as it closed behind them.

* * *

Paxton sat on the floor of a storage hut, his eyes kept fast on the three men who guarded him.

A short while ago, with his hands bound behind him, he'd been pushed through the gates of the ringwork, guided up the muddy path, then shoved through the door of the small hovel.

His feet were ordered tied. Next he was knocked to the floor. After spitting dirt from his mouth, he came to his knees, then angling over, sank to his rump, resting his back and head against a barrel.

He'd led himself into this mess, had done so knowing that Alana was probably fleeing to the protection of the ringwork and her uncle.

Unarmed and alone, he should have returned to the fortress and gathered the force that was needed to breach the palisade and take his wife back—*if* he were able to cross over the river, that was.

But he'd not done what was wise.

Instead, like a fool, he'd charged onward, his anger driving him, his confusion as to why she would flee him plaguing him all the way.

And so here he sat in the clutches of his enemy. Paxton couldn't help wonder if he would live to see the dawn.

The door opened, and three men, including the one who had captured him, ducked inside.

The oldest of the trio looked at the man beside him. "Is that him?"

Aided by the candlelight, the younger man searched Paxton's face. "Aye. 'Tis Paxton de Beaumont."

"Well, well," the older man stated. "Welcome to my lair, Norman."

"I've experienced better welcomes than this," Paxton returned, wondering how the younger man knew him.

The man chuckled. "Believe me: It will only get worse."

Paxton was very much aware of that. Through narrowed eyes he stared at his foe. "You have me at a disadvantage, sir, in more ways than one. You know my name, but I have yet to learn yours."

"Rhys ap Tewdwr," he announced. "These are my sons, Dylan and Meredydd." He'd clamped a hand on each of their shoulders as he said their names. "Now that the amenities are out of the way, tell me: What were you doing in the wood?"

"Taking a stroll," Paxton declared. "Regrettably, I got lost."

"'Tis an error you will soon regret," Rhys remarked. "One you will never again repeat."

"Do you wish to kill him now?" Meredydd asked. "If so, I captured him, therefore I claim the right."

"Nay," Rhys responded in a low voice. "If we slay him here, we cannot carry his body out without Alana's notice. And we cannot leave him here, for he'll begin to stink. We'll wait, and while we do, we'll take pleasure in making his life miserable. Have patience, Meredydd. When the time comes, you will be the one who ends his life. This I promise."

Paxton had strained his ears to hear what was said, but the most he was able to glean was that his life would be made miserable and Meredydd was the one who would eventually end it.

Things didn't look very promising, Paxton decided, then he cursed himself for acting so impetuously. He thought about Alana and wondered if she'd made it safely to the ringwork. Or was she still wandering in the wood, cold, wet, and possibly in peril?

Rhys broke away from his sons and strode across the clay floor toward Paxton. Standing above his prisoner, he glared down on the man he deemed as his enemy. "My niece denies that you in any way harmed her. But I suspect there is more to it than she is willing to tell. Know this, Norman: Your stay with us will be a brief and unhappy one. You might as well start reciting your prayers, for it won't be long before you die."

Hatred gleaming in his eyes, Rhys delivered a backhanded fist to the side of Paxton's face. The blow snapped Paxton's head to the side. Tasting blood in his mouth, he turned his face around, to glare at Alana's uncle.

"That," Rhys said, "was for whatever misery you've caused my niece these past weeks. 'Tis only the beginning, Norman, for I haven't avenged her yet."

His jaw throbbing, Paxton attended the man as he spun on his heel and stalked toward the door. On his way, orders were issued to the guards.

"Strip him from his clothing and boots, then tie him up, and leave him for the night. Make sure you bar the door on your way out. His ordeal will begin at first light."

With that, Rhys and his two sons exited the hut.

It wasn't long before Paxton found himself naked and huddled on the floor, his hands and feet bound, pitch blackness surrounding him.

The dampness and cold penetrated his skin, chilling him to the bone. The one warm spot inside him was near his heart as he thought about Alana and the ecstasy they'd shared.

But even that bit of heat began to cool as he contemplated her motive for running.

Lying there, the impenetrable darkness and heavy silence reminding him of a tomb, he felt his mind whirl with uncertainties.

She'd drawn him from the fortress, across the river, deeper and deeper into the wood.

In the glade, they'd made love, wondrous and free, just the same as in his dream.

Then she was bolting from him again, leading him on, ever closer to the ringwork.

Had that been her purpose all along . . . that he should be captured by the man who hated him simply because he was Norman?

He'd forced her into marrying him by threatening the lives of her kin. That he was now Rhys's prisoner smacked of the ultimate revenge.

Gilbert.

His friend and he had both desired her, had both married her.

Alana.

Was it possible she had betrayed them in the same manner?

Death.

Like Gilbert, he would soon pass into that eternal sleep.

Paxton was inclined to believe that it was the dividend received for his ever having trusted her.

CHAPTER

15

"**E**xplain why you came here," Rhys stated.

Alana lifted her gaze from her food. She, Dylan, and Rhys sat in the rushes beside the hearth sharing their supper from the same trencher. Meredydd and Caradog were situated a few feet away, hovering over their own plate.

"Can we not talk of other things as we enjoy our meal?" she asked. "It has been a while since I've seen you. Surely you have tidings of what has been happening here."

"'Tis the same routine, day in and day out," Rhys announced. "Explain why you fled your home."

Alana glanced at Dylan. He offered her a hint of a nod, affirming that he'd back her in whatever she said.

"The Norman and I don't get along."

Rhys emitted a short laugh. "Did you think you would?"

"I had hoped we could come to some sort of an

accord, whereupon we'd be able to live in peace. But, my father's kinsmen are close to rebellion. I've grown weary of trying to keep them all from each other's throats. I came here to collect my thoughts and seek a much needed rest."

Rhys cocked his head and studied her closely. "Why is it I don't quite believe you?"

"You may accept what I say or not. 'Tis your choice. I have explained my reason for coming here. So enough said."

He looked at Dylan. "Did she tell you more than she's willing to tell me?"

Dylan's dark eyes settled on Alana. "Only that the fight has gone out of her because of all the worry."

Rhys grunted. "By her belligerent manner, I'd say she's regained her nerve."

"I'd not be snapping at you," Alana said, "if you'd stop these incessant questions the way I'd asked you earlier. Please, Uncle, just let it be. I am weary and I don't want to think about these past several weeks. Nor do I wish to talk about them."

"Then we shall discuss something else," Rhys said.

"And what is that?" Alana asked.

"Your marriage."

Alana's gaze skittered to Dylan. His face was a stoic mask. Had he told his father about Paxton and her, even after he swore he wouldn't?

"My marriage?" she questioned, hurt that Dylan would betray her.

"Aye," Rhys said. "'Tis time—"

"Father, is this really necessary?" Dylan interrupted. "In the short while since her arrival, you've hounded Alana perpetually. Can you not allow her some time to enjoy herself?"

"I do desire she enjoy herself," Rhys insisted. "I also want her to be happy . . . free from this worry she says is weighing her down. That is why I think it's time she remarried." He turned to Alana. "I did not approve of your choice of a husband the first time you decided to wed. You are now aware you made a disastrous mistake. I warned you against Gilbert FitzWilliam. He was rude and crude, as all Normans are. The bastard was also treacherous to a fault, which you discovered. Consequently, when you marry again, the man you choose will be Welsh. You've denied my proposals that we join, and I accept your refusal. But you have been widowed long enough. You need a man's protection. Therefore, I've decided you should marry Dylan."

Relief washed through Alana, for Dylan hadn't betrayed her after all. How could she have thought that he would? More importantly, how was she to respond to Rhys?

"Uncle, your concern is most gratifying. And Dylan would make a fine husband. But not for me. Though you may wish otherwise, I cannot marry him."

"Why?" Rhys asked.

"Because after my first marriage, I swore I'd not join with a man again." Which was true, yet her vow, through no failure of her own, had fallen by the wayside. But Rhys must never know that. "Gilbert was enough."

"But—"

"Father," Dylan said sternly, "Alana has spoken on the matter. Now let it rest and allow us to have a conversation of a more pleasant nature."

Before her uncle could agree or disagree with his son, Alana took control and changed the topic. "So, Meredydd," she said, smiling. "When I arrived, Dylan said you were in the wood. Were you hunting?"

The piece of lagana that Meredydd had broken from the larger cake of bread and soaked in the broth on his trencher hung in midair as he attended her with his doe brown eyes.

"Aye," Meredydd responded at last, then poked the lagana in his mouth.

"Did you have any luck?"

He nodded as he chewed. "Aye," he said once he swallowed.

Alana thought he was being most reserved, which wasn't like Meredydd at all. Usually he talked continually. "What did you bag?"

Meredydd beheld his father. "He got himself a fine boar," Rhys answered for his son.

"Would you like for me to help with its preparation?" she inquired.

"Nay," Meredydd stated. "I bagged it, so I'll fix it."

Meredydd seemed irked by her questions. She glanced at each of their faces. They all appeared annoyed by something.

"What's wrong with the lot of you?" she inquired. "Has my coming here caused a problem?"

"Nay," Rhys answered quickly. "It has been a long day for us, and we need to be up before dawn. Once we finish our meal, I think we should retire for the night."

With her uncle's response, Alana noted the deepening lines on each of their brows, as well as around their mouths and eyes. Whether the marks were from the strain of fatigue or from another form of stress entirely, she couldn't say.

She did know that the Welsh worked long and hard throughout the day, resting little, if any. Her uncle and cousins were no exception.

Though it appeared otherwise, warring was not their only task at hand. The hillsides leading up to the ringwork had been cleared of their trees. One area was pasture for the cattle they raised; two others were for the grain—oats in spring and summer, wheat in winter. A fourth, which changed from year to year, lay fallow.

Rhys and his sons spent hours in the field, tending their herd, weeding the grain. Inside the ringwork, whether on the buildings, their tools, or their weapons, there were always repairs to be attended to. Their labors were constant and neverending, as it was for most of her kin.

Thinking it might be her own guilt that was causing her to imagine things, Alana decided to accept Rhys's explanation. In truth she was a bit tired herself. A good night's rest would probably lighten all their moods.

Alana harkened to the patter on the roof. "Listening to the rain outside has made me sleepy as well," she said. "If we're finished eating, I shall clean up our plates while you spread the pallets."

At everyone's nod, she collected the trenchers, then taking them across the way, she washed and dried them, storing them away. When she returned to the hearth, snuffing the candles as she went, she found the pallets were circled around the fire, all of them occupied.

Noting Dylan had saved room for her on his own pallet, she lay beside him. Soon the room's chill forced her to huddle closer to him.

Between the crackle of the low fire near her feet and the raindrops pelting the roof, she soon found herself being lulled to sleep.

As her eyelids grew heavier, so did her heart. For her thoughts were on Paxton. She wished he was the one who lay beside her and not Dylan.

In another life, in another time, maybe there would have been hope for them. But in this life and in this time, with so much standing between them, no hope existed. Happiness would forever elude them.

It was regrettable, Alana admitted, sleep swirling in around her. But lamentably true.

Paxton squinted against the sudden burst of light that streamed into the room when the door was thrown open. Three shadowy figures ducked inside. A flint was struck; a torch blazed to life.

Closing his eyes, Paxton turned his head aside. So accustomed was he to the dark that the brightness hurt his eyes.

This morning marked the second day of his *ordeal,* or so Rhys had termed it.

Thus far he'd suffered several well-placed blows to his face and an equal number of kicks to his ribs. He'd not eaten nor had he been given water.

He was granted a bucket wherein he relieved himself when the need arose, an amenity given to Paxton so he would not defile their storage hut.

Cracking his eyelids, he peeked at the men. Rhys, Meredydd, and the youngest of the brothers, Caradog, were the ones who had entered this time.

"Well, Norman," Rhys said. "I see you are up bright and early. I came by to tell you that you'll not be put to the test today. A pity, for I had such great plans for you. During this respite, I suggest you gather your energies, assemble your thoughts, and make things right with your Maker. Tomorrow, shortly after dawn, you'll be meeting your end."

What was the delay? Paxton wondered. They didn't intend to torment him, so why didn't they just slay him here and now? Through narrowed eyes, he studied Alana's uncle. "Am I to know by what means that will be?"

"I had hoped to spare you the worry," Rhys returned with a rancorous laugh. "But if you insist on knowing, I see no reason to keep it from you. For swine, such as yourself, there is only one suitable conclusion. We plan to roast you, and Meredydd will light the pitch."

Paxton's stomach lurched. Alive and burning—no form of torture could conceivably be as grievous.

The Welshman was aware of that and had devised the mode of Paxton's demise, hoping to administer as much agony as humanly possible.

Paxton had always imagined himself going down in battle, his sword in hand, his king in mind.

But never this. Not death by fire.

"You hate me that much," Paxton remarked.

"Not you, personally, Norman. Just your kind. Had you stayed beyond Offa's Dyke this wouldn't be happening to you. But you trespassed on our soil, and now you must pay the penalty. Tomorrow you'll know the folly of Henry's greed as well as the folly of your own."

The door opened and closed, Rhys and his sons exiting.

Again in the darkness, Paxton pondered his plight.

Greed—one of the seven deadly sins.

Had he been wrong in wanting a fiefdom, wrong in desiring Alana, wrong in thinking he could have both?

According to Rhys, he was.

And, as it stood, Rhys had the last say.

Alana was busy preparing the dough for the lagana, which was baked daily.

Through the open doorway, she glimpsed her uncle and her two cousins as they exited the storage hut. She thought to call out to them, requesting they bring more flour, so she could make several more cakes for Dylan and herself. But, from this distance, and because she was inside the hut, she doubted they would hear her.

By the time she had wiped her hands and had reached the entry, she saw they were well down the path, headed in the direction of the gate.

She really didn't want to face her uncle at the moment. He wasn't pleased that she would be leaving them soon. She sighed, remembering how last night when he'd brought up the subject of marriage again, she'd informed him she wouldn't be staying but moving on to Anglesey.

Just as she had expected, Rhys had grown red-faced, insisting she'd not go. Equally as determined, Alana insisted she would.

The Welsh were not afraid of expressing their views, no matter what their class, and she and her uncle were practically nose to nose in their discussion when Dylan pulled his father aside.

The two men had stepped from the hut for some private conversation. On their return Dylan had presented her with a reassuring nod. Then Rhys allowed that she could go, Dylan accompanying her on her travels.

Though he'd consented, he still wasn't happy about her decision. His moodiness on rising this morning told her it was best she tread lightly while he was around. But no matter his humor, she'd made her choice. At dawn tomorrow, she and Dylan would embark on their journey.

Looking across the way, she decided she'd not trouble anyone about the flour, especially when she could do the deed on her own. After finding a suitable container, she was out the door, whereupon she pointed herself in the direction of the storage hut.

The heavy rain had ended yesterday afternoon, a fine mist supplanting it. To the west, she could see the clouds were thinning. With luck by tomorrow they would again see the sun.

Alana was now at the door of the storage hut. Placing the crock at her feet, she lifted the wooden bar from its braces and set the thing aside. As she reached for the latch, she was grabbed by the shoulders from behind. She gasped as she was spun around.

"Dylan? What in God's name are you doing?"

"'Tis my question to you," he said, still holding her firm.

Alana stared at him, confused. "I used the last of the flour and was going to get more to make some extra bread for us for our trip."

"Take yourself back home," he ordered, nudging her in the direction of their hut. "I'll get the flour for you."

Wondering why he was so emphatic about doing the task himself, Alana hesitated.

"Go on," he said, then gave her a small push. "I'll be there apace."

"As you wish," she said, then started to wend her way back along the path toward her uncle's dwelling.

Halfway to her destination, she glanced at Dylan over her shoulder. With crock in hand, he had his hand on the latch, ready to enter the hut, when a frantic voice called out to him.

Alana looked to the source of the cry. It was one of their elder kinsmen. He was flailing around in the middle of a shock of bundled and bound sticks, which was to serve as firewood for all in the ringwork. Apparently he'd pulled one batch from the cart when the whole came tumbling down on him.

Dylan set the crock aside and loped off to offer his assistance.

Alana watched as her cousin pulled the man from beneath the avalanche. He wiped the mud off himself, Dylan aiding him, then the pair began dividing and stacking the bundles of wood that lay scattered on the ground.

Deciding that Dylan's new project might take longer than her patience could bear, Alana marched back up the path, grabbed the crock, and released the door's latch.

Light flooded into the hut as she pushed the panel wide. Alana ducked inside and froze in her tracks.

In the shadows, across the way, she saw a man huddled against a barrel. He was nude, filthy, and bound hand and foot. He was both squinting at her and shivering against the blast of cool air that had come through the door with her.

"Paxton?"

The crock dropped from her fingers as she rushed toward him. She fell to her knees beside him. Taking his head in her hands, she examined his face which was shaded by the start of a beard.

"My God!" she exclaimed at spying the bruises and cuts on his cheek, on his jaw, and at the corner of his mouth. "What have they done to you?"

"Unlike you, they certainly didn't offer to wash my feet," he rasped.

"If they'd regarded you as a guest, they would have," she returned while attempting to loosen his bonds. Rhys—she felt like murdering her own uncle. "You followed me, didn't you?" Her fingers were still working at the leather bindings without success. "Damn your Norman eyes, why didn't you stay . . . ?"

A shadow fell across them, and Alana turned to see who had entered. The man's back was to the light, and she couldn't make out his face.

"Who goes there?" she questioned, unknowingly thrusting herself between Paxton and the intruder.

The door closed, throwing everyone into blackness.

She heard the striking of a flint. A flame leapt to life atop a candle. Alana was both relieved and angered all at once.

"What is this about, Dylan?" she asked, coming to her feet. "Why are you holding him prisoner? What ever possessed you to do such a thing?"

"He wandered into our territory. Meredydd believed he'd bagged himself a prize. Father did also."

Alana remembered how on her first night here Meredydd had burst through the door, urgently needing to speak to Rhys. Afterward Meredydd, Rhys, and Dylan had gone out into the driving rain. "He's been here all along, hasn't he?"

"Aye—since shortly after you arrived."

"Why didn't you tell me?"

"'Tis the same reason I didn't tell my father that you and the Norman are married. I was sworn to secrecy."

"What does your father plan for him?"

Dylan moved toward her. "Alana, you don't want to know."

"They intend to roast me, swine that I am."

Alana's head snapped around as Paxton's voice rose from behind her. He was sincere. A knot formed in her stomach; her heart sank as panic rose inside her. *This cannot be happening!*

Slowly she turned back to face Dylan. "And you mean to let them?"

"I have no say in it."

"Well, I do," Alana avowed, the fight flowing into her with a vengeance. "You'll not allow this, do you understand? You will help me get him away from here. I shall never forgive you if you let this atrocity that your father has devised to come about. *Never.*"

"What do you propose I do?" Dylan asked.

"When is he to be . . ." She swallowed, unable to say the word.

"Tomorrow, after we leave."

Alana felt the blood drain from her face. "That is why your father was so willing to see me away from here." She caught his arm. "My God, Dylan, you cannot permit this horror. Please, you must help me save him."

Dylan searched her face at length. "All right. I'll help. But I cannot promise we'll succeed."

Alana was again on her knees, trying to loosen Paxton's bindings. "Assist me in freeing him, will you?"

Dylan hunkered down beside them. "Nay," he said, stilling her hands. "If Father comes in here again, which I'm certain he will, all must be as he expects. The Norman must stay as he is. Otherwise my plan won't work."

"But he's cold." She looked at Paxton. "Have you had water or food?" He shook his head. Alana's eyes were again on Dylan. "You can feed him, can't you. Certainly he needs water."

"He'll have both," Dylan said on rising. "Alana, you have to leave here. If Rhys should discover us, he'll put the Norman to death before your eyes." He took hold of her arm, urging her upward. "Come."

Alana's gaze ran over Paxton's face as her fingers lightly touched his lips. "Have faith," she whispered, then came to her feet. At the door, while Dylan scanned the area outside to see if anyone was about, she turned back to Paxton. "I didn't know. Truly, I didn't."

Noting Dylan was waving her into the yard, she hurried from the hut and moved along the path, a sharp ache near her heart.

Blessed Saint David, please watch over him. Protect him as you've always protected me.

The silent prayer, which streamed toward the heavens, was not uttered for the Norman dog who had come to vanquish her as his enemy, but for the man who was her husband . . . the man who was so near to winning her love.

Paxton's gaze was fast on Dylan as he rubbed his wrists in an attempt to regain the feeling in his hands. The leather bindings lay on the clay floor, Alana's cousin having cut them away a few seconds prior.

"Why should I trust you?" he asked, uncertain if this were some sort of trap.

True, he'd been given food and water to replenish his diminishing strength. But that didn't mean Dylan was reliable. Once Paxton was out the door, a dozen Welshman might beset him, their blades driving deep into his flesh.

"Especially since you see me as your enemy?" he finished.

"You are my enemy . . . you and any foreigner who breaches our borders with the intention of claiming our homeland as their own."

"If you feel that way, why are you willing to help me?"

"'Tis not you I'm helping but Alana. For some reason—though I don't fully understand why—she wants you alive." Dylan tossed a pile of clothing, along with a pair of soft leather boots, at Paxton's feet. "Dress yourself, Norman, and make haste. Sunrise is not that far off."

As Paxton pulled on the pair of braies that he'd drawn from the mound of garments, he said, "You know we are married, yet you didn't tell your father. If you despise my kind so much, why didn't you give him the news?"

"I swore to her I wouldn't. 'Tis the same as my not telling her you were our prisoner. What is a man's word if he does not keep it?"

Nothing, Paxton thought as he donned the tunic that he'd grabbed from the pile. He respected Dylan's conviction, but he still didn't know if he could trust him.

"So what is your plan to get me out of here?" he asked, shoving his feet into the boots.

"Put that hood on and pull it low over your brow to hide your face," Dylan said, pointing to the last article of clothing beside Paxton. "When we leave here, I'll take you to a location inside the ringwork where you are to remain hidden. You will wait there until I come for you. The plan, Norman, is that you'll walk out of the gate, alongside Alana, the guards thinking I am beside her. Not a word once we leave here. Now come. We haven't much time. If all goes well, you and your bride will be back at the fortress before noontide."

The hood in place, Paxton indicated he was ready, and Dylan snuffed the candle, throwing the room into blackness. Once they were at the door, Paxton held back while Dylan checked the area outside.

When it was time for Paxton to leave his prison, Dylan caught his shoulder. "Treat her well, Norman," he said. "If you don't, one day you will find yourself staring at the end of my blade. The only deliverance you'll receive from me then will be from this earthly life."

As Paxton stepped into the chilly predawn air, he knew the threat was not to be taken lightly. Then he wondered if that was what had happened to his friend.

Alana's kin—had they killed Gilbert? Had they

then masked his death, making it appear as though he'd drowned?

A possibility, Paxton thought as he followed Dylan to the back of the storage hut, then along behind the line of buildings, toward the entrance of the ringwork. Currently, he wasn't in any position to discover if the concept held any truth.

His own life lay at risk, and until he was free of the danger, he could think of naught else but himself.

"Are you certain this will work?" Alana asked.

The sky showed a faint hue of light on the horizon. Dawn would soon be upon them. Having escaped the hut before Rhys and the others had awakened, she and Dylan were making their way toward the entry of the ringwork.

"I cannot be certain of anything," Dylan replied, "but I'm hoping that what I've devised will see you and the Norman safely on your way."

"How will you explain Paxton's escape to your father?"

"Probably with the truth."

"Do you intend to tell him I'm married?"

"You can't keep it from him forever. Besides, you've made your decision. You're returning to the fortress with the Norman. He won't let you escape him again." Dylan paused. "Do you think he'll punish you for running from him?"

Alana didn't know what Paxton would do. "Nay, I doubt it," she said, not wanting Dylan to worry over her. "He will want an explanation though."

"And what will you tell him, Cousin? That you ran from him because you've fallen in love with him?"

"Nay—never that."

"You know, Alana, the truth might serve you far

better for once. 'Tis all the lies that got you into this trouble in the first place."

She came to a halt. "What would you have had me do? Tell Henry that Gilbert was a treacherous bastard who deserved to die as he did? Do you think Henry would have believed me? Nay, Dylan. I had no choice but to lie."

"I understand your fears, but one day, you may regret you withheld the truth, especially from your Norman."

"It cannot be helped." She searched the sky. "'Tis getting lighter." She wanted to hug Dylan, but simply squeezed his hand, lest someone interpret the show of affection for what it was: a farewell. "Thank you for your help. I owe you much, Cousin."

"Aye, you do. And one day I shall seek payment. But for now, let's get going."

At the gate, Dylan greeted the guards in a genial manner. The men were aware that Alana and Dylan would be leaving at sunrise, since they had been informed the night before.

Amenities exchanged, Dylan said, "We have a long journey ahead. Open the gates and allow us passage will you?"

That was Alana's signal. "Dylan, where is your hood? If the rain comes again, you'll need it for protection."

He gazed at his hands, which held a spear and a sack of food. "'Twas here a moment ago." He looked at the guards. "I must have dropped it along the path. Open the gates. I'll be right back."

"When you find it, put it on so you don't lose it again," Alana admonished as Dylan loped back up the trail. She turned to her kin. "Sometimes you men remind me of children," she commented, then smiled.

"Without a woman to see to your needs, you'd probably forget your heads if they weren't already attached."

Apparently each man had heard the same words from his wife, for they all grumbled an incoherent reply, then set about opening the gates.

Soon a hooded form came loping back down the path and stopped beside her. In the dim light, Alana saw it was Paxton, spear and leather bag in his hands. Nudging him ahead of her, she prayed they got out the gates, down the hillside, and a good way toward the fortress before anyone discovered he was gone.

"A safe journey to you," one of the men called as they passed beyond the palisade.

"Thank you," Alana called back to him while Paxton merely waved his hand.

As she urged Paxton into a northwesterly course, making it look as though they were headed to Anglesey, she heard the gate swinging to. She was close to breathing a relieved sigh, when a shout sounded from inside the ringwork.

It was Rhys.

"He's found us out," she proclaimed. "What shall we do?"

Paxton swore an oath. Dropping the leather bag, but retaining the spear, he grabbed hold of her hand. "Down the hill," he ordered, motioning to the east and the direction of the fortress.

Though a pathway snaked down the hillside, bordered by stone walls separating the fields from each other, it appeared that the best course was a straight one, and Paxton pulled her along to the rock wall. She clambered over the barrier while he vaulted it with ease.

Once on the other side, she yanked up a handful of bliaud and chainse, for she was again wearing her own clothing. Together she and Paxton descended the incline at a full run through the grain as though the devil were after them.

He was, Alana thought, knowing if they were caught, Rhys would probably kill them both. And what of Dylan? Surely Rhys wouldn't slay his own son!

Alana flayed herself mentally.

The peril that Paxton, Dylan, and she now faced was of her own making. She should never have sought to escape Paxton, especially by fleeing to the ringwork.

But who would have thought Paxton would have been so foolish as to risk life and limb by following her into this nest of Welsh who hated his kind with a vengeance? He knew Rhys lusted for Norman blood. So why had he chanced it would be his that Rhys spilled?

The horrifying cries sounded above them as her kinsmen streamed down the hillside after them. *Merciful Saint David protect us!*

The silent prayer lifted as she and Paxton came to the end of the field. Another wall stood before them, higher than the first. Alana groaned, for it was even taller than she.

"I'll never get over," she said as she and Paxton skidded to a halt in front of the wall. "Go. Save yourself. He won't harm me."

"Damned if he won't," Paxton returned. He dropped the spear, then cupped his hands. "Quick. Put a foot in here and I'll hoist you over."

The moments were precious to them both, and Alana didn't argue. Her foot met his hands, and he hefted her high. Her belly hit the top of the stones; the spear sailed over the wall, Paxton leaping and pulling himself up behind it.

"Get going," he said, his gaze centered on her.

But Alana was frozen in place, her own attention held straight ahead. A hissing curse broke from Paxton's lips when he too looked to his front.

There, blocking their way to freedom, were a dozen of Alana's male relatives, weapons aimed directly at them. She imagined they'd heard the shouts from atop the hill and had come from their positions in the wood where they guarded against a possible attack.

Glancing back over her shoulder, she saw Rhys was now behind them. "'Tis finished," she said to Paxton, tears welling in her eyes. "Why did you follow? Why?"

"Because I had to know why you ran," he said. His hand settled over hers, giving it a gentle squeeze. "Why did you?"

Alana had no time to answer, for Rhys was ordering them from the wall. Taking hold of her other hand, Paxton helped her down. Afterward he dropped to the ground. Side to side, Alana and Paxton faced her uncle.

"Did you free him?" Rhys asked, his eyes narrowed on his niece.

"Nay, she didn't."

The words came from behind Rhys, and he spun around. Dylan was making his way through the dozen men who had chased Alana and Paxton down the hill, including his two brothers.

"I freed him," Dylan said when he reached his father's side. "I did so at Alana's request."

So furious was Rhys that the veins stood out on his temples and neck. "You, my eldest son, betrayed me?"

"What would you have me do?" Dylan countered. "Betray Alana instead?"

"Why would you betray Alana?" Rhys asked. "The Norman means nothing to her. He is, however, a threat to all of us. Therefore he must die."

"Nay," Alana said as she stepped in front of Paxton. "You are wrong, Uncle."

"What do you mean?" he inquired, his attention now centered on her.

"He's not a threat to you."

His lip lifting beneath his mustache, Rhys sneered at her. "You must be mad, Niece. He comes here claiming for Henry the land that was your birthright. Next he'll be reaching farther and farther, until he declares the soil on which we stand as his own. He can't do that if he's dead." Rhys cocked his head. "What happened to your loyalties, Alana? Do your kin and your heritage mean nothing to you?"

"My loyalties are the same as they ever were. Likewise, my feelings about my kin and my heritage have not changed."

"Yet you protect the Norman, even after he's stolen from you."

"He has stolen nothing from me. What is mine is his by law."

Rhys snorted. "You mean by Henry's law! The bastard does not rule here."

"Nay, I mean by God's law. And He will smite you if you attempt to undo what has been done."

"God will not smite me for killing a Norman." He waved his sword. "Stand aside so it may be done."

"Would you kill your own kinsman?" she asked, standing firm.

Rhys grew very still. "What are you saying?"

Alana took a step closer to her uncle. "If not by blood then by marriage he is now your kin. Paxton de Beaumont is my husband."

CHAPTER

16

"The Norman bastard is your husband!"

Rhys's words rang out in a half question, half statement, as though he couldn't quite accept what Alana had said was true. He turned to Dylan.

"Did you know about this?"

"Alana told me."

"And you said nothing," Rhys declared, accusation resounding in his voice.

"She made me swear I wouldn't."

"I made you swear you wouldn't tell her the Norman was here, but you broke that vow."

"He did not, Uncle," Alana interjected. "I found Paxton on my own."

"How?" Rhys queried.

"I went to the storage hut in search of some flour to make more lagana for Dylan and myself to take with us on our trip."

"I came upon her inside the hut," Dylan said. "She was very angry, Father, at finding her husband bound and naked and beaten."

"And I suppose you told her what was to happen to him?"

"Nay," Paxton stated as he stepped forward. He'd been listening to the exchange quietly, but it was now time for him to act. "I told her. It was only fair to let my wife know what her uncle had planned for her new husband."

Rhys's eyes narrowed on him. "If you think her marriage to you will stop me from slaying you, you are wrong, Norman."

Paxton heard Alana's gasp as the tip of Rhys's sword met the center of his chest. Paxton did not move, but announced, "You show a great deal of courage, Welshman, especially when facing an un-armed man. Yet I wonder if you'd stand the test if we were matched weapon to weapon."

A dark smile spread across Rhys's face. "Do I detect a challenge in your words?"

"Aye," Paxton stated, knowing he braved much. But if he'd guessed right, Rhys was the sort to take the bait. "A challenge to see who is better with his sword," he finished.

"And what prize is the victor to claim?" Rhys asked.

"If I win, you will allow me safe passage back to the fortress. If you win, you may do with me as you like. Either way, you will give me your word that my wife will not be harmed—not now and not in the future."

Alana caught his arm. "Paxton, no! Because of what he put you through, you're not as hale as you were when you were first captured."

Paxton surveyed her. "You misjudge my ability,

Wife. Even in the most weakened state, a Norman knight is able to stave off his enemy. This Welshman will present no problem."

"Ha!"

The abrupt exclamation broke from Rhys's lips, and Paxton regarded him again. Could he goad him into the fight? If so, he'd have a chance. If not, his next breath might very well be his last.

"I take it you disagree with what I've said," Paxton commented.

"You have a bloated sense of yourself," Rhys declared.

"Then prove it, Welshman. Meet my challenge and let us see which of us is the better with a sword."

"Agreed," Rhys stated. He swung back to Dylan. "Give him your sword."

Dylan shrugged. "I didn't wear it."

Rhys addressed his second son, "Meredydd, your sword—give it to the Norman."

Unlike his brother, Meredydd was able to comply. He pulled the weapon from the leather scabbard at his waist, then handed it hilt first over his forearm to Paxton.

Taking the sword, Paxton noted it was far lighter and about ten inches shorter than his own sword. He and Rhys would be in much closer quarters because of it.

"To first blood?" he asked of Alana's uncle.

"Nay—to the death."

A whimper sounded in Alana's throat; Paxton gazed down at her to see tears shimmering in her eyes. "Stand away, sweet."

"But I don't want you to die. Rhys either. Must you do this?"

He touched her cheek. "Have faith, Alana. 'Tis what you told me."

On Paxton's nod at Dylan, Alana's cousin came forward. Taking her by the shoulders, he moved her to a safe spot, away from the ensuing fray. At the same time, everyone else backed off, forming a wide arc around the two combatants.

Slowly Paxton turned to face Rhys. "Do you accept my terms, Welshman?" he asked.

"Aye."

"Then swear it to all here so that there is no mistake."

Rhys's gaze swept over his kinsmen, his words uttered loud and clear. "If the Norman wins, he is to go free, my niece with him. That is the bargain." Then he was glaring at Paxton. "Whether you had met your end by burning or whether you meet it now by my sword, it matters not to me. Prepare to die, Norman. For it will be so."

Dawn burst across the horizon just as Rhys struck the first blow. Metal smiting metal, Paxton deftly deflected the blade with his own, and the battle for supremacy was on.

Rhys, Paxton discovered, was well-skilled, as good as any opponent he'd ever met. Prowess, agility, force, and cunning were the traits needed to win this fight. Alana's uncle was invested with all of these.

But so was Paxton.

The blades clanged in the crisp morning air, sparks erupting with the potency of the need to either kill or survive.

Paxton could feel the shock of each brutal impact as it traversed his arm, the wave jolting his shoulder. With the next swing, he felt the sting of Rhys's blade as it sliced through the tunic and across his arm.

Riotous anger filled him. Thus far he'd taken a defensive stance. Now it was time for him to attack.

Gritting his teeth, he wielded the sword with all the fury that had risen inside him.

Battling his opponent and causing him to retract, Paxton promised himself that Rhys would not win. He had far more to lose than his life.

There was Henry's pledge of the fiefdom. But even more than that, there was Alana.

He knew now that she hadn't purposely led him here. She never intended that he should be taken prisoner by her kinsmen. He understood that the instant she found him. The stunned look on her face as she fell to her knees beside him, along with her demands that Dylan help free him, had quelled his suspicions.

But the one thing he didn't know is why she had run from him in the first place. The answer would be given him only if he lived. *That* was the reason he had to win.

Striking out at Rhys with all his might, he backed the Welshman across the field toward the ring of observers. Rhys thrust his sword at Paxton's heart, but Paxton managed to veer the blade from its appointed mark, circling it upward.

The quick action brought the two men together, chest to chest. Their harsh breaths blew into each other's faces, eyes glaring with enmity. Fair play was the last thing on Paxton's mind. Hooking his leg behind Rhys's calf, he shoved the man to the ground. Apace, his foot was atop Rhys's belly, the tip of his sword pressing against the man's throat.

"Be done with it, Norman swine," Rhys declared, his words gritting through his teeth.

Paxton noted there was no fear in the man's eyes. To die by the sword would be an honorable end indeed. "Nay, Welshman," he said, lightly drawing the blade's tip from Rhys's neck up to his chin. He brushed the point of Rhys's nose before he withdrew his weapon altogether. "Today you will live."

His foot came away from Rhys's stomach. Alana's uncle rolled to his feet to face him. At the same instant, Alana came rushing up behind Paxton. She peered around his shoulder at Rhys.

"Is the bargain met?" she asked her uncle.

"Aye, Niece," he answered, his eyes narrowing on her. "You may go with your Norman, and this time you may pass safely. But I tell you this: You have disappointed me yet a second time. As of this day, I no longer consider you my kin. Be gone with you."

Rhys retrieved his sword from among the sickly looking tufts of oats that he and Paxton had trampled into the earth as they fought. Motioning to his men, he began marching up the hill, the others following.

Paxton gazed down at Alana and noted her crestfallen expression as she watched Rhys go. That she'd been disowned by her uncle had hurt her deeply. She'd been lotted to suffer the emotional trauma all because of him.

"I'm sorry he was so hard on you," Paxton told her as he embraced her shoulders. "In time, he may have a change of heart."

"I doubt it," she said, her voice choked. She gazed up at Paxton with tear-bright eyes. "Come. Let's leave here before he has a change of heart of a different kind."

By now Dylan was beside them. "I'll go with you . . . at least part of the way, until I know you will be safe."

Alana touched Dylan's arm. "What do you think he will do to you once you return?"

Dylan shrugged. "At the very worst, he'll disown me just as he did you."

"Oh, Dylan, I never meant that he should turn

against either of us. But I could not allow him to slay Paxton."

His fingers brushed Alana's cheek, then he captured her chin. "Don't fret, Cousin. His temper flares then subsides. In time, he will forgive us both. I'm sure of it."

While Paxton listened to the interchange, he felt a growing envy inside him. The two cousins were close—very close. He wished it could be the same between Alana and himself. After the scare they'd just sustained, maybe their relationship would flourish, becoming more secure, more intimate. Paxton hoped this would be the case. Otherwise happiness might always elude them.

"Let's be going," he said, urging her up the hill. "If the river is down, Graham might decide to cross over and come looking for us. If possible, I'd like to avoid another confrontation between Welsh and Norman. For now, anyway."

Once they reached the upper wall, Paxton assisted Alana over the stones. He and Dylan followed. They waited as Dylan walked the few yards and snatched up the leather bag that Paxton had dropped earlier. On his return, Paxton extended the hilt of the sword that he still held.

"I believe this is your brother's," he announced.

"Keep hold of it," Dylan said. "You still might need it."

Then the threesome wended their way down the trail toward the wood, Paxton attending his wife carefully. She held her head high. Not once did she look back. Inside, though, he knew her heart was breaking. To be ostracized by her family was a difficult shock to endure. For her sake, he hoped Dylan was right: Rhys would one day forgive them both.

They had traveled a long distance through the wood

in silence and without incident when Dylan stopped. "We're well over halfway to the river," he said. "'Tis best I leave you here."

Again Paxton attempted to return the sword to him.

"Nay," Dylan declared as he held up his hands in refusal. "You have close to two miles to go. You might have use for it." Then he pulled Alana into his arms and kissed her cheek. "Take care, Cousin. Be happy." His gaze met Paxton's. "Remember, Norman, what I told you about treating her well."

"Aye. I'll remember."

Releasing Alana from his embrace, Dylan pressed the leather bag into her hands. "In case you get hungry." Then he strode back through the wood whence he came.

Both Alana and Paxton watched until he disappeared over a rise.

"Do you wish to rest or continue on?" Paxton asked, his gaze now on his wife.

"Nay," she answered, quickly brushing away her tears. "Not unless you do."

Paxton's heart ached for her, but he said not a word about Dylan as he took her hand in his. "Come, then, and show me the way. We'll rest once we are at the fortress."

In due time they came to the river. Paxton noted how the water rippled swiftly by their feet. It was high but not so high that they couldn't cross over. Still, the memories Alana retained of her near drowning might make her wary.

"Do you want to attempt it?" Paxton asked on turning to her. "If you'd prefer, we could wait and see if the flow abates somewhat."

Alana shook her head and gazed up at him. "There's no need to tarry. If you'll offer me your assistance, I'm sure we can make it to the other side."

His knuckles feathering across her cheek, Paxton smiled down at her. "You risked your life to save me, my wife. Helping you ford this stream is the least I can do in return."

Her wide, beguiling eyes entranced him as he continued to stare at her. A strange sort of warmth filled his heart. It was then that Paxton knew the question had to be asked.

"Why did you run from me, Alana?" When she tried to look away, he caught her chin. "Why?"

"Because you frightened me," she said.

"Frightened you? How so?"

Her brow furrowed slightly. "Must I really say?"

Paxton could tell this was difficult for her, but he wouldn't relent. "Yes. I want to know."

She set her jaw, then released her breath. "The feelings inside me—after we, uh . . . well, after we, uh . . ."

"Made love?" he prompted.

"Yes, after we did that . . . well, I didn't know what to think. I've never felt that way before. It frightened me."

Paxton chuckled. "You'd better get over your fears, Alana. Once I've bathed and shaved this growth from my face, we will again be making love. In fact, we will be doing so each and every day for as long as we live."

A blush crept across her cheeks, and Paxton laughed anew.

"Does the thought cause you embarrassment?" he asked.

"Nay. 'Tis just that I cannot imagine living very long if you're forever taking my breath away as you did the first time."

Paxton allowed his grin to fade. She had not an inkling of what was to come. The ways in which he planned to make love to her were as varied and as wild as anyone could imagine. Just thinking about her being beneath him again, soft, alluring, and welcoming, caused his loins to stir.

"You'll live, sweet," he said, his voice noticeably husky. "And you will enjoy every moment we are together. The pleasure attained and remembered on those occasions will be everlasting. This I promise you."

A shout sounded across the river. Both Paxton and Alana looked to its source. Sir Graham stood on the opposite bank, along with several Norman men-at-arms. Madoc was there. Aldwyn also.

"We'd better get across," Paxton said, then plunged the tip of Meredydd's sword into the earthen bank. He spied the sack in Alana's hands. "What's in there?"

"Some cheese and the bread I made for Dylan's and my trip."

The recollection of her saying almost the same to her uncle came to Paxton. And so did a frown.

If her fears were no more than the way he made her feel when they made love, why then was she so set on traveling through Wales, a perilous journey indeed?

She'd not been truthful with him, Paxton decided as he studied her.

Something else had chased her into the wood and away from him. Something that struck such dread in her that she would risk her life to flee him. Even more so than before, he was determined to discover what it was that had made her run, for it damn well wasn't his lovemaking.

He took the sack from her and offered her a faint smile, hoping it would mask his rising suspicions. "Since you made the bread yourself, we'll take the bag with us," he said, pulling the looped ties up his arm and over one shoulder. He presented his back to her. "Hop on and I'll carry you to the first boulder."

Placing her hands on his shoulders, Alana jumped up and straddled his waist. He caught hold of each leg just behind the knees as her arms clamped around his throat.

"Not so tight, sweet. You're choking me." When she relaxed her grip, he inquired, "Ready?"

"Aye."

"Then hold on and close your eyes."

"Nay, I think I'd rather watch. At least then there won't be any surprises."

"Have faith, Alana. We'll make it."

On those words, he walked into the rushing stream. The water lapped over his boots, to his knees, then to his thighs. Attempting to keep his feet from shifting out from under him, Paxton fought the current as it pushed against him. One slip, and they'd both be washing down the river.

Slowly, steadily, he plodded onward, Alana holding on to his neck in a death grip. She was again choking him, but he said nothing, for he understood her fear.

Reaching the first boulder that jutted from the riverbed, he set her on its top, which crowned a few feet above the water. After he dragged some air into his lungs, to replenish the breaths that he'd lost, he pulled himself onto the large rock. Standing, he helped Alana to her feet, then he bounded to the next boulder. He stretched his hand out to her, assisting her across.

When they reached the last of the stepping-stones, Paxton again took Alana on his back. The last several yards were more difficult than the first, the current being far swifter on this side of the river.

He slipped once; Alana gasped, and Graham reached out to him. Releasing Alana's one leg, which was wrapped around his waist like a snake constricting its meal, he grabbed the proffered hand. Graham pulled him up onto the bank.

"There," Paxton said, allowing Alana to slide from his back to her feet. Turning around to face her, he saw she had gone quite pale. He touched her cheek. "We made it across, sweet. I told you we would."

She pressed her face into his hand, and Paxton thought he felt the brush of her lips against his wrist.

"You did, my husband. For your care, I thank you. If you will excuse me now, I shall see there is hot water for your bath."

His hand fell to his side. "Then go. I'll be along shortly."

Paxton stared after Alana as she, Madoc, and Aldwyn began climbing the trail to the fortress. At the same time, Graham started in with a series of questions and statements, all concerning his worry over the couple and his inability to cross the river to come searching for them. Though Paxton was listening to the knight, his eyes remained on his wife.

The gentle sway of her hips seduced him as she ascended the hill. His loins again stirred as he remembered their interlude in the glade. Not unexpectedly Paxton found he was eager to repeat the magic of their first joining, to feel anew the ecstasy that was theirs.

And more, he thought. Much more.

"Excuse me, Graham," he said, cutting the knight off in midsentence while turning toward the path and the fortress. "I'll explain all that has happened later. Right now, I want nothing more than to be alone with my bride."

A lengthy sigh echoed through the closed chamber as Paxton sank into his bath.

Standing only a short distance from the wooden

tub, Alana watched as he ducked beneath the steamy water. A second more, he broke through the surface, wiped his hands down his freshly shaven face, then up again, sweeping his hair back from his brow.

As he lazed there, with his eyes closed and his head propped against the tub's rim, Alana worried her lower lip with her teeth.

She'd lied to him . . . again.

Alana amended the thought.

She didn't lie exactly, just told him a half-truth as to why she'd run away.

His lovemaking did frighten her. Excited her as well. But it was her fear she might be falling in love with him that had driven her into the wood. That, and the worry over what he would do to her if he ever learned the truth about Gilbert.

She'd been foolish to go to Rhys. Had been even more unwise to think Paxton wouldn't follow. She was his wife, his possession—at least according to the Church and his king, she was. It would stand to reason he'd give chase.

As she viewed his dark head, beads of water dripping from his sleek locks and puddling on the floor, she wondered what he expected of her next.

"Sweet," he said, lifting his arm from the rim of the tub where it rested. His hand stretched toward her. "Come bathe me as a dutiful wife should."

Alana felt her heart jump. Was he capable of reading her thoughts? She hesitated at first, then moved toward him. To honor his request was only fair, especially after everything she'd put him through.

Beside the tub, she shakily knelt and pushed the sleeves of her chainse well above her wrists. Wetting the sponge that she'd taken from the stool next to her, she squeezed out the excess moisture. Then she stared at Paxton's face.

His eyes were again closed, his head yet resting against the tub's rim. But it was his bruises and cuts that drew her attention, for they were far more noticeable since he'd shaved.

Alana's heart ached unbearably. Oh, what he'd suffered because of her. Notwithstanding she knew it could have been worse. He might have died.

Swallowing the sob that had risen to her throat, she drew the sponge across Paxton's wide brow, then more gently over each eyelid, down his straight nose, and very lightly over his one cheek that bore the most injury. Next, she dabbed at his chiseled lips, taking care not to reopen the cut at the corner of his mouth, whisked the sponge over his squared chin, then up his other cheek.

"You're treating me as though I were a wee babe," Paxton declared, his eyelashes parting. "Are you afraid I might break?"

The way he gazed at her with his entrancing blue eyes made the breath still in Alana's breast. That strange feeling, where she went all warm and liquidlike, erupted inside her again.

"Nay." Her nerves atwitter, she looked at the water and dipped the sponge anew. "I was merely taking care so there wouldn't be any pain. 'Tis my fault you bear those bruises and cuts. I wouldn't blame you if you punished me for the misery I've caused you."

With her eyes downcast, Alana didn't see the smile that teased Paxton's lips. "So, you admit I have good reason to chastise you?"

Thus far he hadn't shown any anger toward her, which surprised Alana. Had he been Gilbert, he'd be ranting at her about her stupidity, threatening to discipline her soundly. "Aye," she answered on a nod. "You are my husband. 'Tis your right."

"What penalty do you think would be appropriate?"

She shrugged. "'Tis your choice."

Paxton sat up in the tub. "While you wash me, Wife, I'll decide on what punishment I shall mete out. Now attend to my needs."

Taking the soap, she lathered the sponge, then beginning at his neck, she worked from there over his broad shoulders, down one sinewy arm, across his muscular chest, masking the black springy curls with suds, and onward to the other arm, taking care not to disturb the superficial gash inflicted by Rhys's sword. Finished with those areas, she sidled around the tub and washed his back.

All the while, Alana tried not to think about Paxton or his exceptional body. But the attempt was fruitless, for vivid pictures of him nude in the glade kept flickering in and out of her mind.

She again saw each remembered aspect of him while he made love to her: the sinew in his arms bulging and trembling slightly as he held his weight above her, the throbbing pulse in his throat as his sexual excitement increased, and his handsome features contorting as though he were in agony when he spilled his seed deep inside her.

Then there was his brief expression of amazement.

It was as though he'd never experienced anything quite so ultimately satisfying in all his life.

Alana knew he would come to her again expecting her to submit. Along with punishing her, that also was his right.

She had no choice but to defer to him, just as she'd done with Gilbert, allowing Paxton the use of her body to appease his needs. There was, however, one difference between the two men. She had abhorred

Gilbert. Yet with Paxton—well, he evoked feelings inside her she never knew existed.

Miserably, she was aware she couldn't shut Paxton out the way she had done with Gilbert. And that was what alarmed her so. Hence, it wouldn't be long before her new husband—the man who was supposed to be her sworn enemy—had won her heart completely, and she'd be lost to him forever.

Damn Henry for sending him here! she railed in silence while she rinsed the soap from Paxton's back. Why couldn't Paxton's king have dispatched a man who was old and unappealing? If she'd been forced into a marriage with someone such as that, she wouldn't have any need to fear losing herself.

Moving back around the tub, intending to rinse his shoulders and chest, his arms as well, she again noted the discoloration on Paxton's face, tokens of Rhys's rage against all Normans. She groaned inwardly, her heart twisting anew. She wished she could rescind her impulsive actions, take back her sudden desire to flee, revoke everything that Paxton had suffered because of her.

It was then the dawning occurred.

For all her mental meandering, all her worry over losing her heart to this Norman, Alana understood that it was too late.

She *already* loved him.

That was why she'd been so tormented at finding him in the storage hut, why she'd been so distraught at knowing he'd soon be put to death, why she'd demanded that Dylan help free him, even if doing so put all their lives at risk. Had he been any other Norman, she doubted she'd have reacted the way she had. She'd been frantic to protect him.

What was she to do?

"Alana."

On hearing her name, she blinked. Paxton, she noticed, was studying her intently. "Yes?"

"Has something unsettled you?" he questioned.

More than you'll ever know!

She wanted to shout those words but held them inside. The revelation that she loved him was far too new to her, and she remained cautious, for she felt at her most vulnerable. "W-why do you ask?"

"Your expression—dumbfounded is how I'd describe it. What has astonished you so?"

Alana feared the truth was written in her eyes. To avoid his seeing it, she once more gazed at the water. "Nothing has astonished me," she stated. "You're imagining things."

She needed to be away from him so that she could calm her thoughts and gather her wits about her. Splashing water over his chest, rinsing away the soap, she dropped the sponge into the tub and started to rise, but Paxton caught her hand.

"You forgot my legs," he said, thrusting one muscular limb into the air before her.

Her eyes narrowing ever so slightly, Alana retrieved the sponge and gathered the soap. Couldn't the blasted rogue bathe himself?

"I've come to a decision about your punishment," he said.

Alana looked up from the task of scrubbing his leg. He'd been so matter-of-fact in his announcement she assumed he was no longer interested in learning why she appeared *unsettled*. She was relieved yet guarded.

"And?" she inquired when he did not expound further.

"Obedience is something a husband should expect from his wife, correct?"

"I suppose so."

Paxton chuckled. "Suppose so? Alana, as I recall you vowed to obey me the day we were married."

"I wasn't given much of a choice in the matter."

"On that I'll agree. But you swore to obey me and naught can change that."

"And what does my obeying you have to do with my punishment?"

"Henceforth, whatever my request, whatever my demand, you will honor it, without question, without objection, without hesitation. Not one word will pass from your lips, except that of acquiescence. You will be submissive to me, my wife, in all things."

Alana stared at him, confused. Had he expected her to be a complete shrew, defying him at every turn? Not even with Gilbert did she attempt to usurp his authority over her . . . not until his treachery was made apparent. "I don't understand what you're saying."

"The significance of my meaning will soon become clear. Right now you may wash my other leg."

Its length rose from the water as he plunged the other one into the tub. Methodically, Alana took to scrubbing the leg he'd offered. When she was done, she tossed the sponge into the water and stood.

"You are bathed, milord husband. Is there something else you need?"

Paxton glanced at the water as though viewing what was hidden below its surface. "You missed a few spots."

"I think you are capable of attending to those yourself."

"I am quite capable, but I want you to attend to them for me."

"But—"

"Obedience, Wife, in all things that I request. Remember?"

Clenching her jaw, Alana drew a deep breath. Once again, she lowered herself to her knees. Latching on to the sponge that was bobbing around the tub, she soaped the thing.

Without hesitation.

The words came to her as she was pondering how she should go about this.

"Would you like for me to stand?" Paxton inquired.

"Nay!" she blurted and plunged the sponge beneath the water.

She blindly bathed his lower ribs, the side of the hip facing her. As she reached around to run the sponge over the other hip, her hand made contact with his manhood, which to Alana's dismay was erect.

Her hand popped from the water, and she jumped to her feet. "'Tis done," she announced on a squeak, her face feeling as though it were afire.

"In a haphazard fashion, yes," Paxton said. "For the moment, however, it will do."

He leaned back against the tub's rim, Alana watching him with care. Thinking he intended to say more, she waited. Save for the lapping of the water as he idly raised his knee then lowered it again in a nonchalant manner, there was silence.

"Is that all?" she inquired, praying it was.

His lazy-lidded gaze raked her from head to toe. "There is one more thing that I demand," he said.

Alana was immediately wary. "A-and what is that?"

"Remove your clothes and join me in my bath."

CHAPTER

17

Alana's heart slammed once in her chest, then seemed to stop altogether. When it started again, it thumped in her ears.

"Remove your clothes and join me," Paxton repeated.

"I'd prefer to bathe separately," she answered after she found her voice.

"But I prefer the opposite," he countered. "Obedience, remember?"

"And what if I choose not to comply?" she asked.

"You'll pay the consequences."

"Which are?"

"What rights are usually extended to a man whose wife is considered unruly?"

Alana stared at him. Surely he didn't intend to beat her! So far nothing in his character gave the impression that he was purposely brutal. In fact, Father Jevon's disclosure on how the whip had fallen from

Paxton's hand before the call came announcing Sir Graham and the others were safe indicated he was anything but!

Filled with bravado, Alana challenged him. "You jest."

"Do I? Persist in defying me, and we'll see if I'm jesting."

Noting how Paxton continued to laze in the tub, Alana glanced at the closed door. As she tortured her lip with her teeth, she wondered just how far she could get before he pounced on her.

Not far, she decided, aware he was lithe, agile, and way too swift. Remembering also how he'd toppled Rhys as they stood face-to-face in battle, she knew that he would use whatever ploy was necessary in order to win.

Oh, why was she fretting over something as inconsequential as this? They'd been intimate before. Though she had hoped he'd allow her more time, she was aware he'd be making his demands known sooner or later. Unfortunately it was earlier than she'd wanted.

"Well, Wife?"

Sighing, Alana removed her bliaud, her chainse, her slippers and stockings. Pulling the combs from her hair, she dropped them atop the pile at her feet. She now stood in naught but her chemise. Nervous fingers caught its hem, and Alana pulled the final article of clothing over her head.

Her chemise fell from her fingertips and drifted to the floor. "Satisfied?"

Not yet, Paxton thought, his ardent gaze wandering over her exposed beauty. But soon he would be the most contented man in all Wales.

He extended his hand to her, palm upward. "Join me, sweet."

She was hesitant at first, but directly her hand

slipped into his; Paxton steadied her as she stepped over the tub's rim.

"Now what?" she asked.

"Straddle my hips," he responded while tugging at her hand.

"Nay."

"Alana, don't argue. Just do as I say."

He captured her other hand, urging her to comply. Her foot moved through the water above his belly, then she was lowering herself to sit astride him.

For an instant, Paxton's breath caught in his chest when they connected. Alana's eyes closed and she swallowed with force. They were touching intimately, but not joined. As he gazed at her face, noting the small puckers along her brow, he wondered what thoughts were traversing her mind. The answer came to him forthwith.

"Why are you so intent on embarrassing me this way?" she asked as she viewed him.

Her words were but a miserable little moan that tugged at his heart. "I have no intention of embarrassing you. My purpose is to show you that you have no reason to be afraid of me . . . nor of my making love to you."

"You certainly have an odd way of going about it."

"I suppose you and Gilbert never—"

"Nay, we didn't," she snapped.

Paxton realized he shouldn't have mentioned Gilbert. Still, by Alana's reaction, it was made quite plain that her late husband had never thought to seduce his wife by inviting her into his bath.

Was Gilbert really such a dullard when it came to lovemaking? Was he so self-absorbed that he only sought to take and never to give in return? If so, it was another mark against the man whom he once thought of as his friend.

In light of this, Paxton was more determined than ever to put Alana's old memories of Gilbert to rest. Her new memories would be of him, and him alone, the pleasure he gave her overriding all else, her fear gone forever.

"We'll see if you think that the way I'm going about this is *odd* once we're through, sweet." He took up the sponge and soaped it. "Gather your hair, so I don't get it wet."

The ends of her long tresses already dipped below the surface of the water. Still Alana complied. With both hands, she scooped the dark mass together at the nape of her neck. Then she lifted the whole to the top of her head, where she coiled it around, planting her hands atop it to hold it there.

Paxton's eyelids grew heavy as he viewed her thus. Her jutting breasts, each a perfect globe, taunted him. He wanted to taste each tantalizing peak, but quashed the urge—for now.

Inadvertently her hips moved against his. His loins blazed as his manhood hardened to the point of searing pain. Paxton wondered why the hell he just didn't pluck Alana from the tub, here and now, carry her to the bed, and take her there.

Seduction . . . slow and easy.

It was essential for her pleasure and for his.

Taming his lust, he moved the sponge to her throat, over her shoulders, then up each winged arm, then down, in the direction of her ripe breasts.

The sponge met one sphere, and he bathed it gently. As he did the same to its twin, he viewed the first. Rivulets of suds skimmed down her wet skin, catching briefly on her nipple, then dropping into the water.

Paxton was growing more and more eager to have her. He bathed her ribs, her belly, her navel. Moving the sponge around her waist, he washed her back, then attended her hips and their roundness.

"Raise up," he said, his hand again in front of him.

Alana lifted herself, and he delved between her thighs, stroking her.

"What are you doing?"

Her voice held a hint of breathlessness, and Paxton smiled. "Playing," he said, tempted to release the sponge, allowing his fingers to take its place. "Do you want me to stop?"

Nay, Alana thought.

The most delicious tingles were passing through her body. Why on earth would she want them to end?

But they did.

Water sluiced over her skin as Paxton rinsed her from her neck downward. He did the same with her back. Afterward he tossed the sponge aside. Then he was pulling her to him.

Alana shivered with delight as his mouth opened over one breast. He suckled lightly, then his tongue flicked against the nipple. She felt it harden. Sensation licked to her core.

Then he was attending the other breast in the same manner, and Alana could no longer suppress the groan that had threatened several times to escape her throat.

Releasing her hair, she gripped Paxton's shoulders. "This is madness," she whispered as she tried to push from his hold.

"Nay. 'Tis pleasure, Alana. Relish it. Allow yourself to experience it fully, the same as you did the first time we made love."

Memories of the glade burst around her; her hands relaxed. Alana surrendered to the wants of her body by giving herself over to Paxton.

His hand was working between them. Finding her, his fingers glided through the folds which were slick from the water and the hot moisture that had seeped from within her. He probed, one finger entering her. He withdrew it, then as his thumb rotated the bud, he entered her again.

Alana could not resist the magic his sensual play evoked. Soon she was moving, increasing her pleasure. She moaned when he removed his hand. Then she felt his other hand on her bottom. He was lifting her and positioning himself at the same time. When the crown of his manhood was at her entry, he pressed her hips down.

He was filling her, deeper and deeper. "Kiss me," he entreated, his passion-glazed eyes connecting with hers.

Alana wanted nothing more than to taste his lips. She leaned forward. Their bellies touched; her breasts pressed into his chest. Then he caught her head, pulling her to him.

Hot and wet, his lips opened to devour hers; Alana responded eagerly to his kiss. As their tongues probed and played and teased, Paxton's hips moved. She yielded to the rhythm he orchestrated, his hand lifting her bottom, then pushing her down. His strokes were sure, firm, and unerring, and Alana luxuriated over each new sensation as it came.

With a growl, he pulled his mouth from hers. "This is impossible," he muttered as he set her from him.

Startled, Alana could do naught but stare at him. "Why?" she questioned at last.

"I cannot make love to you the way I want—not in this tub."

The words came from him as he rose to step over the tub's rim. Alana gasped when he lifted her from the water, then set her to her feet. He jerked up the toweling and dried her. Next he dried himself and threw the scrap of linen aside. Afterward he swept her into his arms and carried her to the bed.

She floated downward, sinking into the center of the mattress onto the wadmal cover. Paxton was quickly above her, settling on his knees between her outstretched thighs.

"This is far better," he said, before his lips met hers. They lingered briefly, then sluiced to her neck to play at her pulse. He kissed each breast, nibbled on toward her waist, where his tongue probed her navel.

Alana had no idea what he was about, but he was driving her witless. Then his lips met her curls; his fingers were opening her. She jerked when she felt the flick of his tongue against her.

"What are you doing?"

"Loving you as you've never been loved before."

His hot breath fanned over her, and before Alana could say yea or nay to this new assault to her senses, his lips and tongue were on her, teasing, probing, and tasting her.

At first her fingers stretched, then they curled into the bedcover as her breath was suspended in her chest. Soon she was reaching for his head and threading her fingers through the thickness of his hair, urging him closer.

Her hips writhed, and her heart threatened to burst. Flames of fire licked through her, promising to consume her. In a daze, she saw Paxton was now above her. His hot erect member slid into her.

"Pleasure me," he said.

How could she refuse, loving him as she did?

She welcomed him into her arms, her legs encircling his narrow waist. Their bellies met, warm flesh against warm flesh. His hand burrowed beneath her hips bringing her closer.

"Whatever you desire," she said in response, prompting his lips to hers.

He gazed deeply into her eyes. "Alana."

Her name was a soft plea uttered before their mouths met in a sizzling kiss. Hearing it had acted as the most potent aphrodisiac of all. He moved inside her once, and Alana swore she was melting. Spasms of ecstasy pulsed through her whole being. At the same instant, she felt Paxton's body convulse. His deep, trembling groan flowed past her lips as he climaxed with her.

Spent, they lay quietly. But it wasn't long before Paxton rolled to his side, taking Alana with him.

After a bit, she asked, "Did I pleasure you the way you had hoped?"

Christ yes, he thought, knowing this time was even more wondrous than the first.

Smoothing several errant strands of hair from her face and settling them over her shoulder, he smiled at her. "I'm gratified by your simply being near me. But in response to your question: Aye, you pleasured me the way I had hoped. Even more so."

She nestled into his shoulder and yawned. "I'm glad," she said, her eyes slowly closing.

Paxton's hand covered Alana's where it rested in the center of his chest. "Sleep, sweet," he whispered, kissing her brow, then pulling the edge of the bedcover over her hips and shoulders.

Alana nodded. Soon she drifted into the realm of dreams.

As Paxton lay there, his wife snuggled against him, he examined her face.

Long lashes feathered against the delicate skin beneath her eyes. Light breaths blew between her softly parted lips, stirring the hair on his chest.

Mesmerized, Paxton studied her features, discovering the little nuances of each.

Lovely didn't fully describe her. Yet her outward appeal wasn't what had attracted him. The fiery passion within was what had attracted him from the first.

He recalled how she'd stood up to Sir Goddard, how she had held her own even against him. Likewise, she'd taken on her own uncle, along with the rest of her kin, determined to save his wretched hide from a hellish death.

For a small slip of a creature, her courage was unsurpassed. As a warrior, Paxton admired her tenaciousness.

But was that all?

A strange sort of warmth blossomed inside him. He felt it spread through his whole being.

Nay. There was far more, he decided.

Bemused by the perplexing emotion that was now filling his heart, Paxton grew very still.

Damnation! Was it possible? Was he actually falling in love with her?

To Paxton's delight and amazement, the answer was a definite . . .

Yes!

CHAPTER

18

Alana stood with Paxton at the edge of a bluff overlooking the river that lay a good hundred feet below them. On her husband's arm, which bore a leather gauntlet, perched a hooded female falcon, eagerly awaiting its release.

Viewing Paxton, who was searching the sky and distant landscape for the falcon's prospective prey, Alana felt that familiar warmth flood through her once again.

In the three weeks since they'd returned from the ringwork, the month of June had faded. July was now upon them. And in those three weeks, Alana could rightly say she had experienced the most wondrous time of her life.

Love.

She never thought the emotion could be so magical, so energizing, so all-consuming. But it was.

And all because of Paxton.

As she continued to watch him, she was struck by a twinge of melancholy. If he only loved her as well, she thought, hoping that perhaps one day he would.

"There, girl," he said, moving his arm in the direction of the pinpointed prey. "A nice fat grouse."

Paxton plucked the hood from the falcon's head. With keen eyes, the hunter spied her target, then launched herself into the air. On rapidly beating wings, she took aim from above her prey, then swooped with unimaginable speed. Talons sank into the startled grouse, then the falcon was headed back their way.

"She lures well," Paxton commented as the falcon dropped the limp grouse at his feet, then perched on his raised arm. He replaced the hood and leashed the jess, which was attached to her leg. "Who manned and trained her?"

"I did," Alana said, retrieving the grouse from the ground, placing it into a leather bag with the three others that had previously been snared. When she rose from the waist, she found Paxton staring at her. "Are you surprised?"

"Nay, sweet. Nothing about you surprises me. Not anymore. Though, I must confess, ofttimes I do find myself extremely delighted—enchanted, in fact."

Knowing he referred to their lovemaking, Alana blushed. Then she noticed that certain gleam in his eyes. He wanted her. Again! Amazed by his stamina, she wondered if he ever tired of their sexual play, which went on several times a day, and sometimes half the night through.

"Do you ever think of anything else?" she inquired as an unexplained bout of shyness overcame her.

"Not recently," he said, grinning. "And certainly not while you're around. It seems, my lovely wife, that I cannot get enough of you."

His gaze darkened to a midnight blue, marking his desire, and Alana's flush deepened as her heart tripped a little faster. To cover her embarrassment, she blurted, "Well, I say you should quell your lust for now." She raised the bag. "We need to get our catch back to the fortress, so it can be cleaned."

"In good time," he said.

Paxton urged the falcon into the small cage sitting beside him. He tossed in a scrap of raw meat as a reward for the bird's excellent performance, then secured the door.

Removing the heavy gauntlet, he wiped his hands on a scrap of cloth, afterward announcing, "Presently I have other plans." He reached for her, pulling her into his arms. The game bag dropped at their feet. "And they all have to do with you, sweet."

Small tremors of joy were quaking through her, for his lips were traveling the side of her throat. "You're very bold, sir," she said. "Had you ever thought that someone might see us?"

"Let them," he said, his hand inching her skirt up to her thighs.

She caught his hand. "Paxton—not here. We're fully in the open."

He drew back to look at her. "Then let's find ourselves a nice big tree to hide behind."

Alana uttered not a word as he began leading her from the bluff, down into the wood. She had no objection to his loveplay. In fact, she welcomed it. But she had the oddest feeling they were being watched.

A large oak stood in front of them. "Is this acceptable?" he asked, drawing her around its thick trunk.

"Aye," she said.

"Good," he returned as he pressed her against the rough bark. "For I doubt I could have gone another step farther without at least tasting your delicious lips."

His mouth was instantly on hers, and Alana marveled at the mastery of his kiss, just as she always did. As their tongues mated, she felt his hand lifting her skirt. Soon his fingers were between her thighs, ardently exploring her. She moaned into his mouth as he elicited a sudden flow of moisture from within her.

Alana felt the evidence of his arousal against her belly as he leaned into her. Not one to be greedy, she lowered her hand and found him. She would have preferred to touch him, to feel his hard hot flesh in her hand, but the way they were positioned prevented such, so she stroked him through his tunic instead.

A scant moment later, Paxton dragged his lips from hers. "Sweet Jesus, I want you."

"Now?"

"Aye. *Now,* Alana."

As eager for their joining as he, she nodded.

Paxton eased his hand from between her thighs and started to pull her away from the tree, intending to find a soft spot of earth for their bed, when a flash of color caught both their eyes.

Startled, Alana gasped. Beside her, Paxton froze.

"I didn't mean to intrude," Gwenifer said as she kept to her place, which was no more than twenty feet away.

Glancing at Paxton, Alana noted his harsh frown, along with the tic in his clenched jaw. She understood his anger, for she felt the same herself. Simple *courtesy* dictated that if a person came upon an intimate scene, such as the one she and Paxton were sharing, the person would withdraw as quickly and as quietly as possible. It was apparent that her cousin didn't know the meaning of the word.

"What is it you want, Gwenifer?" Alana asked.

"I came searching you out to tell you that I'll be departing from here for Clwyd on the morrow. It's time I returned home. I was hoping we could perhaps visit for a while this afternoon. I had no idea that you were—well, I've embarrassed the two of you, as well as myself. I'm sorry."

She turned to go, and Alana looked inquiringly at Paxton. Seeing his nod, she called out, "Gwenifer, wait." Her cousin halted, and Alana walked toward her. "Go on back to the fortress. Paxton and I will be along soon. First we need to collect the falcon and the kill."

"I do hope he'll allow you to spend some time with me," Gwenifer said. "I've hardly seen you these past three weeks."

Alana had been surprised by Gwenifer's announcement that she was leaving. Yet, in truth, she knew she'd been a terrible hostess since her marriage. Still, it couldn't be helped. When it came to her husband's needs versus her cousin's, Paxton was the one who would win out every time. And so it should be, Alana acknowledged.

"I'm sure he will," Alana replied, now certain it was best her cousin left. "Run along, so I may speak to him."

With a nod, Gwenifer began her trek back through the wood toward the trail. When she disappeared, Alana gazed up at Paxton, who'd made his way to her side.

"I believe she's angry with us for ignoring her as we have."

"She couldn't possibly be half as angry as I am with her. I should thrash her soundly for prying as she did."

"I'm sure she was too stunned by what she saw to manage a coherent thought. She is a virgin, after all."

Paxton snorted. "That is most questionable."

Alana gaped at him. "Do you have firsthand knowledge that she's not?"

"If you are asking if I bedded her, the answer is no."

"Then how can you say she's not intact?"

"A man knows these things."

"How so?"

"The look in a woman's eye . . . the way she comports herself—your cousin has far more knowledge of what transpires between a man and a woman on an intimate level than you realize, my naïve wife."

Alana sputtered in protest. "Just because *you* perceive a certain look or a particular mode of behavior to mean a woman is unchaste doesn't mean it is so."

"If that is what you want to believe, especially about Gwenifer, then you have my permission to do so. God's wounds, Alana! She threw herself at me constantly."

"Only because I asked her to."

Alana nearly bit her tongue in two once the words were out.

"May I ask why?" Paxton queried, his expression one of amused certainty.

Alana couldn't face him. "'Twas when Father Jevon told me about Henry's edict. I asked that she stick close to you to see what she could learn." She met his gaze. "So if you believe she was throwing herself at you for purposes other than gaining information from you, which she brought directly to me, you are wrong."

Paxton chuckled. "You've confirmed my suspicions, Alana. I was sure you had set her on me. Although what you had hoped to learn, I haven't the slightest inkling. Yet, that doesn't explain her actions prior to your learning about our ordered nuptials."

Alana's eyes narrowed. "You still persist in denigrating her. Why?"

"'Tis only a feeling I have."

It was Alana's turn to snort. "A feeling? Is that all you can muster in way of proof?"

Paxton shrugged. "Sometimes it is enough. However, I will tell you this: If it had been you who was bedeviling me with your feminine charms the way Gwenifer had attempted to do, *you* would have been beneath me in a trice. Such brazen coyness from a woman rarely goes unrewarded, unless the man is not attracted to her. I wasn't attracted to Gwenifer. But *you,* sweet, have intrigued me from the start. Which reminds me. I believe we were in the throes of passion before we were so rudely interrupted. Are you ready to begin anew where we were made to leave off?"

Alana sighed. "I promised Gwenifer we would return to the fortress." She caught his hand. "She's leaving tomorrow, Paxton. Can I not spend the afternoon with her? I may not see her for a very long while."

He smiled at her. "Aye," he said, fingers smoothing an errant strand of hair from her face. "You may spend the afternoon with her. But only after you've seen to me first. Once we return to the fortress, we will go to our chamber. Spare me one half turn of the hour glass and the rest of the day is yours. Agreed?"

Pleased by his proposal, Alana smiled in return. "Agreed."

Paxton had just deposited the falcon at the mews, afterward handing the kill over to one of the castle cooks whom he saw in the yard, and was now striding into the hall, eager to find Alana.

On entering the outer gate, he'd sent her on ahead, promising to join her once he'd finished with his tasks. Not seeing her anywhere below, he assumed she had gone to their chamber.

Paxton's thoughts took flight as he envisioned her nude, lying abed, waiting for him. He loped toward the stairs. At their foot, he met Madoc who had just descended them.

"Is your mistress in her chamber?" Paxton inquired.

"Nay, she's in the kitchens."

"Why there?"

"One of the women sliced her thumb a good one. My mistress is tending it while I fetched the medicinals." He raised the chest high for Paxton to see. "It was left in her room from when she minded your cuts and bruises."

Her room. The connotation nettled Paxton. That Madoc would denote his and Alana's chamber as such meant the man still had not accepted their marriage. But Madoc was not the only one. It would be a while before the Welsh trusted him. This Paxton understood.

"When you see her," he said, "tell her I've gone upstairs."

Madoc grunted and moved aside; Paxton took the steps two at a time. Admittedly he was rather puzzled by his enthusiasm. In fact he felt like the lad of five-and-ten that he was when he'd had his first sexual encounter. But then with Alana everything was a new awakening.

Once inside the chamber, Paxton removed his sword and stripped from his tunic, then headed for the basin to prepare for Alana's return and their interlude of love.

After washing himself, he rubbed his cheek, making

certain it was still smooth from his shave that morning. His bruises were gone, the cuts healed, Rhys's punishment all but an annoying memory.

Next Paxton took up a piece of green hazel and cleaned his teeth as the Welsh did and as Alana had showed him. He then wiped them with a small scrap of wool.

Halfway to the bed, he unbuckled his spurs and pulled off his boots. The spurs fell to the floor, while one boot landed in the corner, the other near the door as they flew from his hands. Dressed in naught but his braies, he dove toward the bed.

The ropes groaned, the siderails threatening to break, as he landed in the center of the mattress on his belly. As he rolled to his back, he spied a scrap of cloth stuck to his chest. He hadn't noticed it before because it was nearly the same shade of yellow as the bedcover.

His brow furrowed as he pulled the cloth from his chest. The square of wool, he decided, was in sad shape: the edges burned, holes in the center, stained with grass and mud. What caught Paxton's eye, though, was the silk embroidery that ran from top to bottom and side to side, nearly covering the swatch.

The design appeared familiar. Turning the square toward the window and the light, he traced the pattern several times.

Paxton sat up with a jerk.

A *salamander?*

He stared at the wool.

The creature's head and tail were missing, but the curved body, flames shooting away from it, was intact. Indeed, the embroidered portion *was* a salamander. Which meant this piece of cloth once belonged to Gilbert, for it was the emblem he wore on his tunic and carried on his pennon.

Paxton plunged a finger through one hole then another. Cuts from a dagger? He inspected the stained edges. Blood. Faded but evident.

Cursing, Paxton was on his feet, his thoughts whirling in disbelief.

Impossible! But then he was attacked by his own words: *'Tis only a feeling I have. Sometimes it is enough.*

He had ignored his instincts and had thrown caution to the winds, thereby allowing himself to believe that Alana was not the treacherous witch that he'd first deemed her to be—all because he lusted after her. All because he thought he was falling in love with her.

But the truth could no longer be denied. The proof was here in his hand. The irregular square of wool, with its scorched edges and stains of grass, mud, and blood; the lacerations in the cloth, along with the telltale emblem, brought everything into complete clarity: This was part of the tunic that Gilbert wore on the day he died.

Paxton heard the latch release on the door; his narrowed gaze shot toward the panel. Flushed, breathless, and smiling, Alana stepped inside their chamber.

"I'm sorry I was delayed," she said, closing the door. "One of the women cut her thumb quite badly. Madoc and I had to attend to it forthwith before she lost too much blood."

Paxton's eyes were hard upon her, for as she spoke she was reaching for the hem of her bliaud. Should he allow her to strip? Should he then pin her to the bed and take her with the force of all the fury that was roiling inside him—just this one final time?

"Hold!" he commanded sharply.

About to pull the garment over her head, Alana stilled. She stared at him in obvious confusion. "What is it?" she inquired, releasing the hem. "What's wrong?"

He thrust the woolen scrap forward. It dangled from his fingers. "This is what's wrong."

Her confusion increased, the furrows in her brow deepening. "What is it?"

"Come see for yourself, Wife."

With cautious steps, Alana came forward. As she reached for the square, Paxton's jaw clenched to the point of snapping. He examined her as she looked it over. In an instant, her fingers began to tremble. Her face suddenly went pale. Her wide gaze jumped to his.

The truth was written in her eyes, yet Paxton wanted to hear it from her own tongue. "Gilbert didn't drown. He died by the blade, didn't he?" Tears sprang to her eyes, but Paxton ignored them. When no response came forth, he grabbed her shoulders and shook her as his voice thundered through the room, "Answer me, woman! 'Twas by the blade, wasn't it?"

A sob broke from his wife's lips and so did her reply, *"Yes!"*

Paxton's body grew taut. One name came to mind. All he needed was confirmation. "Who killed him?"

There was silence, then he felt her shoulders square beneath his hands. Her gaze met his, firm and steady.

"I killed Gilbert."

CHAPTER
19

"Liar!"

The word jolted through Alana as Paxton shook her anew. She thought to hear a thousand other slurs from his lips but not the one that came forth. Frightened by the fury in his eyes, she pushed at his chest. "I told you I killed Gilbert. Isn't that what you wanted?"

"I want the truth."

"It is the truth," Alana insisted, perjuring herself again.

"You couldn't have possibly inflicted that many wounds on Gilbert, let alone one. He was stronger and larger than you. He was a knight—a skilled warrior. Now tell me who killed him and why it was done."

Alana swore he'd not receive the indictment he sought. He could beat her senseless, but she'd not say the names. "I killed Gilbert," she repeated.

With a growl, he shoved her from him and spun away. Alana tripped back two steps. Her eyes fast upon him, she watched as he thrust his fingers through his hair in obvious frustration. Apace, he turned on her again.

"It was Rhys and your cousins who killed him, wasn't it?"

"Nay!"

"Christ, woman! Why are you protecting them?"

Because they were defending me!

Though the words screamed through her mind, she held them inside. Even if Rhys had disowned her, she'd not allow him or his sons to suffer the devastation that would befall them, a product of Henry's anger. It was her fault. If she hadn't married Gilbert, unwisely hoping to secure her inheritance, none of this would have taken place. And if justice prescribed that a life be given for the life taken, it would be hers and no other's.

"Paxton, hear me. I killed Gilbert. I did so because he tried to kill me."

"Kill you—why?"

"Apparently he hated me."

"Appar—" He cut himself off. "Don't you know for certain whether he did or not?"

"He must have hated me, for that's the only motive I can think of as to why he would want me dead." Which was true.

Paxton scrutinized her, his jaw again clenched. "I think you had better explain all, Alana. Tell me exactly what happened the day Gilbert died."

Memories came rushing in—the struggle, the fall. She closed the door on them. "Perhaps I should start at the beginning of Gilbert's and my relationship. Maybe then things will be more clear to you."

"If that is what you want, I will allow it, but start somewhere and do it now."

His patience was waning, and Alana prayed she

could convince him that Gilbert died by her own hand and no other.

Her insides were churning, yet drawing a deep breath, Alana began speaking in a calm, steady voice. "I didn't love Gilbert when I married him. Likewise, I don't think he ever loved me. Our union was a selfish one on my part." She waved her hand around her. "All this that you see and the land beneath and around it was my inheritance.

"When Gilbert and the others arrived, I saw it slipping away from me. I thought that if we married I could ensure for my children, who would be half-Norman, half-Welsh, that none of this would be taken from them, nor would it be taken from their children and so on. I also hoped our joining would bring peace for my kinsmen.

"At first our relationship was amicable. But it wasn't long before Gilbert began to grow distant. He barely spoke to me. At the slightest thing, he became angry with me. I never knew why. As for my plans ensuring my posterity would never have to leave this land—well, like my marriage, those disintegrated as well."

"I explained why you probably didn't conceive," Paxton stated. "It was Gilbert not you, Alana. Tell me about the day he died. What transpired?"

The doors opened again in her mind, the memories streaming forth. Along with them came the terror she'd experienced, as well as the fear and the anguish. Knowing she had no choice but to apprise Paxton as to what occurred, she forged ahead.

"We had experienced heavy rain for several days on end. The morning of the day Gilbert died the rain had stopped briefly. He came to me, asking that we take a walk. I was surprised but concurred with his request.

"After leaving the fortress, we went down by the

river to the outcrop of rock that I showed you. We were standing there, watching the raging current, when Gilbert shoved me. I nearly fell but caught his sleeve. He forced my hand away. We struggled, but he was far too strong. I was suddenly falling toward the river. I—"

Alana stopped as she recalled the horror of it all. She saw herself again tumbling through and beneath the waters, clawing her way to the surface, gulping in fragments of air, only to be dragged to the bottom again. The terror was eternal. Even now, almost a year later, she was quaking the same way she did when she had pulled herself from the violent eddy that nearly ended her life.

"Alana?"

Hearing her name, she blinked. She looked up to see Paxton was in front of her. Grasping her arm, he guided her to the bed, seating her on the mattress. He stood above her in silence; Alana glanced away.

"Are you able to continue?" he asked at last.

"Aye," she said, her fears being replaced by her anger at Gilbert's treachery.

"Then do so."

Alana clasped her hands in her lap and squared her shoulders. All the while she was creating a fabrication, for this was where the lies would begin.

"Well?"

"I don't know how long I tumbled along or how I managed to keep from drowning. By some miracle, there was a limb stretching before me. I somehow grabbed hold of it and, with effort, pulled myself from the river." That much was true. "I lay on the bank for a while when I heard—"

"What side of the river?"

Paxton shot the question at her, and Alana frowned at him. "This side. Why do you ask?"

He waved her query away. "Go on."

"It wasn't long before I heard footsteps. I saw it was Gilbert and, fearing he would shove me in again, I drew my knife. When he was upon me, I stabbed him."

Lies, she thought, knowing it hadn't happened that way at all.

In actuality, she lay there, weak and exhausted, but fearing Gilbert would find her, she crawled to the then existing footbridge, which wasn't very far away. Literally dragging herself to the other side, she managed to pull herself into the wood where she hid, attempting to renew her strength.

Not long afterward, she saw Gilbert striding along the opposite bank, and she drew her knife. Luck was with her, for he didn't cross over but continued on downstream, apparently searching for her body.

Once he disappeared, she pushed herself to her feet with the aid of the tree she was secreted behind and stumbled on through the wood. A watcher found her. Fortunately, he was on horseback. Drawing her up in front of him, he took her straight to the ringwork and Rhys's protection.

Gilbert may never have been punished for his heinous act. Had he been smart enough to secure himself behind the fortress walls, Rhys probably would not have been able to touch him. But it was Gilbert's own stupidity that brought about his demise.

For reasons Alana couldn't quite fathom, nor could anyone else who was involved, Gilbert had made his way to the ringwork on foot. His rationale may have been to appease his wife's relatives by showing his insurmountable grief over Alana's sudden, tragic loss, thus preventing any suspicion to fall on him.

If that was his plan, Gilbert had erred, and grievously so, for Rhys was aware of his treachery. And though Alana had not been there to witness Gilbert's death, she had been told what had happened after the fact.

A watcher had sighted Gilbert, sending word on ahead to Rhys through a companion. Leaving Alana in the care of several women inside the ringwork, her uncle and her three cousins set out to intercept Gilbert.

They came upon him in the wood. Tears streaming down his face, he told his story of how Alana had slipped and fallen into the raging current, how he'd made a frantic search but couldn't find her, how he could only assume his lovely wife had drowned.

It was then Rhys accused Gilbert of perfidy, announced that Alana lived, told him he was aware of the truth and that Gilbert's lies and betrayal would not go unpunished.

Stunned by all that Rhys had told him, Gilbert sought to flee. But he found himself surrounded. He begged for mercy, but Rhys, Dylan, Meredydd, and Caradog were set on revenge.

Their blades plunged repeatedly into Gilbert's treacherous heart. When their anger had subsided, they carted Gilbert's body to the same river that he claimed had taken his wife's life and tossed him in.

When Alana learned of Gilbert's fate, she felt no remorse over his demise. But she did become fearful of Henry's wrath once he learned of Gilbert's death. That was when she'd insisted on returning to the fortress with the concocted story that Gilbert had drowned, praying that Henry would accept her accounting as true.

Gazing at the woolen square in Paxton's hand, Alana wondered how it had gotten here. Madoc had destroyed the tunic—at least he'd attempted to. The rain had started again, and he'd buried what he couldn't burn. Someone else had known the truth all along. But who?

"Alana!"

Her trance was broken. "What?"

"I asked how many times you stabbed him."

"I don't know—a dozen, maybe more."

He pressed his lips together. "I don't believe you."

He had to believe her, Alana thought. "Why not?"

"I saw the river when it was stirring with a force so great that it is hard to believe anyone could survive its current. You told me the water was far worse on the day Gilbert supposedly drowned. You said that you and Gilbert struggled but he was too strong. You say also that 'with effort' you pulled yourself from the river. Thus, it is not conceivable for you to have inflicted that many wounds on a man who was none the worse for wear."

Think.

"I waited until he was on his knees and pulling me over," she said, the answer coming to her in a trice. "'Twas then I struck at his faithless heart. He died at once, for he nearly fell atop me."

"What of the other wounds?"

"I wanted to make sure he was dead," Alana stated with conviction. "The bastard tried to kill me! What would you have done?"

Undoubtedly the same thing, Paxton concluded. But he still didn't accept her story. At least not the part about her having killed Gilbert.

He kept picturing the water and how it swelled and dipped with raw fury. After pulling herself from the fierce current, she would have been far too weak to manage so much as a scratch against Gilbert.

Yet fear and the need for self-preservation could in itself muster energies that no one thought existed.

Nay.

She was covering for Rhys. He was certain of it. And unless he could refute her claims, there was little he could do to help her.

Then he remembered something. "Tell me, Alana: If you killed Gilbert on this side of the river how did his body get on the other?"

She met his gaze squarely. "'Tis simple. I rolled him into the water. The current carried him downstream."

He hoped he could trip her up, but he'd failed. Damnation! Why was she doing this? Why would she risk her life for someone like Rhys? The man had disowned her for Christ sake!

Loyalty, he decided. It was the same kind of allegiance he would soon have to address in himself. He had to make a decision. He had no alternative. His oath had bound him to his king. And though he would attempt to defend her, plead that Alana's actions were justified, Paxton knew it would be Henry who decided whether Alana lived or, God forbid . . .

Died.

"Are you sure this is your sworn testimony to me—that it was you, and you alone, who killed Gilbert?"

"Aye. I swear it."

Paxton noticed that she didn't even blink. He stood there quietly, staring at her.

"What will you do with me?" she asked, the silence having stretched on for a time.

"'Tis not my choice, Alana."

"What do you mean? I thought you were overlord here. Doesn't that make you my judge?"

"I wish it did. Before I came here I swore an oath to Henry. If I learned that Gilbert had died by any other means than by drowning, if I became aware that you were involved, I pledged I would take you to my king just as he ordered me to do. Knowing that, are you still willing to swear you killed Gilbert?"

She pressed her jaw together and gazed up at him with eyes that appeared to be glazing with tears. "Aye," she said at last. "I still swear it."

"Then prepare yourself for your journey, Alana. Tomorrow, we leave for Chester."

"Chester! Why there?"

"Because that is where you'll face Henry and, unfortunately, your fate."

CHAPTER

20

Plains of Chester
July 1157

Alana was overwhelmed by the sight that lay before her.

The once vast, open plain was naught but a sea of tents. Smoke from a thousand campfires curled toward a cloudless, late afternoon sky, while an untold number of men moved about the encampment with serious intent.

It was obvious what was happening here. Even so Alana had to ask. From atop her gelding, she looked at Paxton, who rode beside her, and queried, "What is all this?"

Paxton didn't respond but stared straight ahead. His silence was in no way surprising to Alana. He'd been thus since they'd left the fortress in the pre-dawn hours that morning, well before her kinsmen had awakened. On their journey, he'd barely spoken to her, attending her little, if at all.

His deliberate coldness struck a sharp ache in her

breast. Had he plunged a knife into her heart, she doubted it would be anywhere near as painful.

With her confession, she knew their relationship would change. In fact, she expected to be subjected to the effects of his anger: a scathing rebuke, a harsh denouncement of her and her ilk, perhaps even a physical blow. But after his initial flare of rage, he'd displayed no emotion toward her whatsoever.

To her extreme anguish, he'd become glacial, distant. It was as though she no longer existed. Considering the uncertainties she faced, Alana felt lost, deserted, and completely alone.

Though she'd vowed from the first not to show any outward signs of fear, Alana had to admit that she was frightened by what might lie ahead. It would be gratifying to have someone whom she trusted and loved standing there beside her to offer his comfort and his strength.

That someone was Paxton.

Yet, because of his quick dismissal of her, Alana was well aware she'd have no such encouragement. She'd been left to fend for herself. Knowing as much, she questioned whether he ever cared about her at all.

Perhaps he did once, she conceded. But that was before he'd learned she'd murdered his friend.

The group of twenty riders, which, besides Paxton, herself, Sir Graham, and Father Jevon, included Gwenifer and Madoc—both having been apprised of the situation by Paxton, then sworn to secrecy, whereupon they insisted they come along to testify on Alana's behalf—were drawing ever closer to the encampment.

Scanning the wide area again, Alana was determined to have a response from Paxton. "Henry plans to invade Wales, doesn't he?" she blurted.

"Aye," Paxton stated, his tone clipped. "Soon he

and his knights, along with most of those you see before you, will ride against Owain Gwynedd to reclaim the territory that the Welsh prince has usurped from him. A victory should be Henry's in a matter of days."

Thinking Paxton was a bit overconfident in his assumption, she frowned at him. "If your king is foolish enough to believe the same as you've said, he is in for a rude awakening. Mark my words: In Owain Gwynedd he will meet his match." She again looked to the encampment that was now only a hundred yards away. "You knew from the start Henry was planning to invade my country, didn't you?"

"Aye. That is why Henry returned to England from Normandy. And that is why I knew to bring you here to face him."

While Alana held the reins to her gelding, Paxton had tied a leather lead to its bridle. His action stated that he didn't trust her to ride quietly. He expected her to bolt at any time. Just why he thought she'd be foolish enough to charge off into the wood, with so many to give chase—including him—she couldn't say. As he now slowed his destrier from a canter to a trot, then into an easy walk, he tugged on the lead, making certain she followed suit.

When they entered the camp and began making their way toward its center, Alana's senses were at once assailed by the delectable aroma of roasting meats and rich stews as they turned on their spits or simmered in their caldrons over the open fires for the untold suppers that would be served that night.

Her appetite had abandoned her after Paxton's accusations and her erroneous confession, and she'd had nothing to eat since well before noontide yesterday. And that was only a small nibble of cheese.

In objection to her self-imposed fast, her stomach

grumbled loudly; her mouth watered almost painfully. But by the heaviness in her chest that dipped deep
into her belly, Alana doubted she'd eat much, if
anything at all, on this day either.

A woman's playful squeal rose into the air. Alana
turned toward the sound. A plump wench was
sprawled across a soldier's lap, his hand working its
way beneath her skirts.

Alana wasn't surprised by the sight, for wherever
such a large army had amassed, there were the ever-
present camp followers.

Though sometimes wives or entire families, who
desired to be near their husbands or fathers, were
among them, ofttimes the largest following were wom-
en of questionable reputation.

Besides the one she'd thus far spied, Alana saw
there were several other women making bawdy advances toward a like number of soldiers. A few were
attempting to entice an entire group. In all cases, the
men appeared more than eager to pay a coin for the
slatterns' services.

A particularly attractive young woman, who was
indeed the exception to the others in both her looks
and in her cleanliness, had caught Alana's attention,
mainly because she'd just been swept up into the arms
of a handsome knight and carried into his tent. The
flap closed with haste behind them.

Alana wondered if Paxton, when finding himself in
similar circumstances—far from home and prior to a
battle—had ever eased his needs by way of a camp
whore. More to the point, would he have the same
inclination since he was married?

The thought that he might be unfaithful, bedding
one woman after another with delightful ease, upset
her terribly. But, then, if Henry were to exact punishment on her to the fullest degree, which was Alana's

greatest fear, he'd be free to do whatever he wanted, whenever he pleased. It would, after all, be rather difficult for her to make protest about his actions from the grave.

Alana sighed. Fretting over Paxton's past and future actions seemed rather fruitless. It was probable her husband believed he could do whatever he chose, here and now. For any obligation he might have felt toward her as his wife, as well as any hope that he would one day love her the same way she loved him, had surely disintegrated the instant she confessed to killing Gilbert.

A deceitful, murdering bitch—that was how he no doubt saw her. That was why he'd become so cold, so distant. He could no longer abide being near her.

Alana didn't blame him for feeling as he did. Were their situations reversed, she'd most likely react in much the same manner. From the start, she knew her world would come tumbling down around her. The truth always had a way of making itself known. With Paxton hating her as he did, Alana could genuinely say she cared little if she lived or if she died, the latter being a strong possibility, depending on Henry's mood.

The gelding came to a halt beneath her. Emerging from her thoughts, Alana saw they had weaved their way to a less populated area of the camp. She looked at Paxton whose gaze was fixed on an area just past her. Sir Graham had urged his horse up alongside her, where he'd reined in. She now sat between the two men.

Paxton had refused to acknowledge her. Not even so much as a furtive glance came her way. Alana's misery increased. More and more she felt the outcast. Her dejection deepened. Then she heard Paxton say to

Graham, "Watch her. If she vanishes into this tangle of tents and bodies, we'll never find her."

At his words, something sparked inside her, which surprised Alana. Locked in her gloom, she thought sadness was the only emotion she could feel. She was wrong. That he would assume she was bent on running had nettled her, for in effect he was calling her a coward.

If her original intent was to escape facing Henry on a charge of murder, she would have cast the blame on Rhys, on her cousins, on anyone who might have seemed a worthwhile suspect. She certainly wouldn't have incriminated herself by confessing to killing Gilbert.

"You malign me, sir," she said, her eyes narrowing on Paxton. "I have no fear of confronting Henry, hence there is no reason for me to run."

His icy blue gaze raked over her. "A fool's words, fraught with bravado," he returned. "Had you an ounce of sense, woman, you'd fear facing him, as you damned well should." He attended Sir Graham. "Keep an eye on her, just in case she suddenly regains her wits and tries to flee. I shall soon return."

Alana stared after Paxton as he rode off through the camp. Once he disappeared behind some tents, she looked at Gwenifer, who had guided her gelding to the spot where Paxton's destrier once stood.

"Why is he being so cruel to you?" her cousin asked.

"The obvious reason is my admission to felling Gilbert. Beyond that, Gwenifer, I imagine he now rues the day he ever married me."

Quick to dismount so that Gwenifer would not see the tears that had gathered in her eyes, Alana wished she could claim the same about Paxton.

Unfortunately, she could not.

* * *

A fiery rage roiled inside Paxton unlike any he'd ever known. It was contained only by the mantle of ice encrusting him.

Alana's deceit was the spark that set the emotion aflame; her continued lies simply added more fuel. But the main source of his fury was the damnable oath he'd taken.

God's wounds! Why had he ever made such a vow?

Before him sat the large tent that bore Henry's banner. He reined his destrier to a halt a few yards from it, but instead of dismounting, he kept to the saddle and stared at the canvas monstrosity, pondering what course he should take.

Paxton believed Alana when she'd said Gilbert had shoved her into the river. She was lying, however, about having killed Gilbert herself. The true culprits were Rhys and possibly his sons. Paxton was sure of it. The problem was how to convince Henry of these things without drawing suspicion of a conspiracy.

Alana's false claim that Gilbert had drowned made her a willing accomplice. The other strike against her was a solid reason as to why Gilbert would want her dead. Unless she could provide such a motive—one more fitting than she *imagined* her late husband hated her—Paxton feared Henry would dismiss her testimony as to Gilbert's treachery. Instead his king might see her as a faithless wife who contrived to murder her husband. The results would prove disastrous. Alana would undoubtedly be hanged.

His oath.

Paxton knew he was bound by it. Yet of those who owed their allegiance to Henry and had made the trip to the Chester plains, only Graham knew about Alana's confession. He could ask his friend to forget what was told him. Certain Graham would comply,

Paxton could then return to the fortress with Alana, where together they'd begin their life anew.

Maybe.

There was the subject of trust, which now stood between them. She'd deceived him from the start about Gilbert, had played with his emotions, and had finally convinced him that her late husband had drowned.

She also had run from him on the day of their wedding, intending to go much farther than the ringwork if she could. He understood now it was because she feared he'd discover the truth: Gilbert was murdered.

Yet Paxton couldn't help but wonder if the affection she'd shown him during all those wondrous days and nights that she'd spent in his arms and in his bed was no more than a ruse actuated so as to keep him off guard until she could flee him again. The possibility was strong, but was it realistic? Was he discrediting her simply because he feared it was true?

Even if the matter of trust could be resolved, there was this affair with the tattered scrap of tunic. Somebody other than one of those whom he suspected were the actual five players in this macabre event was also aware that Gilbert had been murdered. Whoever had placed the evidence on his bed wanted to make certain Alana's duplicity was exposed. Considering that, Paxton doubted the person would rest until Henry also knew about Alana's lies.

Who could it be?

One of his own soldiers who had previously been afraid to come forward? One of Alana's kinsmen who was still angered by their marriage?

Madoc?

Gwenifer?

Aldwyn?

But what would be their purpose?

"Well, well, well. If it isn't Paxton de Beaumont. I thought I saw you ride in alongside the Welsh whore. What brings you here from the back of beyond?"

Recognizing the voice, Paxton looked at its source. "So, the snake has slithered from his hole," he commented, his gaze narrowing on Sir Goddard. Of all people, the knight was the last he wanted to see. "I shall inform Henry that Chester Castle needs sturdier locks on the cells in its dungeon."

"Don't bother," the man said. "'Twas Henry who set me free."

"A momentary lapse, I'm sure," Paxton said as he dismounted.

Sir Goddard blocked Paxton's path and sneered in his face. "You didn't have the authority nor the power to keep me imprisoned."

"It was always Henry's choice as to what happened to you. 'Twill be my choice, however, if you continue to stand in my way. Move aside before I lose my temper. You felt the effects of it once—or was it twice?" Paxton frowned. "Nay, I believe it was at least a half dozen times my fist met your face, all totaled. If you don't want it to do so again, I suggest you make haste and depart."

Sir Goddard stepped from Paxton's path. "Whatever the great overlord wishes," he jeered.

Already leading his destrier toward the tent, Paxton paid the man's parting words little heed. He handed the reins off to one of the sentries, while he announced himself to another. The man ducked beneath the open flap into the tent. A bit later, he returned, bidding Paxton entry.

He hesitated.

Should he or shouldn't he?

He thought of his oath, then of Alana. He clenched his jaw as his gut twisted. Like it or not, he had no option but to comply.

Paxton stepped into the tent.

"Why won't you tell him the truth?"

Alana stopped her pacing inside the tent where she was held prisoner and turned to look at Madoc. It was the first time they had been alone together and able to speak freely since they had left the fortress.

In the hour since she'd last seen Paxton, a cart had arrived at their location inside the camp. Three tents were delivered, along with some pallets, compliments of Henry. The canvas structures—a small one for Gwenifer; a large one for Paxton's men, including Madoc and Father Jevon; a medium-size one for her, and she presumed for Paxton—were quickly erected and set in order. Alana was immediately placed inside her tent, a guard posted just outside.

"Why won't I tell him the truth? Because, Madoc, I will not allow anyone else to face Henry but me," she said.

"Why?"

"If I claim I acted in self-defense, I have a better chance of receiving clemency. I will tell Henry everything that actually transpired, up to a point, but I will not bring Rhys and my cousins into this. The more people Henry finds are involved, the more likely he'll think it was a conspiracy against his vassal."

"You're risking much, girl," Madoc said. "If you don't want to name the ones who really killed the bastard, at least tell Gilbert's king it was me. I've lived my life. 'Twould be a waste if you were hanged. You're too young."

Alana was moved by his offer. He had served her well over the years, just as he had done with her father. No one could be more loyal than Madoc. But she'd not allow him to stand in her place. "And what reason will you give for slaying Gilbert?" she asked.

"I could say I was defending you."

"That would mean you were also at the river the day Gilbert died. I'm sure Henry will question why Gilbert would try to slay me in front of a witness. Suppose Henry asks you what your feelings were toward Gilbert—what will you say?"

Madoc sneered. "You know I despised him."

"Yes, but will you tell Henry that? If you do, your fate will be sealed. Again Henry will take your words as proof of a conspiracy against his vassal. And if you lie, saying you respected Gilbert, your testimony will be refuted.

"Henry is said to be most cunning, and your temper, Madoc, tends to erupt with ease. You couldn't possibly hold your tongue on how you feel about those who seek to take our land from us. You hate all Normans and you hate their Angevin king. Henry's own temper is renowned. Once you have expressed yourself, as I'm certain you will, he'll probably kill you then and there.

"Nay, Madoc, I will not let you perjure yourself. I am the one who must face him. And I shall do it alone."

And alone she'd be, for she doubted Paxton would speak on her behalf.

Oh, why had he come into her life? She'd never felt such pain as this before, loving him as she did, knowing he didn't feel the same. The ache in her breast was unbearable. Would it never end?

Only with her death, she surmised.

She heard voices outside the tent. The flap lifted, and Paxton stepped inside. He glanced her way, then his gaze settled on Madoc. "Leave us, please," he said.

His tone was somber, and Alana felt a trickle of fear run through her.

"You can't allow this to go forth," Madoc declared, his eyes narrowing on Paxton. "She—"

"Madoc!" Alana admonished, certain he was about to tell all. "Leave us, as my husband has asked."

"Nay," Paxton declared. "What were you about to say, Madoc?"

With her eyes, Alana pleaded with her servant not to divulge anything that would betray her. His lips pressed tightly together, Madoc presented her with a hard stare in return.

"'Tis nothing," Madoc announced, then turning on his heel, he stomped from the tent.

"Did you wish to speak to me about something?" Alana asked, once she and Paxton were alone.

"I have just come from seeing Henry. I am to take you to him shortly."

The declaration triggered a sense of alarm inside her; Alana quashed the feeling, knowing she had to remain calm. "And what was his reaction when you told him I confessed to killing Gilbert?"

"He wasn't surprised by the admission, but he wasn't pleased by it, either."

"Are you saying he was angry?"

"I've seen him angrier." Paxton cocked his head and studied her. "You said you weren't afraid to face him. If that's true, why the concern over his mood?"

Alana's heart was starting to race, her trepidation rising anew. "I'm not afraid of facing him," she stated. Maybe if she kept saying the same aloud, she'd soon convince herself it was so. Then maybe not. "I simply wanted to know what I'm up against."

"Being hanged," Paxton said flatly.

She stared at him. Hearing his declaration made the possibility seem more real. She swallowed what she thought was her heart. "You doubt he will believe my story."

"Since it is a lie, you can be assured he won't believe it."

"'Tis not a lie!" Alana insisted.

Paxton was on her in a trice. He grabbed her arms, pulling her to him. "Your persistence in perpetuating this falsehood is naught but foolishness, Alana," he said, his hard gaze boring into her. "Your life is at risk. Or are you too dim-witted to understand that?"

"Do you care?"

Her question took him unawares. "What?"

"Do you care if I live or die?"

"What nonsense is this?" he asked, still stunned. "Certainly I care. The last thing I want is for you to die."

"Why?"

His frown deepened. "Because you've done nothing that warrants your being hanged."

It wasn't the reply she'd hoped would come. And though she chanced hearing the words that would devastate her completely, Alana had to know. "What about us, Paxton? What if Henry decides to show me leniency, will you still want me as your wife?"

"Our vows stated 'until death do us part.' And thus it shall be."

"That's not an answer," she snapped. "I want to know if you'll ever forgive me for playing you false about Gilbert's drowning. Will there ever be affection between us again?"

His gaze skimmed her face. "In all honesty, I don't know. The trust has been broken. Whether it can be repaired remains to be seen."

Alana's heart sank. Why was she doing this to herself? In all likelihood, she was going to be gibbeted.

Did she have some perverse desire to torture herself all the more?

"I do know, Alana, if you don't tell the truth, there won't ever be the chance for you to see what the future holds for us."

There was still hope, she supposed, for he hadn't closed the door on their future. But the inflection in his voice didn't sound promising. Maybe it was because he held more certainty about her fate than she did. "You want me to say Rhys killed Gilbert, is that it?"

"Only because it's true."

"Suppose I told Henry my uncle killed Gilbert . . . that he did so to avenge the attempt on my own life—are you able to assure me that Henry will not see it as a conspiracy, especially since I, being in full possession of my senses, lied to him, telling him that Gilbert had drowned?"

"I cannot give you such an assurance."

"Why?"

"Because you have yet to present a motive as to why Gilbert would want you dead."

Alana knew that. She just needed confirmation. "Then the truth is as I told you: I killed Gilbert."

Clenching his jaw, Paxton shut his eyes. When he opened them again, he released her. "'Twill be as you've said." He strode to the entry. "Come, Alana." He motioned to her while lifting the flap. "Henry awaits you."

CHAPTER
21

Paxton was livid. And with good reason.

When he and Alana had entered Henry's tent, they had come face-to-face with Sir Goddard. The knight had been summoned by Henry to give testimony about Gilbert's death, and Alana had been instructed by Henry to wait outside, with the explanation that she would be called directly. Under guard, she'd complied.

To Paxton, it seemed strange that she couldn't face her accuser—which he knew was exactly what Sir Goddard would be—so that she could disprove whatever was said in error. Though his wife wasn't being given the chance to defend herself, Paxton decided he'd act in her stead.

"Are you able to give me an idea what Sir Gilbert and the Lady Alana's relationship was like?" Henry asked the knight, who stood beside Paxton, both men facing their king.

304

"Aye," Sir Goddard replied, "I can tell you about Sir Gilbert's relationship with his wife. 'Twas not pleasant. She was a veritable shrew, constantly nagging at him. They always argued, mainly because she instigated the row. Considering his lot in life, Sir Gilbert tried valiantly to keep the peace between them. He was most patient with her. I never saw him raise his hand to her—not once. Had she been my wife, I wouldn't have been so kind."

Paxton's gut twisted on hearing those words. He doubted any of it was true. But how could he refute the knight's claims? He had no firsthand knowledge as to what had actually transpired between Alana and Gilbert to give testimony to the contrary. But there was one thing he had witnessed.

"Sire," he said, intervening, "this evidence comes from a man who is naught but a slovenly drunk, lax in his duty as a knight. He has spoken most vilely of the Lady Alana since I first met him, mainly because she is Welsh. And I am able to attest that he tried to defile the Lady Alana. I pulled him off her myself, then exiled him to Chester Castle to await trial and sentence for his misdeeds. This man's testimony is no doubt fraught with lies."

Henry's gaze snared Sir Goddard. "What have you to say to Sir Paxton's charge that you attempted to rape his wife?"

"His wife?" Sir Goddard asked. "She wasn't his wife at the time. And I didn't attempt to rape her. 'Twas the other way around. The slut tried to seduce me."

Paxton's restraint snapped. He grabbed Sir Goddard by the tunic, his fist raised. "You lying bastard," he said between clenched teeth. "'Twas rape and you know it."

"Cease!" Henry shouted. "Release him, Sir Paxton —now!"

Paxton's fingers uncurled from Sir Goddard's tunic. He shoved the man from him. "He lies, sire," Paxton said, again attending Henry.

Henry raised his chin. "Your testimony, Sir Goddard, is suspect. I know Sir Paxton. He is a man of honor. If he says you attempted to rape the woman who is now his wife, I believe him. You were released from the dungeon at Chester Castle because I am in need of knights to ride with me against Owain Gwynedd. You will still do so. But if you manage to survive the battle, I will see that you are punished for your offense. And do not think to flee, sir, for you will be guarded even on the field of battle. Is that clear?"

"Aye," Sir Goddard grumbled.

Henry turned to Paxton. "You honored your oath to me and brought me word that the Lady Alana confessed to killing her late husband, albeit as she claims in self-defense. She will stand before me soon. What I am trying to acquire here is an understanding of Gilbert's and her relationship, along with the events leading up to his death. So unless you have personal knowledge of these things, I ask that you not speak. Your wife will have the opportunity to defend herself. I am interested in justice, not revenge, Sir Paxton. Remember that."

"Aye, sire," Paxton said, knowing Alana's fate was questionable. Once all was said and done, he hoped his king would be not only just but merciful as well.

"Sir Goddard," Henry addressed him, "I want you to tell me of the day Sir Gilbert died. Do so without embellishment, without slurs, without commentary as to what you *think* may have happened. Tell me only what you actually saw and heard."

The knight relayed the information according to

Henry's wishes, telling how Alana and Gilbert had left that morning, how Alana returned that night alone, how they searched for his body at the river without result, and how the next day they found Gilbert a mile downstream.

"Did you see any blood on his tunic, any sign he'd been stabbed?" Henry asked.

"Nay—only mud and grass stains. But we weren't looking for signs of treachery. We were told he'd drowned."

"And what was the Lady Alana's response when you brought the body back to the fortress?"

"She cried and carried on as though she were grief-stricken. She insisted on preparing the body herself—she and her servant, Madoc. Afterward, Sir Gilbert was buried."

Madoc, Paxton thought. Naturally he would have been with Alana when Gilbert's body was prepared. He knew exactly how Gilbert had died and by whose hand. But getting the man to tell everything that had transpired would be next to impossible. Madoc was far too loyal to his mistress.

Even if he could convince Madoc to reveal the truth, were the man to go before Henry, his temper might erupt and his distaste for Gilbert, for Paxton, for any man who sought to conquer his homeland could be exposed. In such an event, his testimony would prove more of a hindrance than a help to Alana.

"Sir Paxton?"

"Sire?"

"Is this Madoc fellow also in your company?"

"Aye, sire. As is the Lady Alana's cousin, Gwenifer."

"'Twould be good if I spoke to them also," Henry said.

Just then a messenger strode into the tent. Henry beckoned the man forward, whereupon he whispered in Henry's ear. Henry nodded as the man stood aside.

"I fear something of great import has come to my attention. My undertaking against Owain Gwynedd is my first concern, so I must end my questioning for this day. I will summon you and the Lady Alana on the morrow, Sir Paxton. Along with you, I want to see this Madoc and Gwenifer as well. Now good eventide."

"The same to you, sire," Paxton said, bowing. He turned and exited the tent.

"Does Henry wish to see me now?" Alana questioned.

"Nay." Paxton noticed the sun was close to setting. "An important matter has claimed his attention. He will summon us tomorrow."

Sir Goddard came from the tent; Alana stiffened when she saw him. Protectively, Paxton placed his body between the knight and his wife.

"I always knew you killed him," Sir Goddard declared. "You'll soon get your comeuppance. I hope Henry gibbets you, then pikes your head. 'Tis what you and all your kind deserve."

His comments made, the knight strode off into the camp.

"I cannot imagine why Henry would free such a vile man," Alana said when Paxton again faced her.

He nodded at her guards, then took Alana's arm and began guiding her toward their tent. "He's in need of knights to fight against your countrymen."

"Your king must be desperate indeed. With the likes of Sir Goddard at his side, 'tis certain he will not succeed. Owain Gwynedd will be the victor, just wait and see."

Her damnable Welsh pride, Paxton thought, his anger rising. He saw they were a half-dozen yards from their tent. With effort he held his tongue until they were inside, whereupon he spun her around and gripped her shoulders. "Henry's quarrel with the Welsh prince should be the last thing that's on your mind. When will you get it through that thick head of yours that you're going to be hanged! Is that what you want? To die for another's crime?"

"'Tis not another's crime," she insisted. "'Tis mine."

The rage he was holding inside was near to erupting. "Always loyal to your kin, aren't you? What about me, Alana? I'm your husband. Your allegiance belongs to me, first, last, and always. And it belongs to our child."

"Child?" she asked, startled.

"Aye. Did you ever think that you may have conceived? We did make love, you know. And quite frequently. Therefore the possibility does exist."

Surprise still lit her face. "I'd been disappointed so many times with Gil—well, I hadn't thought . . . I'm barren. There is no child," she said with certainty.

"You don't know that," Paxton countered. "You withhold the truth, believing that you're protecting Rhys and his sons, when in reality you're being selfish. You didn't kill Gilbert, but you'll be killing my heir if you continue with this pretense."

"Nay," she said on a moan. "I cannot conceive."

In the dim light within the tent, he saw tears glistening in her eyes. "'Twas Gilbert who could not sire a child. *I* can. Think about it, Alana. Think about all those long nights we spent in each other's arms. Remember the ecstasy we shared. Besides our child, do you want the pleasure of our lovemaking to be lost to you as well?"

"I don't want to lose any of it," she whimpered.

"Then why do you persist with the lie?"

"You don't understand."

"No, I don't. Explain."

"'Tis because Henry might think that we all conspired against Gilbert. Not just Rhys, Dylan, Meredydd, and Caradog, but everyone at the ringwork, everyone at the fortress. You saw the army that is here. What is to say Henry won't send a portion of his warriors to destroy all my kin? Why should so many die when one can stand in their place?"

If he could only get her to confess to Henry that she hadn't been the one to wield the knife; swear also that she was unaware of Gilbert's death until after the fact, his king might see fit to show her clemency.

"So, you do admit that Rhys and his sons are the culprits," he declared.

"Nay! I killed Gilbert."

Paxton wanted to shake her until her teeth rattled. "You stubborn little fool. The scenario I see is far different from the one you're trying to paint."

"What do you mean?"

"I mean, Alana, I recall how you ran to your uncle on the day we made love in the glade. I imagine you did the same the day Gilbert died. I see you pulling yourself from the river, crossing the once existing footbridge that Sir Goddard told me about. Somehow you made the lengthy journey to the ringwork, maybe with the aid of one of the ever-present watchers who are stationed throughout the wood. When Rhys learned of Gilbert's duplicity, he and his sons set out to find your faithless husband in order to avenge the attempt on your life. He accomplished the feat, too, didn't he?"

Her eyes widened before she shook her head in denial.

"Didn't he?" he persisted, shaking her at last.

"Yes!" she confessed. "But if you tell Henry such, I shall say you are the liar."

His frustration had met its limits. "You still insist on dying for the greater good of all, do you?" Though the light was dimming, he noted how she obstinately lifted her chin. "Then here is a memory you may take to the grave with you. When the noose is tightened around your neck I want you to know exactly what you'll be losing forever."

Paxton pulled her to him; his mouth covered hers in a hard, angry kiss. The rage inside him was barely leashed. He'd be damned if she'd die before he had her one last time.

His tongue plunged between her lips as he cupped one breast and kneaded it. He thought she would fight him. Instead he heard her moan. She was kissing him. The passion inside her at least equalled his, if not surpassing it altogether.

Drawing back, he helped her strip from her clothing. His own followed. Then sweeping her up into his arms, he carried her to the large pallet that had been sent with the tent.

He laid her on the rough bedding and settled his knees between her outstretched thighs. "Remember what you're losing, Alana," he said, his fingers priming her.

Then he was inside her, his hips moving. Each thrust went deeper and deeper; she matched his rhythm, eagerly.

He lifted her hips, bringing her closer. "Remember," he whispered before his lips again met hers in a heated kiss.

The fire and fury inside him conjoined. His blood seared through his veins. Alana arched beneath him, her spasms of ecstasy enticing him. *Damn her for wanting to leave him.* The thought streamed through his mind as his whole body jolted with his climax.

His heart still thundering in his ears, Paxton rolled away from her. He lay there, his eyes searching through the shadows to stare at the canvas ceiling. Not a word was said, and Alana soon turned her back to him. Paxton felt the heaviness in his chest grow even more cumbersome.

Anger and desperation had driven him to take her the way he had—hard and fast. He doubted he'd hurt her—at least not physically. Emotionally? He didn't know.

What did it matter? She was bent on destroying herself, destroying their future, destroying their child, if she had conceived. Foolishly, she refused to have it any other way.

Weary of thinking, Paxton allowed his mind to go blank, but after a while, he began to wonder if Alana's strategy might not be the best one after all. If she admitted that Rhys and her cousins killed Gilbert, Henry may indeed see it as a conspiracy. If she claimed self-defense, Henry might in fact believe her and show leniency.

But what was Gilbert's motive for wanting her dead?

Sir Goddard had described Alana's and Gilbert's marriage as an unhappy one, but not from lack of Gilbert's trying. It was Alana the knight blamed for the misery the couple shared. Though Paxton had been able to discredit the knight, he knew if the testimony that was yet to come from Madoc and Gwenifer showed a similar pattern of discontent, Henry may see the killing as an act of a disagreeable wife who wanted her husband dead.

Growing restless, Paxton raised up from the pallet.

He leaned over to view Alana. Her eyes were closed, soft sounds of slumber whispering through her lips. Rising, he donned his braies, then snatching his tunic from the ground, he covered Alana's naked form. Next he crept, barefooted, from the tent.

The chilly night air washed over him. Paxton drew several cleansing breaths. On releasing the last, he hunkered down beside the entry of the tent to idly pluck at the grass.

The scrap of tunic, which now was in Henry's hands—who placed it on the bed, and why?

Paxton searched his mind for an answer. Not a name came to him. Then he pondered Gilbert and men in general.

Why would a man want to kill his wife? Because he hated her, as Alana had suggested? Or, which Paxton saw as the more likely choice, because of another woman?

Was that Gilbert's intent: He wanted Alana dead, so he could marry someone else?

Gwenifer, perhaps?

From all he'd gleaned, Paxton knew the pair was quite friendly. Likewise, he doubted she was a virgin. Could Gilbert and Gwenifer have been carrying on an affair behind Alana's back? Did they scheme to kill Alana together? A possibility, Paxton decided. But to prove such was another matter entirely.

Conjecture was not hard evidence. If he accused Gwenifer, she'd deny the charge. Without tangible verification, Paxton couldn't show she was lying. Besides, considering the minor argument he and Alana had over whether or not Gwenifer was chaste, Alana would probably side with her cousin, insisting there was naught but friendship between the pair.

Paxton found he was back where he'd started.

Staring across the way at an unattended campfire, he felt his frustration rising anew. His mind again a blank, he watched as a man stumbled into view.

The newcomer was aimed at the campfire. He paused to drink deeply from a skin of wine. Wiping his mouth on his sleeve, the man continued on, then plopped onto the ground before the fire, his back to Paxton. He drank from the skin again. Lowering the container, he weaved a little, then seemed to nod. He jerked himself awake.

Drunk, no doubt, Paxton thought as he started to look away. A shriek caught his ear. He looked to the campfire anew. Paxton bounded to his feet and ran toward the man who had set himself afire.

Instead of dropping to the ground and rolling to extinguish the flames, the man was spinning round and round, his horrendous screams filling the air.

The sound drew others from their tents. Several onlookers ducked back inside, then reappeared with blankets in hand.

By the time Paxton reached the hapless man, he was totally engulfed—a human torch! Knowing it was the same death Rhys had meant for him, Paxton shuddered.

Water from a bucket was tossed onto the flames; Paxton grabbed a blanket from a stunned bystander's hand. He charged forth, knocking the man to the ground, then snuffed the remaining fire, but he feared it was far too late.

Pulling the blanket away, Paxton almost retched at the stench of burned flesh. Holding his breath, he eased the man onto his back. The sight was indeed grisly. Suddenly Paxton realized he knew the man. The near-lifeless eyes that stared back at him belonged to Sir Goddard. Mercifully came the death rattle. The knight would suffer no more.

Paxton spread the blanket over Sir Goddard, covering him from head to toe. He came to his feet. Though he'd never wished that sort of death on anyone, it was apparent to Paxton that Sir Goddard, for all his maliciousness toward others, had in fact received his due.

He turned away and headed toward his tent, desperately needing the comfort of Alana's arms.

It was late afternoon of the next day, and Alana stood listening to Madoc's testimony as it was given to Henry. Gwenifer was beside her. Father Jevon and Sir Graham were also in the tent, while Paxton was situated only a few feet behind her.

Last night, after he'd taken her to the pallet, their passions erupting hot and fast, he'd left her, thinking that she slept. On his return, he'd come to her, his body shaking. Not until this morning had he told her what he'd witnessed, explaining Sir Goddard was dead.

He held the horror inside, telling her only that he wanted her. The second time his lovemaking was tender and caring yet there was a fervor in his kisses and caresses that said he desired her like no other. Still, he never said the words she so wanted to hear. Much to her regret, Alana supposed she never would.

Drifting from her memories to the present, she heard Henry ask of Madoc, "Did your mistress and Sir Gilbert argue?"

"Sometimes."

"Who instigated the argument?"

"Why Sir Gilbert did. He was always cold and critical of my mistress. No matter what she tried to do to please him it wasn't good enough. A body can take only so much. Then they have to defend themselves."

"Did Sir Gilbert ever raise his hand to his wife?"

"I saw him do so once."

"Did he strike her?"

"Nay," Madoc admitted. "He just got that hard look in his eyes, lowered his hand, and walked away."

"There were no children from this marriage, correct?" Henry asked.

"Nay," Madoc answered.

"Do you know if they shared a bed?"

"'Tis a rather personal question to be asking," Madoc said with a frown.

"I'm trying to establish if the Lady Alana refused her late husband his conjugal rights," Henry returned.

"'Tis still personal."

"Answer anyway," Henry stated.

"They didn't sleep together, but he went to her often enough. He wasn't with her long, but it was long enough to ease himself."

"And what is your opinion of Sir Gilbert, Madoc? Did you respect him?"

"Had he treated my mistress better, I might have. But he was rude to her. 'Tis hard to respect a man who treats his wife that way."

Henry crossed his arms over his chest and rolled back on his heels. "What do you think of Normans, sir?"

Alana held her breath.

"I try not to think about them at all," Madoc replied.

"When you do, what crosses your mind?" Henry countered.

"'Tis not polite to state the words in mixed company," Madoc responded. "Therefore I won't say."

"Spoken like a true Welshman," Henry stated.

"That's what I am. And proud of it."

"I believe you, sir," Henry said. "Tell me about the day Gilbert FitzWilliam died."

"The heavy rain we'd been experiencing for several days straight had stopped, and Sir Gilbert asked my mistress to take a walk with him. 'Twas early morning when they left the fortress. The next I saw her was that night when she returned alone."

"Did she say anything to you about what had transpired?"

"That Gilbert had shoved her into the river."

A half-truth, Alana thought, knowing she'd said far more than what was just reported. Madoc was hedging.

"She didn't say she killed him?"

"Nay," Madoc said, truthfully.

"Who prepared the body once it was taken from the river?"

"My mistress and I."

"Then you saw the wounds?"

"Aye."

"Did she say she killed him then?" Henry asked.

"Nay."

"Didn't you ask?"

"Nay."

"Seems strange that you would see the injuries and not inquire about them."

"Maybe to you. My responsibility is to serve her, not to question her. The bastard got what he deserved for trying to kill her. I helped clean him, dress him, and bury him. That's the way it was."

"Perhaps," Henry said. "Then perhaps not. You may stand aside, Madoc." His gaze shifted. "Alana of Llangollen, please step forward."

Though she tried not to show it outwardly, inside Alana was trembling. She moved to stand before Paxton's king, whereupon she curtsied. Afterward, she looked him square in the eyes.

"Your confession has been given to me by Sir

Paxton. As I understand it, you admit to killing Gilbert FitzWilliam, my knight and vassal, in an act of self-defense, is that correct?"

"Aye."

"Tell me exactly what occurred."

Alana told Henry the story, which was half-truth, half-fabrication, making certain she didn't vary from the accounting she'd given Paxton: Gilbert had attempted to shove her into the river, they struggled, she eventually lost the fight and fell to tumble through the water. By luck, she caught hold of a limb and pulled herself onto the bank. "When I heard him coming, I feared he'd toss me into the water again. I sought my knife, then waited. He turned me over and that's when I struck at him. Afterward, I rolled him into the water."

"Why the pretense of drowning?" Henry asked, his gaze hard upon her. "If he made an attempt on your life, there seems little reason for you to lie."

"I am Welsh. Because of it, I feared you would not believe my report of the events, even though it was true."

"Why did you marry Gilbert FitzWilliam in the first place?" Henry asked.

"I had hoped the marriage would bring peace to my kinsmen."

"It had nothing to do with your desire to retain control of the land on which the fortress is built?"

Alana frowned at him. Did he think she killed Gilbert in greed?

"I am aware that your father, Rhodri ap Daffyd, claimed the land," Henry said when she didn't respond immediately. "On his death, it became part of your inheritance. When you married Gilbert did you hope to keep control of your legacy through him?"

"I cannot deny that I wanted to secure my inheritance for my children, who would be half-Norman, half-Welsh."

"So in effect, you married him for selfish reasons," Henry stated. "Except you did not bear Gilbert children, did you?"

"No, I did not."

"You did not refuse him his conjugal rights, then?"

"No, I did not."

"Did you love Gilbert?"

Alana stared at Henry. "No, I did not."

"Why do you think Gilbert would try to kill you?"

"Because he despised me," she said.

"Did he ever say such to you?"

"Nay, but his actions were most revealing. He showed me no warmth nor did he grant me any respect."

"Did he ever strike you?"

"Nay."

"Do you hold a natural malice toward my Norman knights?"

"I married another of your vassals, didn't I?"

"Only because I decreed it, right?"

"Aye," Alana said, knowing at the time it was true.

Henry examined her intently. "You may stand aside," he declared.

Gwenifer was called next.

As Alana passed her cousin on her return to the spot where she once stood, Gwenifer seemed unable to look her in the eyes. Alana believed that Gwenifer was simply nervous.

Turning to face Henry, Alana felt Paxton move closer to her. From behind her, he reached out, caught her hand, and squeezed it, offering his reassurance. The action was welcomed by Alana, for it meant he cared.

"Maid Gwenifer," Henry addressed her after she

curtsied, "you are summoned before me to give testimony. In whatever you say, I will expect you to speak true. Do I have your word to this?"

"You have my word."

"Do you live at the fortress with your cousin?"

"Nay, but I visit her on occasion. I was there when Gilbert died."

"Then you know of the mood of their relationship just before his death, correct?"

"I saw and heard things, yes."

"Was Gilbert cruel to your cousin?"

"Not cruel, nay."

"Was he purposely rude to her?"

"Their relationship was strained, but 'purposely rude'? Nay, not that I noticed."

Henry scrutinized Gwenifer. "Did they argue?"

Gwenifer chewed at her lower lip.

"Answer me with the truth. Did they argue?" he repeated.

"Alana became short with him."

"When?"

Again Gwenifer hesitated.

"When?" Henry inquired anew.

"On the eve of Gilbert's death."

"Do you recall why your cousin became angry with her husband?"

"Nay."

"Do you recall anything that was said?" Henry asked.

Alana had forgotten that she and Gilbert had argued. In fact, she'd even forgotten what may have passed from her lips. She attended Gwenifer carefully, wondering what she would tell Henry.

Gwenifer again gnawed at her lip. "'Twas said only in the heat of the moment," she blurted. "I'm sure Alana didn't mean it."

"What was said, Maid Gwenifer?"

Silence.

"What was said?" Henry barked.

Gwenifer jumped at the sharpness in his voice. "Alana said she rued the day she had married Gilbert. She said his death would be a relief. I'm sure she didn't mean it. 'Twas only words."

The incident came flooding in on Alana. She and Gilbert were in the hall. He'd made some hateful comment about her being barren—that she was useless to him, and as a woman, she was unappealing.

Alana had countered with the statement that she rued the day she married him. Told him his attempts at lovemaking were laughably inept, stated that he made her skin crawl whenever he was near, announced that his death would be a relief, for it would assure that he'd never touch her again. She said these things even though he'd not approached her for months on end.

Gilbert's reply was that she'd not have to worry about his coming to her ever again. His plan to kill her was probably already set in his mind.

Though she recalled all this, she didn't remember Gwenifer being anywhere near to hear either Gilbert's or her words. But then their voices might have carried through the large room. Others may have heard them as well.

At the same time these memories streamed forth, Alana felt Paxton's hand withdraw from hers. In effect he had deserted her on Gwenifer's declaration. Did he now believe that she killed Gilbert, her heart filled with hatred and malevolence? Did he think her claim that Gilbert had first made an attempt on her life was naught but a ruse?

Alana refused to turn and look into his eyes, for fear that the answer to both her silent questions would show in the affirmative. The coldness in his gaze would destroy her.

Dejection filled her, as did an unbearable feeling of loneliness. Paxton had withdrawn his support and Henry would no doubt pronounce that she would be hanged, for Gwenifer's testimony was most damaging.

Alana's heart raced with trepidation when she heard Henry say, "Alana of Llangollen, stand before me."

With halting steps, she moved to the place where Henry pointed. She felt suddenly cold and was shivering. Still she lifted her chin and met him stare for stare.

"Is what your cousin said true? Did you say you rued the day you married my knight? Did you say his death would be a relief to you?"

Alana could not refute the words, for it would be a lie. And Henry, she knew, was far too discerning. "Aye, I said those things."

Several gasps were heard from those who were congregated in the tent, before Henry questioned, "And you admit to killing Gilbert FitzWilliam?"

Alana felt she had no choice but to continue the lie. "Aye, I killed him, but it was done in self-defense. He attempted to kill me first."

Henry was quiet for a long while as he scrutinized Alana, who in turn wondered what his verdict would be. His face was unreadable, and Alana concluded that he was a master at disguising his thoughts and emotions, an admirable trait for a man who was king.

"My decision is made," Henry said finally.

Offering prayers to Saint David, Alana held her breath.

CHAPTER

22

Alana of Llangollen, by the testimony given me and by your own confession that you killed Gilbert FitzWilliam, I find that you did so with malice aforethought and not as claimed in self-defense. You will, therefore, by my decree, be hanged for the crime of murder. May God have mercy on your soul."

His words ended, several things happened all at once. Father Jevon began droning a litany in Latin; Alana's knees buckled as two of Henry's knights latched onto her arms; Gwenifer burst into tears, ran to a nearby bench, and sank atop it; Madoc cursed Henry soundly; while Paxton shouted, "Nay! 'Tis a travesty of justice!"

The tent, which was abuzz with voices, grew suddenly still. "Do you question my verdict and my authority, Sir Paxton?" Henry inquired.

"I do not question your authority, sire," Paxton

announced as he stepped before Henry. "I do question your verdict and the sentence you have pronounced. I have remained silent too long, therefore I feel it is imperative that I be allowed to speak."

"You may do so," Henry declared. "But I doubt anything will change."

Paxton glanced at Alana to see her gaze was fast upon him. She knew what he was about to say. She also knew she was going to die, and Paxton hoped she wouldn't be foolish enough to deny his words once they were all said.

He looked at Henry. "My wife confessed to killing Gilbert FitzWilliam in self-defense. I do not believe her claim that it was her hand that wielded the knife. However, I do believe she speaks true when she says Gilbert attempted to kill her."

"If not by hers, then by whose hand do you think Gilbert was killed?" Henry asked.

"By her uncle's and her cousins' hands in an act of revenge against Gilbert's attempt on Alana's life."

"Nay! 'Tis a lie!" Alana cried. "I killed Gilbert."

Paxton's gaze shot toward her. "God's wounds! Would you for once keep your tongue still, woman! That damnable Welsh pride and stubbornness of yours is taking you to the gallows as it is. Now keep quiet!"

Alana pressed her lips together, and Paxton again attended Henry. His king's brow was arched, his lips twitching as though he were amused by Paxton's display of temper toward his misbehaving wife.

"I'm most interested, Sir Paxton, in hearing your version of what you think happened to bring about Gilbert's death," Henry said. "Proceed."

Paxton explained what he thought transpired that day, telling his king about Rhys and his sons, how they lived in a ringwork across the river. He even included how Alana had run to her uncle on the day of their wedding to show she had probably done the same when Gilbert attempted to kill her. He did not let it be known that Rhys had captured him with the intent of burning him at the stake. To do so would not advance his cause but obstruct it instead.

"Has your wife admitted these things to you?" Henry asked once Paxton was finished.

"Aye, she has."

Henry circled his gaze to Alana. "Do you concur with your husband's testimony?"

It was Paxton's turn to hold his breath.

"Nay. I killed Gilbert in self-defense."

"She denies your story, Sir Paxton."

"She would, sire."

"And why is that?" Henry asked.

"'Tis as she's stated," Paxton returned. "She feared you wouldn't believe her if she told the truth. In this case, she was certain you'd see Gilbert's death as a conspiracy perpetrated by herself and her kin."

"It does smack of a conspiracy," Henry stated.

"How so?" Paxton inquired.

"I have yet to hear a valid reason as to why Gilbert would want his wife dead. Sir Goddard, rest his beleaguered soul, described their marriage as being disharmonious. Despite that, according to Sir Goddard's testimony, Sir Gilbert tried to keep the peace between them. It is admitted by all who were asked that Gilbert never struck her. Though Madoc's testimony paints a different picture of my vassal, showing him as rude, cold, and disrespectful of his wife, I am still told they argued, which Sir Goddard said was instigated by her.

"But setting those two testimonies aside, Gwenifer's is the most damning of all. Your wife admitted that she said what Gwenifer reported: In essence, she wanted Gilbert dead. Whether by her hand or by her uncle's and cousins', I'd say she got her wish. I also say it was deliberate and not an act of self-defense nor was it an act of revenge because Gilbert sought to kill her first. There is nothing to say he tried anything of the sort. Thus, Sir Paxton, my verdict stands."

Paxton couldn't believe what he'd heard from his king. "You saw the scrap of tunic that Gilbert wore the day he died. You've heard the ordeal she went through as she was dragged along through the river. Heed me when I say I've seen the water's turbulence firsthand after a heavy rain. It was a miracle she survived its fury. Therefore I ask you this: Do you really believe, in the weakened state she was in, that she could have inflicted those wounds on a man who was stout and hale and who was nearly twice her size?"

"I can believe anything of a woman who is bent on treachery," Henry replied.

"Then you are a fool," Paxton bit out.

When the gasps settled there was naught but a ponderous silence. Paxton's hard stare was locked with Henry's. To all who looked on, it was difficult to say who was the more angry of the two.

"'Tis treason you risk, Sir Paxton. One more word against me and I shall have you gibbeted alongside her," Henry threatened. "Is that what you want?"

"Treason it may be, sire, but a man is not a man if he does not speak out against an injustice. There is no equity in what you do. You seek revenge for no reason."

Henry's face reddened perceptively. "No reason!" he thundered. "She's confessed to killing my vassal."

"Simply because your vassal attempted to kill her first. Besides, her confession is false. She is protecting her kin. They are the culprits."

"She denies that."

"She's lying."

Henry set his jaw. "'Tis only her word to say that Gilbert acted against her. She offers no motive for Gilbert wanting to kill her, except she believes he despised her. Two have testified that Gilbert was essentially kind to her."

"Pah!" Paxton returned. "One was a drunken sot who hated all Welsh. He attempted to rape her."

"Sir Goddard claimed she tried to seduce him."

"A lie," Paxton shouted. "You have accepted my testimony that it was."

Henry's eyes narrowed. "So I did. But what of her cousin? Are you able to refute her testimony?"

Paxton could not. Of the two witnesses to whom Henry referred, one speaking against Alana, the other supposedly for her, Gwenifer's testimony was indeed the most damaging. How could he stop this madness from advancing to its intended end?

"You seem at a loss for words," Henry stated. "My decision is made." He looked at the men who held Alana. "Take her to the gallows and see she is hanged."

"Nay!" Paxton cried, and found himself suddenly held by two other knights. He was ready to use any means to protect Alana and keep her from dying needlessly. "You would not kill a woman who may be with child, would you?"

"By her own admission, she is barren. That she dies is a favor to you. You can take another wife, one who will bear you sons. Take her out," Henry ordered again.

"Nay!" Paxton shouted anew.

Henry's face grew redder than before. "I ask again, do you question my authority?"

"I question your wisdom."

Several gasps were heard again at his statement, which could be construed in no other way but as treasonous.

"Then I presume you wish to die alongside her?"

Paxton knew the answer the instant the question was asked. As his gaze ran over Alana's lovely face, his heart ached with the knowledge that she'd soon be lost to him forever.

Turning hard eyes on Henry, Paxton said, "I'd prefer death over life without her, aye. And I'd certainly prefer death over serving a king who knows not the meaning of justice."

"Then so be it," Henry decreed.

"Nay!" Alana cried, fighting against the hands that held her. "He knows not what he says. Hang me but spare him. Please. I beg you."

Her pleas coursed through Paxton, but he knew they would have no effect on Henry. Paxton had sealed his own fate by challenging his king as he had. It mattered not. Life without Alana was no life at all. In death they would be together forever.

"Strike his spurs and take them to the gallows," Henry ordered. "Priest, start praying for their souls."

As Paxton felt the symbols of his knighthood fall away from him, Father Jevon reciting his prayers again, he heard Alana's cry, "Nay! You must not do this." When Henry turned away from her, she looked at Paxton. "You are the one who is the fool. Why did you do this, Paxton? Why?"

Though he wished he could take Alana into his arms one last time, he knew that would be impossible. His hands were being bound behind him, the same as were hers. "There's only one answer, my wife," he said, a bittersweet feeling surging inside him.

"And what is that?" she asked, tears brightening her eyes.

"I did it because I love you."

A sob broke from her lips. "And I love you," she said in return, her eyes locked with his.

Even though their bodies were held apart, in that instant their hearts touched in an everlasting promise of faith and devotion. Paxton absorbed the feeling as it was extended to him across the distance that separated them. He returned it to Alana by way of his abiding gaze.

Then, roughly, they were being turned toward the tent's entry. "I'll be with you forever, Alana," Paxton told her. "Know that I will, love."

"And I with you, my love."

Somewhere behind them could be heard Gwenifer's soft sobs. Overriding those were Madoc's snarls of protest. Other than Father Jevon's uttered litany as he led the way from the tent, the rest was silence from all who watched their departure.

Over Father Jevon's shoulder and beyond the raised flaps, Paxton could see the waning sun. It would be their last sunset, he thought, praying it was a glorious one indeed. Then, the opening was filled with men, each one entering separately. Alana's and his pathway blocked, their progression was halted.

"Out of my way, Priest," the first one said as he shoved a startled Father Jevon aside.

"Rhys?"

The query came from Alana, her surprise evident. Paxton stared at the man. Beside Rhys stood each of his sons, Dylan included. Behind them was Aldwyn.

"Aye, Niece. I am here," Rhys stated. "I could not let this travesty go forth." Then he looked to the area at large. "Where is Henry?"

Henry's voice boomed through the tent, as he asked, "Who inquires?"

"Rhys ap Tewdwr," Alana's uncle announced. "I

have come to give testimony on my niece's behalf." His gaze ran over both Alana and Paxton. "It appears I have arrived just in time."

"Come forward, Rhys ap Tewdwr," Henry declared. "You men"—he motioned at Alana's and Paxton's guards—"bring the condemned." Once everyone was standing before him, he eyed Rhys as though gauging him. "I have made my decision in this matter. Your niece has confessed to killing my vassal, Gilbert FitzWilliam. She has been found guilty of murder and is sentenced to be hanged. Your testimony is too late."

"Not too late," Rhys said, "just delayed. Or are you the sort who is unwilling to admit he has erred in his judgment? If so, you will be putting an innocent person to death simply to avoid acknowledging your mistake."

Henry glared at Rhys. "The previous testimony offered against her is what convicted her. You may speak, but I warn you this: If you do not convince me of her innocence, she will be hanged."

Rhys arrogantly inclined his head. "You might be king of England but you are not king of Cymru," he said, referring to his country in his own language. "Since I am not one of your subjects, I intended to speak with or without your permission."

For a third time the tent was a cacophony of gasps, then dead silence. As Henry and Rhys stared at one another, neither man backing down, everyone held their breath, waiting for Henry's infamous temper to erupt.

They were disappointed, however. For reasons known only to him, Henry appeared to respect Rhys's tenaciousness. "Your point is well taken, Welshman," he said at last. "We shall address this man-to-man and on an equal level. But when I make my decision, it will be as king, for we are on English soil, and Gilbert FitzWilliam was my vassal. Now have your say."

"Rhys, no," Alana interjected.

"Hush, Niece," he commanded, turning on her. "This time you will hold your tongue." He again faced Henry. "Alana did not kill Gilbert. I did."

"And I," Dylan stated.

"As did I," Meredydd confirmed.

"I, also," Caradog added.

"A lie," Alana chimed.

"Be quiet," Henry ordered at her intrusion. He looked back to Rhys. "Why did you set yourself on my vassal?"

"He attempted to murder my niece."

"She has said as much, except she claims she killed him."

"Unlikely. She just pulled herself from a raging torrent after being shoved into its current by Gilbert FitzWilliam. With what little strength she had, she dragged herself across a footbridge and hid in the wood. She was found by one of her kinsmen and brought to me. She told me all that had transpired. Your fool of a vassal erred when he came to us with the story that his 'beloved' Alana had drowned. For his treachery, he received his due."

Henry was quiet. "Did you see Gilbert shove your niece into the river as she has claimed."

"Nay," Rhys stated. "They were alone."

"Then there is still no proof that Gilbert attempted to murder her."

"And why is that?" Rhys questioned.

"There is no reason for his wanting her dead."

"There is a reason," Rhys countered. "It came to my three sons and I in the form of a name. It was the last utterance Gilbert ever breathed."

"And what name is that?" Henry inquired.

"Gwenifer."

All eyes turned on the woman who had been quietly listening to the exchange. "Nay! 'Tis not true!" she cried, bounding from the bench on which she sat.

"They were lovers," Rhys accused. "What better reason is there for a man to want his wife dead than that of his wanting to marry his whore?"

"'Tis a lie," Gwenifer insisted as two of Henry's knights approached her, ready to take her prisoner.

"Hold," Henry commanded of the men just as they started to grasp her arms. "Gilbert could not have married this woman. The Church would have prohibited such a union. She would be too closely related. She is after all his wife's cousin."

"Perhaps in England you abide by such edicts from the Church. In Cymru, we intermarry all the time. 'Tis to ensure our blood isn't tainted by outsiders," Rhys said with a sneer. "With Alana in her grave, Gilbert would have married Gwenifer, and no one would have objected. As I said, he erred. Alana still lives, and Gilbert is dead, payment for his faithlessness."

Henry pinpointed Gwenifer with his harsh gaze. "Is this true, woman? Were you Gilbert's lover?"

Paling, Gwenifer shook her head.

"Do not lie to me," Henry thundered. "The proof is easily delivered to me. An examination by my own leech should tell us whether you are a virgin or not."

When Gwenifer didn't respond, Henry ordered the man forward. "Nay!" she yelled on his approach. "Do not come nigh!"

"Your refusal impeaches you, woman!" Henry shouted. "'Tis true: You were Gilbert's lover!"

"Yes!" Gwenifer fairly screamed the word, then she pointed her finger at Alana. "But she killed him!"

Alana was stunned by Gwenifer's confession and

subsequent accusation. Then the realization came: The friendship between Gilbert and Gwenifer was far more than it appeared. Remembering all the occasions on which she saw them together—Gilbert smiling at Gwenifer, his laughter ringing freely, hers doing the same—Alana now knew that they were in fact lovers. How very stupid of her not to have known sooner.

"You both wanted me dead," she said to Gwenifer. "You knew Gilbert had schemed to kill me, didn't you?"

"Yes, I knew," Gwenifer said, struggling against the hands that now held her arms. "We arranged the plan together."

At Henry's nod to the men who held Alana, her arms were released. She stepped toward Gwenifer. "You would kill me simply to marry Gilbert?"

"I loved him and he loved me. But nay. Not 'simply' to marry Gilbert. I wanted revenge."

"Revenge? Why?"

"Because of what your father did to my father. I hated Rhodri for killing my sire. But I avenged Hywel's death by making certain his murderer met his own end."

Alana stared at her. "You! But you were nowhere near my father when he fell from his horse."

Gwenifer raised her chin. "'Twas no accident that he did. I cut the cinch to his saddle. That is why he fell. That is why he broke his deceitful neck."

Alana recalled how each time Gwenifer came for a visit something terrible occurred. Her father's death was the first of three such happenings. The second was Alana's near drowning, and Gilbert's subsequent death. And now this. As to the first, that Gwenifer blamed Rhodri for her own father's demise was madness, pure and simple.

"Hywel died because of his own treachery, Gwenifer. He was dissatisfied with the portion left to him on our grandfather's death. He tried to usurp his own brother's inheritance and incited a fight between them. Rhodri had no choice but to defend himself. It was Hywel's greed that killed him. Naught else."

"That land was my father's," Gwenifer insisted, obviously unwilling to accept the truth. "Just as it now should be mine. You stole it from me. I hate you for taking all that I ever valued: my father, the land, Gilbert. But in good time I made certain you were found out."

The piece of tunic, Alana thought. Gwenifer was the one who placed it on the bed. "How did you come by Gilbert's clothing?" she asked.

"I saw Madoc leave the castle after he helped you prepare Gilbert's body for burial. I followed him into the wood and watched as he tried to burn the evidence. The rain came, drowning out the fire. He buried the remaining scraps, which I unearthed the moment he disappeared from sight. I saved the most damning piece, waiting for the right time to deliver it into the proper hands. Your Norman husband suspected you from the start. I thought it only fair to present it to him when you both appeared so very happy. It worked, for I shall soon see you hanged. 'Twill even the score, Cousin."

"Nay!" Henry interjected, and all eyes turned his way. "Based on the new evidence presented here, Alana of Llangollen will not hang. You have perjured yourself in your testimony, young woman. You lied with the intent of seeing an innocent person put to death. You and Gilbert connived to kill his wife. You have also confessed to murdering your own uncle. Gilbert received his deserts." He looked at Rhys. "Which, I might add, was fair and just." He turned back to Gwenifer. "But you have yet to receive yours. Therefore, by my command, the sentence that was once passed on your cousin is now passed on you." He waved his arm. "Take her to the gallows!"

The blood drained from Gwenifer's face; she appeared to faint. Holding her limp form between them, the two knights dragged her to the bench and laid her upon it. While one sought something with which to fan her, the other went in search of some water. It was then that Gwenifer sprang to life.

Her knife drawn from its sheath at her waist, she bounded from the bench. Her once beautiful face was contorted with rage, her eyes glassy and wild. "I hate you!" she screamed, the blade aimed straight at Alana's heart.

Alana stood rooted to the spot as she watched her cousin come at her. Behind her Paxton shouted her name, then cursed the men who yet held him. From the side, she felt Rhys's and Dylan's hands attempting to jerk her aside. Then before her, she saw Gwenifer falter. Her eyes widened as her features became a frozen mask of disbelief. In a trice, Gwenifer fell face first in the dirt at Alana's feet, a quarrel protruding from her back.

Her heart hammering in her ears, Alana looked to the man who had cast himself directly behind Gwenifer. Henry's stance was firm, his jaw set. He slowly lowered the crossbow from his shoulder.

"Woman, thy treachery is met," he said, gazing at Gwenifer's lifeless form. Then he looked at Alana. "Though either means of her delivery might be considered by my hand, she sustained a far easier death this way than she would have by hanging. She will be given a proper burial."

Handing off the crossbow to another, Henry motioned to the two knights who had once restrained

Gwenifer; Alana turned away as they lifted her cousin's body and carried it from the tent, Father Jevon following after them. Wanting to feel her husband's arms around her, Alana gazed beseechingly at Paxton. But he could do naught to comfort her, for he was still held fast by his guards.

"Release my knight and untie his hands," Henry stated from behind her. "And untie his lady as well." While the leather bindings were removed, he motioned to Sir Graham, who had come from the rear of the tent. "You, there, pick up those spurs and bring them here," he ordered, his hand outstretched and waiting.

Once Sir Graham complied, Henry commanded Paxton and Alana forward, ordering everyone else back. After removing the straps from his own spurs to replace those that were cut away on Paxton's, Henry knelt before Paxton and began restoring the symbols of knighthood to his vassal's heels.

Henry looked up at Paxton as he worked. "You called me a fool and questioned my wisdom before everyone here," he said for Paxton's and Alana's ears only. "I could still have you hanged for treason, sir. But I will not. You believed in your lady. You were even willing to die for and with her. I admire that sort of faith. However, know this: Based on what was told me, I had no choice but to find her guilty. Fortunately her uncle arrived and exposed the lies that were uttered by your lady's cousin. Know this also: I am always interested in justice, thus the change in my verdict. I am, therefore, restoring your spurs, myself. I also forgive your error in denouncing me. But do not make me strike your spurs again, for there will be no mercy from me a second time." He rose to meet Paxton face-to-face. "Is that clear?"

"Aye, sire," Paxton declared. "'Tis perfectly clear.

My actions were those of a desperate man. That I'll admit. I am gladdened you have forgiven me. But you should know that whether it is in defense of my wife, my king, or some lowly serf, if the circumstances are such again, I will react in the same manner with the same sort of conviction. 'Tis a matter of loyalty to what one believes in."

Henry searched Paxton's eyes. "You are honest, sir. 'Tis a virtue I wish all my vassals possessed. I am also pleased that you have included me in those to which you extend your loyalty." He patted Paxton's shoulder. "You have always served me well, and I can truly say I am honored to have you as one of my knights. All that I once promised you is now yours. I wish you a long and happy life, Sir Paxton. Your lady as well. And since you insist it is possible, may your marriage be blessed with many sons and daughters. Now, my friend, whenever you are ready, you may take the Lady Alana home."

Bowing to Henry, Alana and Paxton squeezed each other's hands. When they looked to the man again, they saw his blue eyes twinkling with mirth.

His deep laughter rumbled forth. "Is that the best the two of you can do?" he questioned, cocking his head. "God's wounds! You were staring death in the face, professing your undying love for each other at the same time. Don't be shy. Show us the joy of that abiding affection you hold for one another, so we may share in it ourselves."

Paxton turned to Alana and gazed deeply into her eyes. "My king has ordered this. And it is with great pleasure I do his bidding."

With that, he pulled her into his embrace and kissed her with such depth of emotion that the effect streamed through Alana all the way to her toes. Cheers and roars erupted around them, stating the approval of all who watched. Then, beneath her hand, she felt the laughter rising in Paxton's chest. Ending the kiss, he pulled back and let his merriment fly through the air.

"Why such mirth?" she asked, smiling, for his joy was contagious.

Lifting her, he twirled her around. "Because, my beautiful wife, I'm the happiest man alive."

"Rhys ap Tewdwr, come forward."

Henry's voice rose above the din, once Paxton had set Alana to her feet. She watched as her uncle approached Paxton's king.

"I presume, sir," Henry addressed Rhys, "that you traveled here under a flag of truce."

"Nay. I came prepared to fight my way in, if I had to. I had no intention of disguising my purpose under a false flag."

Henry arched his brow. "You showed great courage, Rhys ap Tewdwr, for you braved much to save your niece. I grant you safe passage back to your homeland, and I pray the next time we meet it will be in friendship and not in battle. If that were to occur, it would be a terrible reckoning for us both, I fear. Sir Paxton and the others will offer you their protection and escort you past Offa's Dyke."

"Considering what is developing here, once in Cymru, the Norman and his men may be in need of our protection," Rhys commented.

"I will take it as a personal favor if you'd see to their continued good health." Henry's gaze swept the lot of them. "God's speed to you all," he said, and made for the entry.

As Henry and his bevy of attendants and knights marched past them, Alana dipped a curtsy while Paxton bowed. Rhys, Dylan, Meredydd, Caradog, Madoc, and Aldwyn remained erect, their Welsh pride preventing any show of respect to the English king.

When they were by themselves, Alana looked to Aldwyn. "I had never thought to see you again, let alone with my uncle. Where were you when I departed the fortress?"

"He was dashing through the wood bent on alerting me as to what was happening," Rhys stated.

"But how did you know, Aldwyn?" Alana asked. "I told no one except Gwenifer and Madoc, and they were both sworn to secrecy." Slowly she looked to her servant and friend. "Someone did not keep his word."

"'Tis a good thing I didn't," Madoc announced. "Or you and your knight would be gibbeted by now."

She shifted her attention from Madoc to Aldwyn. "Thank you for seeking aid on my behalf. I appreciate your concern and care."

"Friends always help friends when in need," Aldwyn announced.

Alana hugged Aldwyn, then turned to her uncle. "If you knew about Gwenifer, all this while, why didn't you tell me?"

Rhys glanced around him to see if they were truly alone. "I didn't know."

Alana frowned. "What are you saying? You told Henry that Gilbert died with Gwenifer's name on his lips."

"I lied. Gilbert was too busy begging for mercy to say anything else."

"Then how—?"

"While we were traveling here, Aldwyn questioned what Gwenifer's true purpose was in insisting she journey with you to Chester. I responded by saying that I supposed she hoped to testify in your behalf. That is when Aldwyn said he distrusted Gwenifer's motives, especially when she and Gilbert were more than mere cousins and friends. The lad saw them coupling in the wood, not long before Gilbert died."

"And you never told me," Alana said to Aldwyn.

"I didn't want to cause you hurt," Aldwyn replied with a shrug.

"Well, I'm certainly glad you thought to tell Rhys about what you saw. I fear otherwise Paxton and I would have been hanged." Again she looked to Rhys. "You never trusted Gwenifer yourself, but you never said why."

"Our countrymen's nature is a passionate and vindictive one. You know as well as I that no affront, recent or past, goes unpunished. Considering what occurred between your father and hers, I always thought she was too quick to forgive. In other words, I didn't believe she was playing you true. Obviously, she wasn't."

"Yes, obviously."

From behind her, Paxton's hands settled on her shoulders. His touch was light yet reassuring; Alana sighed. Gwenifer's beauty masked the ugliness growing within her. Alana could only imagine the depths of her cousin's hatred toward her for Gwenifer to do and to say what she did. Certainly she had fooled Alana. Thankfully she didn't fool Rhys.

"Why did you come here, Uncle?" she asked, putting thoughts of Gwenifer aside. "You told me that you had disowned me."

"I couldn't let you die for killing Gilbert when it was my hand that plunged the knife. That doesn't mean I have forgiven you for marrying another Norman." Rhys's gaze raked Paxton up and down. "Though I'll admit, of the two, he is the better."

"I think so—definitely," Alana said, gazing up at her husband. His love for her shone through his eyes.

Never had she felt this happy, this cherished. The feeling was like no other.

"Well, Norman, are you coming back to Cymru with us?" Rhys asked.

"'Tis Alana's home and now my home," Paxton stated. "Yes, I'm heading back to Cymru."

"Then let's be on our way," her uncle announced.

Madoc, Sir Graham, Aldwyn, Rhys and his sons exited the tent, Alana and Paxton following. When they stepped outside they heard the makeshift gallows that was hastily raised from tent poles, a cart serving as its base, come crashing down.

Alana looked at Paxton. "He really meant to hang us, didn't he?"

"Aye, because of your stubbornness he did."

"You were equally stubborn, sir, hounding him as you had. Calling your king a fool—what did you hope to accomplish?"

"One way or the other, you were not going to leave me, Alana of Llangollen. Those dark Welsh eyes of yours captivated me from the first time I looked into them. Do you think I could bear to see the light perish in their depths? Nay. I would have fought the angels of Heaven and the demons of Hell to keep you beside me. And if that also meant my death, I would have gladly faced and accepted it just so we could be together always."

Alana's heart thrilled to his words. "You love me that much do you?"

He looped his arms around her. "Aye . . . through eternity, and beyond."

"Though I never would have believed it possible, I love you equally as much"—she winked— *"Norman."*

Paxton chuckled. "It does seem hard to believe—

first enemies, now lovers." His eyes narrowed slightly. "Tell me something, Wife. Why did you really run from me that day in the glade?"

Alana gazed up at him through her lashes. "Must I?" she asked, while plucking at the front of his tunic.

Paxton nodded. "Yes, you must."

She sighed. "Well, after we made love, I discovered I was falling in love with you. The realization scared me so badly all I could think to do was run."

Full laughter rumbled from his chest. "Let's go home, Alana," he said, urging her toward their tent so they could gather their belongings. "'Tis there I'll teach you that you have nothing to fear from me."

"Do you swear that is so?"

"I swear."

At that moment, the rays from the setting sun burst across the sky in an aura of light to paint the clouds that streaked the horizon in brilliant golds and vivid oranges.

"Oh, look, Paxton," she said. "Isn't it beautiful?"

"Aye," he returned, viewing the magnificent spectacle of nature, his arm around Alana's shoulder. "But tomorrow's sunrise will fascinate me even more."

"How so?"

"It will mark the commencement of all the glorious days that lie ahead of us, Alana. Right now, it seems too far away."

She understood what he meant. For with the setting of this day's sun, all the deception, all the uncertainties, all the strife, all the fears that once plagued them would vanish along with the dimming light.

And tomorrow, by way of the daybreak, came the promise of a new beginning for Paxton and for her, one filled with love and trust and devotion that would last through time everlasting.

Alana could hardly wait for the coming of the dawn.

EPILOGUE

Northern Wales
Autumn 1157

A hawk soared through an azure blue sky, searching diligently for its prey.

On the bluff overlooking the river that snaked alongside the old Norman fortress stood its overlord. From behind, he embraced his lady just beneath her full breasts and above her expanding stomach. In silence, they watched the graceful bird that was not part of the castle mews, its freedom ever assured.

"He's beautiful," Alana said.

"He might be a she," Paxton countered, his hand caressing her belly.

"I was speaking of the hawk."

"And I was referring to our child . . . you know, the one you said we would never have."

"I was wrong."

"Yes, you were. You should have been more trusting when I told you that you weren't barren. It simply took the right man to make certain you conceived."

She smiled up at him. "Apparently so, and he has done a fine job of it. Your seed took from the first."

"I told you it did."

"And I nearly ruined it for all of us," she said.

"Don't think about what might have been, Alana. Only about what is. We are alive and so is our child. That is all that matters."

"Aye, you're right." She was silent for a bit. "I heard from Rhys yesterday by way of messenger. He says they are all well. He sends me good wishes."

"I'm not included in those, I suppose."

"Give him time. It took a lot for him to admit you are better than my first husband, considering your heritage."

"How kind of him to see that . . . since I'm Norman, I mean." He released a long breath. "At least he was there when he was needed most."

"And he'll come to our aid again if the need should arise. Besides, those here hail you as a hero. You saved my life by risking your own. When they learned such, they were most pleased and are now forever beholden to you."

"As they should be," Paxton stated. "I am after all their overlord."

For a moment there was silence.

"How is Dylan?" Paxton asked. "Has Rhys finally forgiven him?"

"Their relationship is still not as amicable as it once was, but things are slowly getting better. Dylan has promised to come visit us. I hear he is building his own hut at the ringwork in anticipation of one day taking a wife."

"It will be good to see him again. Of all those across the river, I like him the best."

"'Tis the same with me."

"Imagine, sweet," he said, sweeping his hand before

him, gesturing toward the land. "All this is ours. And it will one day be our son's, and his son's, and so on."

"In Wales, the sons share in their inheritance. If there are no sons, then the daughters inherit."

"And we are in Wales, aren't we?"

"Cymru, actually."

"Which means we must act accordingly, correct?"

"Yes, it does." She paused, then nodded at the valley below them. "Is this the reason you married me . . . to have yourself a fiefdom?"

"'Twas part of the reason, but only the smallest measure, I assure you."

"And what was the greatest measure?"

"You, sweet."

"You really expect me to believe that, don't you?"

He turned her around to face him. "I do." He smiled engagingly as he drew her closer. "Which reminds me. I have always wanted to make love to you here, high on this bluff. What do you say? Will you allow it, this time?"

Alana blinked. "In broad daylight, so all the world can see."

"No one will see," he said, his mouth growing ever closer to hers. "Trust me."

Their warm breaths mingling, Alana answered with all the sureness in her heart, "Always, my valiant Norman knight. Always."

AWARD-WINNING AUTHOR OF
<u>DEEPER THAN ROSES</u>

Charlene Cross

☐ SPLENDOR ....79432-9/$5.99

☐ DEEPER THAN ROSES ....73824-0/$5.50

☐ LORD OF LEGEND ....73825-9/$5.50

☐ ALMOST A WHISPER....................79431-0/$5.50

☐ EVERLASTING............................79433-7/$5.99

AVAILABLE FROM POCKET BOOKS

POCKET
B O O K S

Simon & Schuster Mail Order
200 Old Tappan Rd., Old Tappan, N.J. 07675
Please send me the books I have checked above. I am enclosing $_____ (please add $0.75 to cover the postage and handling for each order. Please add appropriate sales tax). Send check or money order—no cash or C.O.D.'s please. Allow up to six weeks for delivery. For purchase over $10.00 you may use VISA: card number, expiration date and customer signature must be included.

Name _____

Address _____

City _____ State/Zip _____

VISA Card # _____ Exp.Date _____

Signature _____

833-03